CATHY TULLY

Dr. Shine Cracks the Case

A ChiroCozy Mystery: Book 1

First published by Visions & Revisions Unlimited 2020

Copyright © 2020 by Cathy Tully

All rights reserved. No part of this publication may be reproduced, stored or transmitted in any form or by any means, electronic, mechanical, photocopying, recording, scanning, or otherwise without written permission from the publisher. It is illegal to copy this book, post it to a website, or distribute it by any other means without permission.

This novel is entirely a work of fiction. The names, characters and incidents portrayed in it are the work of the author's imagination. Any resemblance to actual persons, living or dead, events or localities is entirely coincidental.

Designations used by companies to distinguish their products are often claimed as trademarks. All brand names and product names used in this book and on its cover are trade names, service marks, trademarks and registered trademarks of their respective owners. The publishers and the book are not associated with any product or vendor mentioned in this book. None of the companies referenced within the book have endorsed the book.

First edition

Cover art by Daniela Colleo of www.StunningBookCovers.com

This book was professionally typeset on Reedsy. Find out more at reedsy.com

This book is dedicated to my parents. Their love of reading mysteries is in my DNA.
To Don & Carol. Gone but not forgotten.

Contents

Acknowledgement   iv
Map of Peach Grove Georgia   v
Cast of Characters   vi
CHAPTER ONE   1
CHAPTER TWO   7
CHAPTER THREE   15
CHAPTER FOUR   18
CHAPTER FIVE   23
CHAPTER SIX   33
CHAPTER SEVEN   39
CHAPTER EIGHT   46
CHAPTER NINE   52
CHAPTER TEN   59
CHAPTER ELEVEN   69
CHAPTER TWELVE   76
CHAPTER THIRTEEN   84
CHAPTER FOURTEEN   88
CHAPTER FIFTEEN   92
CHAPTER SIXTEEN   97
CHAPTER SEVENTEEN   103
CHAPTER EIGHTEEN   109
CHAPTER NINETEEN   114
CHAPTER TWENTY   118
CHAPTER TWENTY-ONE   124

CHAPTER TWENTY-TWO	131
CHAPTER TWENTY-THREE	137
CHAPTER TWENTY-FOUR	143
CHAPTER TWENTY-FIVE	151
CHAPTER TWENTY-SIX	160
CHAPTER TWENTY-SEVEN	173
CHAPTER TWENTY-EIGHT	178
CHAPTER TWENTY-NINE	188
CHAPTER THIRTY	194
CHAPTER THIRTY-ONE	200
CHAPTER THIRTY-TWO	212
CHAPTER THIRTY-THREE	218
CHAPTER THIRTY-FOUR	227
CHAPTER THIRTY-FIVE	236
CHAPTER THIRTY-SIX	239
CHAPTER THIRTY-SEVEN	246
CHAPTER THIRTY-EIGHT	252
CHAPTER THIRTY-NINE	258
CHAPTER FORTY	268
CHAPTER FORTY-ONE	273
CHAPTER FORTY-TWO	279
CHAPTER FORTY-THREE	283
CHAPTER FORTY-FOUR	288
CHAPTER FORTY-FIVE	295
CHAPTER FORTY-SIX	300
CHAPTER FORTY-SEVEN	304
CHAPTER FORTY-EIGHT	310
CHAPTER FORTY-NINE	315
CHAPTER FIFTY	321
Gluten-Free Recipes	329
Gluten-Free Flaxseed Crackers	330

Gluten-Free Blueberry Muffins	332
Gluten-Free Peach Cobbler	334
Misalignment & Murder . . . Sneak Peek	336
A Zombie in the Sand	341
About the Author	346
Also by Cathy Tully	347

Acknowledgement

I want to acknowledge the numerous writers who have helped me in ways great and small.

Most importantly my Cozy Guppy friends, Alli Stone & Denise Todd. Next in line, the women of the Secondary Characters Group: Vikki Walton, Tonya Marie Agerton, Danielle Botz, Janie Pritchett Clark, Peta Flanigan, Stacy Stewart, and especially Rose Dewar, Erin Scoggins and Mary Pat Smith.

Map of Peach Grove Georgia

Cast of Characters

Susannah's Clan

Dr. Susannah Shine — Chiropractor at Peach Grove Chiropractic
Larraine Moore — Dr. Susannah Shine's Office Manager
Tina Cawthorn — Assistant to Dr. Susannah Shine
Henry the Eighth — Susannah's Betta fish pal
Rusty — Office rescue cat

Peach Grove Business Association

Fiona Bailey — Owner of the Long Branch Stable
Olivia Franklin — Accountant and payroll specialist
Daniel Kim— Owner of Southside Insurance Agency
Bitsy Jean Long — Proprietress of Peachy Things boutique and Susannah's BFF
Marcie Jones — Co-Owner of the Wing Shack and President of the PGBA
Billy Jones — Co-Owner of the Wing Shack. Husband to Marcie
Hayle Jones — Daughter of Marcie and Billy Jones
Colin Rogers — Owner of OK Automotive

Cantina Caliente

Anita Alvarez — Owner of the Cantina Caliente
Pilar Alvarez — Mother of Anita Alvarez

Dolores Alvarez — Daughter of Anita
Tomas Perez — Head waiter at Cantina Caliente

Peach Grove Police Department
Randy Laughton—Police Chief
Keith Cawthorn—Police Officer and husband to Tina
Owen Chaffin—Police Officer
Detective Varina Withers—Detective
Little Junior Long—Desk Sergeant and cousin to Bitsy

Henry County Hospital
Roman Broady — Ex-Marine and Childhood friend of Bitsy
Iris Duncan — Assistant at the medical examiner's office

CHAPTER ONE

Dr. Susannah Shine's hand shook as she keyed in the password again. The ear-piercing *whoop* made it hard to think. *Third time's a charm.*

Behind her, Police Chief Randy Laughton shouted, "Will you please shut off that alarm!"

The whooping ceased, and Susannah turned to face him, trying to think of something to say that wasn't an outright lie. She knew that her cat, Rusty, had triggered her clinic's security alarm, but she didn't want to admit it. Randy already treated her like an incompetent.

"The cat must have gotten locked inside and tripped the alarm," Susannah said, biting back her shame.

Pulling himself up to his full six-foot-two, Randy peered down at her. She blinked up at him. "I reckon," he said, hands on his belt. "Seems like they would have gone over securing the premises in your training in New York City." He drawled *New York City* as if the words left a foul taste in his mouth.

She leveled her gaze on the police chief, on his gray-blue eyes set in a long ruddy face marred by acne scars. She resisted the urge to speak.

"Doc," Randy said, jutting his chin toward Rusty, who was

now lying on his back at the edge of the parking lot, the picture of innocence. "If you don't get control of that critter, I may have to stop responding to these alarms. This is the second time this month."

His eyes drilled into her as if daring her to contradict him. She didn't. She started to inch door closed.

He sighed. "I'll take a look inside for you."

"That's not necessary. It's clear that Rusty was the culprit," she said, forcing a smile out of muscles that would have rather scowled. *Remember your Southern charm training. It's okay if smiling hurts.* "No need to come inside."

A car door slammed, and a woman leaned against Randy's patrol car. She wore an expression of barely suppressed boredom.

"Who's riding with you today?" Susannah asked. A light breeze stirred the pine trees and lifted the woman's blond hair off the collar of her Peach Grove PD windbreaker. Susannah felt a chill and stepped inside, shielding herself with the door.

Randy's jaw tightened, and his thick nose reddened. "The mayor hired a new detective. I was giving her a tour of the town when the call came in to respond to your alarm."

"Well," Susannah said, distracted by the rumbling of her stomach. Because of the alarm, she had run out of her house without eating a thing, and she thought of the gluten-free snacks she kept in the kitchen. "I guess you should get back to official business."

Randy cocked an eyebrow. "This *is* official business. If you'll let me get on with it."

"Really, no need." Susannah had lived in Peach Grove for years but sometimes still felt like an outsider. Randy would always see her as a bumbling law enforcement wannabe, even though she had been a part of the NYPD.

Randy shrugged and turned, fingering his radio as he made his way back to his car. With a glance over his shoulder at her, he got in the car and sped out of her parking lot.

As she closed the door, a streak of orange announced Rusty's return. He rubbed against her calves, causing a flank-to-slacks fur deposit. Allergic to the core, Susannah felt her eyes begin to itch, but she patted the animal's orange head anyway. She couldn't resist a hard-luck story. Pulling a tissue from her bag, she walked him through the office to the break room, where she kept his kibble.

"Mrow," Rusty commented. He danced about her legs as she filled his dish and placed it outside the rear door.

"You're welcome," Susannah said, shutting the door before he could re-enter the building.

In the kitchen, she grabbed a gluten-free blueberry muffin, ripped off the top, and pushed it into her mouth. Still chewing, she entered her office and fed her betta fish, Henry the Eighth. He wagged his tail fins as she checked the tank's temperature and gave him a ration of food pellets.

Nibbling on her muffin, she gazed out the window at the orchard where early risers were queuing up to pick their own peaches. She smiled. Her adopted hometown, Peach Grove, Georgia, was everything that Brooklyn, New York, was not. Blue skies, green grass, orange mud, and locally grown peaches beat out cement, dirt, and rattling trains any day of the week.

She didn't understand why her family worried about her, especially her mother, who said the rosary daily for her safe return. Adjusting spines in Georgia was far safer than defending New York City subway trains from perverts.

She also didn't understand Chief Laughton's disdain for her. Her training with the NYPD's Transit Patrol had been solid, and so had her performance—until a health issue compelled her to leave the force after just one year. But here in a small town on the rural side of Atlanta, there was no reason for military-like precision when locking up her chiropractic practice. Peach Grove was a safe town that rocked peach blossoms and pastureland, not breaking-and-entering gangs.

Besides, she was a doctor now.

She turned to her computer and began work on some insurance reports. An hour later, a loud *blam* shook the building. Susannah rushed from her office and raced down the hall to the waiting room. Every eye in the room was on Marcie Jones, who steadied the door with one hand, ignoring the mark on the wall where the knob had hit. Fiona Bailey, already seated, put down her magazine. There was a mischievous gleam in her eyes.

"What did that door ever do to you, Marcie?" Fiona asked.

Marcie sneered, tossing her light brown bob and rolling her eyes. She folded her arms, scowling at her husband as he entered. Billy Jones lumbered through the doorway, leaning on worn metal crutches, escorted by Rusty, who circled him, mewling.

Tina Cawthorn, Susannah's assistant, shooed the cat away while a smile warmed her heart-shaped face. She placed her slender hand on Billy's shoulder. "Dr. S. wants me to help you—"

"I'll help him," Marcie interrupted. "I left the store to bring him up here. He doesn't need the both of us hanging on him."

"Yes, ma'am," Tina said, her brows peaked, her bronze skin flushed. She cast a look at Larraine Moore, the office manager, who perched behind the counter and tapped at a computer. With a shrug, Tina turned and strode down the hall without a word.

Larraine stood, took off her glasses, and put them on top of her head, burying them purposefully between soft ringlets of white hair. She was taller than Tina and older by forty years, and she was invaluable to Susannah because her long service to her church had taught her to smile effortlessly in all circumstances. She smiled now at Billy and came around the counter into the waiting area.

"Come on in, darlin'," she said, stepping in front of Marcie and ushering Billy down a hall. "We'll get you fixed up."

Marcie followed closely as Larraine led Billy into a treatment room and assisted him onto the chiropractic treatment table. Larraine left the room and returned with an ice pack.

"He needs his back popped." Marcie scowled her neck rigid and pursed her lips. "We have plenty of ice in the coolers at the Wing Shack."

"I'm sure you do," Larraine said, placing the gel pack over Billy's lower back. "The doctor wants him to ice his back. She reckons it helps with the pain. But I expect there are some pains that don't never go away." She locked eyes with Marcie, resettled her eyeglasses on the bridge of her nose, and marched out of the room and into the hallway, where she pressed a bony finger to her lips. "Lord forgive me," she whispered. Her complexion, powdery-white at the best of times, turned momentarily translucent. She looked up to see Susannah standing in the hall. "Have you been there this whole time?"

Susannah nodded, and Larraine looked away, a pink tinge testifying that blood actually circulated to her face. She pulled her white cardigan tighter around her light pink scrub top and returned to her station behind the front counter.

Susannah had treated Billy many times before, and her technique was always the same: a tall order of chiropractic adjustments served with a short stack of ignoring Marcie. She entered the treatment room with a smile, nodding at Marcie, who sat with her arms folded across her chest. After Susannah greeted Billy, her experienced hands probed his back and efficiently manipulated his vertebrae. Holding out her hand, she helped him to his feet; he took two steps without the crutches and gave her a wan smile.

"Finally," Marcie blurted. "Now maybe I can get back to my day."

"That's better," Billy said, cutting his eyes to her and giving Susannah a sympathetic shrug. "Thanks, Doc. You're a lifesaver."

"It's what I do," Susannah replied, winking at Billy. She turned to Marcie and added, "I'll see you tomorrow at the Business Association meeting."

Marcie jutted her chin, mumbled a response, and steered Billy out.

CHAPTER TWO

Anita Alvarez, a dark haired, full-lipped woman, suffered from a perpetually cheerful personality. *She should at least have the decency to look tired at 7:30 a.m.,* Susannah thought. But she never did. The Peach Grove Business Association met monthly in her restaurant, the Cantina Caliente, known to most locals as simply "the Cantina," and Anita was usually the most chipper person in attendance. Susannah, who found it hard to be chipper at any hour of the morning, bristled, knowing that Randy would be speaking for the Peach Grove Police Department. She dreaded confronting him again and wished she hadn't told Bitsy Long, her best friend, that she would attend the meeting. She imagined herself still in bed with a pillow over her head. At least the pillow would stifle the big hair she was experiencing because she hadn't had time to use the flat iron. It felt like she had a brunette lampshade on her head.

Anita touched Susannah's elbow, interrupting her ruminations on her hair, and offered her a cup just as Susannah's stomach rumbled.

"Hot *café* to start the day," she said in a clipped, singsong way with hardly a trace of her native Mexico. Susannah wished she had the ability to make simple statements sound like jingles, but that was not in her skill set.

Today, as they hid in the kitchen pass-through and sipped coffee, Susannah noticed Anita's hand trembling. *Maybe she imbibed too much latte*, Susannah thought. The coffee, brewed from Mexican espresso, mixed with hot milk, and topped with a sprinkle of cinnamon, packed a wallop. She sighed, inhaling the bracing aroma.

"I'll be back," Anita said, sloshing latte foam onto the floor as she pushed through the swinging door. Before the door even stopped swinging, Susannah heard Anita's raised voice coming from the kitchen. A man's tenor hollered a response. Susannah tiptoed away from the doors and turned her attention to the meeting. A few minutes later, Anita returned, sipping through a clear plastic straw that jutted from a plastic cup. She lifted it in a toast. "I felt like something cold. You want?"

"No, thanks," Susannah said, recognizing the Mexican version of iced tea Anita preferred. She tipped her cup toward Anita. "I prefer my drink hot."

Anita was about to reply but slipped on the floor where her spilled latte foam had congealed into a small slick spot. She slid into Susannah and then regained her balance. "Would you?" She handed Susannah her cup while she grabbed a few paper towels from the server's station and mopped up the spot. "There."

They resumed their beverage sipping, but after several minutes, Tomás, Anita's assistant, glared at Anita and beckoned to her. His gaze shot to Susannah, and the scowl shifted to a weak smile. His dark hair flopped over one eye.

"Ah," Anita said, "trouble in paradise."

CHAPTER TWO

Anita re-entered the kitchen, and Susannah sauntered off to the dining room, turning her gaze on Randy, who stood at the hostess's podium addressing the room. The Peach Grove Business Association, known to locals as the PGBA, was preparing to stage their biggest project—the Independence Day Festival—and the Peach Grove Police Department would provide security for the event. She glanced around the dining room. Most members focused their attention on the police chief, and she hoped she could slip into a seat unnoticed.

Susannah sipped her coffee, observing Marcie at her game. Marcie's brown bob swung into her face as she dragged a stool over from the bar and placed it directly in front of Randy. There she perched, shaking her head to straighten her hair before peppering him with questions, her green eyes boring into him and the veins in her neck bulging.

Susannah's shoulders relaxed. Perhaps Randy wouldn't notice her. Let him throw some sass at Marcie; she was impervious to snide comments. She scanned the tables, also hoping to avoid the new detective, who had accompanied Randy to the meeting; for some reason, the woman gave her gooseflesh. She rubbed her arms, taking a moment to identify club members from behind. Colin Rogers, the local auto shop owner, sat alone, his hands wrapped around a ceramic mug. At the next table, Daniel Kim, the Peach Grove insurance guru, sat with his associate.

Susannah took another sip, reveling in the sensation of espresso warming her body. No sign of Fiona Bailey; Susannah couldn't remember the last time the stable owner had attended. Billy Jones was also absent, but that was no surprise. Even when he wasn't in pain, he appeared only occasionally, preferring to fade into the background while Marcie flaunted her position as PGBA president.

A flicker of color caught her attention as Bitsy Long settled an orange shawl over her shoulder. Bitsy owned Peachy Things, a themed boutique in downtown Peach Grove, which supported her addiction for all things peachy. Keeping her eyes down, Susannah crossed to Bitsy's booth and slid in, asking, "What did I miss?"

"I'm not sure," Bitsy said, licking a blob of sour cream off her thumb. "I've been busy with this breakfast burrito."

"How did you get that?" Susannah looked around. "The kitchen isn't open yet."

"If you know the right people, it is." She chuckled, the smattering of dark freckles standing out on her rich brown skin. "My girl Anita took pity on me."

Susannah turned her attention to the podium, where Randy had stopped speaking. He ran his thick fingers through his light crew cut and stared at Marcie, whose usual workaday attire of khakis and a polo shirt went by the wayside when she was performing her duties as the PGBA president. Today, she wore a charcoal-gray skirt suit with sheer black hose, which made her look like she was on her way to a big job interview at a Fortune 500 company. As usual, her white blouse was so stiff Susannah wondered if she had bought a new one for the occasion. Marcie acted like local royalty because she came from one of the oldest and wealthiest families in Peach Grove, but in reality, she was a small-town girl who ran a chicken takeout shop.

"It's not only the watermelon seeds, Marcie," Randy said with a frown.

Susannah shot a questioning look at Bitsy, who raised her eyebrows in confusion. Marcie sponsored the Watermelon-

Eating Contest at the festival and gave out free slices of melon to practically everyone on the fairground. Susannah knew that running the contest brought Marcie a huge return on her money because she flooded the festival with coupons to the Wing Shack. Marcie had once confided to Susannah that buying a few watermelons was cheaper than running an ad in the local shopper.

"I simply don't see how you can blame slip-and-fall accidents on the contest," said Marcie. "Watermelons don't injure people. If you ask me, we have to keep the wrong kind of people away from Peach Grove. You should give out tickets for littering with a hefty fine. Problem solved." She swished her hands together as if washing the problem away.

Bitsy nudged Susannah with her knee. They both were aware of Marcie's penchant for blaming all the ills of Peach Grove on out-of-towners: they drove recklessly, they were rude and inconsiderate, and worst of all, they bypassed the Wing Shack for fast food franchises.

"It's not that simple, Marcie," Randy said. "I need all my manpower during the festival to focus on other safety issues. I can't spare any officers to follow watermelon eaters around, waiting for them to spit seeds or drop rinds on the walkways." He paused to take a swallow of coffee and caught Susannah's eye over the cup; he gave her a nod. Nothing derogatory there. Bitsy was right—she should just relax. Glancing around the dining room, Susannah saw that all eyes were front and center except for one person, who occupied the very spot where she and Anita had been standing moments earlier. It was the new detective. Her lean build conveyed a slight and unassuming appearance, but the heavy-lidded, downturned eyes gave her a viperous aspect.

Susannah looked away, pretending not to notice. Now there were two people in town who thought she was a bumbling idiot. Her empty stomach clenched. She glanced at Bitsy's plate and wondered if Anita would take her order too.

As if on cue, Anita appeared with a plate in one hand and a coffeepot in the other. She winked at Susannah and placed an order of huevos rancheros on the table. "I heard you were hungry." Susannah blushed and mouthed her thanks.

"Anyway, it's a done deal," Randy continued, an elbow on the podium. "The City of Peach Grove was sued twice last year over slip-and-fall accidents at the fair. The Watermelon-Eating Contest is canceled. Y'all can have some other kind of contest."

"Ooh, I think we should choose peaches," Bitsy cooed. "I think that makes more sense, don't you?"

Marcie shot her a glance, her green eyes the color of a troubled ocean. "Whoever heard of a peach-eating contest?"

"We can make it peach pie, can't we? I can see it now, y'all." Bitsy bumped her way out of the semicircular booth, the fringe on her peach-colored shawl jouncing along with her. She raised her hands, spreading her fingers wide, framing an imaginary scene.

Susannah ate her eggs while watching Bitsy. One of the first people she had met when she moved to town, Bitsy was her polar opposite in virtually every way. Never at a loss for words, she approached life with an effervescence that Susannah was unable to muster but always enjoyed watching.

"We can build a stage and frame it with peach-colored bunting. With a banner that says PEACH PIE-EATING CONTEST, decorated with pictures of peaches. And on the dais, big ol' piles of peaches on display, all juicy and beautiful."

CHAPTER TWO

The room was silent.

"Come on. Y'all know how much I love peaches. I have bolts of peach-themed fabric in storage. I'll do all the decorating myself." She folded her arms across her chest as if it had been settled.

Anita broke the silence. "But where will we get so many peach pies? It's not like watermelons. Even the biggest *gordo* can hardly eat one full melon, right?"

Other voices joined the debate.

A bang erupted from the front of the room. Susannah glanced around as a second and then a third bang followed. Marcie was half off the barstool, banging one of her black high heels on the podium. Past her, Randy stood with his hands on his utility belt, his face as pink as it had been the day before, his eyes hard and gazing over Marcie's head. Susannah turned and saw the detective shake her head and walk out of the restaurant. When she turned back, Randy had moved away from the podium, his color returning to normal.

Bitsy, one hand now on her hip, faced Marcie and asked, "You banged?" Bitsy was a free spirit, a big personality who dressed in bold colors and wore her hair in short spiky dreads and her nails long and painted in the color of the minute. When she had an idea, she took up three times the space of an ordinary human, using her entire body for emphasis.

"This discussion is not on the agenda. We are here for the Preliminary Safety briefing," Marcie said, pointing to her copy of the agenda.

"I'm spitballin' here," Bitsy said breathlessly. She despised the parliamentary procedures of motions and seconds, and she often clashed with Marcie over this. "You know, throwing out some new ideas." She inhaled, ready to go for a second round.

"You know the procedure," Marcie shot back, chin jutted defiantly. "You can raise a motion, and we can vote on it and put it on the agenda for the next meeting."

Bitsy raised her hand and waved it to and fro like a human windshield wiper. Marcie ignored her while she bent down to replace her shoe and then looked up, an expression of surprise on her face as if she had expected Bitsy to vanish. "The chair recognizes Bitsy Long."

"I motion we do a peach pie-eating contest."

"Those in favor of placing the peach pie-eating contest on the agenda for discussion."

Susannah eagerly raised her hand.

CHAPTER THREE

Susannah was stowing her boarding pass in her laptop bag when the phone rang. She frowned. No one called her landline anymore. She glanced at the caller ID and cussed.

The alarm company. Again.

"It can't be!" she spat, lifting the receiver and verifying her security code with the representative. No way had she locked that cat in again; there had to be another explanation. She clearly remembered Larraine shoving the cat out the door. Had Tina let him in? *Could I have missed him?* she thought, and then froze.

Could an actual burglary be in progress?

She glanced at her watch. Nine forty-five. She had allotted thirty minutes for her drive to the airport and now regretted cutting it so close. Atlanta's Hartsfield Airport was notoriously busy, and traffic was bad at any time of day. If she left now, she could make it, but if there was a break-in, she might never leave Peach Grove.

She scowled. Booking at the last minute had been a harebrained idea, brought about by an overwhelming desire to spend time with old friends. She gunned the engine of her Jeep, spewing pebbles out of her driveway and onto the lawn. Grasping her cell, she dialed Larraine, who answered immediately, saying, "I thought you would be on a plane by now."

I wish I was, she thought. "I'm on my way to the airport, but the alarm company called."

"Must be old Rusty." Larraine laughed. "I knew that fat tomcat was going to set off the alarm by lying on the windowsill crying for kibble. He needs to go on a diet."

"Mmm-hmm, not sure if we can blame Rusty this time." The left rear tire veered into a rut, and it took all her strength to hold the wheel steady and not drop the phone. "I hoped you could do me a favor and go reset it."

"I'd love to, sweet pea, but I'm in a church van halfway to Stone Mountain. We're having a picnic and then watching the laser show."

Susannah chuckled, imagining Larraine's white coif reflecting the bursts of color during the popular light show. At least that made her smile. "That's all right. Have a good time. I'll see you when I get back."

Dust swirled around her as she executed the quickest three-point turn in memory, cursing herself for not heading straight to the office. She checked the dashboard clock. Three minutes had elapsed since she left the house. Would Randy be waiting for her when she arrived, one hand on his hip, the other on his radio, smirking? What did he like to say? *"I see we've had another episode of the cat burglar."*

She jammed the gas pedal to the floor. She had to beat him there, check the building, reset the alarm, then hightail it to the airport before he showed up. If old Rusty was locked in the office overnight, so be it. She turned onto Highway 42 and sped into the front parking lot at the ten-minute mark.

The Jeep slid to a stop, front tires encroaching on the pathway to the main entrance. If Rusty had triggered the alarm, the premises divulged no signs of him. She rattled the doors, but they didn't budge. The windows gleamed, undisturbed. The alarm tech had told her that alarms went off all the time for no reason, but in her office, Rusty was the obvious fall guy. She examined the windows again. They showed no telltale signs of feline tomfoolery.

Susannah rounded the building to check the north-facing side, jogging on the grass, eyeing the side of the structure.

Nothing.

Her watch showed twelve minutes gone, and she still had the rear of the building to inspect. She exhaled, almost spitting. So far, her luck had held. Perhaps the Peach Grove PD was occupied with an actual crime. Maybe a fistfight had broken out over a parking place at the local supermarket.

Now, to reset the alarm and *skedaddle*, as Larraine would say.

A flicker of orange caught her attention, and she turned. Rusty stood about twenty-five yards off, his tawny coat standing out against a shock of green grass that grew in a drainage ditch at the side of the road.

"Well, I'll be," she said. "There's my troublemaker." Hearing her voice, he raised his chin in her direction and flicked an ear. At the same time, she heard a thud behind her. Before her brain could process the sound, she felt a blinding pain, and all went black.

CHAPTER FOUR

Susannah's head throbbed, and though she told her eyes to open, they refused to cooperate.

Ugh. I feel like I've been hit in the face with a frying pan. And not in a good way.

A voice called from a distance. She unscrunched her lids, but bluish light drove pain deeper into her neck, and nausea bubbled up her throat. She squeezed her eyes shut and flattened herself against her bed.

Why am I still in bed?

The voice called again, and she sat up. This time, a violent surge of nausea seized her, and she rolled over, narrowly avoiding vomiting on herself. She wiped her mouth on the back of her hand and groaned. The vertigo was back. She wanted to scream and rail against the condition that had changed her life, but something was different. The spinning immobilized her. When it passed, she forced herself up, unsealing her eyelids one more time. This time it took.

She wasn't in bed.

She recognized Keith Cawthorn, Tina's husband, dressed in his police uniform. His six-foot-five frame loomed over her, his face devoid of the usual warmth in his copper complexion.

CHAPTER FOUR

A smaller woman wearing the dark blue of Peach Grove Fire and Emergency squinted while touching Susannah's head with gloved hands, and then she handed Susannah a tissue. The pulsating lights of an ambulance and two police cars danced against the pines. "Keith? What's going on?"

"I hoped you could tell me," he said, his eyes assessing her in a way she had never seen. Behind him, the female detective with the snakelike eyes, dressed in cream-colored slacks and a white blouse, peered at her and listened impassively.

"I don't understand," said Susannah.

"What were you doing here?" Keith asked.

The alarm. She had wanted to beat the Peach Grove PD to the office so she could reset the alarm. Obviously, that had not gone to plan. Randy had sent Keith in his place. She eyed the detective, who now wore a sour smile, and froze. Something was amiss.

Susannah shook her head, and the spinning returned, forcing her thoughts away. Her hands rested on the cool grass. She was on the ground outside the building with a blinding headache. This wasn't an attack of Ménière's disease. She could hear, and there was no ringing in her ears, but there were flashing lights. She blinked. The blue light bars atop the police patrol cars were flanked by red ambulance lights. Officers in black windbreakers milled about the lot. An attendant removed a stretcher from the ambulance.

How did I get here? "I work here," she said. It was true.

"The office is closed," said Keith. "You're supposed to be in Florida."

"My flight," she moaned, struggling to sit up. "I'm going to miss my flight. What time is it?"

The EMT placed her gloved hand on Susannah's shoulder,

keeping her from moving. Keith leaned in, frowning. "You need to let her finish checking you out."

Susannah waved them away. Her head pounded, and she blew out a breath. The nausea was subsiding. She inhaled deeply and looked up at Keith. She saw concern in his eyes, but it was not enough to keep her on her back. Before she'd retired from the NYPD, she had gone through a lifetime's worth of medical exams, which left her as ornery as an octogenarian with her own health. She knew she had the right to refuse care. "I'll sign whatever you want, just let me get up."

Keith squinted at her, offered his oversized mitt, and helped her up. The detective stepped up, squeezing between Susannah and Keith. "I'm sorry," she said, lingering on each word, her reptilian smile giving Susannah a chill. "You can't leave until you answer some questions."

Susannah swallowed. Had Randy shared his opinion of Susannah with this woman? The nausea returned, and Susannah coached herself to aim for the detective's shoes.

"I know you're not feeling well, Doc," Keith said, "but we need to know why you were here."

Susannah touched her head, finding a knot the size of a lemon. "I got a call from the alarm company as I was leaving for the airport. I came over to check it out." She looked at Keith curiously. "Then, I think someone hit me."

Keith raised his eyebrows and then glanced at the detective. "What's all this about?" Susannah asked.

"Doc," Keith asked, "were you planning on meeting anyone before your flight?"

"Here?" Susannah shook her head. Sparks flew down her neck. *Don't do that again.* "Why would I meet someone here?

CHAPTER FOUR

I was on my way to the airport when I got the call."

The detective moved closer, removing a business card from her jacket pocket. "Varina Withers." She handed Susannah the card and tilted her head. "Maybe someone needed a quick prescription refill?"

Susannah drooped, exhausted, and squinted at Keith. "Do I have to tell her?"

"Tell me what?"

"Chiropractors don't prescribe drugs. They give adjustments."

A raspy chuckle escaped the detective's lips. "And if the adjustment doesn't work?"

Susannah rolled her eyes, and her head pounded out a new rhythm. *Don't do that, either.*

Focusing on Detective Withers, she inhaled, ready to explain that chiropractic was a system of realigning joints that depended on the skill of the practitioner and not the use of prescriptions. But her thoughts were leaden, and her tongue felt thick.

"Or, maybe someone couldn't get an adjustment because you were going out of town," Detective Withers continued, her tone patronizing. "So you helped them out with a script."

"We don't prescribe drugs. It's not in our scope of practice."

The detective smirked, bobbing her head in acknowledgment. "So you're not qualified to prescribe?"

Susannah's throat tightened as she bit back rising anger and resentment. *Who is she? And why is she such an ass? Her attitude makes Randy seem downright neighborly.* Susannah had practiced in Peach Grove for over a decade and was a respected professional and active in the community. "Why am I being interrogated?" She turned to Keith. "I have to get to the airport."

Detective Withers leaned in, and Susannah smelled peppermint on her breath. "Oh, you'll know when I interrogate you." She narrowed her eyes and walked away. Over her shoulder, she said to Keith, "You tell her."

"Tell me what?"

"Doc, you aren't the only person we found lying on the ground. Anita Alvarez is in your parking lot, and she's dead."

CHAPTER FIVE

Susannah steadied herself. The bump on her head smarted as she watched Bitsy through Peachy Things' glass door. She had spent the morning answering the detective's questions. The shock of seeing Anita face down in the parking lot of Peach Grove Chiropractic was made worse by Detective Withers's insinuation that Susannah had somehow been to blame. Shaky and nauseated, she couldn't bear to eat anything and had skipped lunch in favor of a call on Bitsy.

The idea that she could have saved Anita if she had only gone to the back of the building first taunted her. That, mingled with an intermittent fear of arrest, spurred her desire to leave the office and find solace with her friend.

Susannah understood that she had stumbled upon the crime in progress, but somehow the police didn't see it that way. The detective had even told her she shouldn't leave town—as if she were their primary suspect. On the quick drive from her office, she recalled the raised voices she had overheard in the Cantina Caliente: Anita and Tomás quarreling in the kitchen. At the time, she had assumed it was a minor spat. Anita had laughed it off as "trouble in paradise." *More like a devil in your midst*, she thought, then bit her lip. Could Tomás have been so angry with Anita that he had killed her? That was one possibility.

Through the window, Susannah spied Bitsy leaning over the checkout counter, a cell phone clamped to her ear and worry lines intensifying her frown. A peach-colored wrap adorned her shoulders, and the tasseled edges swayed as she tapped a fine-tipped marker on her lip. Bitsy had grown up in a rural part of the county on a small family farm. She had a large family and seemed to be friends with everyone who had ever attended her high school. Though she had left Georgia for the big city to pursue her dreams of becoming a fashion designer, when she returned to Peach Grove, it was as if she had never left.

Bitsy hung up, and Susannah pushed the door open; tiny bells jingled, announcing her presence. Bitsy dropped her marker and rushed around the counter with open arms. She pushed past a tangle of leather shoulder bags, rocking the stainless steel rack on which they hung. The high-end bags, which to Bitsy's credit were in a variety of colors besides peach, convulsed spasmodically as she grabbed Susannah, squeezing her arms hard enough to bruise.

"Oww," Susannah said, trying to wriggle out of her grasp.

Bitsy released her and stepped back. "Goodness gracious. You look like you've seen a ghost," she said, crushing a burgundy-colored bag between them as she pulled Susannah in for a hug. She waved a hand over Susannah's bandaged head. "Shouldn't you be in the hospital? I thought you had a concussion."

"Who told you?" Susannah was not surprised. Gossip traveled through town faster than the Norfolk Southern

CHAPTER FIVE

freight trains.

"My cousin Junior works at the police station. He called me soon as he heard."

"I thought your cousin Junior drove a wrecker."

"That's plain Junior. This here is Little Junior."

Susannah nodded. Bitsy had cousins in every nook and cranny of the county, most with equally odd nicknames.

"Are you sure you're all right? Junior told me Anita Alvarez is dead and you were knocked out flat. Why aren't you at the hospital?"

"I refused to go."

"Refused to go? Why wouldn't you go?"

"Because I'm fine."

Bitsy took Susannah's hand and led her past the peach-speckled tote bags with their matching wallets and through a curtain that led to the back room where she stored her inventory and ate her lunch. She ushered Susannah into a folding chair and patted her hand.

"Stop." Susannah wriggled her hand from Bitsy's steely grasp. "I need to talk."

"Girl, give me a second, then I'm all ears." Bitsy strode to a heavily painted cupboard and wrenched the knob. Warped from age, the door was long and narrow; its hinges squawked, and the bottom edge scraped along the floor. She stuck her head into the closet, delving into its dark recesses. "Oof," she grunted as parts of her ample upper body overflowed the meager doorway. As she withdrew, her shawl snagged a nail, and she yanked it free. The building that housed Peachy Things belonged to the historical district and was over a hundred and fifty years old. Susannah had never understood why a style maven like Bitsy didn't tear out the crooked wooden cabinets and creaky pine board floors and replace them with materials from the twenty-first century. Even the twentieth century would do.

"I got something special for you." Bitsy brandished a black drawstring pouch on her palm as if she were balancing a plate on a stick. Her hand trembled from its weight. She glanced excitedly at Susannah as she placed it on the table and set her long fingernails to work untying the string.

"What is it?"

"This here is an old family recipe. One sip and you'll be good as new." She pulled out a mason jar filled with a clear liquid and twisted open the lid.

"Is that moonshine?"

"You've heard of it, hunh?"

"You know I don't drink this early in the day."

"This isn't drinking—it's medicinal."

Susannah was doubtful. "I'm fine."

Bitsy raised a brow and peered into Susannah's face. "Humph. You're not fine. I know you think some gluten-free vitamins and a massage can fix everything, but I can see that ghost-scared look in your eyes."

"Fight evil spirits with some evil spirit, eh?"

"You shouldn't mock the spirit world." Bitsy regarded her through narrowed eyes, as if assessing her impact on the spirit world.

Susannah didn't answer.

"I see you're not arguing with me."

"I'm still not drinking that."

Bitsy glared at her. "Well, someone has to." She lifted the jar to her lips and took a small sip, shuddering as she swallowed. She placed the jar on a small table and screwed the lid back on. "What did you want to talk about?"

"When you were at the Cantina the other day, did you notice any problem between Anita and Tomás?"

"No. Why?"

"Because I heard them arguing in the kitchen. Tomás stuck his head out of the kitchen door, and he was so angry his face was red. Anita just laughed it off."

Bitsy nodded. "So you think Tomás might have done her in?"

"Well, when you put it that way, I'm not sure."

"Me neither. You know how hot-tempered restaurant workers are. You ever watch Gordon Ramsay? Were they telling each other to piss off?"

Susannah chuckled at her reference to the volatile tempers in the reality TV kitchen. "Maybe I am making too much of it."

Bitsy's cell rang, and she removed it from her pocket, answering with a deft swipe of the thumb. "Uh-huh. Uh-huh. Okay." Her eyebrows peaked as she listened.

Susannah turned away to give her privacy and found herself contemplating piles of purses, clutches, and totes. A low wooden shelf held cardboard boxes and sealed plastic bags filled with boutique fodder. Bitsy loved accessories as much as Susannah loved chiropractic equipment.

Susannah had spent many years in this town as a healer, a vocation that suited her much better than her short-lived career as a police officer had. That choice seemed preordained by growing up in a family of law enforcement officers. Some of her first memories were of being captured and tied up by her older siblings in their games of cops and robbers. As the youngest of four children, she had been relegated by her brothers and sister to the role of the bumbling robber—an opinion one brother maintained as she grew into adulthood. Sadly, her career in law enforcement had done nothing to change this opinion. She had pushed away the humiliation she felt when she resigned her position with NYPD. Chiropractic school had been her true calling, and it had delighted her to discover that she was a natural healer.

However, there was nothing delightful in what happened today. Her office had been the location of a repugnant act, one that stained her reputation and hurt her soul. What was worse, it had been perpetrated against someone she knew and liked.

Bitsy ended the call and shot Susannah a pointed side-eye while jamming the phone into her rear pocket. She gave the mason jar a wistful parting glance and crammed it back into the bag, then closed the warped door with a kick. "Let's go. I'm taking you home." She hurried to the front door and with a flick of the wrist flipped the OPEN sign to CLOSED.

They left the shop and crossed Main Street to where Bitsy had parked her black Ford Explorer. Susannah, trailing behind, asked, "Who was on the phone?"

"That was Junior again. Seems a detective by the name of Weathers was kicking up a fuss about Anita's murderer."

"It's Withers."

Betsy stopped next to her truck, her peach-shaped key chain dangling from a manicured finger. "That's what I said, Weathers."

"I already talked to her. I think Junior is relaying old news."

"No. This is new news. Junior has his ears on the situation, and he says Detective Weathers has been trying to convince

Randy to bring you in." She looked down, avoiding eye contact with Susannah. "Junior says she's ranting about how alternative doctors are dangerous because they take advantage of sick people by taking their money and keeping them away from real doctors. Junior thinks she's—" She pointed to her temple and twirled her finger to signify *crazy*, then opened the passenger door for Susannah and pushed her in. She got in the driver's side, started the truck, and gunned the engine. "Junior heard Keith tell her he's been in your office many times. He told her that him and Tina get their backs cracked."

"I don't know how that changes anything." She fingered the bandage on her head as Bitsy maneuvered out of the parking place. "I thought Anita died from head trauma like me."

Bitsy slammed on the brakes. The truck pitched and stopped. She faced Susannah, grabbed the flesh of her upper arm, and squeezed, twisting like she was wrestling with a key stuck in a lock.

"Hey!" Susannah slapped her hand away. "Stop doing that." She reached out and pinched Bitsy above her elbow, grabbing a piece of her peach-colored shawl in the process.

"Ow!" Bitsy cried, slapping Susannah's hand away. "I'm making sure I ain't talking to no ghost."

"What do you mean?"

"You said, 'Anita died, like me.'" Bitsy sailed out of the small lot and onto Highway 42. She shot a look at Susannah. "You for sure alive."

"I meant, I thought someone hit her in the head, like they hit me."

Bitsy smoothed down her shawl. "Why do you think that? Did Keith tell you that?"

"No. Not exactly." Susannah tried to remember his words, but her phone interrupted her thoughts. She stared at the number in surprise. "It's Randy." Susannah frowned.

"How does he know your cell number?" Bitsy asked, alarmed.

"We were on that planning committee last year." Susannah chewed a cuticle. "Maybe I should go talk to him."

"No." Bitsy grabbed Susannah's phone without looking at the display and tucked it under her thigh. "I'm gonna have to do your thinking for you, on account of this concussion." She pointed at Susannah's head. "If the police want to talk to you, you do *not* want to talk to them. And no fleeing the jurisdiction. You can hide, but you better not run."

"It's Randy. He knows me," she said, though her voice wavered. Randy had never been more than an acquaintance, and his snide remarks about her former occupation had revealed disdain, not friendship. He never let an opportunity pass to joke about her training with the NYPD. She bit her lip. Maybe he felt a smidgen of professional rivalry. Inept or not, the NYPD *was* the largest police force in the country.

Stupefied, she realized that she had no idea what he actually thought of her. She'd lived in Peach Grove for years, but Randy always talked to her like she had moved in last week. She tugged at her blouse and swallowed. She didn't need him sniffing around the NYPD to find out how her career had ended.

Bitsy pointed at Susannah, shaking her finger while she drove. "Randy is the Chief of Police, but the mayor hired this detective. That means she wants to make the mayor happy, not him."

Susannah's face fell. She and the mayor were not on the

CHAPTER FIVE

best of terms thanks to a slight misunderstanding. "Maybe you're right. Maybe I should lie low for a while. Let them find out what happened to Anita before I talk to that woman again."

"You can come home with me until you figure out what to do next." Bitsy edged the truck across the railroad tracks with a gleam in her eye. "I'll cook you up a mess of greens and some cornbread, dripping with butter."

The truck rattled over the last rail, and a stabbing pain struck Susannah's neck, making her eyes water. Her phone rang. She cast her eyes down at Bitsy's thigh. "Half a mile away from the police station is hardly off the grid."

"Oh baby girl, if you want to get off the grid, I can help with that too." She pulled in front of her Queen Anne cottage, a Victorian style of architecture common to rural Georgia. Painted light blue with bright white trim, it had an understated look, at least from the front. Originally constructed in 1890 with no indoor plumbing or heating, subsequent residents had added on to it, giving it a haphazard flow that Bitsy called eclectic. "I'll park the truck way behind my gardening shed, and no one will even know that I'm here."

Bitsy loved to garden. Her shed was her pride and joy, a prefabricated aluminum unit that looked like a gingerbread house trimmed with blue tulips. She felt it gave her an edge against the archenemies of Georgia gardeners: fire ants and their hungry cousins, termites.

She turned into the rutted drive, which at first glance appeared to be a two-track dirt road running alongside a row of overgrown hedges. Despite her slow speed, the truck rattled and bumped over the hard clay soil. Susannah shut her eyes and stifled a moan as pain shot from her neck to the top of her head.

"Hang on, we'll be on the grass in a—"

Susannah opened her eyes to see Bitsy's truck nose to nose with Randy Laughton's cruiser.

CHAPTER SIX

Randy Laughton met Susannah's eyes and lifted his thick fingers off the steering wheel in acknowledgment. The bent grass at the foot of the cruiser told her he had not been waiting long.

Bitsy shifted into reverse, her hand clenched on the wheel, her foot poised over the accelerator. Without taking her eyes off Randy, Susannah tapped Bitsy's hand. "Don't," she said, her mouth dry, the rules of her former profession coming back to her. "We can't run."

A woman was dead, her body discovered on Susannah's property. The police were disregarding the fact that she had been assaulted. If she didn't cooperate, she would appear guilty. Besides, the more she mulled it over, the more questions she had. Why had Anita been at her office? Was she meeting someone? Perhaps someone who had access to the office? Larraine was two counties away at the time of the murder, but what about Tina? It horrified Susannah to think Tina could have had anything to do with such a vicious crime, but Tina knew the building would be deserted and was one of only three people who had a key.

She felt guilty for even imagining that it could involve her assistant. Her thoughts were sluggish, like boots stuck in Georgia mud. Were Tina and Anita even acquainted? And if they wanted to meet, why not do so at the restaurant?

Her eyes connected with Randy's. Normally blue-gray, today they appeared the color of steel. She felt a tingling in her neck. Could the police suspect Keith? A fellow Peach Grove police officer and husband to Tina, Keith would have known the office was closed and about the secluded nature of the back parking lot. He could have gotten Tina's key off her key ring without her knowing. She swallowed. Could Keith have been meeting Anita for a rendezvous?

Bitsy's voice roused her from her thoughts. "We could hide until we figure this out. I know every backwoods road around here."

"And Randy does too." Randy and Bitsy had attended the same schools and had spent years on the rural roads of the county. It was tempting but not realistic. "You should know that."

"I know what I know, and I know what Randy don't know."

"I have to talk to him."

"You're makin' a mistake."

Susannah shot her a look. "Anita's dead, and I need some answers."

"Don't get in his car." Bitsy exhaled. "Meet on neutral ground." She threw the truck into park, her fingers tapping. "Keep away from them handcuffs. If he touches you, you yell, 'Police brutality!' and raise your hands up so he don't shoot. I'll come running and record the whole thing on my phone. One time, my Uncle Moses Long—"

Susannah put a finger to her lips, stopping what she knew would turn into a rambling history of the Long family's

CHAPTER SIX

dealings with the law.

A rap on the driver's-side window sent the fringe on Bitsy's shawl shuddering like a frightened tabby. "Ladies." Randy stooped, peering into the truck.

"Randy," Susannah said, the word sticking in her throat. Bitsy tried to smooth her shawl, her fingernails tangling in the decorative weave.

"I thought I might find you together."

"That ain't no feat of detective work," Bitsy mumbled.

Randy placed one arm over the other and leaned his elbows on the car door. "Susannah, I've been trying to get in touch with you."

"Humph," Bitsy said, shifting her leg to make sure that her thigh covered the face of Susannah's phone.

"Could I have a word in private?"

Bitsy turned to Susannah. "You have the right to remain silent. You do not have to talk to him." She turned back to Randy. "We know our rights."

"I'm not fixin' to arrest her. I only want to talk."

"That's what they said to Uncle Moses."

Susannah got out, slammed the passenger-side door, and glared at Bitsy through the windshield, silently urging her to stay put as she followed Randy to the side yard. He stopped next to Bitsy's monster privet hedge, which bowed under the weight of fragrant white flowers. There was a formality to his bearing, a stiffness to his posture, and a seriousness in his manner Susannah had never seen. Whatever he meant to say, she wasn't going to like it.

"Ms. Susannah, we've known each other awhile."

She tried not to bristle at being called *Ms.* instead of *Doctor*. Using *Ms.* with a woman's first name was common in Georgia, but she felt the slight like a slap in the face. She forced a slight smile, all the while imagining her *Ms.*-sized hands throwing him into the hedge and pummeling him.

"This is strictly off the record." He glanced over at Bitsy and turned his back to the truck. Susannah saw her lean her elbow on the truck's door frame, unabashedly jutting her head out the window.

"I'm glad to hear that because I have some questions that I would like answered."

Randy shook his head. "I can't give you any information in an ongoing investigation."

"I thought we were off the record," she retorted, turning away.

"Listen to me," he said, reaching out to her. "I'm off the case. Detective Withers is in charge now."

"She is?"

He nodded. "You best watch yourself."

"What does that mean?"

"I just mean cooperate with her."

"Am I a suspect?"

Randy hooked his thumbs over his belt. "Right now, you are a person of interest."

"What? Why?"

"Keith told us you closed the office and were going out of town. Detective Withers looked into your flight arrangements and noticed you have a one-way ticket to Tampa."

"And?"

"She thinks you are a flight risk." He looked down at his hands. "It's mighty suspicious."

"It's a last-minute vacation. An old friend talked me into coming along on a family fishing trip. He had already

CHAPTER SIX

chartered a boat, and I wanted to get there fast, so I decided to fly. I paid for a one-way ticket because I was going to rent a car to meet up with my friend and drive it back."

"Ummm," he said noncommittally. "Do you have your car rental agreement?"

"I thought this was off the record. Why are you asking me this?"

Randy said nothing for a moment. When he finally spoke, his voice was a whisper. "Detective Withers is new in town and doesn't have a dog in this fight, which is why she's in charge."

Susannah's brow tightened. Even thinking about the woman gave her a headache. "I was only going to be gone a few days. I have patients scheduled next week." She heard her voice getting louder but didn't care. In fact, it felt good.

Randy put up his hand in a "lower your voice" gesture. "Can't you see that it might look suspicious?"

"Someone taking a vacation looks suspicious? I rarely leave my practice. I'm overdue for a vacation."

"That's not what the detective sees. She sees someone who is deviating from her normal pattern."

"The only reason I'm not already out of town is because whoever attacked Anita almost killed me." Her hand flew to the bandage on her head. "I'm a victim too."

Randy's eyes widened. "Then act like it."

Susannah was stunned. "What does that mean?"

His face flushed, turning his nose a deep shade of pink. "Go to the hospital. Refusing to be treated makes it look like you're hiding something. Withers thought you were more worried about going on your trip than the dead woman in your parking lot."

"I didn't know anyone was in my parking lot!" Susannah snapped, stepping back, wobbling as her heel settled into a patch of soft Bermuda grass. Randy reached out to steady her, but she waved his hand away. She heard a squeak and glanced at the truck to see Bitsy's elbow slide down the door panel as she leaned her upper body out the window. "Keith and the detective withheld that information from me."

"Susannah, I have to be objective here." He turned away, rubbing a thick forefinger over his lip. When he turned back, there was a determination in his eyes that frightened her. "Keith is off the case because his wife works for you. It's Detective Withers's case now. I can't stand in the way of her investigation, but I'm giving you a little friendly advice."

Susannah's shoulders sagged, and a weight pulled on a spot behind her breastbone that turned her words to dust. Perhaps she should be grateful for the warning, but she was angry. "That would be?" Her voice sounded rough.

"Get your affairs in order at home and in your office."

Susannah opened her mouth to object but said nothing. His words struck her to the core. Why was she a suspect? She thought back to her encounter with Detective Withers. The woman seemed to dislike her immediately. If two women were attacked in the same way, what would make one of them a suspect?

Randy jerked a thumb over his shoulder at Bitsy. "Have her bring you to the hospital. The EMT thought you had a concussion. Let a doctor make the diagnosis official, then go home and stay there."

CHAPTER SEVEN

Randy nosed his black-and-white out of the drive, and Susannah watched him speed away. She chewed on her lip, reviewing the day's events in her mind: the call from the alarm company, the drive to the office, and the terrible mistake she made by not going around the building immediately. Anita's killer had been hiding. If she had driven straight into the back parking lot, might Anita be alive right now? And what about the alarm? Rusty had not been locked inside the office; he was not the wrongdoer this time. So who was? Had Anita been banging on the door, hoping someone was inside the building? Surely she already knew the building was empty.

"I shouldn't be telling you any of this," Randy had said before he left. "I believe our new detective is barkin' up the wrong tree. But you're going to have to prove it to her before she moves on."

Susannah felt weary. It took all her strength to climb into Bitsy's truck and shut the door. The clicking of Bitsy's nails on the steering wheel got her attention.

"So, what did you learn?" Bitsy asked.

"Nothing." Susannah grasped the door handle to steady

herself. "Except Randy thinks I should go to the hospital. He's doing me a favor by telling me what I already know."

"Well…" She peered at Susannah, a clear *I told you so* expression on her face. "Let's go." She put the truck in gear and headed toward the hospital. "What else did he say?"

"You mean, besides that Detective Withers suspects me?"

"Uh-huh, besides that."

"He couldn't disclose any information because of the 'ongoing investigation.'" Susannah put air quotes around the words *ongoing investigation.* She didn't care if she was using air quotes incorrectly.

Apparently neither did Bitsy. "So let's go over what we know."

Susannah inhaled and then nodded. She held up a finger. "I know the office was closed and locked, and a lot of people knew it. I know Anita was in the back parking lot, and someone, maybe Anita, tripped the alarm."

"And we know you showed up and made someone mad, so they clocked you," Bitsy offered. "But we don't know who or with what."

"Right. The detective wouldn't give me any information. Neither would Randy or Keith. Whatever it was, it couldn't have been very big." She flinched as her fingers massaged the spot on her head. "Or I would have been a goner."

"What else do we know?"

Susannah paused, not wanting to divulge her suspicions about Tina and Keith. She gazed out the window, letting the scenery calm her. They passed stands of evergreens, a staple of the Georgia landscape. Puffy white clouds dotted an azure sky. A beautiful June day, ruined by a horrible incident. She closed her eyes and dozed off. The car stopped, and she looked up, surprised to find herself at Henry County Hospital.

"I'll meet you inside," Bitsy said.

Susannah made her way to the admissions desk, where a young woman with straight brown hair handed her a clipboard stacked with forms and pointed to a seating area. Susannah retreated to a plastic chair, sitting next to a five-year-old covered in grass stains who jabbered to himself. He and a little girl, presumably his sister, appeared to have been dragged across a wet lawn. The girl wailed, fat teardrops sliding down her dirt-streaked cheeks.

Susannah put her head down and went to work, ignoring the boy, who waved as he danced toward the entrance, his tongue touching his top lip.

"Tommy," his mother called, "come here."

"Mama, that lady in the orange cape is waving at me."

"Come back here before I give you a lickin'."

"Mama," the boy said, "the lady is waving at the policeman now."

Susannah looked up and saw the boy pointing at Bitsy, who stood outside the automatic glass doors, gesticulating at a security guard. He pulled his nightstick from its holster as Bitsy shook her finger at him.

"Mama, is she a superhero? She has a cape."

The boy's mother grabbed his hand and pulled him across the room, a look of alarm spreading across her face. Susannah rushed through the doors and was ready to drag Bitsy away from her own brush with police brutality when the guard sheathed his stick and let out a bark of laughter. Bitsy beamed and threw her arms around the guard's neck. She broke off the hug when she saw Susannah.

"This here is my old friend, Roman Broady." Roman turned

to face Susannah. Deep-set eyes and a stubbly beard gave him a gruff, forbidding look, but a broad smile illuminated his long face. His complexion was a few shades darker than Bitsy's, and he sported a few freckles in almost the same pattern. He could have been one of her many cousins, but the twinkle in his light brown eyes testified to a different relationship. Bitsy said, "We've known each other since we were kids. When he gets a break, he's gonna give me a tour of the campus."

"Nice to meet you, Roman." Susannah smiled.

"I better get you inside," Bitsy said, and she waved her fingers at him and shooed Susannah into the waiting room.

"A tour?"

"Don't worry. I'm here to help you as much as you need." She perched on the chair that the little boy had vacated. He stood nearby, wide-eyed, enthralled by her every move.

Susannah lifted the clipboard. "I'm fine. I eat paperwork like this for lunch."

Bitsy rubbernecked while Susannah wrote. "You missed one." She tapped the page with an orange fingernail, and the clipboard clattered to the floor. The admittance clerk looked over at them with a scowl. "You need to hold on to this." Bitsy handed Susannah the clipboard, frowning. "Your grip strength is going."

"So is my patience," Susannah said. It was her turn to shoo.

Bitsy stood tentatively. "Well, maybe I'll run to the restroom."

"Go on your tour, please. That would help me."

"Only if you're sure," she said, already three feet away. "Roman will be so excited. This is his first real job since he got out."

"Out?" Susannah said, absentmindedly.

"Discharged from the Marines."

"Uh-huh," she said without looking up. Bitsy disappeared, and Susannah finished the forms and returned them to the clerk, who pushed her glasses up the bridge of her nose and took her time reading each page.

Susannah turned away, making room for an enormous man with a bloody neckerchief wrapped around his hand. He leaned forward, raising his hand at the clerk, and asked, "How much longer do I have to wait?"

"The doctors are working as fast as they can," the clerk said. Susannah gave him a sympathetic shrug and headed to her chair, but before she could reach it, Bitsy intercepted her.

"That was a quick tour," Susannah commented.

"I think you should take it too." She guided Susannah away from the admissions area and down a hall past the restrooms. Roman leaned against the wall next to an elevator bank. He straightened up and mashed the call button. The door slid open, and he got in. Bitsy followed. She turned to face Susannah. "Come on, you want to see this."

The elevator descended one floor, and the doors slid open. Roman motioned for Susannah to go first and held the door while Bitsy followed. The hall was brightly lit and smelled of disinfectant. "Dr. Shine," Roman began, "Bitsy tells me how much you've supported her over the years."

"Well, that's what friends are for," Susannah said.

"You got that right, girlfriend." Bitsy lifted her upturned palm for a high five.

"Seriously?" Susannah asked.

She lowered her hand.

"I agree one hundred percent." Roman nodded, indicating they should proceed down the hall, which ended at double doors. His eyes sparkled, "My girl Bitsy had my back when we was young'uns. Kept me from a hide whipping, a time or two."

Susannah laughed, and he continued, "Now it's time for me to return the favor," he said, patting Bitsy on the shoulder.

"Oh, you on the right track," Bitsy said, leaning into his shoulder and nudging him with her elbow.

Susannah observed their behavior, amused. Suddenly Bitsy straightened and looked past Susannah's head. A tall, muscular woman stood before the double doors. Her black hair was pulled into a severe ponytail, and her scrubs were smudged. She held a surgical mask in her left hand, and her black eyes bored into Susannah's skull.

Susannah stepped back. She hadn't heard the door open.

"This is Iris Duncan," Roman said. "We served in Iraq together. She helped me get this job."

"I told him there was an opening." She turned her gaze to Roman, who stood with his feet apart and hands flexed. "He got the job on his own. It was the least I could do. He saved my life."

Roman shook his head dismissively, and his full lips flattened. "Tell the doc what you told me about the lady who was found down in Peach Grove today."

Iris glanced down the hall. "Preliminary findings are unremarkable. Cause of death is pending."

Susannah gasped. "I thought she was bludgeoned."

Iris shook her head. The muscles around her eyes tightened as she replaced the face mask. "No signs of trauma. The ME sent blood labs out with some detective looking over his shoulder. Never seen her around here before." She snapped the elastic band over her ponytail and turned to Roman. "I

CHAPTER SEVEN

have to get back. Don't come here again."

CHAPTER EIGHT

Susannah, a bag of frozen peas balanced on her head, scooped Ben & Jerry's nondairy Cherry Garcia into her mouth with a tablespoon. Thankful that her treatment for a mild concussion had gone smoothly, she had rebuffed Bitsy's offer to spend the night. Instead, she wrapped herself in a blanket and sprawled on the couch, watching Turner Classic Movies. When she was a child, her Nana had instilled a love of old action movies and film noir in her, and *Murder, My Sweet* played in black and white. She let the twisted tale play out as she pondered the questions that had been swirling around her mind all day.

Why was Anita at Peach Grove Chiropractic? Because of the many PGBA meetings at the Cantina Caliente, Susannah knew that Anita opened the restaurant on certain weekdays, arriving before anyone else. By 9:30 a.m., she should have been in the kitchen, drinking espresso, arguing with Tomás, and prepping for the Cantina's lunch crowd. Had she left the restaurant, or was she on her way there when she stopped off at Peach Grove Chiropractic? She wasn't a patient, so she would not have known that the office was closed on this particular Friday. Did her car act up, causing her to detour to the office, hoping for help? Had she banged on the door and set off the alarm, or had something more nefarious happened? Surely, she would have noticed if someone was following her and called the police instead of parking in the back lot, hidden from view.

In her mind's eye, Susannah imagined an assailant—a mugger or carjacker—attacking Anita. Susannah saw her pleading for help, beating on the window. She shook off the image; it could not be right. The medical examiner had found no trauma. Could Anita have died of natural causes? If she had, how long would it take a medical examiner to reveal this information? Susannah stretched her neck. Most likely, they would wait until those toxicology tests returned. That could take weeks.

She licked the last bit of cherry off her spoon. Detective Withers suspected Susannah because it was logical to think an encounter had taken place. True, there might have been a meeting, but it had not been with Susannah. She clenched the spoon, knowing that she could not mention her suspicion of Tina or Keith to anyone until she spoke to them first. Just because Tina had a key to the office did not mean that she'd been there.

It was with a deadly seriousness that she realized it was up to her to find out who Anita had been with—and why. Finally, comforted with the knowledge of what she had to do, she punched the remote, placed Ben & Jerry in the freezer, and went to bed.

#

The next morning, Susannah stood at the rear entrance to her office. A sense of foreignness came over her, as if this were the first time she had been there. Rusty lay on the bench and lifted his head, then rolled over. She scratched his chin and checked to see that he had food in the blue plastic dish.

The door opened, and Tina pushed past Larraine and rushed out. Her round, wide-set eyes lent her face an innocence that disappeared as her hand flew up to her short-cropped hair in the exact place where Susannah's head throbbed. "Dr. Shine, why aren't you home resting? Keith told me you had some knot on your head when he found you."

Susannah felt her face burning with guilt. Much as she did not believe Tina or Keith could be involved, she couldn't be certain until she had more information.

Larraine put her hand on Susannah's shoulder. "Dr. S.," Larraine said. Her pale, sinewy fingers held Susannah tight. "Lord have mercy. Look at that bump."

Susannah imagined what she must look like: her hair was modified bed head, her eyes were red from lack of sleep, and she was bloated from too much Cherry Garcia. But Larraine wasn't looking at her waist. Susannah touched her head for the hundredth time. This bump was no badge of honor; it was a badge of stupidity. "I'm fine, really. I'd rather not hear any more about it."

Larraine opened her mouth as if to speak and then seemed to think better of it. She touched Tina's arm, and something unspoken passed between them. "Do you want to work today?" Larraine asked. "I've had two new patients call in for appointments. Everyone else still thinks you're on vacation."

"Yes, I'll need something to do," Susannah said, too late realizing that she should pay a visit to the Cantina.

She saw concern in Larraine's icy blue eyes; Larraine knew that a murder in her parking lot could be a harbinger of bad times for her chiropractic practice. "Good. Tina and I were going to purge the files."

"Sure." Susannah nodded. It was probably best for all of them to keep busy. "Purge away."

The two women headed for the file room, but Susannah interrupted them with a question. "There's something I've been wondering," she said, making eye contact with each woman in turn. "Is there some way Anita Alvarez would have known that the office was closed?"

Speaking Anita's name seemed to release the tension from the room, and Larraine wiggled her shoulders, fingered the buttons on her cardigan, and exhaled.

"Well, it wasn't a secret," she said, thinking aloud. "I called everyone who had been in last week to remind them." She waved a hand in Tina's direction and gave her a thoughtful look. "And Tina sent a blast email out to our entire list of patients."

"But she wasn't on our list," Tina said. "Was she?" Her brown eyes shone with flecks of gold as she looked at Larraine for clarification. "I don't remember seeing her name."

"No," Larraine said, "she was never a patient."

Susannah steadied her gaze. "Did she call here that morning? Contact either of you?"

"No," Tina said. "I forwarded the office number to my cell phone. There were no calls until after, uh, the accident."

Susannah forced herself to ask, "Are you sure?"

Tina nodded. "Yup. Keith and I ate breakfast with my phone in the middle of the table, so I wouldn't miss any calls." She looked at Susannah sheepishly. "Keith plays the TV hella loud while he gets ready for work." She rolled her eyes. "But he got called in early that morning, so I know I didn't miss any calls on account of him. He was out of the house before 7:00

a.m."

Susannah nodded, relieved that Tina and Keith had been accounted for at the time of the murder.

"But I was thinking..." Tina tilted her head in Susannah's direction, color rising in her dark complexion. "Maybe Ms. Alvarez came here because she wanted to get adjusted. Or maybe she wanted to talk to you. Y'all are in that business club together, right?"

"Now hang on," Larraine interrupted. "If she wanted an appointment, why was she in the back parking lot?"

Susannah's eyebrows went up. "That's exactly what's been bugging me. Why wasn't she at the front door?"

Tina shook her head.

"I have no earthly idea," Larraine said. She fingered her cardigan again. "Patients always park in the front parking lot. Most of them don't even know that we come in this way." She tilted her head to indicate the back door.

"Maybe she didn't park in the front because she didn't want to come in," Tina whispered. "Maybe she parked there so she *wouldn't* be seen."

All three women turned to look at the door. Tina pulled the curtains aside, and they watched as the sudden movement caused Rusty to scamper away with his tail down. He crossed the gravel lot slowly, and Tina held the fabric aloft until his paws touched the grass of the field next door.

"It's secluded," she said. "Keith always tells me that the back lot is too secluded. He can't see it when he drives by because of the trees that line the pasture on Piney Grove. He wants me to park in the front lot when we're working late."

"But Anita was here in the morning. Why would that matter?" Larraine asked.

CHAPTER EIGHT

Tina tittered. "Ms. Larraine, you so sweet."

Larraine looked confused.

"If she met someone, it wasn't me," Susannah said, looking at Larraine pointedly. "She didn't want to be seen."

"Oh," Larraine said, blushing. She shook her head, making a soft *tsk-tsk* sound. "Y'all should know better than to gossip about someone who's passed."

"Let's say it's speculation," Susannah said. "And it stays inside these walls. All we know for sure is that she was here, and she didn't park in the patient lot. We *think* she didn't want an appointment, or she would have been at the front door. And we *think* she was meeting someone in secret."

Tina nodded her agreement. Larraine pursed her lips and then leaned toward Susannah and said, "Speculation is just a fancy word for gossip."

Susannah took Larraine's hand in hers, drinking in her fair face. "It's not gossip if we don't tell anyone else."

Larraine thought it over and allowed herself a slight smile.

The three women parted, each with their own thoughts.

CHAPTER NINE

Susannah sat at her desk watching Henry swim about his tank and search out hiding places. She had considered buying him a snail or a ghost shrimp for company, but in the end had settled on a moss ball. The round green plant was a colorful addition to the environment. Henry seemed satisfied. She, on the other hand, was not.

She swiveled her chair and gazed out the window at the peach orchard across the street. The fruit hung heavy on the trees, the earliest varieties already ripening. Watching locals lug bushels of peaches to their cars was preferable to writing insurance reports. She pushed away from the desk.

This is a colossal waste of time. I need to get out of this office and start asking questions.

Bitsy picked up on the first ring.

"How about we meet for a late breakfast?" Susannah asked.

"Just what I was thinking," Bitsy said, and Susannah could hear her smiling. "Just give me a few minutes. Andrea is due here at eleven."

Susannah was about to reply but gasped as a familiar vehicle came into view.

"What is it?"

CHAPTER NINE

"We might have to put off lunch. Detective Withers just pulled into my parking lot."

"I'll be right there!"

Susannah crept down the hall as two thoughts battled for dominance. The first registered danger and urged her to flee. *Waffles sound good right about now*, it said. The second thought came from her upbringing in a house full of law enforcement officers. *Stand your ground*, it said. *Nothing good comes of cowardice.*

She entered the waiting room, a layer of perspiration on her upper lip. The detective leafed through a pamphlet, which she tucked back into its Lucite holder as she faced Susannah, her eyes giving nothing away. Today her kinky blond hair was collected into a loose bun, her face sharp angles with those poisonous eyes.

"Dr. Shine, I wanted to have a word with you about Ms. Alvarez and why she was here the other day."

"As I told you, I don't know why Anita was here."

The detective grunted low in her throat. "You told me that when you arrived here, you weren't aware that Ms. Alvarez was in your parking lot?"

"That's correct."

"She didn't contact you?"

"No."

"When did you speak to her last?"

"At the Business Association meeting," Susannah said. "Wednesday morning."

"What did you discuss?"

"Nothing much, just chitchat."

"*Chitchat?* Could you be more specific?"

Susannah sighed. "Chitchat, you know, 'How are you,'

'Thanks for the coffee,' 'See you later.'"

"Mmm-hmm." The woman excelled at nonverbal expressions. "I understand that you and Ms. Alvarez were by yourselves for part of the meeting, and that was all the conversation you had?"

"Yes." Susannah swallowed. She didn't think admitting that she told Anita the story of Rusty, the "cat burglar," could be integral to a murder investigation. "She was busy. She was in and out of the kitchen. There was some kind of issue going on in there."

"What do you mean?"

Susannah explained that she had heard an argument coming from the kitchen and that Tomás sounded upset.

"And you didn't get involved in this issue?" The detective asked, emphasizing the word *issue*.

"No."

"Could you hear any of the argument?"

"No."

"Did you perhaps peek into the kitchen to see who was in there?"

"No."

"Did you go into the kitchen at the Cantina Caliente at any time?"

"No."

"Did you get involved in this 'issue'?" The detective lifted her head and jutted her chin.

"No. Why would I?" The hum of a vehicle interrupted her thoughts. A door slammed. Footsteps neared, and the outer door flew open.

Here we go, Susannah thought, as Bitsy's figure loomed large in the doorway.

CHAPTER NINE

"Oh, am I interrupting?" Bitsy said, crossing the room and clasping Susannah's arm. She smiled at the detective. "We had a Waffle House date."

Detective Withers stood with her feet apart and her hands folded in front of her belt and regarded Bitsy.

"We're almost done," Susannah told her.

The detective raised an eyebrow but said nothing.

Bitsy flopped into a chair. "I'll wait." The chair groaned as she shifted and plucked her phone out of a side pocket of her handbag.

"Are you finished?" the detective said, her words sharp and final.

Bitsy swiped at her phone. "You two go right ahead, you won't bother me none."

Detective Withers didn't move for a few seconds, but when Bitsy didn't look up, she faced Susannah. "I won't take up much more of your time, Doctor," the detective said. "Getting back to Wednesday morning, were you in the kitchen with Anita Alvarez?"

"No."

"So, to make it clear, you weren't curious about what you heard, and you didn't look into the kitchen?"

"I was curious, who wouldn't be? But it was none of my business, so I went to sit with Bitsy."

"That's right," Bitsy interrupted. "I can vouch for that."

The detective gave Bitsy a prolonged deadeye but got no reaction, as she never wavered from her game. "Dr. Shine, did you argue with anyone at all while you were in the restaurant?"

"No, Detective. I didn't get involved in Anita's argument or in anyone else's conversation. Why do you keep asking me this?"

"Because according to witnesses, after a somewhat rancorous discussion about…" She held up a finger and then reached in her pocket, making a show out of removing her notebook and flipping through a few pages. "Ah, here it is. A peach pie-eating contest," she continued, shooting a quick glance at Bitsy, who had momentarily stopped tapping. "You left the restaurant looking…" She glanced at the notebook again, cleared her throat, and read, "'As jittery as a june bug.'"

She flipped the cover of the notebook closed. A look of satisfaction crossed her face but was soon replaced by irritation as a loud guffaw filled the room. Bitsy jumped up with a surge of unconstrained energy and approached the detective. One hand clutched her phone, which displayed small colorful gems moving across the screen.

"Who all said that?" she asked, grinning. "That expression is so country. I haven't heard that one in a dog's age. It had to be Johnnie Turner. Was it old Miz Turner?" She pushed Susannah to the side and approached the detective, her dreads bouncing airily, but there was a cold gleam in her eyes.

"I'm not at liberty to say."

"Well, whoever said it was wrong. I was right there, and I sat with Dr. Shine and walked out with her. She wasn't jittery as no june bug."

Detective Withers gave Bitsy a frosty look, but she didn't break. "And you are?"

Bitsy reached into her purse and pulled out a business card with a peach logo. "Bitsy Jean Long," she said, "proprietress of Peachy Things, a boutique in downtown Peach Grove." The detective took the card and gave it a fleeting glance, then shoved it into her rear pocket. Her gaze returned to Bitsy, who scrutinized the detective's shoes and pants with a pained expression. She shook a finger at the detective's shoes. "You come and see me, and I'll fix you up with some real dainty shoes. Just because you have a blocky foot doesn't mean you can't wear a pretty shoe."

The detective's jaw muscles bulged. Her expression didn't change, but Susannah could see the displeasure in her eyes. Susannah knew that Bitsy wanted to get a rise out of Detective Withers, like she did to Marcie at the PGBA meetings. Those who didn't know her thought Bitsy was an airhead, but the detective was not falling for it.

"Excuse me. I need the little girl's room." Bitsy turned, in that way that she had that was part ballerina swirl and part graceless stumble, and scurried away. Her footsteps resounded down the tiled hall.

Detective Withers watched her go. "A very entertaining person," she said dryly, then narrowed her eyes. "Returning to the argument in the kitchen, did Ms. Alvarez tell you what it was about?"

"No. She didn't say anything about it, and I didn't ask."

"She made no comments to you of a personal nature?"

"No."

"And she didn't contact you about an appointment?"

"No."

Detective Withers said nothing, but she jotted a few words in her notebook. She placed the notebook in her pocket and as an afterthought said, "Dr. Shine, are you an herbalist?"

"No, I'm a doctor of chiropractic."

"You sell herbal medications out of this office, is that correct?"

"Yes."

"But you are not an herbalist. Are you a nutritionist? Do you have some kind of certification to sell supplements?"

"I sell supplements under my license as a chiropractor."

"I see."

Susannah didn't like the sound of that. She tried to think of something to say to change the direction of the conversation. "Detective, you never said how Anita died."

"I'm not at liberty to discuss the details."

"So it could have been natural causes?" As soon as she said the words, Susannah knew that she had erred.

The detective faced Susannah, her gray eyes hard. "Would I be talking to you if she died of natural causes?"

CHAPTER TEN

"What was that all about?" Bitsy asked as Larraine and Tina trailed Susannah down the hall. They joined Susannah at the window as she watched the detective drive away.

Susannah shook her head, tapping a nail on the glass until the detective was out of sight. "I don't know."

"I think she's trying to rattle you," Tina said. She twisted her wedding ring around her finger, scowling. "I don't like her. Keith's not fond of her either."

"You heard?"

Tina and Larraine nodded guiltily.

"How much?"

"All of it," Tina said. "We didn't mean to spy on you."

Bitsy placed one hand on her hip and scolded Susannah with the other. "You needed ear-witnesses. You know, in case they try to entrap you and claim you confessed when you didn't."

"I don't think—"

"Don't you worry none." Bitsy sat down, swiping at her phone. "We're all looking out for you. Little Junior has his ear on the situation too. He knows to call if anything serious comes up."

"So that wasn't serious?" Larraine asked, her face powder barely covering blue veins.

"You know what I mean, Ms. Larraine. She was just fishing around, trying to get Susannah here to incriminate herself."

Larraine grasped Tina's arm, and they both lowered themselves silently onto a sofa.

"How could she think it had anything to do with you?" Larraine breathed. "It seems obvious Anita was meeting a man, once you think about it."

Bitsy's eyes went wide, and Susannah filled her in on the conversation she'd missed.

"So y'all think she was seeing someone on the down low?"

"That's what we think." Tina looked serious, worry lines creasing her brow. "But there's no way to prove it."

"With all the questions about what happened in the kitchen, do you think something illegal could be going on at the Cantina?"

"Like maybe drugs?" Larraine asked.

"I don't rightly know," Bitsy said, rubbing her hands together, thinking. "I never heard anything like that. My family has its finger on the pulse of the county, but it's a healthy pulse."

Susannah gazed around the office, replaying the detective's questions in her mind. From growing up in a law enforcement household, she knew that reticence was a common trait among those "on the job." Her father had been a man of few words, and her brothers had followed suit. But sometimes, what they didn't say spoke volumes. She inhaled. Could something illegal be happening in the kitchen at the Cantina? "You know what else I want to know?"

CHAPTER TEN

"Why a detective dresses like she's going hiking?" Bitsy interjected.

Tina laughed, and Larraine shook her head disapprovingly but said nothing.

Susannah's eyes bored into Bitsy, urging her to be serious. "No. I want to know who hated Anita enough to kill her. I also want to know what is going on in that restaurant. Maybe Anita stumbled onto a drug ring operating out of the kitchen. We've got to get over to the Cantina and talk to some servers."

Bitsy shook her head. "There's a sign in the window saying they're not open for the next few days."

"I'd love to talk to Anita's family," Susannah said. "I know her mother lived with her, but I can't just knock on her door."

"Why don't we go get some wings? I can't think on an empty stomach," Bitsy said, looking from Tina to Larraine to Susannah. "And much as I hate to admit it, Marcie Jones always has the gossip. Maybe she knows something."

Larraine politely declined. "Too early for me. I never eat before noon," she said as she headed back to her computer.

Tina mentioned that she had a lunch date with Keith. "But you're right. If there are any nasty insinuations in the air, Marcie would know."

\#

Bitsy pulled up to the Wing Shack and wedged her Explorer in next to a red Ford F-150. In the passenger seat, Susannah chewed a cuticle while replaying the detective's last comment.

"You coming?"

"Remember," Susannah said, narrowing her eyes as Bitsy's stomach rumbled, "when we see Marcie, don't tell her the detective was at the office. I want to ask the questions. The last thing I want to do is give the Queen of the Peach Grove

Grapevine more gossip to use against me."

"Don't worry. I promise to keep my mouth shut. Except for when I'm eating."

At the door, Bitsy pointed to the stenciling on the window glass, which proclaimed the wings to be the hottest in six counties. "I don't know about all that. My cousin Paul Smoot makes deliveries for a Vietnamese barbecue joint and—"

The door opened, and out stepped Billy Jones, who filled the doorway with his bulk. He was clad in a bright red apron that came down to his knees. "Y'all coming in, or are you going to stand out here jawin'?"

"Don't mind if I do," Bitsy said, stepping through the door with a quick bow. Susannah chuckled, but she followed Bitsy as Billy held the door open with his hip.

"How's the back?" Susannah asked.

"Much better." He smiled, lifting his apron to expose the wide brace that underpinned his polo shirt and single-handedly held his pendulous gut aloft. "This thing is a lifesaver."

Susannah smiled. Bitsy scraped the feet of a steel-backed chair across the linoleum floor and plopped onto the red padded cushion. Her large frame swallowed up the round seat. Susannah worried that the tiny chair might not hold Bitsy's weight, but Billy showed no sign of alarm.

"Now what can I get you?" He spread his dimpled hands and indicated a laminated menu affixed to the countertop with cellophane tape. Behind him, a sallow-faced teen in an identical red apron placed wings into a fryer. There was no sign of Marcie. Susannah ignored the menu.

"I'll have a grilled chicken salad, mild please."

Bitsy looked aghast. "You don't come here for mild and

CHAPTER TEN

greens." She blinked at Billy. "You come here for the heat and the meat. Don't you, Mr. Billy?"

He played along with Bitsy, folding one arm against his waist and taking a theatrical bow. "Sure enough," he said, rounding out the vowels so that *sure* became *show*, and then pulled a pen out from behind his ear and pointed it at Bitsy. "Triple order of the nuclear?"

"You bet."

"French fries, slaw, *and* hush puppies?"

"You got it."

He grinned and turned to his cook, Zach Johnson. "Three orders down." Billy wrote the order on a paper ticket and pointed his pen at Susannah. "Doc? Anything to go with that salad? Sweet tea or cola?"

"She never drinks sweet tea," Bitsy informed him. "When we order tea, the sweet is for me," Bitsy rhymed, pleased with herself.

The rear door opened, and a teenage girl with long blond hair entered. She wended her way through the kitchen and gave Billy a hug. "Hey, Ms. Bitsy," she said, pushing her hands down into her pocket.

"Hey, Miss Hayle," Bitsy said. "Come and see me. I got some new purses."

Hayle nodded. She pulled Billy aside and spoke to him quietly. He reached into his pocket and handed over a twenty-dollar bill. She grinned and left.

"We heard about Anita. Marcie and I were shocked," Billy said, shaking his head as he filled paper cups with ice. "Simply shocked." He kept his gaze on Susannah and returned to the table, placing the drinks down, concern in his eyes. "How are you, Doc? I don't mean to pry, but I heard you were injured."

"I'm doing fine." She tipped the cup in Bitsy's direction. "She's taking good care of me."

Bitsy beamed at her. "It's what I do."

"I heard you were there when Anita was killed. Did you see anything?"

"No. I had no idea anyone else was around." Susannah dropped her gaze, feeling queasy, not from the concussion this time but from a jab of guilt. What good was it to have police training if you couldn't remember any of your skills? She sipped on her water. "I wish I had gone to the back of the building first. Maybe I could have helped Anita."

Bitsy reached across the small table and patted her arm.

Billy wiped his hands on his apron. "Let me get your salad," he said. He shifted his weight as if to leave, and then asked, "Do the police know how she died? It wasn't on the news."

Susannah shrugged. "No idea."

"What's gonna happen to the Cantina, I wonder?" Bitsy mused.

Susannah tried to imagine the Cantina Caliente without Anita. She turned over the thought that Tomás could be the culprit. Could he be selling drugs out of the kitchen? Was that why they had been arguing? It didn't seem likely. Anita would not have been so flip about that kind of "trouble in paradise," would she? Susannah knew that Anita had a teenage daughter, Dolores. Would she inherit the restaurant, or would Tomás have the opportunity to buy it? She glanced at Bitsy, who scrutinized the cook as he placed her wings in a fryer basket.

"Tomás is keeping it open for now," Billy said.

"Really?" Bitsy asked, pulling her eyes off the food and glancing at Billy.

"Yes," he continued, his brilliant blue eyes sparkling as he piled Susannah's salad greens into a bowl. "Marcie called over to Tomás when we heard."

Bitsy arched her eyebrow. Susannah mirrored the action.

"You know," Billy continued, "to ask if she could be of any help. Marcie's thoughtful like that."

"Uh-huh," Bitsy replied, eyes returning to the fryer.

"Tomás said that Anita's family wanted to keep the restaurant open."

So the family is still in charge, Susannah thought. A bang interrupted her thoughts. Zach eyed the rear door nervously. Billy busied himself at the grill as Marcie, dressed in khakis and a polo shirt, entered the kitchen. Taking in the kitchen and dining area in one glance, she glowered at Billy, who turned his head away.

"The trash bin in the parking lot hasn't been picked up," she said, pulling an apron off a peg and slipping it over her head. She stood at a small sink and bent to let the water cover her slender hands as she snatched up a small brush and scrubbed with such vigor that Susannah thought she might be readying to perform surgery.

Zach dumped a basket of wings into a large metallic bowl and drizzled the contents of a red squeeze bottle over them. Marcie shut off the faucet with her elbow and in one step pulled the bottle from the boy's hand. "We measure the sauce," she told him, shooting a withering look at Billy, who returned the glare.

Susannah was surprised to see a reaction out of Billy. He always seemed immune to Marcie's bullying.

"Y-yes, ma'am," Zach said, his voice quivering.

Bitsy leaned into Susannah. "I told you she was skimpin' on the hot sauce."

They watched as Marcie lectured Zach.

"Sucks to be him," Susannah murmured.

Billy came around the counter, placing their order on the table with a tiny flourish. Susannah noticed the slightest tremor in his hand. He avoided making eye contact and left without his usual quip. There was no doubt that Marcie could be daunting. Susannah would have to ignore it if she wanted information.

Bitsy snatched a wing from the top of the pile and cleaned the bone in seconds flat. She reached for another, and Susannah started on her salad. Marcie stepped to the counter and frowned at the sauce covering Bitsy's fingertips. She wiped her hands on her apron and fixed Susannah with an eager expression.

"A shame about what happened to Anita," Marcie said, but the glint in her eye said the exact opposite. Marcie lived for gossip, and nothing gave her greater pleasure than sharing it. "Couldn't be good for your business."

"It sure ain't good for Anita's business," Bitsy muttered through a mouthful of chicken. She licked hot sauce off the tip of her thumb. "Or for Anita."

"No, of course not." Marcie waved a hand at Bitsy apologetically. The refrigerator behind her kicked on, throwing an electric buzz into the air. "It's terrible. But you know how people love to trash talk. And before you know it, your livelihood suffers." She glanced at Billy with a knowing look.

Susannah regarded them.

"Who's talking?" Bitsy asked.

"Well, I don't want to say," Marcie began, as if she would enjoy spilling her guts, "but I heard that the Peach Grove PD is fixing to get a search warrant." She cut her eyes toward

Susannah. "Randy's waiting to get the go-ahead."

Susannah felt her ears getting hot but forced herself not to flinch. She was sure Detective Withers would love to search her office.

"Old news," Bitsy said, piling her food onto her plate. "It's Detective Winters who's in charge now. Not Randy."

Marcie's face brightened, her eyes filled with anticipation.

"Yessir," Bitsy continued, ignoring Susannah's kick, "my cousin Little Junior told me that the mayor's gonna fire Randy."

Marcie gasped. A crescent-shaped lock of hair spilled forward onto her jaw. "How can that be? I was just talking to him," she cried, realizing too late that she had divulged her source.

Bitsy shook her head as if considering this. She lowered her voice, "Maybe he doesn't know yet. Junior says they're keeping him in the dark."

Marcie's face fell. She turned away from them and pulled her phone out of her apron pocket.

"Why did you say that?" Susannah hissed. "She's over there group-texting the entire town."

"I got carried away. Let's get out of here before she finds out I'm fibbin'." Bitsy looked down at her plate, which was empty except for a small pile of French fries. "I guess I don't need no takeout boxes today." She grabbed the remaining fries and tossed them in her mouth.

Susannah sighed. The lunch hadn't been a total failure. She had found out that Tomás would still manage the Cantina for the family. Perhaps that was one less motive for him, but it left the question of whether drug dealing or other crimes were taking place in the Cantina. She pushed the door open, making a mental note to leave Bitsy at home the next time she questioned Marcie.

CHAPTER ELEVEN

Susannah entered treatment room three, glad to have a patient to treat. Since Marcie's comment that the Peach Grove Police Department wanted to search her office, she had been jumpy and distracted. Finding out she was high on the suspect list was not what she had expected when she decided to pay a visit to the Wing Shack. She had wanted to gather some tidbits on Tomás and discover what was going on in the kitchen at the Cantina Caliente, but her search for nasty insinuations had bitten her in the butt. She pushed her worries aside and greeted Fiona Bailey, who lay face down, waiting for an adjustment.

"Good morning," Susannah said.

"Good morning, Dr. Shine," she replied, not bothering to turn her head. Her soft Irish accent gave her words a soothing rhythm. Fiona wore a denim work shirt with black and gray jodhpurs. Her strawberry-blond hair fell down her blouse in a long braid. She was a horsewoman and regularly turned up in jodhpurs and riding boots. As usual, her attire was spotless. If she didn't already know it, Susannah would never suspect that Fiona spent most of her day in a barn.

"Good to see you, Fiona," Susannah said, reviewing her chart. Fiona had frequented Peach Grove Chiropractic since its opening, and Susannah reviewed her history of spills and injuries related to her equine endeavors. "Neck acting up again?"

"You know it is. It's only been a week, and those knots are killing me."

Susannah steadied her fingers, lightly palpated Fiona's upper back, and forced herself to concentrate. She put some pressure on the right side of Fiona's neck, and Fiona flinched. "I see," commented Susannah. "These knots in your neck have knots."

Fiona chuckled, and Susannah smiled, relaxing. She had this. Palpating muscles and adjusting spinal segments was second nature to her, and she moved her fingertips along Fiona's spine like an artist exploring an untouched canvas.

"I know you're going to fix me up," Fiona said.

Susannah performed the adjustment, which caused a resounding pop. Her skills as an adjuster were excellent, and Fiona sat up, smiling, and flexed her neck.

"Better?"

"Oh, yes. I dare say it is." She pronounced *dare* as *dar* and rolled it into the next word, making it sound like the name *Darcy*. "Thank you."

"You're welcome."

"You know, Dr. Shine, I wanted to let you know that you're welcome at the stable anytime."

She got up off the adjusting table and wiggled her shoulders. "That feels great." She grabbed her purse and smiled. "Come on out, and I'll give you a riding lesson."

"Oh, I haven't been near a horse in years," Susannah said,

not in the least interested in learning to ride. She considered horses elegant and beautiful, but not a form of transportation she was keen on using. The mere thought of balancing on top of a moving beast made her queasy and gave her vertigo flashbacks.

"We have to change that," Fiona said. "I'll chose a gentle mount for you."

Susannah was about to protest, but Fiona drew closer and lowered her voice. "Besides, I have a few things I'd like to tell you. Not to speak ill of the dead," she began, pronouncing the words *spake ell,* and then crossed herself with a bent forefinger, "but just because someone dies does not mean they were a saint in life."

Susannah found herself tongue-tied.

"You might be surprised to learn that Anita had more than a few enemies."

Susannah blinked. "How do you know that?"

"Because she owed me a lot of money, and I'm not the only one. She got into disputes with her vendors and was at odds with a few merchants in town. In fact, I heard she had a run-in with Colin Rogers at the restaurant one evening. You can ask Tomás about that." She tapped her phone to check the time. "I'm running late. Come and see me when you have time, and we'll talk."

Susannah's heart skipped a beat as Fiona left the room. She had thought Tomás was the missing piece to the puzzle, but now other pieces were falling into place. The Cantina wouldn't be open until Wednesday, when Anita's family planned to hold a memorial service, so speaking to Tomás would have to wait. In the meantime, there was a new name on her radar.

"*Ciao, bello,*" she greeted Henry as she entered her office. She checked the temperature of Henry's tank and gave him a wave. She eyed the green moss. "*Ciao, verde.*" The man at the pet store had told her the round plant's growth rate was five millimeters per year. That meant it would slowly go from the size of a golf ball size to a tennis ball. She pulled out her phone and snapped a picture. A Marimo moss ball baby picture.

She put the phone aside and eased into her chair. Staring out the window, she planned her next move. A bee, apparently diverted from its trip to the peach orchard, buzzed against the glass. "Buddy, you're in the wrong place," she said aloud.

"Maybe he's just where he's supposed to be," Tina replied from the doorway. She smiled timidly and knocked softly before she entered.

Susannah beckoned her in and grimaced as Tina placed a few file folders on the desk. Tina was dressed in a bright set of scrubs, the top decorated by a parade of topsy-turvy penguins; the whimsical design suited her personality. She turned to leave and then paused, twisting her engagement ring around her finger. She and Keith had been married a year, and sometimes Susannah saw her worrying that ring as if she were wishing on a magic lamp.

"Is something on your mind?"

"I-I can come back. I don't want to interrupt you."

Susannah crinkled her brow, intrigued. "I could use the change of topic."

Tina stared at her hands, finally leaving her ring alone. "I know you have a lot on your mind, but I have something to tell you."

"Go on."

CHAPTER ELEVEN

"I'm pregnant," she blurted and then smiled. An enormous grin spread across her face and lit her brown eyes. Almost as soon as her face brightened, it collapsed into tears.

Susannah came to her side and took her hand. "What's wrong? This is happy news."

"I know, I know, but…" Tina swiped at her tears. "I haven't told Keith yet."

"Is there some reason he shouldn't know?"

Tina looked up, tears glistening on her lashes, and laughed. "No, no. Nothing like that." She swatted at Susannah like she was swatting away an annoying fly. "You so bad."

Susannah led her to a chair, and she sat. "Why haven't you told him?"

"You see, when Keith and I got engaged, I made him promise not to go on active duty again." She snuffled, an undainty, phlegmy sound.

Susannah nodded, pursing her lips, determined not to interrupt again.

"I was so worried all the time. When I was a kid, my dad was with the Atlanta Police Department. I watched my mom worry every time he left the house. Every shift, she walked him to the door, and she kissed him like she would never see him again. When I was thirteen, my dad transferred to Peach Grove PD. My mom became a new woman. It was like a weight was lifted from her shoulders. When Keith went into the Army, I felt that same weight on me."

"So, now you're worried that there's a killer in town."

She frowned, her fingers finding her ring again. "Yes and no."

Susannah frowned back at her. "Yes and no?"

"Yes I am, but that's not the only thing I'm worried about."

She met Susannah's eye, her hands quiet in her lap. "The Peach Grove PD doesn't pay a lot of money. We both knew that in advance. But we love it here, and it's safer than other areas, so I was thrilled when he signed on. I promised Keith I would work for a while, and we would hold off having kids until we got some money in the bank. But with one thing and another, like my car..." She lifted her hands in a gesture of frustration. "We haven't done a very good job of that."

"I'm sorry you're so worried," Susannah said, "but you don't have to go through this alone. Keith will make a great daddy. He's going to be overjoyed when he finds out."

Tina smiled. "You think so? I don't want him to think I went back on my word."

Susannah squeezed her hand. "It takes two to tango. I think you should let him in on the secret, so we can all celebrate. If it makes you feel any better, your job here is always open. Plus, you have two built-in babysitters for when you need a night out."

Tina threw her arms around Susannah, grinning. "I'm going to tell him tonight," she said. "I'll fix his favorite meal, and we'll have us a nice little talk."

"Good," Susannah said. "Is there anything else?"

"Since we're done for the morning a little early, is it okay if I go to lunch?"

"Sure."

Tina scooted out the door, listing off ingredients she needed to buy for Keith's dinner. Susannah checked the time on her phone. There was plenty of time to put her plan into motion. She closed the door and leaned against it, making a gun out of her forefinger and thumb and aiming at Henry as he poked at the moss ball. Henry the First had been her good luck

CHAPTER ELEVEN

charm. They had been through thick and thin until he went belly-up. Henry the Eighth gave her a swish of the fin, and she responded with a determined grunt.

This office needed to stay open, not just for Susannah's sake but for Tina and Larraine's as well. She would have to make sure it did.

Bitsy picked up on the first ring.

"Do you still need an oil change?"

CHAPTER TWELVE

The sky had turned overcast as she and Bitsy turned into the parking lot of Colin Rogers's shop, OK Automotive. Susannah ran her fingers through her hair, hoping to quell the volume brought on by the increase in humidity.

Stevie Duncan peeked out the door, his eyes wide. The logo for OK Automotive was stenciled on the door in blue. Behind it, Stevie shook his head. His disheveled shoulder-length brown hair swayed from side to side but failed to hide his protruding ears. "We're closed," he said to Susannah and slammed the door shut with a whump, two large bells slapping the glass.

The women looked at each other. They had rehearsed different scenarios that would allow them to question Colin about his relationship with Anita Alvarez. None of them included having the door slammed in their faces.

Bitsy looked at her watch. "That don't make no kind of sense. It's eleven thirty on a Monday morning. How am I gonna get my car inspected?" She banged on the door and waved at Stevie, pointing toward her SUV. He blinked rapidly and licked his lips. She put her hands up in prayer posture,

CHAPTER TWELVE

mouthing the words *please, please, please.*

He scowled at them and swallowed, his Adam's apple bobbing. He turned and rushed through the door to the garage. They waited, but he didn't return.

"I see that impassioned plea worked." Susannah dialed the phone number stenciled on the window. It was a typical automotive shop, a brick building that housed a small office on one side with four massive roll-up doors on the other. Signs for oil change and inspection hung over each of the doors. All had small oval windows embedded in the ribbed steel. The farthest door was deeply dented and streaked with blue paint. The potholed parking area was riddled with oil stains but sat empty except for two used cars and Bitsy's SUV. The answering machine picked up but after a few words the line went dead.

"If Stevie's here, Colin must be in there."

They approached the first roll-up door. No light shone through the windows, but Susannah heard music. She cupped her hands and peered inside. Bitsy did the same. "Why is this place so dark in the middle of the day? Is this a zombie garage?" Bitsy asked.

Through the window, Susannah saw a late-model Toyota up on a rack. Colin worked in the pit beneath, a shop light illuminating his work area. Susannah tapped on the glass, hoping to get his attention. He continued working.

"You have to make more noise than that. My cousin Cenetta owns an auto shop in Alabama, and she's half deaf from working around them pneumatic drills."

Susannah pounded harder, and Colin climbed out of the pit and yelled something over his shoulder, then disappeared.

Bitsy crossed her arms. "He doesn't move like the undead."

"Hey, y'all," a voice called.

Stevie cowered behind the glass door, which he held against his chest like a shield. He craned his neck. "Mr. Colin says he's fixin' to call the police if you don't get."

Then he was gone, the lock thrown into place before they could move. Bitsy pursed her lips, hands on her hips. Susannah banged harder on the window and paused, then banged again. Colin reappeared and grabbed something off his workbench. The door lurched up with a rattle of chains, retracting faster than Susannah would have thought a garage door could move, and as it went higher Colin stepped toward them, holding a crowbar poised to strike.

Bitsy grabbed Susannah's arm. "I have my Smith & Wesson, but I used all my ammo shooting at zombie targets."

Susannah placed her hand over Bitsy's, which was already digging inside her purse where she carried the 9mm pistol.

Colin slowed as he came out of the garage, squinting in the sun. "Why don't you leave me alone?" He stopped. "Ms. Long? Dr. Shine?" He looked from her to Bitsy, then back. "What are you doing here?"

Susannah pointed to Stevie, whose face was red with exertion from yanking the overhead door skyward in Guinness World Record time; his hands still gripped the chain. "Didn't he tell you? Bitsy needs an inspection."

Colin shook his head. "He told me there were two crazy women banging on the door." He pulled a dirty rag out of his pocket and wiped his hands. "We've had some trouble, and we're both a little rattled." He looked at his assistant. "Stevie, this is Dr. Shine, the chiropractor, and Bitsy Long, the woman who owns the shop you were telling me about." He turned to Bitsy. "His girlfriend favors some of those scarves in your shop."

Bitsy softened. "You tell her to come see me. I'll give her a ten percent discount if you get me my inspection today."

"I'm sorry, I can't." Colin frowned and studied his hand as he dragged the rag across his palm. "Someone broke in and vandalized my computer. They won't leave me alone."

Susannah took a step toward him. "Who won't leave you alone?"

"I don't know who it is." Colin slumped, his face falling. "And the police have been no help."

"Is that new detective hounding you, too?" Bitsy asked.

"Who? No." Colin straightened and inhaled. "Come on in. The least I can do is offer you a drink. I know I can use one." He led them through the garage. The light still hung under the Toyota, and Susannah glanced down into the pit. Colin said, "Shut the door, Stevie."

The younger man threw a latch, and the door rolled down with the same rattling of chains that had accompanied its ascent. Colin tapped his temple. "He's a good worker, but none too bright."

He waved them into a supply room, which held floor-to-ceiling shelves stacked with the shop inventory. Used auto parts commingled with new ones. A desktop smudged with dark fingerprints held a catalog the size of an old-fashioned city phone book alongside a computer monitor. A mini fridge sat in the corner of the room, decorated by a faded bumper sticker that read: MY GRASS IS BLUE. Next to it were two plastic chairs. Colin opened a cabinet and with trembling hands pulled out a glass and a bottle of Jack Daniel's. He poured himself a double and took a quick sip before putting the bottle down and setting two smaller glasses on the workbench. He tilted the bottle toward Susannah and Bitsy. "Y'all drinking?"

"No thanks," Susannah said with a slight flick of her hand.

"I don't want to ruin my appetite," Bitsy said.

He took another short sip and then leaned against the counter. "I'm so sorry, y'all. I didn't recognize you with your face on the glass like that. I've had to call the police a few times, but by the time they get here, the troublemakers are gone." His eyes darkened. "Explain that to me, when my business is practically across the street from the police station."

"Are you saying that they're not answering your calls on purpose?" asked Susannah.

"No. They answer, but in their own time."

"Why?"

Colin scowled. "The same reason why everyone is avoiding me and my business has dried up: Tomás," he said, and took another drink, banging the glass down on the counter. "That man is spreading lies about me, and there's nothing I can do about it. He's telling everyone that I killed Anita."

"Ain't no way Mr. Colin kilt her," Stevie said. He moved past Colin, retrieved a can of Red Bull from the mini fridge, and popped the top. "We was here working the whole day. I done told that to Chief Randy, but nobody minds me."

"You got that right," Colin said. His voice, etched with whiskey, had a deeper edge to it.

"I seen them tear up the parking lot and crash into the bay door," Stevie said, hanging his head. "The police won't do nothing 'cause I didn't get no tag number."

"That ain't your fault, I didn't get it neither," Colin said, motioning to the shop. "You go do me a favor and make sure the doors are locked. I'm done for today."

"Sure thing, Mr. Colin."

Colin watched him go. "That detective lady made him feel stupid cause he couldn't remember the tag, like he's soft in the head or something." He lowered his voice. "He can read good as me, but he ain't worth a dang around people. Anyway, he knows enough to help me out around here." He nodded at the auto parts catalog.

"You think they're not investigating because they believe Tomás?"

"I'm thinking they're looking for someone to pin the murder on so they can close this case right quick and look like heroes," he said, walking to the end of the desk and looking down the aisle that Stevie had exited. "Stevie wouldn't make no good witness for me. Put him in a room with that detective, and he'd say whatever she wanted him to say. He knows it too. He's been shaking like a dog with fleas since he met her"—at the mention of fleas, Bitsy looked around, alarmed—"and my alibi would be gone, along with the truth."

"Surely Randy wouldn't let that happen," Susannah said, feeling a prickling on her neck. Would Detective Withers coerce a confession to make an arrest? Susannah wasn't sure. "He's honest. He wants to find the truth."

"Keep telling yourself that, Doc." His words came slower, and Susannah thought he'd had more than the three sips of Jack Daniel's she had seen. "I told Randy he had the wrong guy. I told him what happened that night with Anita."

Bitsy's eyes were round. "What happened?"

He glanced over at her. "Well, I got nothing to hide. Tomás is telling everyone the first part. I might as well finish the story." He spread his fingers as if considering their callouses and dirt for the first time. "I was for sure at the bar." He pointed in the direction of the restaurant. "I was having a few drinks, and I got lit. I admit it. Getting drunk at a bar ain't no crime that I ever heard. I wasn't driving. I keep a cot here, in case I don't feel like driving home." He waved his hand in the direction of a door.

"What happened?" Susannah asked.

"He's sayin' I pushed her, but I never pushed her. I was leaving, and she was walking me out. She was good like that, Anita. She didn't judge me, like some people. She liked having me there, even if I was half in the bag. She said it made her feel safe."

"Safe from what?"

"I'm not sure. She never would say." His eyes were glassy, and he reached for the bottle.

Susannah had to keep him on track. She leaned past him to reach for one of the empty glasses and thrust it under the bottle. "I think I will have that drink now." She gave Bitsy a nudge with the toe of her shoe and nodded at the empty glass.

"Me too," Bitsy chimed in. "I'm sure my appetite will be fine."

Colin grunted and poured.

"She never said what she was afraid of?"

"No, but I think it had to do with the dark blue sedan."

"Dark blue sedan?"

"I told Randy I didn't push her that night. She slipped. She walked me to the door, and we saw a dark blue sedan pull up. Looked like a Hyundai, but I couldn't be sure. It was plumb dark out. As soon as she saw it, she turned around so fast she had me spinning. She must have slipped on something,

CHAPTER TWELVE

and she hit the bar." Colin looked down, inspecting his hands again. He pulled a pocketknife out of his pocket and dug the blade under his thumbnail. Bitsy stifled a tiny gasp as she watched Colin scrape the dirt from the blade and wipe it on his pant leg.

"And then what happened?" asked Susannah.

"Well, I ain't proud of it," he said, his tone getting morose. "I was more'n a little drunk, and I almost fell on her. But I didn't. I grabbed the bar to steady myself, and I helped her up. Then suddenly Tomás came in, yelling in Spanish. Anita yelled louder. I don't speak no Spanish, but I could tell they was fightin'. She waved him away, and he went back into the kitchen. You ask me, Tomás could be the one who killed her. That night, he had hate in his eyes."

"And then what?" Bitsy asked, mesmerized by the story, her hands clasped around the drink, which she hadn't touched.

"And then I left."

"That's all?"

"No, there's one more thing, and here's where I think Randy and the detective think I'm lying."

"What is it?"

"I saw that same blue car later on. I came here and watched TV for a while." He indicated the door with a jerk of his chin. "When I went out to get some stuff out of the truck, I saw that same car. So I watched it."

"What did it do?"

"It went to the Cantina. It was closed by then, the lights were out, and I wondered, 'What is this person up to?' I was about to call the police when a funny thing happened."

"What, what?" Bitsy said.

"Anita came out and got into the car, and they drove away."

CHAPTER THIRTEEN

A flashing blue light blinked through the window, strobing off Larraine's white coiffure and dancing in her glasses. Her hand flew to her mouth, and the file she held fell to the floor. "Stand back," she said, pulling Susannah away from the door. A loud rap rattled the glass. Her frown deepened. "I'm glad Tina's not here."

Susannah shot her a quizzical look. What was that supposed to mean? Tina had taken the day off to deal with some auto repairs. Larraine studied her hands, and Susannah pushed the curtain to the side. Keith Cawthorn's ham-sized hand rapped again. His piercing black eyes scanned the office as she opened the door, and he bent his frame to get through. Behind him, three police vehicles crowded the lot. Randy stood to the side, looking into the distance. A man and a woman dressed in plain clothes were being lectured by Detective Withers.

Keith took a tentative step forward and handed Susannah an envelope. "Dr. Shine, this is a search warrant," he said, clasping his hands together in front of his belt. Susannah appreciated his attempt to appear nonthreatening and quasi-human sized. Keith stood six feet five and had the wingspan of a jumbo jet. He nodded at Larraine and then met Susannah's eye. "Don't fuss with them none," he said gravely, his expression pulled into a tight mask.

Larraine stepped out of the way with a small squeak.

"Let them be, and we'll be out of here quick." He leaned down and said, "Don't give her an excuse to get destructive or seize any of your equipment."

Susannah tried to read the document, but the print swam before her eyes. Anger and humiliation burbled up from deep inside. For over a decade, she had thrown herself into a new career, working with her patients and forsaking memories of her police career. At the time, she believed that leaving law enforcement was the right thing to do, but it was a painful and humbling time in her life. She had lost face before her father and one brother, though her other brother was ambivalent. Tone, her partner, had encouraged her to work through her health issues and remain on the job, but in the end he respected her decision. He and his wife, Irma, had been her biggest supporters in her change of career, which had made her even more ashamed to admit that fear of failure as a law enforcement officer had motivated her exit from the force and eventual departure from her hometown. In the intervening years, Randy's taunts had stung, and she had reassessed her decision many times and found her present occupation much more suited to her personality. She was older and more confident. Fear did not motivate her actions anymore. At least she had told herself that enough times that she believed it.

Then why were her knees shaking and her mouth suddenly parched?

She had been expecting this since Marcie had tipped her off, but it still made no sense to her. What were they looking for? Anita had never been a patient, so there was no medical file pertinent to her. They could return with her name embossed in gold and there wouldn't be anything in the office related to her. Besides, what reason would she have had to kill Anita?

A *rap-rap-rap-rap* interrupted her thoughts. Detective Withers leaned into the doorway, her compact frame taut, an enormous flashlight in her hand. Wisps of dirty-blond hair escaped her bun and waved around her face. She retracted her lips in a movement that was three-quarters pained grimace and the one-quarter Louisiana debutante.

"Officer Cawthorn is correct," she said, pointing the flashlight for emphasis. "Y'all stay out of our way, and we'll be outta here in two shakes of a snake's tail." Her lips receded, displaying small but menacing teeth.

Susannah tried to return the smile, but it didn't work. Her dry mouth wouldn't allow her lips to slide. She cleared her throat instead. "Detective," she said, working to keep the shaking out of her voice. "Federal regulations protect the personal health information of my patients. I can't give you open access to all my patient files."

Detective Withers's smile faded but did not completely diminish. "You are aware that there are exceptions for reasons of police investigation." Her tone was soft Southern charm mingled with a shade of female Terminator, and the words gave Susannah a chill.

"Certainly," Susannah said, aware of the rough New York inflections she could not shed. In a game of dueling accents, she would lose.

"A crime was committed on these premises," Detective Withers said, holding up the warrant and shaking its pages.

CHAPTER THIRTEEN

"This warrant gives me legal authority to search this office and seize any evidence."

"I'm happy to comply, but when it comes to patient information, your warrant will have to specify which files you want to examine."

Detective Withers's face deepened in color, and she backed out of the doorway, barking a command at a uniformed officer. When she returned, she directed the other officers to avoid the patient files. Susannah got out of their way as they fell on the office, methodically searching every room. After two hours, Larraine reported that Detective Withers was now in the supply room.

"I won't be surprised if she looks in the refrigerator too," Larraine commented. They left Susannah's office and found the detective scowling at a shelf of supplements. Rows of supplement boxes were neatly arranged across several shelves, but what had her attention were the brown glass bottles, filled with liquid herbal solutions, that lined a cabinet in the corner.

She motioned to a colleague in the hall, the debutante grimace reappearing. "Take those bottles," she said, indicating the shelf that held the liquid herbs. Her eyes glinted as she faced Susannah. "I wonder what you'll think of the federal regulations that prohibit a quack like you from practicing medicine without a license."

CHAPTER FOURTEEN

"That woman is lower than a snake's belly," Larraine said, drumming her fingers on her arm while she leaned against a file cabinet. "There's no way you are practicing medicine without a license."

Susannah studied her office manager. The smile lines around her mouth had hardened into a furious scowl. Even her white hair seemed to darken a shade.

"I'm not worried about that," she said, trying to convince herself as much as Larraine. At least her knees had stopped shaking. Again, she relived her days with the NYPD and remembered the caution and vigilance that had been ever by her side. She never spoke of the unexpected health problem that had made her unfit for duty, preferring to focus on the present. But this was a fear that she had lived with since the day she had taken a tumble down a long flight of underground stairs and woken up in the hospital. It was a fear of not being able to measure up. It was the voice that told her that she would crash and burn, bringing the roof down on top of her and her staff.

But now, it was fight back or roll over, and she was not someone who rolled over.

CHAPTER FOURTEEN

Larraine stopped drumming and leaned forward, propping her glasses up on her curls and examining Susannah. "Well, I'm glad to hear you feel so confident," she said.

"I don't feel confident at all." Susannah's voice had an unfamiliar edge to it, and she regarded Larraine. "Did you hear the glee in her voice? She was thrilled to think she had something on me."

Larraine bobbed her head and cleared her throat.

"I wondered if she was setting me up as the bad guy from the beginning, but now I'm sure of it."

Larraine pulled her glasses down and swiped at her nose. "I hope not," she said, a slight catch in her voice. "I've been praying for the detective. It wouldn't hurt you to pray on it too."

Susannah nodded. Larraine had a faith in prayer that Susannah simply did not share. Action had always guided her life and solved her problems. She massaged her chin, thinking. There was not a modicum of evidence in her office that could point to her involvement with Anita's death, but law enforcement officers could misconstrue simple facts—like Detective Withers had done about her trip out of town. They merely had to be convinced they were right. She shivered.

What was it that had the detective convinced she was right? There were people who thought chiropractors were quacks that broke patients' necks and gave them strokes, but none of that was relevant here. Obviously, Detective Withers didn't have confidence in her abilities, but why had she confiscated bottles of herbal supplements?

"I'm not going to take this," she said, surging out of her chair and wincing when it hit the wall.

Larraine frowned. "What are you going to do?"

Susannah paused, her hand smoothing her hair. "I'm not sure, but I can't sit by while this detective trumps up a case against me. I've been thinking I need to fight back, but what I need to do is solve this thing."

"Maybe you should hire a lawyer instead," Larraine offered, looking over her glasses at Susannah, a trick she used to look intimidating. Susannah bit her lower lip to keep from laughing; she loved Larraine, but a tough cookie she was not. "My son-in-law's daddy is with Buchanan, Hinton, and Norris. In fact, he's the Norris. Winston Norris. They have a reputation for being the toughest law firm in the county. I could give him a call."

"Sure, that would be fine," Susannah replied, but her voice trailed off. She knew Larraine's suggestion was sensible, but lawyers were expensive. So were emergency room visits; she glanced at the spot where she had stuffed the hospital bill. A sour taste flooded her mouth as she remembered Marcie's comment about destroying a business with gossip. She needed this to be over—and soon.

"Larraine," she said, taking a breath, "we don't have the luxury of letting lawyers duke it out. By the time they're finished, it may be too late." Everyone knew that lawyers dragged their cases out. The longer it took, the more money they made. Her stomach twinged. She had no choice but to dig in and solve this thing herself. "I need your help."

"Anything, sweet pea."

"Fiona tells me Anita wasn't as well liked as we thought. She didn't pay her vendors on time and found herself in disputes with local merchants. Then the detective questioned me about the argument I heard at the restaurant. I need to know what else Anita was hiding. Could you use that church

CHAPTER FOURTEEN

grapevine to dig up some details?"

Larraine blanched, something Susannah wouldn't have thought possible. "I'd like to help." She paused. "But you know I don't cotton to gossip."

"I understand." Susannah nodded. "Don't think of it as gossip, think of it as helping me with an investigation. I'm not asking you to spread rumors. I'm asking you to ferret out some information."

Larraine looked intrigued.

"If we don't get some answers soon, we will all be out of a job."

CHAPTER FIFTEEN

Iris Duncan emerged from the side entrance of the lower level of Henry County Hospital with her car keys in hand. Her black hair was sleeked into a high ponytail like she had worn the first time Susannah had met her.

"That's one hungry girl," Bitsy commented, as they watched her stride into the parking lot with purpose. They had been sitting in the parking lot for an hour, waiting for Iris's shift to end, and Susannah thought she saw cracks in Bitsy's patience. Her hands, which had been draped loosely over the steering wheel, now gripped it so forcefully that her fingernails dug into her palms. Her foot was poised over the accelerator, and there was an excited gleam in her eye.

After Detective Withers's appearance at her office, Susannah knew she had to discover what killed Anita. Last night, over coffee and a dessert of gluten-free peach cobbler, Susannah had told Bitsy, "The key is to find out how she died." She scraped her fork across her plate, sweeping up the sticky remains of the cobbler. "So let's call Roman, and we'll go have a talk with Iris Duncan."

"We don't need him. Let's ride up to the hospital and talk to her ourselves."

CHAPTER FIFTEEN

"Shouldn't we wait until Roman is on duty to go?"

"I don't want to bother him with this." Bitsy waved Susannah off. "He's got the PTSD and needs to keep things chill."

"Chill? He's spending time with *you*." Bitsy and Roman had resumed their previous close relationship. Without being told, Susannah knew a romance was blooming.

Bitsy preened. "I know how to kick back and help a man relax."

Susannah eyed her friend. "Are you sure you know what the word *relax* means?"

"Shoo." She waved her nails. "I'm worth a little extra stress."

So now they sat, watching Iris get closer. As she neared, Bitsy shot out of the parking place, immediately jamming her foot on the brake, laying the shortest stretch of rubber that anyone would ever see. Susannah, arms outstretched, braced against the whiplash injury she knew she had just sustained.

Iris stopped in her tracks only feet from the Explorer, one hand on her hip. In one quick motion, she pulled a semiautomatic pistol from under her scrubs and aimed it through the passenger-side window. Iris's lips flattened and her nostrils flared.

Susannah raised her hands in surrender. "Are you crazy?" she gasped, her breathing short and fast. "I said *ask her to dinner*, not *use your truck to ambush her*."

Bitsy waved. "Hey, Miss Iris, it's me, Bitsy, Roman Broady's friend."

Iris blinked.

"That's a real nice pistol you got there. Is that a Sig Sauer? I like your holster too. Is that one of them Thunderwear holsters?"

93

Iris lowered her shoulders and nodded. She replaced the two-tone gun in its holster beneath her navel.

"Anyways, you won't be needing it," Bitsy continued. "We only wanted to invite you to dinner."

To Susannah's surprise, Iris's face relaxed, the color returning to her olive complexion. She threw back her head and barked with laughter. "Roman told me you were a wild one." She chuckled, looking past Susannah directly at Bitsy. "You remind me of my brothers." She paused. "I miss them."

Bitsy made a finger gun and pointed it at Iris. "There's more where that came from. Hop in."

Iris was still grinning when she received her value meal from the RicoTaco drive-through. Both she and Bitsy were calmer than Susannah thought appropriate after a near-death experience.

"Where are we headed?" Iris asked, stuffing a burrito into her mouth as Bitsy accelerated down the interstate ramp while chomping on a sugar-covered cinnamon churro.

"This little snack here has got me hungry for a real dessert," Bitsy said, brushing the sugar off her pants and slurping at her sweet tea. "I reckon we could make it to that Dominican pastry shop in Stockbridge."

"What are you doing here, anyway? Roman told me you were going to visit a cousin for few days."

Bitsy inhaled and sputtered sweet tea from her nose. Susannah grabbed the wheel as Bitsy stowed her cup and rubbed at her nose. "That hurt," she said, and then grinned at Iris in the rearview. "I came home early."

Susannah twisted in her seat. "You asked us not to bother you at work."

"Asked? Ordered is more like it. Roman kinda freaked me

out by showing up with you two." Iris nodded, licking her fingers. "I owe him, but I need to keep my job. Anyway, he told me what's going on. I guess you'd want to know about the dige levels, then."

Susannah's eyes widened.

"What's a ditch level?" Bitsy asked.

"Not *ditch*," Iris said. "*Dige*, it rhymes with fridge. Comes from digoxin. It's a chemical compound of a heart medication, and your departed friend ingested enough to stop a clock."

Susannah waited to hear what came next. Digoxin, also known as digitalis, was a drug obtained from the leaves of the foxglove plant. She crumpled into her seat, deflated. The pieces were falling into place. High digitalis levels were harmful to the heart and could cause death. Anita had been found dead outside Peach Grove Chiropractic with no signs of a struggle because she had not been attacked.

She had been poisoned.

Detective Withers had confiscated her herbal products because she suspected that Susannah was hiding poison among the liquid herbs.

"It would be consistent with taking a heart medication like Lanoxin," Iris explained, eyeing the churro in her hand. "She could have overdosed on her medication. It's been known to happen."

"She never mentioned that she took any medications," Susannah murmured.

"Maybe she didn't want nobody to know she had a bad ticker," Bitsy offered, one hand on the wheel, the other on her drink, which she used to punctuate her comments. "Like my Uncle John Coltrane Long. He used to carry his pills around in an empty RC Cola can. You could hear him rattling all the way down the block."

Iris shrugged and took a bite of her her churro. "It's also an active component found in the foxglove plant."

"So what's that mean?" Bitsy asked.

"If she didn't take heart medication," Susannah said, "then she was poisoned."

CHAPTER SIXTEEN

Susannah sat at her computer, head in hand, regretting the shot of espresso she'd downed earlier in the evening. It was time for bed, but the last of the caffeine jitters kept her awake and worried. Detective Withers had not disclosed the high digitalis levels in Anita's blood, but it would inform her progress on the investigation and push her toward certain suspects and away from others. In this case, out of Colin's garage and into Susannah's clinic.

Her eyelid twitched. Perhaps there was a reason to suspect the herbal supplements. She glanced at the massive *Compendium of Plants*, a reference book for herbal medications. If Anita had been taking digitalis, certain herbs could interfere with its actions or even cause side effects. It was imperative that she find out what medications Anita took. She glanced at the screen with dry eyes. Right now, she had to finish her research on poisonous plants.

Both she and the detective knew that anyone could go to a gardening center and buy foxglove, but not many people would be aware they were purchasing a poisonous plant. Some die-hard gardeners would know, as would people who had knowledge of herbal remedies—like herself. She knew that nothing in her office would have traces of digitalis in it, but someone in Peach Grove knew how to use this poisonous plant. The proof was in the blood test.

She glanced at the picture on the right side of the web page. Much to her surprise, information on digitalis was easy to find. She knew, like a punch in the gut, that the detective had visited the same sites. Wikipedia had a page dedicated to it, with a vibrant picture of a dark pink common foxglove plant decorating the sidebar. She tapped a finger on the textbook she had pulled from her bookshelf and considered the poisonous plant. While the shrub oleander had also come up in her search, there were more references to foxglove and its varieties. The plant had been known for centuries by herbalists for its poisonous properties and was associated with death and witchcraft, evidenced by its alternative names: dead man's bells and witches' gloves. Interestingly, its first medicinal use for treating heart disease dated back to the 1780s.

On perusing the images she had retrieved, she found that many varieties of the showy foxglove flowers reminded her of blooms she had seen in this area. If she hadn't seen them in a neighborhood garden, then she had seen something similar. Incredibly similar.

She rubbed her neck and glanced at the clock in the corner of her screen. Eleven fifteen. She rose and entered the kitchen, filling a glass with water and draining it. Plunking the glass on the counter, she returned to her computer and initiated a search for images of other tubular-shaped flowers. Perhaps Anita had been in contact with foxglove, thinking it was some other plant.

She scrolled past bright pictures of tropical flowers, most

of which she didn't recognize. The tubular orange flowers of trumpet vines were fairly common here in Georgia, but a vine could never be confused with the tall, heavy stalks of the foxglove. At the middle of the page, she stopped.

Clumps of pink flowers peeked out from behind grasslike fronds. *Penstemon* had colorful tubular flowers on tall spikes, and Susannah knew if she hadn't been intently looking for differences, she would easily confuse it with foxglove. The hue of *Penstemon* "Garnet" was off, but not by much. It could pass for a sister to the foxglove pictured on the Wikipedia page. A few more clicks brought her to photos of hollyhocks and snapdragons. She remembered hollyhocks from her grandmother's yard in New York, but this variety sported a flower of an almost identical shape to the foxglove's, growing on a single tall stalk. The snapdragons, on closer inspection, would never pass muster as a tubular blossom, but at a glance, the vibrant pink shade growing on a tall stem cut a similar form, especially to an uneducated eye.

She sat back, digging her toes into the carpet, fatigue finally seeping into her limbs. She peered once again at the doppelganger plants.

They were all confusingly similar to foxglove. Anyone around here could add the dead man's bells to their home garden and surround it with some nonpoisonous vegetation, and no one would be the wiser.

She interlaced her fingers behind her neck and stretched, pondering the properties of the poisonous plant. All parts were poisonous, and from what she had discovered, the only creatures that could consume it unharmed were moths and their larvae.

Questions formed in Susannah's mind. How common

was it for people to grow foxglove without realizing what it was? Could Anita have poisoned herself with it? It didn't seem plausible. It seemed more likely that she would be taking medication for heart disease rather than unwittingly poisoning herself.

Chewing a cuticle, she ignored the slight flutter in her stomach. Anita had never mentioned a medical problem, but though Susannah had been acquainted with her for many years, they weren't close. Most of their interactions had been at the Business Association meetings—not the preferred place for opening up about your personal health matters.

She thought about what she knew about Anita and concluded that she could recall very little of importance. In fact, Susannah couldn't remember any personal details that Anita had confided. A melancholy descended upon her. The usual mundane items of life and business came to mind, but no confidential tidbits surfaced. They had chatted, while sharing coffee, once a month for years, but aside from what everyone knew—Anita lived with her mother, who helped her care for Dolores, her teenage daughter—she didn't know much else. Had she even met Anita's mother? Susannah sighed. Unlike some people who quickly became overly familiar, dumping private facts into their conversation too soon, Anita was reserved. One could even say tight-lipped. In all the years they'd been friends, Anita never mentioned how she came to the United States or what had brought her to Peach Grove.

Of course, Susannah had never asked.

Susannah felt another tug of guilt. What kind of friend had she been? Had she ever invited her here? She looked around as if the answer lurked behind the curtains. She didn't have to search for it; it echoed around her brain.

CHAPTER SIXTEEN

No. No. No.

So, why did she think that Anita took no medications? It was possible she had a mild case of heart disease. Many of Susannah's patients took medications to lower blood pressure or statins to lower their cholesterol yet showed no outward signs of ill health.

She reread the medical website, which listed digitalis as a popular treatment for congestive heart failure, and frowned. The symptoms of congestive heart failure were outwardly noticeable, unlike high blood pressure, which was considered a silent killer. But fatigue and weakness were definitely not things she associated with someone as active and vivacious as Anita. The last time they sipped their *café* together, she had looked strained, but Susannah had written it off to the everyday stresses of running a business. There had been no other signs of disease.

Symptoms of dizziness, shortness of breath, and coughing or wheezing would have been obvious. She chewed her cuticle again, this time drawing blood, and revisited her memory for the tenth time. They had shared a coffee. Anita had even stopped to mop up the floor before Susannah took a seat next to Bitsy. A few minutes later, Anita had appeared, fit as ever, and served her a plate of huevos rancheros, balancing the plate in one hand and pouring coffee with the other. No coughing, no wheezing, no signs of anything out of the ordinary.

Susannah smiled, remembering how pleased she had been to quiet her rumbling stomach with those eggs. A tear dripped onto her keyboard, and she sat up, still smiling, unable to stanch the flow of tears.

She would miss Anita.

Another twist of her gut chided her for being a poor friend while Anita was alive. She resolved to make it up to her family; the only way she could do that would be to question them discreetly about Anita's health. But it was no longer a matter of rude comments from Randy. If Detective Withers found out, there would be trouble. She narrowed her eyes, shutting down her computer. For the first time since Anita's death, she had a plan. She felt her body relax and headed to bed.

CHAPTER SEVENTEEN

Susannah opened the heavy wooden door of the Cantina Caliente and stepped into the paneled foyer. Bitsy followed, barely touching the door with her fingertips, letting the weight of the wood fall on Colin Rogers, who entered behind them. Bitsy sped past the wood panels, which were carved with the likeness of saints. Anita had commissioned the work from a Mexican sculptor renowned for his representations of the holy images of her homeland. Carved into one wall stood the Virgin of Guadalupe, her head covered by the traditional turquoise mantel emblazoned with hundreds of tiny stars, which had been painstakingly etched into the wood. Susannah thought that painting the stars gold was overkill, and Bitsy had long ago dubbed her "Our Lady of the Lightsaber." "I know she got those Princess Leia buns hidden under that headgear," she had told Susannah, giggling when Anita had thrown a scowl her way. But after that, Bitsy assiduously avoided looking at the image. "One thing I know from my strict Christian upbringing," she told Susannah earnestly, "is that graven images will send you straight to hell. Catholics might be immune, but us nondenominationals are not."

Susannah paused at the end of the foyer. The middle of the restaurant held two long banquet tables. Chafing dishes sat warming on either end. Most of the attendees congregated at the booths on one side of the room or at the bar on the other, leaving the area around the buffet tables empty. The spotless table linens, the wide-open space, and the subdued voices all gave the restaurant a distinct ambiance. She shivered. Anita's absence was palpable.

At the front of the room, an older woman with gray hair held the arm of a teenage boy who wore a pair of black slacks and an ill-fitting sports coat. It had to be Anita's mother; the resemblance was uncanny.

Susannah nudged Bitsy, pointing out Tomás. "There he is," she said, keeping her voice low. He wore a black suit with a white carnation in the lapel. He bent at the waist, his suit unwrinkled and stiff, as he spoke to Anita's mother.

"I see." Bitsy, garbed in a somber black dress accentuated by a discreet orange-and-black scarf, smiled wide. She spoke without moving her lips. "You can't start asking questions yet. Let everyone get liquored up first." She gave Susannah a nudge and nodded at a group of Business Association members as she made her way to the bar.

Susannah watched her climb onto a stool, and Colin followed her lead. Nolan, the bartender, handed them both drinks. From the size of the glasses, Susannah knew they were imbibing *té tamarindo*. Tamarind tea was a tart concoction invented by Anita, who mixed the flavor of the Mexican tamarind fruit with the Southern staple beverage of sickly-sweet iced tea. It was a Cantina Caliente favorite.

Susannah examined the group of locals. Somber in their formal clothing, even lapsed members of the PGBA had made time for the memorial. They polished up nicely, Susannah thought. She moved away, casually studying the floral arrangements, looking for anything that resembled foxglove. When she had determined that nothing fit the bill, she felt foolish. Surely, if the killer worked at the restaurant, he or she would not have the nerve to put the poisonous plant on display.

She crossed to Tomás, who stood next to an easel that held a picture of Anita. Remembering the detective's interest in what had gone on in the kitchen and the angry voices she had heard the last time she was here, Susannah was eager to question Tomás. He met her eyes, and his smile wavered. He walked away, stopping to give instructions to one of his servers. She caught up with him and placed her hand on his arm.

"Doctora," he said, glaring at her hand.

She held on to his jacket. She didn't want him to get away just yet. "Everything looks beautiful," she said, nodding at the table. "Anita would be proud."

He smiled wanly, glancing around the room. "Yes, she would be."

Susannah couldn't help herself. "These flowers are gorgeous. Was Anita fond of them?"

His eyes fell on the floral arrangements. "Anita loved flowers. She said they reminded her of home." His gaze followed a server who carried a chair. He made a hissing noise, and the man looked over and immediately changed direction. "She liked everything just so. The only place she allowed a mess was on her desk. Papers up to here." He raised his hand to his nose and then shook his wrist in a quick flicking motion; Susannah had seen Anita do the same to express displeasure. His smile faded. "But even there, she always had a small vase of flowers."

Anita kept flowers in her office. Susannah knew Anita's office was on the far side of the kitchen. Had they found poisonous flowers? Was the detective even looking? She cut her eyes to the kitchen and then back to Tomás.

"Tomás, I'm curious about something. Was Anita here the morning she died?"

Tomás smoothed his cuffs. "I work the opening shift on Friday, and Anita closes." He twisted the button on his cuff, his fingers clenched. "But she might have been here and left. At least, I think someone was here. The light was on in her office, and Anita always shut off all the lights. Like I said, everything had to be just so."

Susannah glanced at the archway where she had shared her last cup of coffee with Anita. "The last time I was here, it sounded like you and Anita had a disagreement about something."

"No, that's not right." Tomás hesitated, rubbing his thumb and forefinger together. "I, uh—"

Before he could finish, the door opened and Detective Withers and Randy entered. Randy and Tomás exchanged a glance, and Tomás hurried away, mumbling, "You are mistaken. I must go."

Susannah watched him hurry off. A tap on the arm made her jump, and she turned to see Dolores Alvarez, Anita's seventeen-year-old daughter.

"Dr. Shine, thank you for coming," she said tentatively. "Can I speak with you?"

Susannah placed her hand on Dolores's. Her hazel eyes were flecked with brown, and Susannah saw the weight of her grief in them. "Of course."

"I'm trying to understand why the police say my mother had a heart problem."

"Oh?" Susannah was amazed that the detective had taken the time to rule out a medication overdose. But it was logical. As Iris had said, a medication overdose could happen.

"Yes, a detective came to the house this morning and asked for a list of my mother's medications. I told her she didn't have a doctor and wasn't taking any medications. She never got sick. But the detective insisted." She frowned. "She said *Mamá* must have been taking heart medication. My *abuela* and I told her she never took any pills. The detective wasn't very nice. *Abuela* got angry and threw her out."

"I'm so sorry." A familiar sensation gripped her gut. Guilt, mixed neatly with a modicum of fear and a dash of self-loathing. A recipe for an ulcer, but she still couldn't divulge what she had learned from Iris.

"Did she ever mention this to you?" The girl looked forlorn.

Susannah forced a weak smile. "No, she didn't, but I don't know if she would have shared something like that with me."

Dolores nodded. "I know she trusted you." A tear rolled down her face. "I thought she might have said something."

"I'm sorry." Susannah leaned in and gave her a hug. When she stepped back, Anita's mother stood at her shoulder. Her gray hair accentuated her pale and drawn countenance. She fixed Susannah with deep black eyes.

Dolores said, "*Abuela,* this is Dr. Shine, the chiropractor. *Mamá*'s friend."

The woman held out her hand, her expression softening. "Pilar Alvarez. Thank you for coming." She spoke with the same melodic voice that Susannah had admired in Anita.

Dolores drew closer and lowered her voice. "I asked her if she knew about *Mamá* going to a doctor." She swiped at a tear, and her grandmother took her hand.

Pilar narrowed her eyes, her face darkening. "I told that detective the only complaint *mi hija* ever had was a few days before she died." She sniffed. "She complained of a headache. She said she wanted to see a doctor about that, but I don't know if she did."

Susannah leaned toward Dolores. "I'll be glad to help you figure it out." Pilar had given her the perfect opening, and her gut quietly agreed. "If she saw a doctor, you should be able to access her records and discover if she was taking any medications."

Before Pilar could speak, a petite woman entered the restaurant. She took one look at Pilar, and a wail escaped her, which caused a hush to fall on the assembly. Susannah had never heard such a loud voice come out of such a small person. Pilar and Dolores turned as the woman, whose eyes were ringed with smudged eyeliner, made a beeline for them and threw herself on Pilar, gasping. A solemn-faced man, possibly the petite woman's husband, caught up and stood to the side with his hands clasped, silently staring at his shoes.

Susannah pushed a business card into Dolores's hand. "Call me when you have some time."

Dolores rolled her eyes at the noise and forced a small smile. "I will, and thank you."

CHAPTER EIGHTEEN

Susannah pulled Bitsy into the Cantina's restroom, checked to make sure that all three stalls were empty, and locked the door.

"Why did you bring me in here? You know I hate public restrooms." Bitsy crinkled her nose. "They smell funny and have germs."

"Keep it down," Susannah whispered, interrupting what was sure to degenerate into a lecture on cleanliness and the use of personal-sized hand sanitizer. "I need your help."

"You could have asked me for help while sitting on a barstool," Bitsy grumbled. "They're not exactly being generous with the alcohol. How am I supposed to disinfect myself when I leave here, without no alcohol?"

Susannah picked up some paper towels from a pile on the sink and handed a few to Bitsy. "I have to get into Anita's office," she said.

"Now I know you're losing your mind," Bitsy replied, grabbing the door handle with a towel clenched between her fingers. It rattled but did not budge. "Now you've gone and locked me in a restroom." A look of disgust crossed her face, and she rattled the door again for emphasis.

"You can't go." Susannah pulled her back. "You have to help me."

"Do you hear yourself?" Bitsy crossed her arms. "I am helping you. By not helping you. That detective is out there, and you know she don't like you. What's gonna happen if she finds you snooping around Anita's office?"

"What difference does it make? She already suspects me. I have to find out what's going on in that kitchen. And I need to see her office. Maybe they missed something."

"I know what you're thinking. You want to find some poisonous flowers to prove that Anita wasn't taking no medication for her heart. You want to prove you didn't do it. You think the killer would leave poison flowers lying around, all nice and neat for you to find?"

"Of course not. I just need time to do some snooping. There has to be something the police missed, or they wouldn't be investigating me."

Bitsy took a step toward Susannah and scrutinized her, pursing her lips. "No. I can't see you pulling this off. You're a doctor—you're supposed to be refined."

"Who said that? Did you forget I used to be a transit officer?" Susannah folded her arms and scrutinized Bitsy in return. "I worked in the subway tunnels of New York City."

Bitsy's mouth was a resolute burgundy line. "Hmmmph," she said. "So that's how it's gonna be?"

Susannah watched her expression soften.

"Okay," she said. "But on one condition."

"Whatever it is, I agree."

"No criticizing my methods." With that, she snapped the lock open with paper towel–protected fingers and left.

#

CHAPTER EIGHTEEN

Wedged between a rack piled with saucepans and a fire exit, Susannah stared into Anita's office. With the chef and servers bustling in and out, slipping into the kitchen was easier than she'd imagined. Finding something that linked Anita to the killer would not be as easy. Sweat collected under her arms. She took a breath and stole into the unlit office and closed the door.

The office was a windowless box, white plasterboard walls peppered with scuffs and tinged with gouges where the doorknob had repeatedly hit. A time clock hung next to a bulletin board with the requisite Workers' Comp and OSHA notices. Nothing out of the ordinary there. She searched a desk, finding nothing but a few pens, some paper clips, and a container of Tic Tacs. The desk held no family pictures or personal accoutrements. What did she expect? A day planner opened with the killer's name penciled in?

Voices filtered through the door, and she edged along the wall and turned off the light. Opening the door a crack, she saw Tomás holding a white table linen over his arm. It had a large stain on it, and Susannah wondered if this was part of Bitsy's method or if it was some other mourner's faux pas.

"Why have you not arrested him?" he said. "He's out there eating Anita's food and drinking *té tamarindo*. He should be in jail."

"Now settle down, Tomás."

Susannah recognized Randy's voice. She froze, as he moved into view frowning at Tomás. Afraid to close the door, she held her breath. *Quiet as a church mouse*, she thought.

"Don't tell me to settle down." Tomás pointed at Randy, and then he balled up the soiled linen and launched it into a bin with a grunt. "I gave you information about how he hurt

Anita. I should have told you sooner, but Anita begged me not to call you, and now she's dead."

"We follow up on every lead," Randy said, reaching out to put his hand on Tomás's shoulder. "It takes time."

Tomás shook Randy's hand away, flicking his palm up in a *back off* motion, and walked out of the kitchen. Randy followed.

Susannah exhaled and eased the door closed. She stood for a moment, replaying the conversation. Tomás must be talking about Colin. She twisted the lock and flipped the light on, returning to Anita's desk. She stared at an empty ceramic vase, remembering Tomás's comment that Anita always had flowers on her desk. Susannah barely had room for the patient files that landed on her own desk, and there was no way she would keep a container filled with water near her computer.

Wait a minute. She looked around. There was no computer. She had often noted the electronic order system that the restaurant used. Wouldn't Anita use a computer to review that data? She ran her fingers through her hair. Perhaps the police had taken her computer. What did that mean? She didn't know, but she had no time to waste on worrying about that now.

Fiona said that Anita had billing disputes, so she searched for bills, sifting an assortment of papers in a wire basket. There were three bills for produce, one for meat, and one from a janitorial service. No magical a-ha moment there. She sagged. This was it? Some invoices and an empty vase? She jammed the invoices inside her blouse. *Damn women's suits. If I were a man, I would have pockets.*

Voices carried from the kitchen once more, and she berated

herself for believing this was a good idea. She had found nothing, and now she was stuck in here. Tiptoeing to the door, she again shut off the light and stood, waiting. A deep voice shouted out orders. Were they still setting up the buffet?

She cracked the door. The chef directed his staff with a large stainless steel spoon, like a culinary maestro. Three men carried covered trays, and a tall, chubby woman loaded a trolley with two large coffee urns. Coffee already? Had she been here that long?

She glanced at her watch, grateful that she'd chosen to wear it tonight; checking her phone in a dark room might give her away. *Mental note to self*: *when snooping around, wear a watch.* Only ten minutes had passed. They must be providing self-serve *té tamarindo* with lunch. The chef followed the trolley out of the kitchen.

Now was her chance.

She stealthily exited the office, closing the door as she stepped into the kitchen. A sudden rush of footsteps sent her heart hammering.

"Don't push me," a young male voice squeaked.

She wrenched the doorknob behind her, but it wouldn't give. She had locked herself out and had nowhere to go.

CHAPTER NINETEEN

Susannah pushed through the rear exit and tripped down a single step, sliding knees first into a wooden pallet. A sliver of wood protruding off the pallet snagged the seam of her skirt, and she heard the fabric tear as she balanced herself. Clutching the door, she pivoted, flailing as it swung open. Vertigo descended upon her and she cursed her clumsiness, inhaling deeply and focusing on a point on the ground to regain her equilibrium.

She held tight to the weighty door to keep it from closing. She did not want to alert the kitchen staff to her presence, but she didn't want to be locked out either. How suspicious would it look if she were found lingering in the delivery area? She tried to come up with an excuse, but her mind went blank.

A weight pushed against her, and a leg covered by a long white apron jutted through the exit. No ready stories sprang to mind, and she was sure she wore an expression that looked like the proverbial deer in the headlights. She berated herself: *If you're going to be sneaking around, you can't be a clumsy oaf AND a poor liar.*

Inside, a raucous cry caused the aproned leg to disappear, and the door closed with a solid *thunk*. Even before she tried the handle, she knew that it would be locked. *Two for two*, she thought.

"Well," she murmured, scanning the back side of the building and seeing no one else, "I guess that decides it."

She took in her surroundings. She stood in the rear alley of a strip of shops, which from this side of the building all looked the same. Several metallic doors, each situated next to an electric meter and HVAC unit, interrupted a long beige wall. Behind her, a privacy fence cut off the shopping center from the adjacent property. A large dumpster sat inside a six-foot cinder block enclosure.

She was not only alone here, but she was isolated. Was it possible that the killer had stalked Anita in this alley, waiting to get her alone? The thought raised the hair on her arms, and she pushed it aside. She frowned at her shoes. What had possessed her to dress in pumps, anyway? Her toes scrunched together, and something was wrong with her right heel. She leaned against the cinder blocks, trying to fix her damaged shoe. The smell of rotting garbage drew her attention, and she limped over to the dumpster.

She knew that you could learn a lot about a person from their trash, but she didn't know if the adage rang true for businesses. She peered inside, inhaling the cloying air, which was humid with decaying food. The bin was crammed full of refuse, much of it packaged in black plastic trash bags. Plastic cooking oil containers balanced atop a cardboard box with the logo of La Chiquita tortillas on it. The box sat on several large cans of hot peppers, which wore a green Mamá Linda label. Susannah chuckled. Even with her limited Spanish, she knew the translation of *mamá linda* was "pretty mama." *Pretty Mama's hot peppers* somehow seemed humorous.

Flattened cardboard boxes were shoved up against the side of the metal behemoth, and she scrutinized its filthy depths but saw nothing of interest. She moved along the dumpster, pushing a garbage bag to the side, and then sighed, checking her watch. More lost time with no results. Fifteen minutes had passed. Bitsy would be running out of ways to keep Randy's attention. Giving the dumpster one last glimpse, she stopped as a bunch of dried flowers caught her eye. They were wedged between a trash bag and the wall of the unit. She peered at them, gradually recognizing the downward-hanging bell of the flower. Could it be foxglove?

She wanted to shout, *Eureka!*

Here was her first solid evidence, she was sure of it. She froze, unsure of what to do. As of yet no official report of the digitalis in Anita's blood had been released. If she reported this to Randy, how would she explain her find? Waylaying a county employee and plying her with Mexican food in exchange for information wasn't something she wanted to admit.

Bitsy's voice played in her mind: *"That detective is out there, and you know she don't like you."*

That detective didn't like her, and the presence of these flowers here meant that the detective's investigation had missed them. She pulled her phone out and snapped a picture. That was a start, but she needed physical proof. She pocketed her phone and reached for the flowers, but they were just out of reach. She pulled herself up and leaned in, stretching her five-foot-ten frame across the trash heap. As she leaned, her head began to spin, the familiar sensation of vertigo causing her to flail about, her fingertips crushing the dried petals. She held the edge of the dumpster and righted herself. The world returned to its normal orientation, and she grasped for the remnants of the stems, but they disintegrated into fragments and fell away.

"No!" she cried, as the plant cascaded beyond her reach. Edging back, she dislodged the stack of plastic cooking oil containers, which tumbled down upon her, sprinkling a few remaining drops of oil into her hair.

"Unbelievable," she muttered, straightening her skirt and then patting her hair. Her skirt was ripped, her heel was broken, and now she had a trash can oil treatment for her hair. And she still had to return to the memorial lunch.

Dead bits of foliage stuck to her fingers, and she considered their presence in the trash. It could not be a coincidence. This was evidence, and it had slipped away. She righted herself, tottering on her broken heel. From her pocket, her phone buzzed. As she reached for it, a different kind of noise caught her attention. A dark blue sedan turned into the alley and headed her way. It approached at a breakneck pace, and she was certain it would careen into one of the brick enclosures. But it didn't. Instead, it accelerated, forcing her to jump out of its way. Teetering to one side, she squeezed herself between the dumpster and the wall. In a flash, the car was gone.

She blinked and peeped around the cinder block wall, watching the brake lights flicker as the car sailed around the building and then out of sight.

CHAPTER TWENTY

Susannah placed her hands on her knees and inhaled deeply. She was trembling, grateful she had not been harmed, but berating herself for being outside alone. Maybe she should stick to chiropractic and leave the investigating to the professionals. After all, she had left the NYPD because she could no longer put a partner at risk.

She straightened. This was different. It wasn't her fault this time. That car had aimed right for her. She must be getting close, but to what she did not know. The sound of a car engine startled her. She blinked twice before she recognized Bitsy's Ford Explorer. Bitsy pulled up next to Susannah and rolled down the window.

"What are you doing here?" Susannah gasped.

"Didn't you get my text?"

"No, I was almost run down by a car. Did you see anything?"

Bitsy glanced down the alley. "Not a thing. Come on, jump in. We gotta get movin'."

Susannah clumped over, vowing to purchase a formal pantsuit that she could wear with flats. "How did you know I was here?"

"I didn't. Not for sure, but you were taking so long that I

reckoned I'd creep out here and take a look-see. I didn't know driving back here was such a popular activity." She jammed her foot down on the accelerator. "Now, if we get in there before all the ruckus is over, no one will ever know we left."

Susannah ignored her NASCAR driving. "What ruckus?"

"One of the cooks went loco throwing stuff at one of the servers. Randy and Detective Westers had to pull him off the man."

"You mean Detective Withers."

Bitsy ignored her comment and made a drinking motion with her thumb and pinky. "He must have taken one too many nips of ol' Jose Cuervo."

"Really?"

"Uh-huh. I ran into the kitchen with Randy, and when I didn't see the detective lady dragging your ass out of Anita's office, I thought I'd better check out here."

She rounded the building and stopped in front of Daniel Kim's insurance agency, which was two shops away from the Cantina. A group of people was disembarking from a white church van with the name *IGLESIA DE NUESTRO SEÑOR* stenciled across the side.

"Get in behind that crowd of bereaved, and I'll go park."

Bitsy joined her as she queued up with the group, entering the restaurant behind an extended family. The religious depictions in Anita's entranceway had caused a bottleneck of older Mexican congregants, one of whom pulled out a rosary and crossed herself amid whispered prayers. She and Bitsy circumvented the faithful, following a family who immediately went to the bar and conversed with Nolan in Spanish. Susannah headed to the ladies' room while Bitsy ambled toward the kitchen.

Susannah glimpsed herself in the mirror. Her first brush with stealth snooping had not gone as planned, but she had gotten out of it without being arrested, so she considered it a win. Her ex-colleagues on the NYPD would wet themselves laughing at her pathetic screw-up. She looked rough, but nothing that a hairbrush wouldn't fix. A woman exited a stall and washed her hands, giving Susannah a polite nod before leaving. A minute later, Bitsy entered and scanned the three stalls.

"You're getting sloppy," she said, pulling a paper towel out of the dispenser and locking the door. She pursed her lips with disapproval. "Give me your shoe."

Susannah handed her the damaged pump.

"Randy and the lady detective are in the dining room," she said, realigning the heel and whacking its bottom against the counter with a flick of her wrist. She handed the shoe to Susannah. "A perfect time to show your face."

"How did you do that?"

"My little secret."

Susannah took a few steps to test the shoe repair, while Bitsy pulled a tube of lipstick from her purse and observed Susannah in the mirror. "It's a miracle," Susannah said, taking a few more steps.

"You bet it is," Bitsy said, squinting at her and then slapping Susannah's hand away from the tear in her skirt.

"Ow!"

"Girl, do I have to teach you how to be sneaky?" She smacked Susannah's hand again. "Weren't you ever a teenager?" She stowed the lipstick in her purse. "No, don't answer that. If you leave that rip alone, chances are no one will notice. If you keep touching it, someone definitely will."

CHAPTER TWENTY

Bitsy reached for the door.

"Don't you want to know what I found?"

Bitsy raised her eyebrows. "A lot of trouble, is what I'm thinking." She led the way out. They returned to the dining room and blended into the line at the buffet table. Bitsy handed her a plate. Susannah smiled at the aroma of chicken breasts.

"So what *did* you find?" Bitsy asked as she spooned some rice onto her plate.

"Flowers."

Bitsy's face fell, and she busied herself over the tray of chicken. Someone had hand-lettered cards describing each dish. This one read CHICKEN AND TOMATILLO WITH CILANTRO. Bitsy snagged the largest piece in the pan and then scooped some green sauce over her rice. Susannah passed on the tomatillos but dug into a tray of enchiladas covered in red sauce and served herself a side of black beans. They found a table in the corner.

"What kind of flowers did you find?"

"Well, I can't show you. They got crushed." She stopped, seeing Tomás watching them from across the room. She gave him a smile. "Here comes Tomás. I'm going to stay quiet. I think he may be a little miffed at me."

"I'm on it."

Susannah tried to look contrite as he strode over. Colin was right: Tomás was pointing the finger at him. And from what she'd heard in the kitchen, Tomás was hounding Randy to make an arrest. While she should have been grateful to have the investigation point away from her, she wasn't so sure Colin was the man. After almost being run down by a blue sedan, she was sure there was more to this than met the eye.

Tomás nodded at her but gave Bitsy a warm smile. "I hope you enjoy your meal. I chose some of Anita's favorites."

"I guess Anita enjoyed the tangy foods," Bitsy commented, nodding at what was left on her plate. "What with the tamarind tea and the chicken and tomatillo."

"Anita loved spicy flavors. She grew her own hot peppers. They were a labor of love."

"I love gardening too. I have me a gardening shed—"

Susannah nudged Bitsy under the table. She needed to keep on track with her questions. She couldn't have Bitsy going into a fifteen-minute description of the miniature house with attached porch she called her shed.

"That's right," Susannah interrupted. "Bitsy loves growing flowers. Did Anita grow flowers?"

"No," Tomás said to Bitsy. "She and her *mamá* specialized in pepper plants."

"She didn't have any problems eating all those hot peppers?" Bitsy asked. "I can't eat hot food like I used to."

"No!" Tomás said, laughing for the first time. "Anita always had a hardy appetite until—"

"Until?"

Tomás looked around the room and then back, narrowing his eyes at Susannah. "Anita had no health problems until about two weeks ago." He glanced over at Randy, who was speaking with the mayor. "I told this to Randy, and he says Anita complained about migraine headaches. But I know the truth. It was no migraine."

Bitsy nodded, forgetting about food for once. "What was it?" she whispered. "Did she have one of them brain tumors?"

"No, that *pendejo* Colin…" His gaze slid to the side, indicating the table where Colin sat. Bitsy looked over, narrowing

CHAPTER TWENTY

her eyes over her *té tamarindo*. "About two weeks ago, he got drunk at the bar, and Anita asked him to leave. He didn't want to leave, but she tried to walk him out. He grabbed her. I saw this. She slipped and hit her head on the bar." He touched his temple. "She thought I didn't see, but I did. I told her to report him to Randy, but she refused. Right after that, she says she has migraine headaches, but I didn't believe it. I think it was a head injury. She wasn't eating like she used to either. When I asked, she told me she was fine. And now, well…"

His voice trailed off, and he removed a handkerchief from his inside pocket and blotted his upper lip. "If I find out *este cabrón* had anything to do with what happened to Anita, I'll kill him myself." He looked up at Susannah, his eyes flashing. "I know you heard us yelling the other day." His face drooped, and he appeared tired. All the fire had gone out of him. "But that is how we worked. She yelled. I yelled. No one was angry. If she were here today, we would probably yell." With that, he replaced his handkerchief and walked away.

CHAPTER TWENTY-ONE

Susannah looked at her friends, seated around the break room table. Larraine poured tea, and Tina laid two plates. Rusty prowled the room, tail held high, sniffing at the corners and stalking nonexistent critters. Bitsy, surprisingly calm, cooed at him. Susannah had closed the office to attend the luncheon and had been looking forward to going home for a hot shower…until Larraine sent a text asking her to return to the office. Before she knew it, she and Bitsy were warming their hands on mugs of steaming tea.

"How was the luncheon?" Larraine asked.

"You tell her," Susannah said to Bitsy, picking up her cup and dunking the tea bag.

"Well, one of the cooks tore up the kitchen going loco after a server, and the police had to break it up. It came in handy. It gave me time to rescue you-know-who." Bitsy jerked her thumb at Susannah and sipped at her tea, her gaze landing on the cookie-filled plates. "We didn't get dessert at the Cantina. Are mourners supposed to be on a diet?"

Tina chuckled. "Help yourself."

She grabbed a cookie and munched. "I thought gluten was banned in this office?"

CHAPTER TWENTY-ONE

"No." It was Susannah's turn to chuckle. "I'm a tolerant boss, but the brownies are gluten-free."

Bitsy paused, then grabbed a brownie and nibbled at it.

Larraine crossed her arms and reset her glasses on her nose, peering over them at Bitsy, as if willing her to get back on topic.

"Well, what did you rescue her from?" Tina asked.

"From her own foolish self." Bitsy dunked the brownie. "She snuck into the kitchen to snoop around Anita's office and then had to beat it out the back door. She was out there in the alley dumpster-diving when I came along."

"Oh my." Larraine tilted her head down, peering over her glasses to examine Susannah. "Now that you say it, she does look a bit disheveled."

"'A bit disheveled.' Good one, Ms. Larraine. She's a hot mess." Bitsy nudged Susannah. "Now that I think of it, give me your phone."

"Why?"

"'Cause I'm fixin' to download this Find My Friends app, and you need one too."

"Why do I need one?"

"For real? My female intuition only travels so far."

Susannah slid her phone across the table, which shook as Tina set her cup on the table with a thud. "Well, what did you find?" she asked.

"Nuffin,'" Bitsy said, crumbs spilling down her blouse. "The only thing we found out was that Tomás denies he argued with Anita. Says they just liked yelling at each other."

"That's not true!" Susannah interjected. "I found out a few things. First of all, I spoke to Anita's daughter, Dolores. She says that the detective wants to know about her mother's medical history, like if she took any medications."

Bitsy nudged her leg. "Why didn't you tell me you talked to Anita's daughter?"

"I'm telling you now. The detective wants to rule out a medication overdose. Which means…" She paused for effect. "Anita was poisoned."

Tina gasped. "That Keith Cawthorn, how dare he keep this from me." She looked around the table and sank low in her chair. "Er, I mean, how did you find that out?"

Susannah looked at Bitsy, who suddenly was interested in Rusty's antics. She inhaled, trying to decide if she should tell Tina and Larraine about the information they had obtained from Iris. "According to both her mother and her daughter, Anita wasn't taking any medications and didn't go to the doctor." She looked from Tina to Larraine. "Even Tomás told us she was in good health until recently, when she hit her head. But that caused headaches, not heart problems."

"Wait," Larraine said. "How does all this add up to poison? I'm missing something."

Bitsy grabbed another cookie and whistled for Rusty, trying to tempt him with a cookie. Susannah's resolve weakened. She couldn't keep this from them. They were a team, and they all needed to have the same information.

"You are missing something." She paused. "Let's just say that Anita had a very high amount of a heart medication in her blood. High enough to kill. This particular medication is made from a plant called foxglove. If Anita didn't get the medication from a doctor, it means someone poisoned her using the foxglove plant."

Larraine resettled her glasses on her nose and pursed her lips.

CHAPTER TWENTY-ONE

"Okay." Tina exhaled slowly and sat back, her chair creaking. "What were you doing in the dumpster?"

"Looking for clues, and I found one. I saw a dried-up foxglove plant, but I couldn't reach it. So I took a picture."

Susannah brought up the photo on her phone. She enlarged it and passed it to Larraine, who squinted through her bifocals. "All I see is trash, darlin'," Larraine said.

Tina looked over her shoulder and shook her head, then handed the phone to Bitsy.

"I don't see no poisonous flowers," Bitsy said.

Susannah snatched the phone away from her and enlarged the photo. "There, in the corner of the dumpster. See?"

The three women brought their heads closer to the screen.

"Uh," Tina murmured. "No, ma'am. I don't see flowers."

Susannah scowled and enlarged the picture again, but they were right, all that was visible was a black smudge where the leaves would have been. Susannah sulked.

"Well, I have some news," Larraine said.

"Ms. Larraine." Bitsy leaned back, slurping at her tea. "What kinda spying are you doing?"

"Not spying." Larraine blushed. "Just asking a few questions here and there. First off, a few of the young'uns from the church are servers at the Cantina, and none of them noticed any illegal activities happening in the kitchen."

"Except for staff choppin' up the chef with a cleaver," Bitsy teased.

"Second," she continued, ignoring Bitsy's remark, "remember when I said my son-in-law's daddy is a partner in a law firm? Well, we happened to have them over for dinner last night." Her blush grew deeper, and Susannah knew Larraine had invited them over as a way of questioning Winston Norris.

"I had a chat with Mr. Norris, and it turns out that Anita was a client with his law firm. This is completely off the record, of course. He'll deny he ever said anything, but Anita had a will and left everything to her daughter."

The women went silent, letting that bit of information sink in.

"So what does that mean, Ms. Larraine?" Tina finally asked.

"Well, financial gain wouldn't have been a motive," Susannah answered. "So Tomás wouldn't have murdered Anita to gain control of the restaurant. That is, if he knew that Dolores inherits the restaurant."

The women nodded. Rusty jumped onto the table and sniffed at the plates, his whiskers twitching. "No, sir." Larraine scooped him up and, holding him against her side, opened the door and dumped him next to his supper dish.

Tina put her cup down and shifted in her chair. "I wasn't going to say anything," she said, glancing around uneasily, "but I overheard something the other day when I was at the Peach Grove PD waiting on Keith. He doesn't know about it, so it can't get him in trouble."

Larraine leaned stiffly against the door, Bitsy put down her second brownie, and Susannah held her breath. What now?

"I only want to help," Tina continued, her hand to her chest.

"Out with it, buttercup," Larraine cajoled.

"I heard the detective talking about having Dr. Shine's fingerprints on a cup that they found on Ms. Alvarez's desk. That must be why she thinks you're involved."

All eyes were now on Susannah.

"My fingerprints?"

Tina nodded.

Susannah sat back, her mouth hanging open, and replayed

the last time she'd seen Anita, as she had many times since her death. The cheery banter, the hot latte, how she slipped on the spilled coffee. "The *té tamarindo*."

"*Té tamarindo?*" Bitsy faltered. "You hate *té tamarindo*."

"Anita was drinking it, not me."

Three heads nodded.

"Then, she slipped on some spilled coffee and almost fell. I held the drink for her so she could wipe up the floor. That's all."

The women sat silently.

"What should we do next?" Bitsy asked.

Susannah stood, stretching. There was plenty of daylight left, but she wanted to go home and soak in a hot tub. She turned from Larraine to Tina. "Tomás suspects Colin Rogers. Fiona mentioned him too. Bitsy and I have already talked to him, and I don't believe it's likely that he could have poisoned Anita. However, he was in the Cantina regularly, so it's possible. Larraine, maybe you could make some calls to your church friends and see what you can turn up about Colin."

Larraine's hands fluttered to her throat. "Who would I call?"

Susannah smiled. "I'm sure you'll come up with some church lady who will be happy to, uh, reminisce."

Larraine nodded.

"And Tina, do you think you could subtly pick Keith's brain about whether Colin or Tomás have ever been in trouble with the police?"

She grinned. "I can try."

"Let's call it a day, ladies. Tomorrow morning, I'm going to the stable early to talk to Fiona." She filled them in about Fiona's comment that Anita had enemies. "We can meet back here for a late breakfast. I'll bring some blueberry muffins. Say, around nine? Patients aren't due until after lunch. Maybe by then, I'll know more."

Tina and Larraine said their good-byes and left. Bitsy stood and excused herself and headed for the restroom. When she returned, she eyed Susannah expectantly. "Am I getting super-secret orders? Like *Mission Impossible*-style?"

Susannah laughed. "Well, remember when we talked about Anita not wanting to be seen?"

"Sure, like she was meeting someone on the down low, like she was doing the nasty with a married man?"

"Something like that. We need to figure out who."

"Well, she wouldn't be the only one. You know my cousin Denise? The one who owns the beauty shop? She's all the time telling me about who's doing what with who. For some people, getting their hair done makes them run at the mouth."

"And there we have it. Maybe you could check with a few of your cousins and find out if they heard anything about Anita."

"Like someone who confessed to murdering her? That kind of thing?"

Susannah chuckled. Bitsy's crazy sense of humor contained barbs of truth. "We have to be discreet about this."

"Sneaky, like."

"Exactly."

"I'm on it, Dr. Shine. I'll make some calls."

CHAPTER TWENTY-TWO

Susannah woke early, grabbed a travel mug filled with hot coffee and drove slowly through the cool morning. A vague breeze stirred the trees as she pulled up to the Long Branch Stable. The Long Branch Stable was only a couple of miles from the office, in a part of the county that had avoided development. Fiona's property edged into the hilly countryside that bordered the Long Branch Creek. It was the perfect place to go riding, and taking a mounted horseback tour was a popular activity.

She had taken Fiona's cue and booked a riding lesson but hoped she would convert it into a walking tour of the paddock and stables. *Maybe even leave out the paddock*, she thought. She was not at ease around horses. They were powerful animals and deserved respect, but she had no desire to ride one, and the chance of a vertigo attack made it even less likely that her rump would ever sit in a saddle. She knew many people who had been injured by horses, and she was not keen to join their ranks. Susannah knew that animals could smell fear on a human, and she willed herself to smell confident.

A teenage girl, who wore her blond hair in a long braid, led a reddish-brown pony out of the stable. Susannah gathered her courage. *If a teenager can handle a horse, I can too.*

She approached the building, greeted by the smell of damp earth and wood, and found Fiona grooming a chestnut horse with a white star on its nose. Fiona smiled, motioning for Susannah to enter. The horse shifted its obsidian eyes to her, daring her to take a step. Susannah froze.

"Dr. Shine. Come on in. I'm finishing up with Beau."

Beau snorted, flaring his huge nostrils in her direction. Susannah felt the blood leave her face.

"You're here for a lesson," Fiona said, glancing at her as she scooped feed into Beau's feeder. "Are you okay, then?"

"I'm fine, fine," Susannah assured her.

"Don't let Beau put you off." She stroked the side of his face affectionately and then plucked a carrot from a bag and placed it in her mouth. Beau reached out and grabbed it with his large front teeth, and Susannah shivered. "He's a big teddy bear."

"To be honest, Larraine made me book the lesson. I came to talk."

"I see curiosity got you and the cat." Fiona laughed, pointing at a scrawny black-and-white cat that had stopped in midstride to assess the situation.

Susannah smiled. "After our last conversation, I think I have reason to be curious."

"Of course you do. I told you Anita had enemies. I used that word because it was what she used. She would say it in Spanish: *somos enemigos*. 'We are enemies.' I think she kept a list in her head of her *enemigos*." Her smile faded into a sneer. The expression did not become her.

"How many enemies did she have?"

Fiona shrugged. "Who knows?" She could not hide the

scorn she obviously felt. "Sometimes she acted as though the world was against her. She would take offense with someone and vent about them nonstop."

"Like who?"

"Anyone." Fiona frowned, thinking. "Her hairdresser, her insurance agent, the man who painted her house. You name it. She complained that the vendor who sold cooking oil scammed her by selling her rancid oil. That made no sense to me. If I sell you rancid oil, will you ever buy anything from me again? It's no strategy to build a business on."

Susannah remembered her foray around the dumpster and the large cans of cooking oil; she suppressed a shudder. "Do you think she made someone angry enough to kill her?"

"I don't know. If she got what she wanted, then she felt vindicated and forgot about it. But I don't know if they forgot about her." She raised her eyebrows; wisps of strawberry blond hair rose along with them. "I heard her on the phone arguing. She didn't back down, and she could get ugly. Let me show you something."

Fiona led Susannah to the tack room and pointed to a saddle hanging on the wall. It boasted hand-worked leather and smelled as if it had been recently oiled. The stitching on it was precise and intricate. "It must have cost a fortune," Susannah commented.

Fiona huffed. An action that would have been a nasal snort on anyone else came off as delicate on her. "You don't have to tell me. Anita ordered it and then refused to pay for it."

"Why wouldn't she pay?"

Fiona gave a slight shake of her head and narrowed her sapphire eyes, the slightest hint of sadness playing across them. "Who knows? Maybe I was the enemy by then." She pulled the saddle from its hook and threw it over her forearm effortlessly. Susannah made a mental note that Fiona was stronger than she looked. "Anita insisted on some custom work." She nodded at the roses tooled into the leather. They covered the horn and edged the saddle in a motif of trailing blooms, which must have taken days to complete. The work was intricate, but it had been covered with a vibrant red paint. Too vibrant. It would have been beautiful, but the color glared ostentatiously from the leather.

"It's not so bad."

Fiona's lip curled. She walked across the room and threw it over a saddle stand. "Would you like to buy it?"

"Umm," Susannah hedged. She searched for a polite way to decline. "It's not my style."

"I've heard that before." Fiona threw a disgusted look at it and turned away. "It's unsellable." She paused. "You can add saddlemaker to the list of her enemies. She treated him like dirt."

"How so?"

"He told her not to paint it because it would hide the hand tooling." She ran her hand over her hair, smoothing a flyaway strand. "She blew up at him, called him all kinds of names. Obviously, he gave in."

"Why did you order it for her?"

"She was paying her bills back then, wasn't she? She told me she wanted to buy a mare and board it here." She kicked at some hay on the floor. "I thought she would be giving me business for years. I trusted her."

"Then she reneged?"

"She never even came to look at it. Made up excuse after excuse. Finally, I called and asked her to give me payment

CHAPTER TWENTY-TWO

over the phone. She told me she would call me back with a card number." Fiona shrugged and rehung the saddle on the wall. "I never heard from her again."

They stepped out of the tack room. Two women were standing in front of a stall, coaxing a tall black horse into its bridle. Fiona motioned with her head and led Susannah out of the stable and toward a split-rail fence.

"You know, I've lived here for twenty-five years. I came here when I was only a girl and never thought I'd own a business like this. The land alone is enough to make me happy for the rest of my life." She sighed. "But for a long time, I felt like an outsider. Then one day, that changed. Suddenly, I had been here longer than some of my clients. Now I give lessons to their children."

Her fair face became serious.

"Gossip travels fast. Anita hadn't been dead a day, and I overheard certain folks accuse you. I pick up gossip." She chuckled. "You see, to some people I'm like a redheaded ghost. I fade into the background and disappear when they're on their mounts. I've heard a lot of nonsense over the years, but none as useless as blaming someone for a murder because of where the victim was found."

"I don't know what to say. I appreciate your faith in me."

"Well, let's say I have faith in Jesus, but I believe you're a better person than Anita." She turned to face Susannah, a wistful look in her blue eyes. "My point is I was angry at Anita for a long time. I got over it. Maybe someone else couldn't."

"Can you prove she cheated anyone else?"

"No, but she ran a business. She had to pay vendors and suppliers. Not to mention overhead, repairs, and contractors.

I'd bet my bottom dollar I wasn't the only one she stiffed."

"You told me she had a run-in with Colin. What did she tell you about that?"

"She didn't. I heard it from Tomás. She just told me that he was her barfly. She could count on him to close down the bar a few nights a week."

Susannah nodded. She had learned as much from Colin himself. "What about Tomás? Did she have problems with him? I thought I heard them arguing during the last PGBA meeting."

"Tomás?" Fiona's expression became sullen. "Anita and Tomás. There was never a dull moment with them."

"What do you mean?"

Fiona coughed, avoiding Susannah's eyes while removing her gloves. "Well, she didn't speak much about Tomás, but it was clear that they bickered all the time. From what I could tell, she didn't hold a grudge against him like she did others. Come to think of it, I remember she had a falling out with her bookkeeper, Olivia Franklin. Maybe you could talk to her. She was in and out of the Cantina. She might have more details about Tomás."

Susannah pulled a pen and a small spiral notebook from her pocket. Jotting down the names Fiona had mentioned, she thanked her and turned to leave. "Another thing. Did Anita ever mention a florist or gardener who she bought flowers from?"

"Flowers? No, she never mentioned buying flowers."

Susannah gave her a smile and walked back to her Jeep, wondering if Larraine knew where to find Olivia Franklin.

CHAPTER TWENTY-THREE

Susannah's hair felt heavy with humidity as she carried four Dunkin' Donuts takeout coffees and her homemade muffins into the office. A slight drizzle had descended on Peach Grove, and Rusty sat under the porch with his tail wrapped around his paws. He watched as Susannah disengaged the alarm and returned to fill his dish, and then he set upon the kibble as if he hadn't eaten in a week. She scratched the tabby's chin with the toe of her boot, and he flopped on his side and rolled over, paws bent in a feline invitation to a belly rub.

"Sorry, big boy," Susannah said. "We have work to do this morning."

On the drive back from the Long Branch Stable, she had considered the list of disgruntled tradespeople Anita had left in her wake. Fiona provided the names of seven unhappy Peach Grove residents, and Susannah marveled at the discrepancy between how the townsfolk behaved in public and how they acted in private. Anita was not the only one whose warts were showing. Colin had been revealed as a boozer with a persecution complex. Tomás could appear calm and genial in the dining room but displayed a more aggressive personality when the kitchen door swung closed. And Fiona, someone she had treated for years, acted pleasant and amicable in her office but in her stable demonstrated a contemptuous, disdainful side. Maybe her attitude was understandable, considering how Anita had treated her.

Gravel crunched as Larraine's Mercury Grand Marquis pulled to a stop. She sat in the car patting her hair into place as Tina leaped out of the passenger seat and cooed hello to Rusty. Purring audibly, he quickly got to his feet and met her as she stood still to allow him to rub against her legs in a feline figure eight. The slam of Larraine's door startled the cat, and he scurried across the parking lot and into the field with his tail lowered.

"Good morning, ladies." Susannah greeted them with a wave. "I have hot coffee and homemade muffins." She entered the building.

Larraine caught up to Tina and whispered, "Don't mention that we were just at Waffle House."

"Don't you worry. My gluten consumption is my own private business."

Larraine tittered, and they entered the office together. Susannah pretended she had not heard the comment, instead concentrating on setting the break room table. She set a Dunkin' Donuts to-go cup at each place. Recycled napkins surrounded a plate, which held several wonky-looking muffins. Tina reached for a cup when a loud banging arose from the front of the building, and she froze, looking from Larraine to Susannah. Tina was the first to break the spell, striding down the main hall with Susannah and Larraine on her heels.

"Who is it?" Larraine asked, as Tina peered out one of the

side windows.

"It's Bitsy," Tina said, and threw the door open.

"Why are you banging on my door?" Susannah asked. "Why didn't you park in the rear like the rest of us?"

"No way, sister." Bitsy shook her finger at Susannah as if she were scolding a child. "A chill came over me after I left here the other day, and it would not leave. I refuse to take chances with a spirit who is not resting in peace. I will park in your poltergeist-free lot, thank you very much."

"Whatever," Susannah muttered, backtracking down the hall. "Come on, then. We're set up in the back. I made my blueberry muffins."

"Uh-hmm," Bitsy said. "That's okay, 'cause I already got my quota of gluten-filled baked goods this morning."

Tina giggled, and Susannah threw a look over her shoulder.

"Well, let's get started." Susannah removed the plastic top from her cup and sipped at the latte. A smattering of foam smudged her upper lip. "I have some news about Anita. It seems she had disputes with half the merchants in Peach Grove. But Fiona told me about one woman in particular. I hope one of you can help me find her."

"Ooh." Bitsy rubbed her hands together, an expectant gleam in her eyes. "This is exciting."

"What's her name?" Tina asked. She grabbed a latte with a sparkle in her eyes that rivaled Bitsy's. Susannah was glad to see she wasn't twisting her wedding ring.

"Olivia Franklin," Susannah said.

"Oh," Bitsy said, her face falling. "I thought it would be someone scary. Olivia ain't scary."

"You know her?"

"You know her too. She used to be a member of the Business

Association, a long time ago. Back when we first joined." Bitsy and Susannah had opened their businesses within a few months of each other and joined the Business Association the same year. "I guess you don't remember."

"No, I don't." Susannah drummed her fingers on the table. What kind of investigator would she be if she had a faulty memory? She racked her brain for an image of Olivia Franklin but could not find one.

"I don't think Olivia is much of a suspect, either," Larraine said. "But I know where she'll be in two days."

"You do?" Bitsy and Tina spoke in unison.

She nodded, a mischievous grin crossing her face, the wrinkles around her eyes deepening. "At the church picnic. Remember, I invited all y'all? And I never heard back from any of you." She raised an eyebrow and tried to look stern but failed. "So now you don't have any reason to stay home."

"I guess not," Susannah agreed. "We'll be at the picnic Saturday morning."

Larraine said, "Good, that makes me feel better about 'interviewing' Miss Holliday." She made air quotes around the word *interviewing*.

"Do tell," Bitsy said, picking up a muffin and taking a blueberry off the top.

"She's a neighbor of the Rogers family. Knew Colin when he was a young'un." She tipped her head at Susannah. "You owe me for this, by the way. I invited her to the house and had to listen to her gossip for over an hour. Thank goodness Charles was out. I must have been red in the face listening to her tell her tales out of school."

Bitsy perked up again. "Now, this sounds good. What did she say?"

CHAPTER TWENTY-THREE

"No." Larraine held her hand up and wagged her finger at Bitsy, the same way Bitsy had scolded Susannah. "That family has had a lot of awful luck and tragedy, and more than one of them has taken up the bottle."

Bitsy shook her head but held her tongue.

"Is that it?" Susannah asked.

"According to Miss Holliday, the entire family keeps to themselves and are not the sharpest tacks in the box. She called them 'lazy boozers,'" she said, using finger quotes again. "She told me she had been inside their house many times. I asked if they were outdoorsmen or if mama was a gardener because I reckoned that if they could hunt, or fish, or can food, Colin might have picked up the skills to poison someone. But according to her, none of them can cook worth a lick. They live on junk food and takeout. She said they rarely leave the house."

"Did she say anything about Colin?"

"No. Just that she thought he shouldn't have charged her so much for a tune-up."

Susannah turned to Bitsy. "What about you?"

Bitsy shook her head. "My cousin Denise thinks Anita might have come to her shop to get her nails done, but she can't be sure. I have to get her a picture."

"I'll text you one." Susannah scrolled through her phone and pulled up a selfie she had taken with Anita. It seemed like long ago, but it was only a few months. She gazed at the image and then pressed send. Bitsy's phone toned.

"Got it."

"What about you, Dr. Shine?" asked Tina. "Did you learn anything new?"

Susannah removed the notepad from her pocket and

pushed it across the table to Tina. "Fiona told me that Anita was extremely particular about the goods and services she purchased. Seems she had disputes with half of Peach Grove. I made note of a few names. Maybe you could call and see what you can find out? If you come up with something, then I can go check them out."

"I'll give it a shot," Tina said, reading off the names of Anita's hairdresser, insurance agent, house painter, and saddlemaker.

"Is that it?" Bitsy asked.

Susannah took a sip of her coffee and reached for a muffin. "She told me that Tomás and Anita bickered all the time, which goes along with what he told us. Anita never complained about him to Fiona, but that doesn't mean he couldn't have a grudge against her."

The phone rang, and Larraine rose from her chair, cup in hand. "I better get that."

Tina stood and swiped at her phone. "I'll get on this right now," she said, and disappeared into the file room.

Bitsy scooped up a muffin with a napkin and stashed it in her shoulder bag. "I have to get back to Peachy Things. I'll let you know what Denise thinks about this picture."

Susannah closed the door behind her and made her way to her office, where she picked apart her muffin while silently watching Henry the Eight swish around his tank. So far, they were coming up with dead ends. Hopefully, the church picnic would change that.

CHAPTER TWENTY-FOUR

Olivia Franklin stood looking over the dessert table in the fellowship hall of the Peach Grove Baptist Church. The accountant wore her ash-blond hair in a short bob with blunt bangs. Small square eyeglasses with black-and-gold frames slid down her nose as she prodded various dishes with a bony finger. A flowing white skirt and oversized blue blouse obscured her slight frame; the blouse's drop collar added another layer of fabric where it tied in front.

"That's Olivia over there, with her fingers in the banana pudding," Larraine said, tilting her head down and pursing her lips. She glared across the cavernous gym-sized room like a referee at a basketball game. Susannah knew that if she had a whistle, she would have called foul. "She best keep her mitts out of my potato salad."

Susannah pulled her shoulders back, stretching her neck. Traipsing across the church campus toting ten pounds of potato salad while clutching a plastic salad bowl against her chest had given her neck a kink. Larraine had refused to give up her blue ribbon dish at first, but Susannah insisted. Letting her carry that heavy container would have been like allowing her mother to carry the catering tray of lasagna to the family Christmas party. The younger generation had their crosses to bear. Susannah said, "Let's put this stuff down and go talk to her."

Before Larraine could answer, Bitsy shoved herself between them, and Susannah lost her grip on the salad bowl, which hit the floor and spilled half of its contents. Bitsy bobbled the aluminum pan she was holding but recovered.

"Why'd you stop short like that? Didn't you see me coming up behind you with the ribs?" She teetered on her Christian Louboutin knock-off spike sandals and wrinkled her nose at the frilly green mess. "What is that stuff? It don't look like no salad I've ever seen."

"It's kale salad. It's good for you."

"Well, dropping this tray of ribs won't be good for me." She pivoted on her faux heels, searching the room. "Where is Roman? He was supposed to be helping me."

Susannah, who now had a free hand, steadied her tray. "I don't see him."

"Hmmph! We made up, but we're gonna be arguing again soon."

"Don't worry about it, Dr. Shine," Larraine said, grabbing the bag containing the potato salad and hefting it with a bulge of her biceps. "It's not the first culinary experiment gone wrong, bless your heart. Go on, I'll get the cleanup crew."

Susannah raised her eyebrows, but Larraine scooted away. All around the edges of the room, people had stopped to watch, but Olivia vanished, spooked like a cat treed by a dog.

Bitsy poked at a bit of kale with the toe of her shoe. "Now who would want to eat that?" she asked, moving aside for Iris Duncan, who stepped forward holding a triple-layer

CHAPTER TWENTY-FOUR

chocolate cake barely concealed under a swath of cling wrap. She nodded at Iris's cake. "We're here to sweet-talk information out of the congregation. Not make them think we're spying on them for their cardiologist."

"There's always one in the group," Iris murmured, shaking her head. Her ponytail swayed in agreement.

"One what?"

"Health nut." Iris skirted the mess and headed for the dessert table. "Come on, if I'm gonna consider joining this church, I have to see what kind of a spread they put out. Though having a shooting range on the campus is a big plus in my book."

Susannah placed her half-empty bowl on a table next to a wilted green salad and a carton of cherry tomatoes. She watched as Iris squeezed her cake in between a mound of brownies and two stacks of cupcakes. The desserts were crammed in four deep and six feet wide. Iris's brown eyes gleamed as she mentally cataloged each morsel.

At the entrée table, Bitsy peeled the aluminum foil back from the tray of ribs. She and Iris bowed their heads reverently, and then Iris dipped one hand into the tray and snagged a juicy rib. Caramelized meat barely hung on to the long, flat bone. Before she could take a bite, Bitsy slapped a paper plate into her other hand. "You're in church now," she said, maneuvering the plate under the dripping flesh. "It's a sin to waste pork."

Larraine returned with the cleanup crew, and in short order the floor was kale free. She escorted the group outside, where parishioners gathered under a large pavilion. Weathered wooden picnic tables were heaped with bags of snack foods. A brigade of senior citizens seated in colorful canvas folding chairs clumped together under a large magnolia tree. Beyond them, a knot of tweens played Ultimate.

"I suppose Roman went straight on to the shooting range." Bitsy took in her surroundings, maneuvering her purse across her body like a bandolero. The purse—faux calfskin, trimmed in black leather—matched her faux-Boutin sandals and gave her a cowboy chic appearance. She dipped into the bag and retrieved a black semiautomatic Smith & Wesson. Releasing the magazine into her hand and racking the slide, she peered into the gun. Satisfied that the chamber was clear, she slid the magazine into her back pocket and dumped the gun back into her purse. "Safety first. I never take a loaded weapon to the range. Now, which way is it, Ms. Larraine?"

Larraine pointed toward some small grassy hills, and Bitsy grabbed Iris's arm and led her off, three-inch heels puncturing the turf as she went. Susannah noticed Olivia Franklin sitting by herself at the edge of the pavilion; the accountant perched, ramrod straight, on the edge of a picnic bench.

Larraine collected two red plastic cups of pink lemonade and a plate of corn chips, which she placed on the table across from Olivia.

"May I?"

Olivia toyed with the bow on her blouse. "Yes, of course."

Larraine motioned to Susannah. "Olivia, you remember Dr. Shine, don't you?

"I should think so."

Susannah smiled and held out one hand. "We met at my first Peach Grove Business Association meeting, but I don't remember seeing you after that."

"I don't have much use for clubs," she said, ignoring Susannah's hand. Instead, she fingered the ends of the blue cotton bow that dangled off her blouse.

Larraine cleared her throat. "Livvy was one of my Sunday School students when she was a young'un."

Olivia's eyes darted up, and she gave Larraine a thin smile. "I always enjoyed your testimony."

"Livvy, Dr. Shine would like to ask you a few questions about Anita," Larraine said.

"Anita," Olivia said with an edge of bitterness to her voice. "Now that she's gone, everybody wants to talk about her." She sniffed, keeping her eyes on her hands. She went silent for a moment while she plopped a floppy leather purse on her lap and pulled a Tootsie Pop from its depths. She dropped the crumpled wrapper, and a light breeze propelled it down the table. "Trying to quit smoking," she said, still not making eye contact, as she tossed the candy around her mouth with her tongue.

Susannah waited until the sucking subsided. "Sounds like you didn't like Anita."

She lifted one shoulder in a halfhearted shrug. "I worked for her. We weren't friends."

"I see." Susannah glanced at Larraine, who gave her an almost imperceptible nod of encouragement. "Is it true that she fired you?"

"Anita and I had a disagreement." She lifted her eyes to Larraine and then inhaled, her words spilling out in a torrent. "I advised her many times to get right with the Lord, but she wouldn't hear it."

"And she fired you for that?"

Olivia locked eyes with Susannah and then shifted her gaze back to her hands. "I thought so," she mumbled to herself. "I tried to help her. I told her she should get a partner to help run her business. She was there with Tomás all the time. I told her she should marry him and let him lead the business. A woman is supposed to be a man's helpmate, not the other way around. That's what the Bible tells us." She blinked and raised her chin. "Isn't that right, Miss Larraine?"

"Well, yes, honey. It is," Larraine said sympathetically, "but I suppose she didn't want to hear that, did she?"

"No," she said, her voice flat. "They would have made a good partnership, but instead she spent her time with that Irish woman. An ungodly person if ever there was one." She spat the last part.

"Do you mean Fiona Bailey?" Susannah asked, slurping at her lemonade, feeling at once relieved and guilty that her status as an unmarried businesswoman was being ignored.

"Who else? I suppose it makes sense that two Catholics would find each other." She fisted her hands and then peered across the table at Larraine. "You know, I read that Catholics aren't true citizens of the United States. Once they're baptized, they are citizens of the Vatican, where the Pope lives. Do you suppose that's true?"

Larraine shook her head. "I have no earthly idea."

"Well, I think that woman turned her against the idea of marriage. Once she started spending time with her, Anita became a disgruntled person." Olivia crossed her arms. Her lips turned down with a sour pucker. She leaned closer to Larraine. "She even told me she was thinking about firing Tomás because she suspected him of stealing."

"Stealing what?" Susannah asked.

"Why are you asking so many questions?"

Larraine shifted, placing her hand on the wooden bench. She threw Susannah a questioning glance before speaking.

CHAPTER TWENTY-FOUR

"That new detective seems to think Dr. Shine had something to do with Anita's death."

Olivia tugged on her blouse. "I don't want to interfere with the police," she said. "Besides, I don't know anything. She only mentioned it once."

"Did she say why she suspected him?"

Olivia's eyes migrated up, and the candy went silent. "Yes, now that I think about it, she asked me about programs to keep track of inventory. She said there was a discrepancy at the bar when Tomás closed. She couldn't balance the sales with the inventory. She thought there was a glitch in her inventory tracking system."

"What did you think? Did you ever notice anything out of the ordinary?"

"I've told you all I know," she said, with a sigh, her shoulders slumped forward as if the question were a weight pulling her down. "I'm not a forensic accountant, and I didn't do her bookkeeping. I specialize in payroll."

Susannah sat for a moment, letting that sink in. Anita had noticed something awry and suspected Tomás was involved. Obviously, Olivia did not think that disqualified him as a potential husband, but maybe Anita did.

"I heard that Anita and Fiona had a falling-out," Susannah said, hoping to move the conversation in another direction.

"Is that right?" Olivia said, perking up.

"She never mentioned that to you?"

"Anita made it clear to me that conversations about her personal life were not welcome."

Apparently, Anita didn't like being lectured. Susannah couldn't blame her there. The women sat in silence for a few moments.

A large neon-green Frisbee sailed close to the picnic shelter, and Susannah got up to retrieve it. It felt good to stretch her legs. She tossed the plastic disc back to a gangly boy who waved his thanks. When she turned back, Olivia was gone.

"She never said what she didn't like about Fiona," Susannah said.

Larraine nibbled on a corn chip pensively and then sighed. "Olivia is a God-fearing woman who is only trying to follow her convictions."

"I can see that," Susannah said, sipping at her lemonade and mulling over the conversation. "But why the chip on her shoulder against Fiona? Why would she defend a man who Anita suspected of stealing but criticize a woman who did nothing wrong?"

"Olivia believes homosexuality is wrong."

CHAPTER TWENTY-FIVE

Fiona Bailey beamed as Susannah approached the Long Branch Stable. "Back for round two?"

Susannah ran a hand through her hair. The thought of spending her Sunday morning on top of a creature that could squash her like a bug made her ears ring and her palms itch, but she needed answers that she suspected only Fiona could give. She hoped she could juggle talking and riding.

Fiona pointed to a young woman who held a smaller mount by the bridle. "Dr. Shine, this is Destiny. She'll be giving you your lesson today."

Susannah tried to hide her disappointment. She had returned to pick Fiona's brain, and she did not want to waste her time with Destiny. During her last visit, Fiona had pointed out Olivia Franklin as someone who might have had a motive to hurt Anita. After meeting her yesterday at the church picnic, Susannah felt Olivia was an unlikely suspect. Although there might have been bad blood between them, Susannah had not discovered anything that suggested Olivia had any contact with Anita after their professional relationship had ended. But Olivia's comment about Fiona and Anita having a romantic relationship forced Susannah's hand.

The young woman nodded at Susannah but did not take her eyes off the horse. Her black hair framed a wide, round face, which glistened in the morning sun. She guided the animal toward Susannah.

"Take good care of Dr. Shine. It's her first time on a horse," said Fiona.

"Uh," Susannah began, careful to avoid eye contact with the giant beast Destiny held by a string. "I, uh, thought we could have a chat first. I could use a cup of coffee."

"I don't have coffee, but I could do with a cuppa tea," Fiona said, dismissing Destiny and leading Susannah into the stable. "Now, you know, we Irish drink our tea hot and strong." She smiled over her shoulder and opened a half door into a small private office. Constructed like the rest of the stable, the walls and door were floor-to-ceiling pine. Against the wall, a file cabinet collected bridle bits. Wedged into the corner, a snack table held an electric kettle and ceramic teapot; above the pot, a shelf held three porcelain cups nested with their saucers underneath and a box with a red label. Various objects of horse-related paraphernalia were strewn on the floor and hung on nails that jutted from the exposed beams. The room had an earthy smell. "I'm glad you made the time to learn to ride."

Susannah scowled. "Thanks to Varina Withers, I have plenty of free time."

"Who is that?"

"She's the Peach Grove detective who thinks I had something to do with Anita's death. Thanks to her, the local rumor mill has run amok, and my office is suffering."

"Ah, yes." Fiona tucked a flyaway hair behind her ear. "The

new policewoman. A very unlikable person from what I've heard."

That's putting it mildly, Susannah thought. "The last time I was here, you mentioned that Anita had a falling-out with Olivia Franklin."

"Yes, I remember."

"Do you mind me asking how you knew that?"

"From herself. She cursed that woman a blue streak one day. Told me she had fired her and never wanted to see her again."

"Did she tell you why?"

Fiona picked up the kettle and plugged it in. "I don't remember. Why do you ask? Do you think it's important?"

"I'm not sure. After talking to Olivia, I got the idea that the problem might have been more about personalities than professionalism. She seemed distressed that Anita hadn't married Tomás."

Fiona dropped one of the tea bags and retrieved it with a graceful twist. She tossed both bags into a small ceramic teapot. "Anita and Tomás? I had no idea they were an item."

"As far as I can tell, they weren't," Susannah replied, watching Fiona's expression. Fiona turned away, busying herself with the tea preparations. "It was Olivia's opinion that Anita should have been married."

"That sounds presumptuous of her."

"Yes, I believe that was the reason Anita fired her, not any actual problem with her work."

"I knew Anita was angry with her." Fiona nodded. "I guess she didn't tell me all the details. I sure wouldn't want anyone prying into my personal life."

"I agree, but Olivia's opinions didn't stop at the Cantina."

"What do you mean?"

"She implied that you and Anita were romantically involved."

Fiona froze. The cup and saucer she was holding shook, and her fair skin blushed deep into her hairline. She set the cup down so quickly that the small table rocked, pitching into the wall. She closed the office door and pulled herself up to her full height. "What do you mean by coming here and saying something like that? You yourself understand how gossip can damage a business."

Susannah held up her hand and repressed the urge to apologize. She watched the blush spread down Fiona's neck and into her chest. "I'm only repeating what Olivia said. She suggested that you and Anita had a close relationship."

"What would give her that idea?" she snapped, her blue eyes dulled.

Susannah shrugged, determined to hold her ground. She was not nosy by nature, but if Detective Withers would not investigate Anita's acquaintances, she would have to. It was said that there are no secrets in a small town, but Susannah knew that was not true. There were plenty, but they rarely stayed secret for long. "I suppose she was trying to come up with a reason why Anita wasn't married."

"Well, outing me would be convenient for her, wouldn't it?" The teakettle shrilled, and she prepared the cups while giving Susannah an uneasy glance. She dropped two sugar cubes into one cup and motioned to Susannah, who signaled that she took it black. "I'm surprised you had the nerve to repeat that to me."

"Being accused of murder is making me nervy. I don't care if you two were partners or not. I'm fighting for my practice and maybe for my life. I need to find out if you're telling me all you know."

Fiona looked at her as if weighing something in her mind. She sighed, pulled a chair over, and motioned to Susannah to sit.

"Anita and I had a fling." She stared into her cup. "I was a fool. I should have known better."

"What do you mean?"

Fiona tugged at her shirt pensively. "I already knew what kind of temperament she had. We had been acquainted for a while before anything happened. Then all at once, we were involved. It lasted a few weeks before the fighting started. She could be demanding."

"About what?"

"Everything. She wanted a discount on her lessons. She wanted me to help her negotiate a good price on a mare she had found for Dolores. She insisted I give Dolores a job, even though I couldn't afford to pay her. She thought the girl needed to learn a work ethic." She rolled her eyes.

"She didn't?"

"No. Dolores is a sweet girl. She did everything I asked of her and did it well. She's quiet and unassuming, the exact opposite of Anita." She allowed herself a meager smile.

Susannah nodded. The requests themselves were not unreasonable, but with an overbearing personality, it could become unbearable. She imagined having to work with someone like Marcie Jones and shuddered.

"She had me on the phone night and day. Not lengthy calls, mind you, but it became tiresome. She would ring me here." She nodded at her desk. "I worried that we would be found out. If it got out, it could cause problems."

Susannah opened her mouth to protest, but Fiona put her hand up. "Sure, not everyone would have a problem with it, but enough would. I told you last time, I hear a lot of gossip. People can be ugly and judgmental. What would those same people think if they knew the truth?"

Susannah didn't answer. She had found Peach Grove lovely and inviting, but she knew not everyone was welcoming. There were those who were threatened by newcomers and always saw them as outsiders. She had been called a Yankee a few times, but it never bothered her. Cultural differences made the world interesting. She had always enjoyed traveling and meeting new people. When she landed here, she was lucky to have found Larraine and Bitsy, who welcomed her and helped her navigate the niceties of small-town Southern life. They offered their friendship and, in a way, insulated her against gossip and ill will. Perhaps Fiona hadn't found the same friendships.

Fiona said, "Now, don't be looking at me like that."

It was Susannah's turn to blush. "Like what?"

"Like I'm a redheaded orphan." She stood and poured more tea in her cup, motioning to Susannah, who declined. She placed the teapot down gingerly, then jerked her thumb over her shoulder. "I love this town and this land, but open your eyes, woman. Do ya see who's out there?"

Susannah braced her saucer so her teacup didn't tremble. Horses were out there: large, heavy, beady-eyed, and ferocious. "I—"

"Girls," Fiona interrupted, looking at her oddly. "Girls love horses. Now how would it look if it got out that the owner of the stable was gay? How do you think that would go over at the church picnic?"

CHAPTER TWENTY-FIVE

"Uh—"

"I take a lot of precautions so that there's never a reason for gossip." She tipped her head. "That door is always open. I delegate lessons and encourage the parents to stay and watch. Two staff, at least, are here with me at all times. If I give a lesson or spend one-on-one time with a youngster, it's always out in the open and there's another adult close by. No child can ever claim I got her alone.

"Then Anita came along, and I got swept away. You asked me the other day why I didn't sue her for the money she owed me. The truth is, I was afraid to take her to court."

"Did she threaten you?"

"Not in so many words. She told me if I pursued it, I would be sorry. So I dropped it."

Susannah sat in silence, sipping at her tea. She was seeing a side of Anita that she hadn't seen before. Charming and gregarious as the owner of the Cantina Caliente, behind the scenes she could be manipulative and argumentative. From where Susannah sat, Fiona had an excellent motive for killing Anita: blackmail. Nevertheless, she could not have had the opportunity. If Tomás and Pilar were correct, Anita wasn't taking heart medication. In order to have digitalis in her system, she would have had to consume it without her knowledge. The killer needed access to her meals, and Fiona had not been around Anita for a while.

It occurred to Susannah that the killer might be someone who was a familiar face at the Cantina, and that was not Fiona. "Did Anita ever mention anyone that might have held a grudge against her?"

"No. She never seemed to care what anyone else thought. She was bullheaded, that one. I'm surprised she cared what

Olivia thought."

"Maybe she was like you and didn't want anyone getting too familiar?"

"Perhaps, but Anita had a perfect cover."

"What do you mean?"

"I mean, she had a family. She had a child and lived with her mother. People fill in the missing pieces with a picture that makes sense to them. She told me a lot of people believed she was a widow who was supporting her elderly mother. They admired her for that." A flyaway hair fell in her eye, and she swiped at it. "They don't realize that she was never married or that Pilar doesn't work because she doesn't need to."

Susannah considered this. Had Anita pulled the wool over everyone's eyes? Colin saw her meeting someone after hours, and judging by the quick about-face she had made when walking Colin through the bar, it had been someone she did not want Colin to see. Was this after she had dropped Fiona? Did she find a new girlfriend—one who drove a blue sedan? Would she care that Colin saw her getting into the car with a woman late at night?

Susannah frowned.

"Dr. Shine?" Fiona had put her cup down and was studying her.

"I was wondering if Anita could have been seeing someone new."

Fiona shook her head. "I have no way of knowing."

A soft knock came on the door, and Fiona opened it to reveal Destiny, who shifted tentatively from foot to foot and began tugging on a lock of her hair.

Susannah glanced at Fiona. How long had the girl been standing there?

CHAPTER TWENTY-FIVE

"I don't mean to bother you," she stammered, looking down at her feet. "Patches is getting restless."

Susannah looked at her watch and jumped to her feet. "Thanks for the tea, but I'm going to have to cancel the lesson. I've taken up a lot of your time, and now I've got to get back." She hoped she was a more accomplished liar than Destiny, who glanced up at them guiltily.

CHAPTER TWENTY-SIX

Bitsy tumbled into Susannah's living room and sprawled into an overstuffed chair, removing her spiky sandals and plopping her feet on the coffee table. Susannah handed her a can of Coca-Cola and flopped on the sofa opposite her. Bitsy popped the top with a grin and said, "I see you remember me when you do your shopping."

"Yes, but I'm still not buying you chocolate-covered Oreos."

"Ooh, girlfriend," Bitsy said, slurping the foam off the top of the can, "you don't know what you're missing."

"I think I do."

"Anyway, we have to agree on the name of our crime solving club."

"We don't need a name. We're not a club." Susannah sighed.

"We're a group of like-minded individuals working for the good of the membership. That sounds like a club to me."

"I guess it does."

"I nominate "Ladies Crime Solving Club. When are Tina and Ms. Larraine gonna get here? We need to vote on it."

"In a few minutes." Susannah glanced at the clock. It was going on noon, but her visit to the Long Branch Stable felt like it had occurred days ago. She moved to the back door and

CHAPTER TWENTY-SIX

drew the curtain, glad that she had visited Fiona before the weather had changed. Outside, the sky was overcast above the pine trees that edged her yard. She had chosen this house because of the undeveloped acreage that came with it. Unlike where she was raised in New York, she couldn't see to the end of her property. There, homes sat on a small wedge of grass, hemmed in by fences and within arm's reach of the neighbors. Here, she could observe the weather and the wildlife without another human in sight. Over the years, she had spied the occasional rabbit and once a bushy-tailed red fox from the comfort of her living room window. "I'm surprised Tina isn't already here. She called earlier, and she was full of questions about what went on at the picnic."

Despite the prayers of the faithful, rain had moved in on the picnic yesterday afternoon, not long after her conversation with Olivia. After that, the crowd migrated indoors, which was where she had found Iris and Bitsy, their plates piled with fried chicken, ribs, potato salad, and chocolate cake.

"This food is so delicious," Bitsy had said. "It takes my mind off how disappointed I am by their shooting range."

"All they had was a couple of cans set on an old tree stump," Iris mumbled, taking another bite of fried chicken. "I couldn't try out my new zombie targets."

"Uh-huh," Bitsy said, jutting her chin to indicate the farm that abutted the church. "And you're not supposed to shoot if that old cow is in the field, on account of how it sours her milk."

The three women had laughed and gone their separate ways.

Susannah hadn't spoken to anyone about her conversation with Olivia or about her discovery at Long Branch Stable.

When Tina called this morning, Susannah had declared an impromptu meeting for latte and brainstorming. Bitsy was the first to arrive, bringing the group naming idea with her. Susannah changed the subject with a brief description of her conversation with Olivia and then asked, "What's your take on what Olivia said about single-woman business owners?"

"I never heard such a thing," Bitsy said, banging the Coke can on the table with a hollow clunk and crossing her legs. "As if I need to be married to run Peachy Things." She harrumphed and then went silent, bringing her hand to her mouth, using her fist to muffle a belch. Slowly she sat up, her brows creased and her nose wrinkled. "Then again, now that I think on it, I suppose I have."

"You have what?"

"Heard such a thing. I am a church-going woman." A look of alarm suddenly crossed her face, and she sat up, her heels thunking on the floor. "Remember, I said Roman and I made up?"

"Yes."

"Well, we more than made up. He asked me to move in with him."

"He did? Why didn't you tell me?"

"Cause there're some details I wanted to mull over, so to speak."

"Mull over?" Susannah echoed. She pulled herself up, scrutinizing the woman sitting across from her. Bitsy was the most spontaneous person she had ever met, and the words sounded like Chinese coming out of her mouth. "What do you mean?"

"We have so much fun together. I can be myself with him, and I feel content having him around."

CHAPTER TWENTY-SIX

Susannah blinked. *Content?* Her brain froze, thoughts stagnated as she tried to make sense of the words. Something wasn't right. "What is happening here?"

"And, you know, that PTSD pill has not slowed things down in the bedroom, if you know what I mean."

Susannah rolled her eyes. "I don't need to know what you mean. So what's the problem?"

"He only took the job at the hospital on a temporary basis. He's been interviewing for months, and he finally got him a terrific job offer."

On the surface, that sounded like excellent news. The kind any content girlfriend should crow over, but Bitsy looked troubled. "Go on."

"It's in Phoenix."

"Oh."

"Arizona."

"I got that."

"You know what they have out there in Phoenix?"

"No, what?"

"Hell if I know, but it's hot, and I hear there's a lot of traffic. I can stay here for all that."

"Wait. I thought he wanted you to move in?"

"He does. If he takes the job, he wants me to move to Phoenix with him. But I'm not so sure now." She leaned forward and drummed her fingernails on the coffee table. "He told me I didn't have to work and that he would make enough to take care of everything."

Susannah was silent. This was more than serious. This was walking-down-the-aisle serious.

"What if he's one of these *19 Kids and Counting* kinda guys?" She stopped drumming her fingers. "I mean, I've worked for years to keep Peachy Things going. It ain't no hobby, it's my life. And now he's trying to take all that away and turn me into a baby mama."

Susannah patted Bitsy's hand. "Sounds like you should talk to him. Maybe he's not planning on any of that."

She nodded and looked at her phone. "He's at work," she sighed, slouching so deeply that her chin was on her chest, her head mashed into the cushion. "I'll call him later."

There was a knock on the door, and Bitsy reluctantly slid up the cushion. "You sure you don't have no Oreos? We're gonna need some snack foods for this meetin'."

"I have some gluten-free crackers," Susannah said, heading for the door.

Bitsy sat up, her eyes narrowing. "Gluten-free, again?" she whined. "I'm all in on crime solving, but can't we be gluten inclusive?"

"Do you want them or not?" Susannah asked, struggling to stop as her momentum propelled her across the hardwood floors in her house slippers.

"I guess they'll do."

Susannah went to the door, and Larraine and Tina entered arm in arm. Susannah had often noted how they appeared as visual opposites. Larraine was taller, older, and plumper, with a penchant for light-colored clothing. Tina, who preferred darker, bold-colored clothing, was petite, slim, and wiry. Despite the generations that separated them, they were inseparable. They stood in the foyer grinning.

Susannah ushered them past her office and formal dining room to the kitchen table. The house had an open floor plan, and the large eating area flowed into the living area. The appliances were set into the middle of the house with the table next to a bowed window. The curtains displayed deep green vines and dark purple grapes, an homage to her Italian heritage and her underdeveloped decorating skills. Larraine offered a hug and draped her purse over a kitchen chair. Today, a powder blue cardigan replaced the usual white she wore in the office.

"Can I help you?" Larraine asked.

"No. You relax," Susannah said. "Sit. I'll make the coffee."

Larraine and Tina settled in around the oval wooden table. Bitsy plopped herself at one end. Tina scooted her chair toward Larraine, who made room for her. "I told her we need a name for our club."

"Club?" asked Larraine?

"Ladies Crime Solving Club, is what I'm thinking."

Larraine and Tina exchanged glances.

"Sounds good to me," Tina said.

"Now that that is agreed upon, we also need snacks for the meetings," Bitsy said, "But I think they should be gluten inclusive. All those in favor, say 'aye.'" She raised her hand and looked at Tina, who avoided her gaze, and then at Larraine, who patted her hair and cleared her throat.

Susannah placed a plate of brownies in the center of the table and handed Bitsy another can of Coke. "They're Bitsy inclusive, and that's a start," she said, leaning over the table and wiggling her eyebrows at her friend. Tina giggled, and Larraine sighed.

Bitsy popped the top and grabbed a brownie. "I'm an emotional eater," she said to Tina, who watched in amazement as she ate a brownie in two bites, followed by a few audible *glug*s of soda.

Tina looked as if she was going to inquire about Bitsy's

emotions, but Susannah interrupted with another plate, stacked with thin, oddly shaped orange-brown wafers made entirely of pointy little seeds. Tina blinked, Larraine forced a smile, and Bitsy tapped a nail on one.

"What the heck are these?" Bitsy asked, picking one up and sniffing. "Smells like garlic."

"They're flaxseed crackers." Susannah brought one to her lips. With one hand under her chin, she bit into it. It crumbled into her palm. "See, it's got sunflower seeds and chia seeds—"

"Girl," Bitsy cut her off, "you got to get your flavor profiles in order. I can't have no garlic mixing with the chocolaty-syrupy symphony I got playin' on my taste buds. Y'all go ahead." Bitsy offered the plate to Larraine and Tina. She got no takers. "See, that there is a savory snack. It don't go with coffee and brownies."

"Okay, okay." Susannah tried to hide her disappointment. She loved the crunchy crispness of the cracker. "Let's get back on track. Right now, we have to talk about what Larraine and I learned from Olivia. And what I found out from Fiona."

Bitsy sighed and bit into another brownie, then cocked her head to the side and ran her tongue over her teeth. "I've been going over what Olivia told you. Maybe Anita didn't take so kindly to Olivia's lecturing."

"Did Larraine fill you in on our conversation with Olivia?" Susannah directed the question to Tina and then retreated to the espresso machine and the soothing smell of coffee beans.

"Yes." Tina frowned, touching Larraine on the elbow. "Yes, we were just talking about it on the drive over. You don't reckon Olivia killed Anita for revenge, do you?"

"I don't think so," Susannah said, placing a coffee before Larraine, who smiled and inhaled greedily. "Olivia told us that Anita only paid her to do the payroll. She didn't make that much money."

"But still." Bitsy tapped a nail on the aluminum can. "It probably made Olivia mad."

"Probably did," Tina said. "I asked Keith if he ever heard anything about Olivia, and he said no."

"Larraine, what's your opinion?" Susannah asked, handing Tina a steaming mug. Thanks to the coffee, her house now smelled like a home. Tina nodded her thanks.

Larraine fiddled with the chain that held her glasses, which today was a utilitarian blue cord, and took a breath. "I've known Olivia since she was knee-high, and she never fit in with the other children. But she was never an angry person, and I can't believe she has the wherewithal to commit this kind of crime."

Susannah returned with her coffee and pulled up a chair. "I suppose we can rule Olivia out. She didn't have access to Anita. Remember, we have to work on the assumption that Anita was poisoned."

The women murmured their agreement and sat in silence for a moment. Bitsy picked up the can of soda, closed one eye, and peered inside. "Maybe Tomás did do it."

"I considered that," Larraine piped up, her face remaining its normal powdery white shade. She was adapting to the investigatory challenge of judging others. "After you left the picnic, I found some of the teens who work as servers at the Cantina. Tomás was at the restaurant all that morning. One boy told me he came in before his normal shift to help Tomás set up the bar. He didn't see Anita that morning. So, if Anita was meeting someone outside the office for…" A slight pink shade crept in her cheeks, and she paused uncomfortably.

"Well, it couldn't have been Tomás."

Bitsy rocked rhythmically, as if the problem were traumatizing. "Tomás could have hired someone to kill her. Maybe a phone call lured her away."

"Hire someone to poison her?" Tina turned that thought over, eyeing Bitsy. "Uh, I suppose it's possible. But don't hired guns usually, you know, shoot people?"

"I see your point, Mrs. Cawthorn." Bitsy thought for a moment. "Sometimes they hit them with baseball bats or run them down with cars."

"Uh, that doesn't fit," Susannah said, trying to get control of the conversation. "There has to be something else."

"What do you mean?"

"If someone were poisoning her, why get together at all? Let's say it was Tomás who poisoned her. Why not just give her the poison and wait for her to drop?"

"Maybe she wasn't dropping fast enough," Bitsy said. "I say we should keep him on our suspect list." She looked around the table. Larraine shrugged, Tina nodded, and Susannah gave a thumbs-up as she sipped.

"Colin, too," Susannah suggested. "Tomás told us he saw Colin push Anita, and she slipped and hit her head. Colin admitted as much to us the day we talked to him."

"You all have been busy," Tina said. She stroked the side of her face. "You're right, not everyone could slip poison to Anita. They had to get close to her."

"Not like those drive-by baseball bat murders you hear about." Bitsy chuckled at her joke.

"You're right," Susannah said to Tina, ignoring Bitsy's humor. "That's what we law enforcement officers call *opportunity*."

CHAPTER TWENTY-SIX

"Law enforcement officers?" Bitsy said, springing up in surprise. "I thought you rode subway trains to make sure everyone kept their clothes on."

"That was only part of it," Susannah said, giving her a sidelong glance. She normally avoided getting into details about her former career. Maybe that should change. "I did get trained as a police officer, you know."

Tina leaned in. "Dr. Shine, you were a police officer?"

Susannah nodded. She had to get this conversation on track. She was about to say as much when Larraine spoke. "One of us should jot down a suspect list," she said, handing her empty mug to Susannah. "I'll have another. Extra sugar this time."

Bitsy grabbed her faux calfskin bag and found a pen. "I'll start the list." She removed a small spiral notebook, which looked the worse for wear, from her bag and touched the tip of her pen to her tongue. She wrote Tomás's name and then Colin's name a few lines lower.

"Don't forget Fiona Bailey," Susannah said over the hissing of the espresso machine.

"Fiona? What did she do?" Tina asked.

"According to Olivia, Fiona is guilty of being a single businesswoman," Susannah replied, and this time she couldn't suppress the eye roll. "And possibly an evil lesbian influence." Susannah handed Larraine her cup and placed a sugar bowl on the table as she watched Bitsy write *evil lesbian influence* next to Fiona's name.

"Now, we don't want to malign Fiona," Larraine said. "Olivia has no proof."

"No. But I do," Susannah said. "She admitted it to me. They had an affair."

Larraine's coloration tinged.

"That doesn't seem like enough of a motive to kill Anita," Tina said. "People are much more accepting of being gay these days."

"Yes, but Anita owed her money. That could be the motive."

Bitsy inked in the word *money* on the line under *evil lesbian influence*. "What about opportunity?" she said the word with a slight bounce to it, as if trying it on to see how it felt. "Come to think about it, I haven't seen Fiona at the Peach Grove Business Association meetings the last few months. How would she have been able to slip Anita the poison?"

"I don't know." Susannah shifted and stretched her elbows behind her. "That will be the most important question. Who was close enough to her that they could put a drug into her food?"

"I know, I know," Bitsy sang, raising her hand and inadvertently flinging her pen across the room. She got up to retrieve it from the hardwood floor. "Tomás had plenty of opportunity."

"I know we have to consider him." Susannah paused, running her fingers through her hair. So many things seemed to rule Tomás out, yet they kept returning to him. It was confounding. She inhaled, allowing the aroma of coffee to soothe her. "But then, who did she meet outside my office?"

Bitsy threw her pad onto the table, and it skittered away and bumped into the brownies. "I never realized that this detectin' was so much talking in circles. I'm getting a headache."

Larraine cleared her throat and placed her hands flat on the table. Her short nails, perfectly manicured with clear polish, contrasted with Bitsy's long, colorful ones. "Tomás and Fiona should stay on the list, just in case. Perhaps Tomás *was* poisoning her, and she *was* having an affair. With someone else, I mean. The two things could have been happening at the same time. We suspect Anita was having an affair with an unnamed man, and maybe he was the one who killed her. But maybe she was having an affair and someone else, like Tomás, got jealous and killed her."

"Ohhhh," Bitsy said. "Now that adds up."

"Or Fiona was the jealous one," Tina added, and Larraine pointed at her in agreement.

"I'm gonna need another brownie," Bitsy said, holding up a finger to interrupt. She shoved half the brownie into her mouth and waved for them to go on.

"By the way, I made those phone calls you asked me to, Dr. Shine," Tina said, "and I spoke to a few of them, but no one said anything bad about Anita."

"Is that so?"

"Yes. The saddlemaker retired, and his son is running the business now. He said he didn't remember the saddle. Her hairdresser told me she was a good tipper and that she felt terrible about what had happened. Anita's insurance agent, Daniel Kim, told me to tell you, 'Hey.' He said Anita gave him a lot of business. He admitted she could be demanding but said she had a good business sense."

"I guess that is a dead end."

"Maybe, but I couldn't find out who painted her house, and I have no way of knowing who sold her the cooking oil either. At least not without asking Tomás."

Susannah nodded, remembering the invoices she had taken from Anita's desk. She took them from inside her blouse and laid them on the table. The other women gathered around and read them with her. Nothing unusual was evident. Susannah shook her head. It was unlikely that a salesman would be in the position to poison one obnoxious client. Why would he bother? It would be easier to find a new client who paid without complaint.

"We've collected a lot of information, but we're still missing something."

There were nods around the table. Susannah stood and gathered the coffee mugs and placed them in the sink. "Who's ready for lunch?"

The women at the table considered the question, an uneasy expression passing from Larraine to Tina. Bitsy nudged Tina. "See why you should have voted for gluten inclusive?"

CHAPTER TWENTY-SEVEN

"Have you ever broken any necks?" a gray-eyed boy asked, an engaging grin spread across his face.

"You don't waste any time, do you?"

Susannah turned to the whiteboard and jotted a few words beneath her name, which had been written by a student in perky round letters, a circle dotting the 'i' in *Shine*. She understood that you never turn your back on a classroom, so she angled herself forty-five degrees, keeping most of the class in view. Career Day at Peach Grove High School was not without its stresses.

She finished writing, "Never broken any necks," and laughter erupted. She smiled. Career Day was a diversion from patients and a way to avoid thinking about Detective Withers and her taunting visits to the office.

"Take your seats, please," she said, and the few students who were still standing quickly found a desk.

She enjoyed interacting with teens and had established herself as a presenter at the annual event. Every year, one or two attendees expressed interest in pursuing a career in physical medicine. She enjoyed speaking with them and found the interaction gratifying. If she could help steer one young adult toward a career, it was worth the time. Then there were the others: those who wanted to find out if chiropractic was the quackery they had heard it was. A question about broken bones usually showed up at some point, and she let them know that she was willing to answer it.

"Ever broken any bones at all?" a girl with jet-black hair asked. Her eyeliner tapered up and onto her temple, and she peeked out from under a dark fringe of hair that obscured her eyes. Susannah wasn't sure if she was shy or if she was just embarrassed to admit that she would enjoy a career that included cracking a few ribs.

"Never."

Susannah faced her first of five scheduled classes, juniors and seniors who would rotate in at forty-five-minute intervals. They were on holiday from their regular class load, and there was an air of frivolity that she tried to keep in check. She had learned that if they became unruly, it would be difficult to keep their attention.

"Chiropractic is very safe," she said, not getting any reaction from the cat-eyed girl who now chewed on a black-polished nail. The gray-eyed boy still wore his smile and seemed genuinely interested. "In fact, chiropractic malpractice insurance is much lower than malpractice for most other kinds of doctors."

"Really? What does that mean?" asked a small girl with bushy, shoulder-length hair. She sat in the front row, wearing a T-shirt sporting the image of the University of Georgia bulldog mascot.

"It means that chiropractors as a group get sued a lot less than other kinds of doctors. And if we do get sued, the insurance companies don't pay out as much on our claims because they are usually not as serious, compared to say, a claim made against a surgeon."

The girl bobbed her head and pushed her glasses up her nose as she wrote something in the spiral notebook that lay open on the desk.

"Any other questions before I begin?"

"Yes," replied a boy whose belly hung over his pants. He wore a football jersey and was as tall and broad as a linebacker. "When do we get lunch?"

There were a few chuckles, and Susannah smiled at him. *Class clown and a football player*, she thought. *Impressive*. "You'll have to check your schedule. I'm not in charge of lunch."

She passed around handouts and began a brief lecture. Everything went well, and it surprised her when the bell rang to release the first section. The rest of the classes proceeded smoothly without the broken neck question, and she was thrilled to greet the last section.

Finally, the bell rang to dismiss the last class, and relief flooded her. She'd made it through the day and no one had brought up Anita's death. All the students stood, except for a girl seated in the last row. She had her head bowed and was drawing on a sketchpad. Susannah hadn't noticed her earlier. As she looked up, Susannah recognized her as the girl she had seen leading a horse out of Fiona's stable the first time she had visited. Today she wore her hair loose, and it fell in straw-colored strands onto her sketchpad.

"Dr. Shine," she said. Susannah noticed a pencil drawing of a horse before the girl flipped her sketchpad closed and maneuvered between the desks. "I want to thank you for helping my father."

Susannah neared her, grasping two leftover handouts she had retrieved. She had not recognized Hayle Jones, Billy's daughter. Hayle took a step closer and grasped Susannah's hand and gave it a light squeeze. She shared Billy's friendly grin.

"It was my pleasure to help him. I hope he's doing better."

"He is," she said. "Mom says he's got to stop eating so many French fries and lose some weight," she added, snorting as she chuckled. Her hand flew to her face.

Susannah agreed. "I also have a lot of thin patients who have back pain. His weight is not the only issue. He needs to come regularly. So tell your dad to come get adjusted."

Hayle picked up her pad, wrapping her arms around it. "I will," she said. "He and my mom get so busy at the store, it's hard for both of them to be gone at the same time. I told him I would drive him over to your office before I go to work."

Susannah nodded. "You work at the Long Branch Stable?"

"Yes, ma'am." She glanced down again, and Susannah noticed how she clutched the sketchpad close to her body as if she were trying to protect it. "But I have my own car. I could take him to see you before I go to the stable. I know Ms. Fiona wouldn't mind if I was a little late. She told me how much you helped her neck."

Susannah nodded and switched off the light as they left the room and entered the stream of students rushing to their lockers. The noise in the corridor rose, and Susannah smiled, coming to a sudden decision. "I'll probably see you at the stable," she said. Though she had no desire to get within ten feet of a horse, it made sense to speak to some of Fiona's staff. "I'm going to be taking some lessons if Fiona can fit me in."

CHAPTER TWENTY-SEVEN

"Oh, Dr. Shine, could I give you lessons? Ms. Fiona said I'm ready to work with clients, and I could use the extra money."

Susannah offered Hayle her hand, and she shook it vigorously. "You have yourself a deal."

CHAPTER TWENTY-EIGHT

Tina Cawthorn finessed a file into the overstuffed cabinet and stared. An aging, chewed-up manila file folder had wedged itself into the corner, preventing the drawer from moving. She placed her hands on the hips of her skinny jeans and scowled.

Thursdays were dress-down days, and Susannah peered at her from the doorway, noting that her own outfit of well-worn denim, a white blouse, and sneakers matched Tina's. Clean lines favored Tina's petite figure.

Susannah stepped into the room as Tina dislodged the file and banged the drawer closed with her foot. She noticed her boss and blushed. "Oh, I, uh—"

"Don't worry about it," Susannah said, taking in the room dedicated to processing insurance. A few charts sat on one side of Tina's desk along with a wire basket that just a short time ago had been brimming with piles of paper awaiting filing. In the days since Anita's death and the slowdown of patients, Tina and Larraine had busied themselves filing and posting payments, and the room was tidier than she had seen it in years. She tucked her hair behind her ear, surprised to find herself wishing for the return of piles of filing. Susannah inspected the cabinet. It was a sturdy behemoth. "Those drawers have taken worse than that."

Larraine walked by. "There will be no abuse of my file cabinets in this office."

"Yes, ma'am," Susannah said. "I'm simply passing through."

Tina scooped up two of the charts and followed her boss down the hall, balancing a clipboard under her chin as she walked. Susannah entered her office, turned, and arched a brow at her assistant. "If I ignore you, will you go away?"

"I know, you hate this HMO." Tina smiled. "But I need you to go over these treatment plans today."

Susannah had always been fond of Tina and Keith, but her sense of loyalty toward them had increased exponentially since Anita's death. Their support of her had been unwavering, and she took comfort in that.

Tina took a tentative step toward Susannah, her head lowered and shoulders tucked as if she were trying to make herself invisible.

Susannah made a sweeping motion with her arm, and Tina deposited the files on the corner of her desk. She turned away from Susannah and waved to Henry the Eighth, who swished his tail and swam behind the filter. "See! I knew Henry liked me."

Susannah gave her a thumbs-up and watched her back out of the room and scamper down the hall. She gazed at the charts. Since Anita's death, she had lost her ability to concentrate on the mundane details of life. Every time her mind calmed down enough to sort through these issues, something else happened to throw her off balance. She thought about Detective Withers. Was she going through something similar, trying to make a way for herself? Or was she an evil woman wielding the power of her office to the detriment of all? Susannah didn't know, but she had to stay out of the detective's way long enough to find the killer.

She resisted the urge to flee the office and closed her eyes. As Bitsy had said, her investigation looped back on itself like a dog chasing its tail. Since reviewing all the suspects with her friends on Sunday, she found herself daily reanalyzing what she knew. Perhaps brownies and latte had made her giddy with the belief she could solve this thing. All week, names and motives had been swirling through her head. She slept so poorly that she was becoming exhausted.

A feeling of lightheadedness made her grasp the desk. Stress was messing with her body. The ever-present threat of a vertigo flare-up terrified her, and she shuddered at the memory of that first and worst episode.

"Hold it together, Sister Shine," she said to herself, mocking the Brooklyn accent of her former partner, Anthony "Tone" Mancuso. "It ain't over till it's over." He would tell her that dwelling on the past wasn't the answer.

She forced her thoughts back to the present, where the slowdown in patients meant she had to be extra scrupulous with all the documentation that this HMO demanded. She couldn't afford to let any payments slip through the cracks.

She slurped at the dregs of her coffee and got to work. An hour later, a sense of accomplishment accompanied her as she hustled down the hall and dropped a stack of charts on Tina's desk and squinted at her. "I'll be back," she said, in her best Arnold Schwarzenegger accent.

Tina grinned, but before she could reply, Larraine's voice came from the front office.

"Dr. Shine?" she called. "It's Billy Jones. I know you aren't dressed for seeing patients, but he's doing poorly."

"Have him come in," she replied, trotting back to her desk, aiming to make the pile on Tina's desk higher before Billy arrived.

Fifteen minutes later, Susannah entered the treatment room steeled to see Marcie Jones, but she was not there. Billy was alone, wearing his Wing Shack polo and a pair of khaki trousers, which were dusted with flour. He sat at the edge of the chair, leaning on its arm.

"Thank you for seeing me." He rose, pushing himself to a standing position by walking his hands up his thighs. "I don't think I've ever seen you in blue jeans."

"Dress-down Thursday."

Though he was in pain, Susannah noted that he was not nearly as tender to the touch as he had been the last time she worked with him. She was relieved that he was healing. "I see you're doing better," she said.

"No, not really. I'm in so much pain, I had to leave work." He grimaced. "I'm sorry you had to come in on your day off."

"It's no problem. It's not my day off. Tina has made sure I have enough insurance reports on my desk to keep me busy late into the night."

Billy chuckled. "I'm sorry to hear it. Still, I hate to be a bother."

"You're not." A hiss escaped as a movable segment on the chiropractic treatment table rose into place, lifted by pneumatic pressure.

"I heard you visited Colin's auto body shop," Billy said, speaking face down.

"I wouldn't call it a social visit. I went along with Bitsy because she needed an inspection."

"I didn't know that Bitsy was with you."

"Well, I was with Bitsy," she said, not willing to admit the true reason for going had been to snoop around and question Colin. The table dropped, and she completed the adjustment.

"Be careful around him, Doc. The man is dangerous."

Susannah stopped to make some notes. "He doesn't seem dangerous to me," she said, as she wrote. "He seems like a man who is unhappy and worried."

"He should be worried. Randy and the new detective must know by now what he's capable of. It's only a matter of time."

Susannah looked up. "What is?"

"Before they find a way to arrest him. You know he has a criminal record."

Susannah gripped her pen. "No, I didn't."

"I guess it's not common knowledge. You'd think Randy would have given you and Bitsy a heads-up, seeing as how y'all are friends."

Billy's comment hung in the air. It seemed Anita's death had ignited a bonfire of gossip under normally reticent people. In the past, she wouldn't have encouraged it, but the town had changed, and she had changed with it. Yet while Colin was an unhappy man who drank too much, he didn't appear dangerous, except to himself.

She finished the treatment, and Billy stood up without using his thighs for support. Susannah suppressed a frown at the traces of flour on the adjusting table. "Doing better?"

He shifted his weight and then cleared his throat. "A little," he said. "I know I should come back more often. I get so busy at work."

"I understand," Susannah said. "But you need to follow up regularly until the pain is under control. And I think I figured

CHAPTER TWENTY-EIGHT

out a way to help."

"How's that?"

"I met your daughter at Career Day yesterday. We had a pleasant chat."

Billy stiffened, grimacing at Susannah, his brow pulled together in pain.

"Are you okay?"

"I got one of those sharp pains is all." He bent forward, his hands again on his thighs, and took a few ragged breaths.

"Why don't you sit down and I'll get you some water." She stepped toward the door.

"No, no. I'm fine." He waved her suggestion away. "It grabs when I stand up. It's gone now. You were saying you met Hayle at school?"

"Yes. She was in my Career Day presentation. I saw her at the Long Branch Stable a few days ago, but I didn't realize who she was."

"I didn't know that you ride." He reached for his back brace, and Susannah lifted it from the chair and handed it to him.

"I'm learning," Susannah replied, as he cinched the brace and came to an upright position. "I want to take lessons, and Hayle offered to help me learn. Providing that Fiona will assign her to teach me."

Billy nodded, listening.

"Hayle volunteered to get you here for your appointments before she goes to the stable." Susannah chuckled. "It's a win-win for all of us. Hayle will make some extra money, Marcie won't have to leave the Wing Shack to help you, and I'll get over my fear of horses."

"Win-win," Billy echoed, his face pale and drawn.

"And you'll get better faster." Susannah penned a final note and then placed her hand on his shoulder. "Let me walk you out."

"Thanks, Doc, you're a lifesaver," he said and took a few tentative steps. At the doorway, he turned and looked back. His sandy blond hair fell across one eye. "If you don't mind me giving you some advice, you be careful now. Colin is not as innocent as he pretends to be."

"Why do you say that?" she asked. She wasn't sure if the Peach Grove PD had released the information about Anita being poisoned, but she decided not to let on that she knew. It was doubtful that Colin could have poisoned her, but he spent enough time drinking at the restaurant's bar to make it a possibility. "You know, he was in his shop when Anita was killed. Stevie Duncan was with him."

"I've known Stevie a long time." He waved his hand for emphasis. "He's attached to Colin and would say anything to make sure Colin stays in business and keeps writing him a paycheck."

"You think he would lie for Colin?"

"Dr. Shine, Stevie is a simple guy, bless his heart," he said, using the Southern adage that could be interpreted as a put-down. "I think he'd say whatever he has to say to keep his job."

Susannah hadn't considered Stevie. She didn't know him well enough to be familiar with his personal history, but it was clear he had some kind of cognitive or developmental disability. Did she think he was above telling lies?

"Colin blames Tomás for causing his problems, but Tomás is voicing what a lot of us already think." He moved his bulk off the doorframe. "Be careful around him."

He left the room in halting steps.

CHAPTER TWENTY-EIGHT

She completed her notes and let her thoughts wander. Colin was around Anita enough, but would he have been able to poison her? Anita served him at the bar. Could she have been drinking or eating too? In all the times that Susannah frequented the Cantina, she had never noticed Anita eating while she worked. She sipped a *café con leche* at the PGBA meetings, but at the last meeting, Colin was far from both the kitchen and Anita's drinks. Then again, if he was the killer, it would not have been difficult for him to meet her the day she died. His shop was close by, and Susannah imagined there were plenty of reasons for him to jump into a car he was working on and take it for a spin.

Susannah left the room and found Larraine and Tina, heads together in the insurance room. Tina glanced up. "I heard what Mr. Billy said about Colin," she said, picking up a few papers. She tapped them into order and placed them in the wire basket. "Do you think he's right that Mr. Colin is dangerous?"

"We did keep him on the suspect list," Larraine reminded them, looking over her glasses at Susannah.

Susannah nodded. "We just have to keep looking for evidence. You can't judge a book by its cover, and right now we have no reason for Colin wanting Anita dead."

"Amen to that," Larraine said and made her way back to her computer at the front desk.

Susannah rubbed her wrist. "I'm not sure that he is dangerous," she said to Tina, who was now seated at her desk. The insurance room was Tina's domain, and the wall above her desk held a few pictures; a calendar featuring puppies and kittens was attached to a file cabinet with plastic smiley-face magnets. Susannah's gaze stopped at a framed picture that sat in a clear area on the edge of the desk. Keith in his military dress uniform smiled down on Tina, who grinned back in an off-the-shoulder white wedding gown. Soon there would be baby pictures next to the wedding picture. "But he is worked up, maybe even desperate. That could make him dangerous."

Tina shook her head. "I don't even know. Keith told me that with a crime like this, there would be a lot of gossip. From what I heard, Mr. Billy is living proof of that."

Susannah nodded, hoping he wasn't proof that she was totally off the mark in her assessment of Colin and Stevie. Her theories all had their flaws, but she didn't think Colin and Anita had been an item. Given that she had also seen a blue sedan outside the Cantina, she believed that the mystery person was not Colin. But could he have another motive to want her dead?

Tina interrupted her thoughts, bringing her back to the present. "Ms. Larraine is paging you." She handed Susannah the phone.

When Susannah finished speaking to Larraine, she turned back to Tina. "When you're done with what you're doing, why don't you pick up something for us to eat? You must be hungry now that you're eating for two."

"One and a half," Tina corrected.

Susannah laughed. She watched Tina brighten at the thought.

Tina said, "The first thing my doctor told me was to not get carried away with that 'eating for two' idea. But I've been so good on my diet, I'm going to treat myself to a tea. I've cut way back on the caffeine and sugar, but I think I deserve a big glass of iced tea. Unsweetened, of course."

"I think you do." Susannah beamed. At least there was one

CHAPTER TWENTY-EIGHT

positive event on which to focus. She looked forward to being an unofficial aunt.

Tina sprang up and grabbed her purse. Susannah said, "Larraine will give you some cash. Make sure you get something for her, too. Don't let her tell you she's watching her figure."

Tina chuckled and left.

Half an hour later, Susannah looked up from a file, the rumbling from her stomach spurring her into action. Tina should have returned by now. She picked up the phone and buzzed Larraine.

"Any word from Tina?"

"No." Larraine paused. "Come to think of it, I thought I heard a car come into the parking lot a while ago. Let me go look." The connection went silent; then, soft rock came through the speaker.

Susannah moved her mouse back and forth as she worked through an online insurance preapproval for a patient. Suddenly, a scream reverberated through the office. The mouse shot across her desk as she jumped to her feet.

"Call 911!" Larraine yelled. "Tina's been hurt."

CHAPTER TWENTY-NINE

Susannah picked up her mobile phone from the desk, dialing 911 as she ran. As the dispatcher's voice came on the line, she felt lightheaded and came to a stop. Steadying herself with a hand on the wall, she moved out of her office and down the hall, searching for Larraine, who she found standing in the open doorway waving her out to the staff parking lot. Susannah's mouth went dry.

"911, what is your emergency?" the dispatcher repeated.

"I need an ambulance." She struggled to get the words out as she flew through the back door, pulse pounding. Tina lay sprawled on her back, her face ashen and her breathing labored, gravel powder dusting her gold hoop earrings. A disposable drink cup spilled its contents onto the ground. "My assistant is ill. She's unconscious."

Susannah kneeled beside Larraine, trying to make sense of what she was seeing, but she could not. Larraine's voice came to her over the persistent thumping of her heart in her ears. She was praying.

A siren screamed as the ambulance came into view. She wanted to move, but she could not take her eyes from Tina's face. The EMTs dropped their gear and went to work. Keith

CHAPTER TWENTY-NINE

Cawthorn appeared and pushed Susannah to the side. She dragged herself to her feet and found Larraine, whose face was gaunt and hollow, as if all of her sixty-four years were now stretched across her bones.

A Peach Grove PD car entered the lot, which was already crowded with emergency vehicles, its blue lights flashing. Randy got out of the driver's side and made his way to Keith, his fingers picking at his belt. He clamped a hand on Keith's shoulder and encouraged him to step away. Keith answered with a wild elbow, and Randy dropped his arms to his sides, his jaw muscles working.

Susannah's legs felt heavy and she stooped over, gulping air. At the corner of the lot where the gravel gave way to brambles under an ancient oak, Rusty sat watching, his ears at attention. She put her hand on Larraine's back, and the two watched as Randy pulled at Keith again.

"Give them some breathing room," Randy said. This time, a uniformed officer was at his side, and they pulled Keith to his feet. His tall frame drooped like a willow tree after a storm. "Let them do their job," Randy said. "You come over here with me."

Susannah looked away, shaken to see Keith transformed, broken and forlorn, smaller somehow. She put her arm around Larraine's shoulder and led her toward the open office door. A pain, exquisite and shocking, pulled her up short—a vise grip was being applied inches above her elbow. Susannah jerked her arm, turning to discern the cause. Detective Withers smiled her fragmentary smile and kept her grip.

"Come this way," the detective said, her brow a rigid line setting her face into stone. She stepped in front of Larraine, abruptly cutting her off when she tried to follow. "Not you."

A female officer, wearing a Peach Grove PD windbreaker, appeared to Larraine's right. Susannah did not recognize her; judging by the look of confusion on her face, neither did Larraine. Vehicles now filled the gravel lot and the lawn behind it, and the detective led Susannah toward them. Rusty was nowhere to be seen.

"This way, ma'am." The female officer, face emotionless, touched Larraine gently on the shoulder and guided her toward the office. Larraine protested. Susannah twisted, watching Larraine look around the parking lot and lock eyes with Randy, who turned away. Larraine's face went from pale to pink as anger colored her cheeks, and she caught Susannah's eyes.

"Go ahead," Susannah said. "I'll be all right."

"Well, isn't that kind of you," Detective Withers drawled, as she edged Susannah onward. "Giving your staff permission to be questioned by the police."

Susannah fumed but said nothing. From tidbits gained through Tina's and Larraine's Peach Grove sources, she had learned that Detective Withers was from Louisiana and had a record for closing cases and catching criminals. Keith had let slip that she was known as a persistent and indefatigable adversary. Susannah didn't doubt any of it.

She inhaled, calming herself. The detective was not in the habit of having two-way conversations, and Susannah knew better than to pursue one. She watched the other officer escort Larraine into the office through the rear door and close it with a thud.

Detective Withers directed Susannah to a parked patrol car, opened the door, and shoved her inside. She shut the door and walked away.

CHAPTER TWENTY-NINE

Susannah looked around, curious. She hadn't been in the back seat of a police car in at least a decade. No, she mused, it had to be two decades. She felt old. A lot had changed since she had been on the job in New York and her partner, Tone, had jokingly stuffed her into the back of a 1984 Crown Vic that was being retired. That had been a car; this was a rolling prison. The back seat was one long hunk of molded plastic, the Plexiglas partition was yellowed and cracking, and the windows were sealed so tight the atmosphere was stifling.

Outside the locked doors, Detective Withers surveyed the scene and ground her fists into her thighs. Susannah felt helpless as she watched the EMTs move with efficiency and speed, and wished, not for the first time, that she had never chosen this spot as an office. Outside of town, set back from the road, with her nearest neighbors the animals in a field and the peach trees in an orchard—how had she ever thought this would be a safe environment for herself and her staff? No witnesses to see the perpetrator also meant no one to come forward in her defense. *Maybe if I worked in a strip mall somewhere*, she thought, *Anita's killer would have struck anyway, but not right at my back door.* Now Tina was the victim of...what?

After many long minutes, the EMT stood and jogged to the ambulance, throwing open its door. He pulled out a stretcher and dragged it toward Tina, its wheels grinding small pellets of dirt and dust. Susannah realized she hated the gravel in this lot.

They lifted Tina onto the stretcher, leaving behind a small white sneaker. Susannah stifled a sob. She wanted to cry but couldn't allow herself to break down in the back of a cruiser. She knew the game the detective was playing, and she knew why. Varina Withers had put her there not only to keep her away from other witnesses but also to put pressure on her, and it was working. The air inside the car was thick, the stink of body odor and plastic tumbled together. The dense foam of the driver's seat back dug into her knees, making her want to scream. She closed her eyes and calmed herself. Putting up with this ploy to "make her sweat" would go a long way toward uncovering just what the detective was thinking.

The police milled around, watching as one EMT hovered over Tina. He laid an IV bag on her shoulder and lifted the stretcher. The other EMT helped load Tina into the ambulance while Keith bent himself into the vehicle.

Detective Withers, her arms folded tightly across her chest, stood next to Randy observing the ambulance's progress as it turned onto Highway 42. Randy shot a glance at Susannah and turned away.

The tightness in Susannah's chest rose into her throat, and she knew whatever relationship she'd once had with him was gone. It was one thing to stand out of the way of an investigation. It was another thing to treat her like a criminal with no evidence and no motive.

Susannah felt a deep sense of despair as she watched the detective throw her shoulders back and walk into the office with Randy close behind her. For years, she had reluctantly put up with his comments but always thought envy fueled his banter. Although retired, she was once a part of the largest, most selective police force in the nation. His assurances that he was treating her like "one of his team" had always felt hollow, but she had gone along with things in deference to his office. She shouldn't have been surprised to see him reveal himself, but it hurt. She was startled when the driver's-

CHAPTER TWENTY-NINE

side door opened, and the female officer she had seen with Larraine got in, turned the ignition, and pulled out of the drive.

"Am I being arrested?" Susannah asked.

"I don't know, ma'am," the woman said in a raspy voice, and pulled onto Highway 42 without another word.

CHAPTER THIRTY

The Peach Grove Police Department interview room consisted of a small table flanked by two well-worn chairs. Orange and black scuffs streaked the tile floor, and Susannah stared at them, chewing her lip as she fought to remain in control. The time dragged, and she fingered a bottle of water, which had stopped sweating an hour ago. She tried to ignore the closed-circuit camera in the corner of the ceiling, and she fought down the bile that rose in her throat.

No crappy coffee here, Tone, she thought, remembering how he associated interrogating a suspect with endless cups of bitter cop-shop coffee. She sipped the water, which tasted like it had been stored in the Georgia sun. *Only potentially carcinogenic water.*

Her stomach rumbled, and she closed her eyes and forced another small sip. The lightheaded feeling she had noticed earlier today returned. Opening her eyes, she pondered her belief that stress was primarily to blame for her vertigo, more than any ear crystals or spinal misalignment ever had been. In times of extreme distress, the symptoms resurfaced.

The door opened, and Detective Withers entered, clutching

CHAPTER THIRTY

a handful of papers. She sat down, clearly taking stock of Susannah. "Dr. Shine, thank you for being so patient." She showed the half smile again, her predatory glare belying her uptempo voice. "I hope you don't mind answering a few questions."

"That's why I'm here, isn't it?"

"Certainly." She reviewed the pages she held. "Is it true that you sell products at your office?"

"Yes."

"What products do you sell?"

Susannah shook her head. "What does this have to do with Tina?"

"Humor me. What products do you sell?"

Susannah gripped her seat, hoping the dizziness stayed away long enough for her to leave under her own steam. A question about the products sold in her office had to mean the detective was about to drill down on the herbal connection to Anita's death.

"You know what I sell. You searched my office and confiscated supplements I had in stock."

The detective narrowed her eyes, and Susannah's skin broke out in gooseflesh. The detective pointed her pen at Susannah as if to say *bingo*. "That's right. And how do you keep track of your sales of *supplements*?" She pronounced the word with derision.

Susannah shook her head. Where was she going with this? "Sales? Everything gets put in the computer and charged to the patient's account."

"So if a patient buys a supplement, then I would find a record of it in your computer system?"

"Yes."

"Is there any other way that you keep track of these sales? Like, say, a paper ledger?"

"No, our accounts are computerized."

The detective pulled a sheaf of paper out of the folder on the table and slid it across the desk. "Is this one of your patient accounts?"

Susannah nodded.

"Really, Doctor? Who is Mr. or Mrs. Miscellaneous? Why are you hiding the name of this patient?"

Susannah scanned the page, her throat going dry. "We call the account *miscellaneous* because we need a way to track products or services sold to nonpatients."

"Why would you be providing products to nonpatients?"

Susannah raised her eyebrows and spoke slowly, as if she were talking to a child. "Because sometimes people who are not patients come in and buy things. A massage, for example. Someone who is not a patient won't have an account in our system. Instead of making accounts for each person, we combine the purchases into one ledger. It gives us a place to put the charges in order to match the payments."

"That sounds like a slush fund to me."

"A slush fund?" She scowled at the detective. "I'm not a retail business, Detective. We don't have a cash register. Every dollar we collect has to balance with a charge in a patient account. It takes time to set up patient accounts. So, for example, if a patient purchases a massage to give as a gift, we don't force the recipient of the gift to set up a patient account."

"Is it so difficult to set up an account?"

"It's not difficult, but it is time consuming. And our computer program is designed to store electronic medical records and requires personal information, such as home address and date of birth. Would you want to give out your date of birth to buy a bottle of vitamins?"

The detective crossed her arms and leaned back in her chair. She had not removed the black windbreaker, and the sleeves rustled as she moved. "I am asking you about the sale of products—dangerous products. You hawk herbal preparations, which can have side effects, without even knowing the health history of the person who buys them."

Susannah opened her mouth to protest but said nothing. The detective had a way of making the simplest things appear underhanded. The *miscellaneous* computer file made it easier for a nonpatient to pay for items without having to set up a username and password. That kind of personalization and account protection was not necessary for nonpatients. Besides, the *miscellaneous* account was rarely used. For the most part, it was a place to track the purchase of gift certificates. Susannah had a few patients who would gift their spouses a massage for their birthday or Christmas. Occasionally she sold a couple of bottles of supplements to nonpatients, but the bulk of her sales went to patients whom she had personally counseled.

Detective Withers made a show of pulling a photograph from between the pages she held, and she slid it across the desk. "Do you recognize this?"

Susannah looked at a picture of one of the brown glass bottles she kept in stock. She used them to hold herbal tonics, which were popular with her patients. "What are you saying? That Tina bought some herbs, and it wasn't recorded in the miscellaneous file?"

"No, Dr. Shine, not Tina." The detective pursed her lips. "I'm concerned about Anita Alvarez. You stated that she was not a patient, but you could have sold her some of these potentially harmful substances and placed the sale in your *miscellaneous* file."

"She never bought any supplements from me."

"You said that this ledger keeps track of the item, but not the buyer. Isn't that correct?"

"Yes, but—"

"So Ms. Alvarez could have purchased something from your office, like a pillow, some vitamins, or even a bottle of your so-called herbal tonic, and we would never know that it was Anita who bought them. Isn't that correct?"

"Yes, but that's not how—"

"She could have paid cash for those herbs, and you would show no record that she was ever in your office."

Susannah didn't answer because the truthful answer was "yes." Anita could have walked in and paid cash for supplements or a pillow, and her name would not show up in any accounting ledger. That was exactly what the *miscellaneous* file was for, but in Detective Withers's hands, it sounded devious and unethical. At last, she said, "I don't run a retail store."

"Of course you don't, Doctor. You run something dangerous. A pseudo-medical office. You lure people in with your inferior license. Then you take their money without ever checking their health history to find out whether your concoctions will harm them."

Susannah knew it was futile to continue to speak to the woman. She stood up. The detective would have to arrest her if she wanted to keep her here any longer.

Detective Withers did not break eye contact and did not stop talking. "Doctor, did you know that Anita Alvarez had a heart condition?"

Susannah shook her head. She could not listen to this nonsense.

"No, you didn't know, because you never bothered to ask her."

Susannah pushed past the detective and twisted the knob on the door. For the briefest moment, she thought it was locked. Terror flooded her legs, and the room slipped off its axis. Then the knob turned, and the world righted itself. She put one foot in front of the other and pushed through.

"You wouldn't have known that the adrenal potion you sold her was contraindicated for someone on heart medication."

Susannah walked on. The air felt light and sweet. The detective was right behind her.

"You stopped her heart with your toxic tonic, Doctor."

The detective had made the connection between the digitalis levels and the herbs in the adrenal tonic she sold. Susannah walked away, fearing with each step that she would be pulled back and arrested. But she continued, safe in the knowledge that the detective lacked any evidence proving that Anita had bought these herbs. And that was one piece of evidence she would never have.

"You can run." The detective followed her down the hall. "But I'm right behind you."

CHAPTER THIRTY-ONE

Susannah exited the station holding her head high, relieved to be outside. The sun had set, and the night was clear. She walked into the parking lot, feeling the lingering warmth of the pavement through her shoes. After a few steps, she realized she had no ride. She patted her pocket for her phone and then remembered dropping it in the parking lot as she felt for Tina's pulse.

Head down, she continued walking. Long, determined steps carried her toward the park next to the Peach Grove Municipal Building. She would regroup there and decide what to do next. Her left eye twitched, but at least the spinning had stopped. The detective wanted to rattle her, but Susannah held tight to the one piece of the puzzle that the detective didn't know she had: the connection to the digitalis levels.

According to Iris, Anita had high levels of digitalis in her blood, above and beyond the norm for a medicated patient. No supplement or herbal concoction that she sold contained digitalis or had the ability to raise digitalis levels. The licorice in the adrenal tonic the detective had mentioned could, if taken over time, deplete potassium levels, thus making the effects of digitalis more powerful, but they couldn't put the drug into your system. There were only two ways to do that: with a drug like Digoxin or by ingesting parts of a foxglove or oleander plant.

It then stood to reason that Detective Withers believed that Anita was already taking Digoxin, and the adrenal tonic had increased its toxicity. Susannah had to contact Dolores and help her uncover Anita's health history, and she had to do it soon.

A horn blared, and she flinched, the noise setting her heart racing. She set her jaw and continued walking. If it was Randy, she would refuse a ride. There was no way she would get into a police car again. Unfaltering, she strode on, but the vehicle caught up and the horn sounded again. She narrowed her eyes and turned.

It was Bitsy, one hand on the wheel, the other waving madly at her. Susannah opened the door and flung herself inside the SUV. "Am I glad to see you." She gave Bitsy a weak punch. "You scared me with the horn. I'm still shaking."

"I only tapped the horn."

"Well, tap the gas, and let's get out of here."

Bitsy flew to the end of the parking lot, which abutted the Peach Grove Community Church, and bounced onto one of the small paved paths that ran through its cemetery. She eyeballed Susannah. "Girl," she said, "maybe we shouldn't drive through the cemetery because you already look like you seen a ghost." Reaching deep into her console, she grabbed a bottle of soda and a four-pack of Oreos and handed them to Susannah. "Here's my emergency low blood sugar supplies. My Auntie Natasha says you take orange juice, but Coke works faster if you ask me."

Susannah waved her away.

"Don't give me any of that health martyr stuff. This ain't no frivolous, recreational use of sugar. I can see that you need to replenish your energy pathways."

Susannah laughed. It felt good to let it out, even if it was halfhearted. Bitsy churned up some grass as she turned onto Little Peach Creek Road, winding her way into the south side of town. Susannah clutched the door, and the Coke slipped from her fingers and bounced onto the orange floor mat.

"Don't make me regret entrusting you with my last Coke."

Susannah picked it up and then twisted the cap off and rushed the bottle to her lips. The foam that rose from the neck of the bottle swept into her mouth and settled on her tongue, introducing itself to taste buds that were more used to kale smoothies than carbonated drinks. The liquid was syrupy and sweet, and the foam spilled down her chin. She couldn't remember the last time she'd drunk a cola, but right now it tasted wonderful.

She glanced at her watch. She hadn't eaten all day. "How did you know I was here?" she asked, pushing a few strands of hair off her forehead.

"Oh, my phone's been buzzin'. Little Junior called me as soon as he saw Officer Young bring you in. Ms. Larraine called me as soon as Detective Weathers stopped harassing her."

"Withers," Susannah corrected, staring out the window. "Nice to have family looking out for me."

"You got that right. Now, don't go spilling no Coke on my upholstery."

Susannah put the bottle in the cup holder. "How's Tina doing?"

"No word yet, but don't worry. I got Andrea on it. Now tell

CHAPTER THIRTY-ONE

me what happened in there? Little Junior only told me they put you in one of them interview rooms. Did they beat you?" She pulled her phone out of a pocket in the door. "Do you have any bruises? I can take pictures for our police brutality claim. White lives matter too, you know."

"They left me alone for a long time. I should have left instead of waiting."

"Trying to make you sweat." Bitsy kept her grip on the phone.

"That's what I assume."

"So, no beating?"

Susannah shook her head. "No."

Bitsy looked almost disappointed and put the phone down. "Did they bring in the good cop and the bad cop?"

"Only Detective Withers."

"Just the crazy cop, then."

"Yes, I guess you could say that." Susannah examined the package of cookies. They were tempting. She bit her lip and ignored them. "Do you remember the day that Anita died, you told me that the detective tried to convince Keith that I was dangerous?"

Bitsy nodded, her eyes without their usual sparkle. "That's what Little Junior said."

"She still thinks that. She believes I sold Anita an herbal tonic that killed her. She interrogated me like I purposely poisoned her."

"How did you poison her?"

Susannah glowered at her, snatching the Coke bottle up and taking another sugary sip.

"Allegedly poison her, I mean?"

"I didn't poison her."

"I know you didn't poison her. I'm prepping you for the trial."

Susannah blanched, her knuckles turning white around the neck of the plastic bottle.

"You're getting paler by the minute! I told you, you need to eat them cookies, for Krebs cycle support."

Susannah tried to relax, but the word *trial* had her heart pumping. Still, she was grateful for Bitsy's weird sense of humor. "Krebs cycle support," she repeated, shaking her head. "How do you know about the Krebs cycle?"

"I read your blog," she said with a huff.

Susannah nodded, distracted by the enormity of the situation. Tina had to be all right. She couldn't bear any more awful news.

When they finally bounced into her two-track drive, Bitsy was silent. She shut off the engine, and they sat facing her garden, composed of several raised beds for vegetables. The trials of keeping dry rot and termites at bay would normally elicit a flurry of complaints from Bitsy, but she said nothing.

After a few moments, Bitsy reached over and gently patted her arm. "Andrea's cooking tonight, but first you got to tell me why Detective Weathers thinks you poisoned Anita."

Andrea, Bitsy's niece, often cooked as a way of thanking Bitsy for letting her live rent-free while she attended college. Susannah had often enjoyed her country cooking style.

"I don't know *why* she thinks I did it, but she has some theory on how. She thinks I sold her some herbs that interfered with her heart medication."

"Hmmmm." Bitsy moved the truck closer to a magnolia tree. "Tomás said she was healthy, except for migraines."

"Yes, that's what I told the detective, but she thinks I'm

hiding something."

"Like all those nasty protein bars?"

"No, she means I have a special computer account designed to hide the names of people who buy things."

"You do?"

"Kind of, but that's not how it works."

Bitsy turned in her seat, her hands still gripping the wheel, and examined Susannah. There was a look of respect in her eyes. "Are you holding out on me? Are you a master villain? I never heard of a bad guy who only drinks water and follows a gluten-free diet."

Susannah rolled her eyes. "I drink coffee, too." She hopped out of the truck, her legs feeling as if she hadn't stood up for days.

Bitsy got out of the truck as well and hurried to the front door, jiggling her key in the old lock. "I suppose you could use all that health food and working out as a super disguise." She looked over her shoulder at Susannah as if expecting confirmation that she was indeed a clean-eating evil mastermind. When she got no reply, she kicked the door, which shimmied but remained stuck.

Then the door sprang open, and Andrea's smiling face met them. She wore blue jeans with an orange-and-black Clayton State University T-shirt. She waved at Susannah with an oven mitt in one hand. The aroma of food cooking met Susannah's nose, and her stomach rumbled.

"Auntie Bitsy told me you had some trouble at your office again." Her large brown eyes were tinged with concern. "I'm sorry to hear it. I thought you might be hungry."

"See how smart my girl is?" Bitsy hugged her while glancing into the kitchen.

Andrea chuckled. "It's not hard to figure out. If she's with you, then she must be hungry."

"You got that right, baby." Bitsy threw her bag on a counter and made a beeline for the stove. "How was school today?"

"Fine." Andrea grabbed a spoon from the garishly painted peach-shaped ceramic spoon holder. Bitsy's kitchen was an old-fashioned farm kitchen with a deep sink and solid oak cabinets, heavy on the peachy accents. The table was long enough to accommodate the passel of Long family members who showed up for Bitsy's after-service luncheons. Susannah chose a chair and sank into it. The smell of chicken and roasting potatoes filled the air. She leaned back and looked around the room. "I'm starving," Susannah said, remembering the phone call at her desk, which seemed like days ago.

Bitsy's eyes widened. "See, it was a good thing I gave you my emergency pack."

"Did she try to foist off that old package of Oreos on you?" Andrea grinned, stirring the pot.

Susannah matched her grin. "She did." She looked sideways at Bitsy, who had her hands on her hips as she bent peering into the oven. "But it was for the good of my energy pathway."

Andrea burst out laughing. "Auntie Bitsy, you're crazy." She shooed her away from the oven by waving the orange-and-green oven mitt and opened the door. "I hope you like roasted chicken."

"I prefer fried," Bitsy replied.

"I know you *prefer* fried," Andrea said, removing the pan from the oven and placing it on the stovetop. She picked up a fork and knife and sliced into it. "But roasted is healthier. Besides, I was talking to our guest."

"Oh," Bitsy said, taken aback. She glanced at Susannah

CHAPTER THIRTY-ONE

as if noticing her for the first time and then waved her fingers, tapping Andrea good-naturedly on the nose. "She's not a guest, she's family, so don't get carried away trying to please her with no specialized cauliflower mashed potatoes or gluten-free biscuits. This here is a traditional cooking household."

"Don't worry, I roasted the potatoes with the chicken, like my mama does." She turned and winked at Susannah. "They're both naturally gluten-free."

Bitsy inspected the contents of the roasting pan. "Well, it smells good enough, so let's eat."

Andrea placed the chicken on a platter and spooned the potatoes next to it. Susannah watched the juices run from the bird, and her stomach rumbled. She realized that the last meal she had eaten with Bitsy was also chicken, but that didn't detract from how enticing the food looked and smelled.

Andrea dug a spoon into a bowl of black-eyed peas and handed it to Susannah. Bitsy rummaged around in the refrigerator, found a bottle of sparkling water, and placed it in front of Susannah.

"I see you remember me when you do your shopping," Susannah said, tilting the contents of the bottle into her glass.

Bitsy smiled with a chicken wing already hanging out of her mouth. Andrea and Susannah laughed, and Bitsy chuckled as she cleaned the bones and placed them on her plate. A banging sound stopped the laughter as the three women listened, and Andrea froze in place, a spoon full of black-eyed peas hovering over her plate.

"What's that?" Susannah asked.

It came again, this time louder.

"There's someone at the front door."

Andrea put the spoon down, a sheepish look on her face. She cleared her throat. "I was fixin' to tell you," she whispered, cutting her eyes in the direction of the front door, "Roman stopped by before. He said he's been trying to get in touch with you and—"

Before she could finish, Bitsy was out of her chair. She grabbed a dish towel and wrung it with both hands as she stalked out of the room. Andrea looked at Susannah, who silently placed her fork on the table, raised an eyebrow, and mouthed, *What's going on?*

Andrea shrugged. "Auntie Bitsy's been acting weird about Roman."

Susannah stood and crept to the kitchen entrance, listening as the front door opened. She pictured Bitsy striding through the small hall and into the living room with one hand on her hip, swinging the dish towel like a lasso. The door opened, and she strained to hear; Bitsy had muted her normally loud timbre. "You have some nerve stopping here, Roman Broady."

"I wanted to see you before I leave."

"Well, you saw me. Good-bye."

"Bitsy, please. I don't want to leave with things like this between us. We been knowing each other too long to stay angry like this."

Susannah imagined Bitsy had both hands on her hips now. "What do you want from me? I thought we were having a good time together. I was respectful of your medical condition. I tried to dial back my natural-born exuberance and give you the room you need. You're the one who brought it to the next level when you asked me to go to Phoenix with you. Now, look at us."

Susannah peeked around the corner. Roman stood in the

CHAPTER THIRTY-ONE

doorway, shoulders slumped and head bowed. A streetlight shone behind him, obscuring his face. Susannah caught Andrea's eye and drew back, feeling guilty at her intrusion. Andrea opened her mouth to say something, but Roman's voice stopped her cold.

"Bitsy, I love you, but I don't know if I can live with you!"

Susannah's guilt could not hold her back. She swiveled around the corner, bumping into Andrea as they both watched Bitsy fling the door shut and turn, one hand still on her hip, and head through the sitting room toward them.

"Hnnh," Bitsy exhaled, the noise a challenge to anyone in the vicinity. "As if I'm gonna let some man control me and make me his puppet." She slid an ottoman out of the way with her foot. Susannah retreated to her seat and busied herself eating. She shot Bitsy a "Who, me?" look and chewed ostentatiously as she entered. "Don't bother pretending, I know you heard everything."

Andrea gave her a hug. "Auntie Bitsy, I'm so sorry."

Bitsy kissed the side of her head. "Don't you fret, little one. He'll make up his mind, one way or the other."

Susannah eyed her friend. "That's all you have to say?"

"No," she said, digging into the black-eyed peas. "That man don't know what he wants. I'm giving him some space to figure it out."

Susannah tasted a piece of chicken. "Mmm, delicious," she said, pointing her fork at Andrea.

Andrea blushed, smiling proudly. Then she took a deep breath and said, "What's this about going to Phoenix?"

Bitsy waved her hand. "He's been job hunting. Looks like he got an offer in Phoenix, and he asked if I'd be interested in going with him."

"Going to Phoenix?" Andrea squawked and began to choke. Black-eyed peas bounced off her plate.

Bitsy stood and slapped her on the back, then handed her Susannah's sparkling water. "Don't get upset. He doesn't even know for sure he wants to live in Phoenix. And he's all fixated on our personality issues."

"Personality issues?"

"Baby, Roman and I go way back. He's what you call an introspective person, and I am outwardly motivated."

"Outwardly motivated?"

She sat back and spread her arms, raising her hands as if to confess. "You know me. I am a people person. I love making a house a home, but I don't want to stay in it all day. I need to get out and make things happen."

Andrea nodded, and Susannah used the pause to spoon up more black-eyed peas.

"Me and Roman are completely different. Look at our jobs. I am open to new concepts and ideas. I love fashion and color, and I reach out to bring in-vogue items into my shop. I make friends everywhere, even on the phone hunting down inventory, bargaining for a price, or working with a client." She pointed at various items that added splashes of color to the kitchen. "I surround myself with beautiful, stylish things and help people who want to buy them."

Andrea was nodding as she spoke. Bitsy lowered her arms and picked up her fork. "Now look at his job. He stands quietly while wearing all black."

"I see," Andrea giggled, "but those things shouldn't keep you apart. I thought you liked him."

"I do, sugar cube." She grinned at Andrea and tapped the table. "Come on, this food is getting cold."

CHAPTER THIRTY-ONE

"I want you to be happy. You don't want to turn someone down because your personalities are different."

"I'm not turning him down. At least not yet. The first thing he has to do is figure out if his PTSD can stand him living with my high-energy, voluptuous-woman-type personality."

Andrea's mouth dropped open. "He has PTSD?" She sat for a moment, letting this sink in. "Well, I guess this makes some kinda sense now."

Susannah swallowed a mouthful of potato. "Have you even talked to him about what he wants?"

"He's not sure what he wants. He says he wants kids, but he has to make sure this"—she indicated herself with both hands—"is what he wants. And then he has to understand I ain't giving up my career to raise him no Broady Bunch!" Bitsy looked down her nose at Susannah and then Andrea. "Now, no more about Roman. Did you make those calls?"

Andrea nodded. "Yes, I used my phone so they wouldn't see your name on caller ID and hang up."

"You talked to Little Junior?"

She nodded several times in succession. "He says that the detectives have gone home for the night, so we don't have to worry about that."

"Worry about what?"

Andrea looked down and poked a roasted potato with her fork.

"Junior heard that Detective Weathers was trying to get another search warrant from Judge Gantner, but it's after hours. She already left for home."

Susannah swallowed what was in her mouth. "A search warrant for what?"

Neither Long woman said a word.

CHAPTER THIRTY-TWO

Susannah couldn't move. She didn't want to ask the next question, but she knew she had to. "How is Tina?"

Bitsy looked at Andrea.

"I have a friend who's doing a nursing rotation at the county hospital, and she found out that she is in 'serious but stable' condition."

Bitsy paused with a speared potato halfway to her mouth.

"Stable is good," Andrea assured her. "It's still serious because she hasn't regained consciousness."

Bitsy nodded and bit into the potato.

Susannah exhaled. She hadn't realized that she'd been holding her breath.

"She could get in trouble for snooping into a patient chart because of the privacy laws and all," Andrea continued, "but she overheard a nurse talking to Tina's husband, so she thought it was okay to tell me that much."

"Thank goodness."

Andrea shook her head, the glass of mineral water at her lips. She swallowed and said, "Ceily overheard one other thing." She placed the glass on the table carefully. "Miss Tina's husband was in the ER with her, and so was that new detective. They got into an argument. She said they got super loud."

"Child, what were they arguing about?"

"The husband—I didn't get his name—"

"Keith," Susannah said.

Andrea nodded. "Keith told the detective that she was investigating the wrong people. He told her they were missing the big picture."

"What else?" Bitsy urged.

"That's it. Ceily was in the supply room across from where they were talking, and they couldn't see her, so she stayed and listened. After a minute, her clinical supervisor came looking for her and she had to leave."

Bitsy leaned across the table and gave Andrea a hug. "You did good." She squeezed her. "You're a true Long."

The girl blushed.

Susannah raised her brow at Bitsy.

"This one was easy," Andrea said, her brown eyes, which were rimmed with the tiniest layer of green, sparkling. "Ceily is smart and caring, but she's a bit of a busybody too. I think she wants to be a nurse so she can help people, but she don't mind being all up in their business."

"Well, I suppose that's a good combination for a nurse," Bitsy mused, sucking at a morsel of chicken lodged between her teeth. "She might make a better hairdresser, though."

"Speaking of that," Susannah said, "did your cousin who owns the nail salon ever find out anything about Anita?"

Bitsy looked up. "As a matter of fact, she did. Denise knew Anita, and she told me that sometimes a man came to pick her up from her appointments."

"Did she ever notice his car?"

"She did. She said he had a big white truck."

Susannah's shoulders drooped.

"Is that bad?" Andrea asked.

"No, not bad. I want to find out who owns the blue sedan."

Bitsy put her plate in the sink as Andrea cleared the dishes, handing them off to her. "Where else have I heard of a blue sedan?" she asked, twisting the tap and rinsing the plates.

"Colin saw Anita get into a blue sedan. I thought it might be important because there was a blue sedan at the Cantina when we were there for Anita's memorial."

Bitsy leaned against the sink, frowning. "I don't remember seeing no blue sedan."

"You didn't, but I did. Remember when you picked me up by the dumpster?"

Andrea paused with dirty utensils in her hand. "The dumpster?"

"It's a long story," Bitsy told her, depositing the flatware in the dishwasher. "Dr. Shine here was playing detective."

Andrea assessed Susannah, pursing her lips and placing one hand on her hip. Susannah smiled at the mannerism she had noted so frequently in Bitsy. "You really are part of the Long family," Andrea said with a giggle.

"She could do worse," Bitsy commented.

Susannah said, "The blue sedan practically ran me down in the alley before you rescued me."

"Hunnh. That seems important. Why didn't I remember that?"

"Probably because you were concentrating on your NASCAR driving. Anyway, I hoped someone else might have seen that car."

Bitsy considered this, but the issue was dropped as the

CHAPTER THIRTY-TWO

women tidied the kitchen. When they finished, she drove Susannah back to her office and waited while she unlocked the door and went inside.

Susannah stood in the shadows of her office, watching from the door as Bitsy drove out of sight. She scanned the lot for Rusty, but he was nowhere to be seen. The alarm had not been set, and she double-checked that the doors were bolted and windows locked. The charts Tina had been working on were shelved. Larraine and her busy hands.

In her office, she bypassed the overhead light and switched on the lamp to Henry's aquarium. She dropped in a few food pellets and watched them fall slowly to the bottom of the tank. She remembered the first day she opened for business, after all the permits and renovations had been taken care of. She had chosen exactly the right spot for her desk and splurged on an expensive chair for herself and the best ten-gallon tank for Henry. Over the years, she had lost that sense of newness and triumph, but never the sense of being at home.

Until today.

In the dark, everything seemed foreign and forbidding. Even the joy she normally experienced watching Henry the Eighth had evaporated.

An oppressive sense of failure weighed down on her. She knew she had waited long enough. She picked up the phone and dialed.

"Dr. Shine, thank goodness," Larraine answered. "I'm here with Keith and Tina. The doctors are taking good care of her."

Susannah nodded to herself. The staff at Henry County Hospital was top notch. She heard voices in the background, and Larraine said, "It's Dr. Shine."

The raspy baritone of Keith Cawthorn came on the line. "Dr. Shine? I'm glad to hear your voice." He sounded relieved.

Susannah felt as if someone had lifted a thousand pounds of rock off her shoulders. She wouldn't have been surprised if Keith had lost his temper and gone into a rage at the sound of her voice.

He asked, "They didn't hold you?"

"I got up and left about two hours ago."

There was a pause. "I reckon you did the right thing. I want you to know that I don't think you had anything to do with this."

Another thousand-pound boulder left her back. "I appreciate that, Keith. I'm so sorry this happened."

"Not your fault." He paused, and Susannah heard him inhale. "I have to get back to Tina."

There was a rustling sound as Larraine retrieved the phone. Susannah could hear Larraine scolding Keith before she returned. "I'm back," Larraine said. "Tina's doing as good as can be expected. The doctors are running tests." She lowered her voice, "They're saying she had an electrolyte imbalance that caused a heart arrhythmia, but they don't know why she won't wake up, and Keith is worried sick. He doesn't say much, but I see it in his eyes. Thank the Lord we got her here quick."

Susannah murmured her agreement.

"I think we're going to need to enlist some extra help with this new detective. She kept me in the office asking questions for so long, I thought she wanted me to confess."

Susannah exhaled. The rage in her skull broke loose, and her mind slipped into gear. When she'd left the NYPD, she swore she would never be put in a position where her inaction might harm someone she cared about. The fear of making the wrong move, of not being in control and losing her balance or falling down another flight of stairs, was a career-ending glitch in her brain. She had become a doctor because she wanted her life and career to have predictable outcomes. But her life had somehow gone out of control, and her loved ones were getting hurt.

"When I saw her put you in that police car, I was worried sick." Larraine lowered her voice. "I think that woman has gone off the deep end. How did you get back to the office?"

"Bitsy picked me up. She brought me to her house first and fed me."

"Well, hallelujah. At least someone can think straight. I knew you wouldn't mind that I called her."

"Of course not." Susannah blinked back tears. At least no one would see her meltdown. Larraine, a sixty-four-year-old church lady, with soft white hair and even softer skin, was proving to be her rock. Susannah was the boss. She always tried to keep a thin layer of professionalism between her and her employees, but at this moment it was cracking. "Thank you."

"Don't think nothin' of it," she said, and then inhaled. Susannah knew that storm clouds were brewing above her soft white 'do. "If this woman thinks she can come to our town and point the finger at our folk and let a maniac roam free, she has another thing coming."

Susannah thought she heard a man's voice grunt in agreement.

CHAPTER THIRTY-THREE

Susannah nodded to Billy as she and Bitsy made their way to a corner table in the small dining room of the Wing Shack. Marcie had called a special meeting of the PGBA to deal with some preparations for the Independence Day Festival. No one appeared to mind that they were meeting here instead of at the Cantina. She heard no mention of Anita's death or of the Cantina Caliente. *Maybe Anita's ghost did reside in the restaurant,* Susannah mused, observing how her fellow members were avoiding the topic. She turned her attention to Bitsy, reminding herself not to mention the notion of Anita's ghost or they would never have Mexican food together again.

Bitsy had pressed Susannah into accompanying her for the vote on the peach pie-eating contest. Since her interrogation at the police station, Susannah had felt shaky and nauseated and in no mood for club politics. She steadied the table as Bitsy bumped it with her purse, a swath of peach-colored fabric spilling out and covering the salt and pepper shakers. Susannah tried to get out of the way, and her elbow hit the wall with a smack. She wished again that she was home, working on putting together the clues she, Larraine, and Tina had collected. The Independence Day Festival had lost its charm, and she wondered if she would have the energy to staff a booth or if she should just take a mental health day. It all seemed meaningless.

Bitsy nudged her back to the present. "I smell biscuits," she said, dropping her bag and heading for the counter, squeezing past other association members. The Wing Shack was less a full-service restaurant than a takeout place with tables, and Susannah wondered how all the PGBA would fit.

Billy stood at the counter, his red apron spread across his massive belly, pouring coffee into Styrofoam cups. Susannah longed for one of Anita's special espresso blends but wore her most polite smile as she queued for a cup. But she was too slow, and Bitsy grabbed the last cup.

Susannah smiled at Billy. "Busy this morning, huh?"

Marcie pushed past Billy, her hair plastered to her forehead. Her usual skirt suit was gone, and she was dressed for work in khakis and a red polo shirt. She frowned at the drips of liquid and spilled sugar. "Why don't we have them come back and pour their own coffee?" she said through gritted teeth.

"That's not very hospitable, is it?"

Marcie lowered her voice and leaned into him; Susannah noticed that her apron, also red and covering the lower half of her body, was speckled with white splotches while Billy's apron was spotless. "They're not our house guests. Besides, it would free us up to do other things."

Billy smiled. "Zach's got the tray of biscuits in the oven. We're good for now."

Marcie faced Billy, twisting a portion of her apron through her fingers as she wiped her hands clean. She glanced at Susannah and gave her a surprisingly warm smile. Then she told Billy, "Anita's delivery is here. I need your help."

Susannah looked away, forcing a disinterested attitude. If Anita had a supply order sent to the Wing Shack, she had to get a look at it.

"Yes, dear." Billy nodded and waved Susannah around the counter. "Last but not least," he said, pointing at the coffeemaker and a stack of Styrofoam cups.

Susannah entered the kitchen, feeling like a trespasser in their inner sanctum. This was the second professional kitchen she had entered in as many weeks. She fixed her coffee, surreptitiously taking in her surroundings. As in Anita's kitchen, long stainless steel countertops held cooking equipment with a secondary shelf piled high with supplies, including stacks of takeout boxes. Unlike the Cantina, which used Styrofoam containers for takeout, the Wing Shack used cardboard boxes, some of which Marcie wrapped with red-and-white baker's twine, a large spool of which sat on the shelf near the boxes.

Zach peered into the oven where dozens of biscuits rose on baking trays. Billy and Marcie had stepped outside the back door, and Susannah heard them continue their squabble, which ended with the slam of a car door. She leaned back to get a better vantage to spy on them. They stood with their backs to her, facing a large white truck.

The wall phone rang. Zach reached past her to answer it, blocking her view. He spoke in the rushed manner that all takeout joints seemed to share, loud enough to drown out Billy and Marcie's spat. Susannah wondered who would be calling for wings so early in the morning, but the thought disappeared as Zach hung up the phone and stepped out of her way. Curiosity drove her a few steps deeper into the

CHAPTER THIRTY-THREE

kitchen. Marcie said they were getting Anita's delivery. The Cantina Caliente was open. Why wouldn't they take the delivery there?

Another half step, and the name on the truck came into view: Southern Charm Distributors. The same name on one of the invoices she had found in Anita's office. She leaned back and stirred her coffee with a thin stirrer, then popped the red plastic into her mouth. A timer sounded, and Zach opened the upright baking unit and picked up a towel, sliding two trays out. He glanced at her and smiled.

"Nice and hot." He grinned. "Just what you've been waiting for, right?"

Susannah forced a smile. "Sure, I love biscuits."

"They have to cool a minute." He turned and shut the oven doors.

"Working at a restaurant must be hard." She removed the mangled stirrer from her mouth and forced a yawn. "Do you always get deliveries this early?"

"No." He wiped his flour-coated fingers on his apron. "We usually aren't open for breakfast. Miss Marcie decided to have the Business Association meeting here at the last minute."

"Oh, I thought Mr. Billy was more involved with the group," she said, practicing her best poker face. She didn't want to give away the fib, but she felt a touch guilty. After all, Zach was still in high school, and she was supposed to set an example for younger people. But she pressed on—something seemed odd about this delivery, and she was sure this boy picked up inside information.

"Oh, no," Zach said. "No. Mr. Billy hated those meetings." He wielded the spatula, making a game of removing biscuits from the baking tray. "He always says that Miss Marcie is the master of marketing. He likes to stay in the background cooking."

"Oh," Susannah replied, trying to look thoughtful as if she were searching her memory. "I thought I saw him at the Cantina. I guess I was wrong."

Zach nodded. "Maybe not." He placed the final biscuit on a waxed paper-lined serving tray. "He used to go over to pick up our order." He pointed at the back door with the spatula. "Maybe you saw him doing that."

"Your order?"

"Yes, ma'am." He pulled a flat rectangle of cardboard off a shelf behind him. He manipulated it with his fingers, shifting tabs into place and popping it open with his thumbs. "Miss Anita and Mr. Billy use the same wholesaler. She used to take delivery of our chicken order and store it in her freezer because it's bigger."

"Well, that was generous of her."

"I guess." Zach handed her the closed box, which was warm to the touch. She took it mechanically, all the while mulling over this turn of events.

"But then he would have to go over there all the time to get the wings," she said, more to herself than to Zach.

"That's what Miss Marcie would complain about too." He lowered his voice. "They argued about it sometimes." He shook his head. "But I agreed with Mr. Billy."

"You did?" Susannah asked, conspiratorially.

"Yes." He wiped his hand on his apron again, flour falling in small powdery clumps. Susannah backed away slightly. "He could place bigger orders and use their freezer as a kind of warehouse. Miss Marcie didn't like it, but it made sense to me. The Cantina is only two minutes away. They could store

CHAPTER THIRTY-THREE

a much larger order than our freezer can handle, and then Mr. Billy could go get what we need for a few days."

"But why would he bother?" Susannah whispered, leaning toward the boy. "Isn't that extra work?"

He rolled his eyes and then tilted his head to meet hers. "That's exactly what Miss Marcie would say."

Susannah was chagrined to learn that she thought like Marcie. Though his explanation sounded logical on the surface, it made little sense when she thought about it. Even if the Cantina could store more frozen goods, Billy had to find the time to get over there regularly. Didn't that negate the whole point of placing bigger orders? Instead of taking delivery of several smaller orders at his store, he stored the food at the Cantina and then shuttled it over. That seemed like even more work. No wonder Marcie and he argued about it.

Susannah said nothing, hoping that Zach would continue. He glanced at the back door and then said, "It also gave us space to store other things. You should see it around here when Miss Marcie orders those watermelons." He rolled his eyes, obviously unaware that the watermelon-eating contest had been canceled.

Susannah chuckled, but her mind worked furiously. Anita and Billy had a business arrangement that Marcie didn't agree with. Could that have made her angry? Marcie certainly seemed like someone who liked to be in control. But angry enough to poison Anita? Susannah walked back to the coffee maker and topped off her cup. Marcie would have had easy access to the Cantina. As the president of the Peach Grove Business Association, she was always the first one to arrive at the meetings and usually the last to leave. With access to her own professional kitchen, she could have prepared the poison out of sight of her family and hidden it.

The wall opposite the back door held the walk-in refrigeration unit. Susannah knew little about restaurant management, but from what she had seen in the Cantina, she knew there should be ample space in those commercial units. She swished the misshapen stirrer around her cup, watching Billy as he loaded boxes onto a red steel hand truck. Marcie, wearing her trademark Marcie frown, reviewed an invoice with the driver.

Susannah rounded the counter and bumped into Bitsy, who had her eyes on the box of biscuits in her hand. Bitsy asked, "What have you got there?"

Susannah opened the lid on the cardboard container and felt the heat rise.

"Where did you get that?"

Susannah pointed her chin at Zach, who carried the serving tray of biscuits toward them. Susannah watched Billy maneuver the rubber wheels over the doorjamb and then stop and reach for the latch on the cooler. She shoved the box of biscuits into Bitsy's hands and made a dash through the kitchen, hoping that Marcie would be busy with the driver for a few more minutes. She wanted a look in the freezer.

"Hey," she said to Billy, "let me give you a hand."

Before he could protest, she pulled the handle and the door opened easily. Billy retreated, lowering the loaded hand truck and rolling it backward as the door swung toward him. He brushed past Susannah, puffing.

The room was dim, and Billy shoved the boxes off with a heave of the handle. Susannah peered in behind him, taking stock of the unit, but her spying was cut short as he swiftly exited, shoving the door closed behind him. He hustled back to Marcie, who poked her head in from the alley.

"I'm coming," he said, oblivious to Susannah, who rushed ahead of the hand truck, which moments before had held forty-pound boxes of chicken wings. It nipped at her heels.

"Billy," Marcie barked.

"I said, I'm coming."

Susannah backed away.

"Watch out for Susannah."

Billy stopped in his tracks, his face flushed, glaring at Marcie. He gave Susannah a sidelong glance, as if seeing her for the first time. "I'm so sorry, Doc." He picked up the bottom of his apron and wiped his face with it. "I'm rushing, trying to get this done."

"Well, stop rushing," Marcie snapped, "and pay attention to what you're doing. I didn't open the restaurant early so we could get sued."

Billy inclined the hand truck toward Marcie, who stepped back, nodding an apology to Susannah.

"No problem," Susannah said, returning Marcie's nod and hightailing it out of the kitchen. She didn't know how the couple could run a business together. Billy had always seemed like an easygoing guy, but he was clearly agitated. Marcie could be so demanding and unpleasant that it had to be hell working with her. According to Zach, they had disagreements in front of him, and this morning Billy was so frantic to get the boxes stowed that he practically ran Susannah down with a hand truck.

Bitsy sidled up to her, licking butter off her finger. "Why you looking so deep in thought?"

Susannah explained what Zach had told her about the

freezer arrangement and what she had seen. "Something's not right."

"I'll tell you what's not right," Bitsy said, glancing into the kitchen. "Running your man like he was a pack animal. It's no wonder he ran off to another woman's freezer."

Using the other freezer simply didn't make sense. Why would a businessperson do such an illogical thing? She would have to find the time to speak to Tomás. Maybe he would have some answers about that. And there was still the question of whether he was stealing. That wasn't something she could ask him point blank.

Susannah started when Marcie called the meeting to order with a bang of the gavel. The Independence Day Festival was only a few days off, and she was not surprised that Bitsy got her wish of running a peach pie-eating contest.

Bitsy stood and twirled with delight, bowing to the room. Marcie's green eyes darkened as she gave Bitsy a scathing look. Bitsy sat and muttered to Susannah, "It's never too early to get the stink eye from that woman."

Susannah nodded. Her gaze had not left the kitchen as Billy loitered in the rear of the building, putting away the delivery items and tidying up. As last-minute details were finalized and the meeting adjourned, Susannah was weighted with a list of people she still needed to see. Time was ticking away, and the more information she collected, the more questions she had.

CHAPTER THIRTY-FOUR

"Steady, Ginger!"

Susannah sat perched atop a horse, thighs quivering, feet locked into the stirrups. A drop of sweat trickled down her back despite the coolness of the morning. An incident of vandalism at the stable had prompted her decision to return for riding lessons, but concern for Tina and anticipation of a meeting with Dolores clouded her thoughts and added to her anxiety.

She had contacted Dolores, impatient to uncover the details about Anita's health and medication use. She needed facts to build a logical case and not rely on what Detective Withers would view as a far-fetched story. However, that plan would have to wait, as Dolores was busy at school and not available until Thursday afternoon.

She grasped the reins and shivered.

The image of Tina lying in the hospital haunted her. Susannah knew in her gut that whoever had poisoned Anita was responsible for Tina's medical crisis, but the doctors had denied any connection. They had diagnosed Tina with a heart arrhythmia, which caused a severe drop in blood pressure. There was also concern that her kidneys were under stress because of her pregnancy, and she remained in the hospital under observation. Keith had not left her side, and everyone was grateful that the arrhythmia had not affected the baby.

She could not let Tina down, and she fought to silence the voices in her head, which told her she was inept and lacked investigative experience. She had to solve this case before more people were hurt.

She turned her attention back to her lesson and Destiny, who had replaced Hayle as her guide and teacher. Fiona had given Hayle time off to purchase new tires since her car had been one of several vandalized. Randy thought the attack was the work of teenaged mischief-makers and not connected to Anita's murder, but Susannah was not so sure. And now, she had her rear clamped into this saddle to make sure her fondness for Fiona didn't influence her judgment. She had to wonder if Fiona could be the connection to the murderer. Had she missed a clue when she was here last? She was determined to find out.

The horse shifted, and she squeezed her knees, undaunted. As she had hoped, only when she got a leg up to mount the animal did she feel any dizziness. She glanced down. Practicing perfect posture was the easy part. Hiding her anxiety from Destiny was not.

Destiny took the reins from her but could not hide the pity in her eyes. "Dr. Shine," she said, leading the horse around the ring, "you need to relax and go with the movement. Ginger is our most gentle horse. In fact, the other day I noticed how careful he is around the barn cat."

Susannah smiled. She was no cat. She was a big, quivering mess, and the horse knew it. For the next fifteen minutes, Destiny coaxed Susannah around the ring with promises of a quick lesson and a painless dismount. Susannah visualized a hot latte as her reward, like the proverbial light at the end of the tunnel. She even envisioned an act of ultimate self-sacrifice: she would give Ginger a nice, crunchy apple.

Fiona exited the barn, leading a large gelding. He was bigger than Ginger and he strode, tossing his head. He lifted one hoof, and Susannah blanched. The movement looked like an equine gang sign.

"This is Shadow," Fiona said, as if the two-ton beast could have a comic book name imposed on him.

Susannah's hands quivered, but she camouflaged the movement by grasping the horn of the saddle. Ginger lifted his chin and shook his head, exposing his large teeth. *Step off*, he seemed to say to Shadow, *this gelatinous human is mine.* Susannah sighed.

"Ginger likes you," Fiona observed, nodding at Destiny, who threw the reins up over Ginger's head. They slid down his neck, and Susannah grabbed them with a confidence she didn't feel. *I guess I have to fake it till I make it.* Ginger stomped a foot in agreement.

"Destiny tells me you've done well on Ginger." She gave Shadow a gentle swat with the reins.

Susannah gaped at Destiny. "Well, I—"

"You're doin' fine. Let's walk. We can talk in private."

"I have to get back to the office." All thoughts of crime-solving had evaporated.

"Nonsense. It's a beautiful morning. You want to learn to ride, don't ya?"

Susannah said nothing, ashamed of how much she wanted to be at her desk sipping coffee and eating a warm muffin.

Fiona led Ginger outside a gate. The entrance to the Long

Branch Stable was a dirt road, abutted on both sides by a wooden fence. The fence's large planks, painted dark brown to match the trim on the barn, gave the stable a tidy, well-kept look. The campus had a neat, rustic feel to it, and Susannah understood why Fiona loved it so much. The air was still and quiet, and there was a fullness to the day that was different here. The paddock they occupied was used to groom and saddle the horses. It was separated from an even larger arena where show horses trained in jumping. The jumping ring held the typical obstacles a competition horse must face, like fences, bales of hay, and pools of water. Susannah prayed that Ginger didn't have hopes of flying over fences.

"I read about Tina Cawthorn on Facebook," said Fiona. "How is she doing?"

"She's still in the hospital. The doctors say she's stable."

"I hope she gets better."

"Thank you." Susannah took a breath. She didn't want to get derailed. "I'm here because I wanted to ask about the vandalism. I know the police don't think it's related to Anita's death, but I'm curious. What do you think?"

"I'm not sure what to think. I have to admit, I felt some relief after Anita died. While she was alive, there was no guarantee that she wouldn't get a bug up her bum and cause me trouble just for spite." She patted Shadow's side. "But now I'm wondering if it was all for naught."

Susannah watched her, curious. Fiona stared off into the distance. Why was she relieved that Anita was dead? Could this mean she was involved with Anita's death? "What was all for naught?"

"All the worrying I did. But who knows? Maybe she already let it slip about us, and someone wants me to know they don't agree with my lifestyle." She regarded Susannah. "Other than that, I can't make heads nor tails of it. Why would someone come all the way out here to slash tires unless they had a personal reason?"

Susannah had to agree. The Long Branch Stable was far enough off the beaten path that no one would happen upon it by chance. It had to be personal, and that made her think it was connected to Anita's death. The problem was figuring out how. "Fiona, what kind of car did Anita drive?"

"She had a Toyota. Why do you ask?"

"Colin told me he saw her get into a dark blue sedan."

Fiona shrugged. "She never drove a sedan that I saw. She had a red two-door. A Solara, I think. It was older, but she loved it because it was a convertible."

Susannah tried to picture it. She must have seen it in the parking lot of the Cantina, but she drew a blank. "Did she ever mention her suspicion that Tomás was stealing from her?"

"No. Who told you he was stealing?" She tugged on the reins, holding Shadow steady. "I think I would have heard about that."

"Olivia mentioned it. She said Anita had an inventory problem."

Fiona shrugged. "Maybe it was just an error. Believe me, if it was on Anita's mind, she would have been ranting about it."

Susannah said nothing. Perhaps it had been some kind of counting error. She wasn't sure it mattered anymore. Since Dolores was inheriting the restaurant, how would Tomás benefit by killing Anita? Could he have killed Anita over some missing liquor? "Did Anita talk about any other relationships?"

"No, I've been over this a hundred times in my head. She never mentioned any other lovers, male or female. She always complained about how busy she was. Made herself out to be a martyr for her daughter's sake." She patted Shadow's side again and sighed. "I teased her about it, but I suppose it was true."

They sat for a moment, and Fiona glanced at her watch. "It's only eight thirty. How about a quick ride? I promise to have you back at the barn before nine."

Susannah agreed with a half-hearted thumbs-up. Ginger swished his tail.

Fiona directed Shadow down the path. Ginger tagged along, up a small but steep hill that crested into a field that was delineated only by a barbed wire fence. It went off into the distance toward a line of towering evergreens. Fiona rode closely alongside Ginger and tested Susannah on the basics of equine handling. Once her trembling subsided, Susannah proved an adequate student, and Fiona gave her a smile and then said, "Okay, we're going to pick up the pace."

Fiona kicked her heels against Shadow's side, and he began to trot. Ginger followed along. Susannah bounced hard against the saddle, trying to keep pace as they flew across the fields, the horses' hooves churning up dust along with clods of yellow grass. The air was pleasant against her face, and the terror that had risen up in her throat turned to exhilaration. She could no longer see the stable, and they passed a row of cedars that stood as neatly as if someone had planted a strip of Christmas trees. Nearing the trees, Shadow slowed and Ginger emulated him. Fiona led Shadow into the shade of the soaring cedars. The humid air smelled of decaying leaves and needles and felt a few degrees cooler. A small

CHAPTER THIRTY-FOUR

trail opened up, and Fiona walked the beasts into the woods, which stretched out behind several houses. Soon they arrived at a small brook. She dismounted and led Shadow to the water. Susannah followed suit and walked alongside Ginger.

"See, that wasn't so bad. The boys got some exercise, and your blood is pumping."

Susannah had to agree. "I didn't realize that anyone lives back here." She motioned in the direction of the houses she had seen.

"Ya, I don't own this. My land ends at the tree line." She pointed in the direction they had been riding. "Except for right behind the barn, I don't own any of the forested land." She tilted her head in the opposite direction. "I own fifty acres on the other side of the stable, but this riding is easy and flat. Good for beginners."

"I appreciate that."

Ginger placed one leg in front of the other and bowed his head, putting his lips to the stream. Susannah admired his coloring and his gentle bearing. She gave him a tentative pat on the side. "Your neighbors don't mind them using the stream?"

"Not at all. All this land originally belonged to one family. The owner divided it into parcels years ago so that a niece could build the stable. From what I understand, the homes were built later, and the woods were a kind of shared property. When I bought the stable, they assured me that I could bring the horses in anytime. I try not to take advantage because I have so much acreage. Like I said, it's an enjoyable ride for a novice."

Before Susannah could ask another question, she was jolted by a cold wet spray that hit her face. She blinked back drops of muddy water and backed away from the creek. Shadow was in the creek, splashing at the water with a pawing motion, showering the bank and churning up the mud. Fiona gave him a tug on the reins and led him out of the stream. Susannah signaled Ginger, but he continued to drink, unperturbed.

"Uh—" Susannah watched Fiona walk down the path and yanked harder on Ginger's reins. He looked at her, unimpressed. "I thought we were friends?"

He lifted his head and stepped toward her. *Now how will I get back on?* She had watched Fiona mount, but she struggled to hold the animal steady. The trees around her began to spin as she threw her leg over his back. Wobbling in the saddle, she gripped the reins, closed her eyes and inhaled, willing the vertigo away. When she opened her eyes, the trees remained stationary. She gave Ginger a kick, grateful that Fiona hadn't been there to see this display of weakness. She exited the trees upright.

"Are you okay? What took you so long?"

"Oh, Ginger here was a tad thirsty."

Out of the shade, long tufts of yellow grass grew in disorderly patches between crooked pines and bent cedar trees. The horses chewed on the grasses. Immediately behind them, a row of crepe myrtles formed a line of demarcation between wild untidiness and a groomed yard. Trimmed so that their bare spindly trunks upheld bushy bright pink foliage, they reminded Susannah of bubble gum–colored ice cream cones enticing her in the Georgia sun.

"Ready to head back?"

Strains of "Girl on Fire," Bitsy's ringtone, shattered the cool morning air. Susannah yanked her phone from her back pocket to silence it, but not before Shadow pranced away, swinging his head to and fro.

"Stop the music!"

Susannah sent the call to voicemail, staring as Fiona calmed the fidgeting gelding.

"He doesn't like loud noises."

"I'm so sorry, I didn't realize."

"I should have asked you to mute your phone." She shook her head, patting the animal. "But I never get a signal out here."

Fiona got Shadow under control, and they retraced their route. Susannah felt as though she had been atop Ginger for days and was pleased to dismount and reacclimate to solid land. Fiona had been right. It wasn't yet nine, but she felt energized and ready to face her day.

CHAPTER THIRTY-FIVE

Susannah's good mood vanished when her Jeep rounded the corner on Piney Grove Road and she spied Detective Withers's car sitting in her office parking lot.

"Ow!" she cried out as she ground her foot on the brake and simultaneously bit her lip so hard she tasted blood.

The insufferable detective nodded at her, and she considered an escape but decided a confrontation with the woman was inevitable. Susannah grabbed her phone as she parked, sending a quick text to Bitsy: *911! Come quick.* With Tina in the hospital and Larraine spending all her free time at Tina's bedside, she would have no witness unless Bitsy arrived soon.

Detective Withers exited her car and slouched across the parking lot, her hands in her pockets, the morning sun highlighting the few strands of untamed hair that blew about her face. Susannah rolled down the window, one hand clamped onto her phone.

"You're here early, Doctor," the detective greeted Susannah, making something innocent sound nefarious. "Getting ready for another day?

"That's what I do," Susannah replied lamely. She felt

CHAPTER THIRTY-FIVE

embarrassed using the pat response she and Bitsy shared. It didn't sound nearly as witty when staring down the countenance of her enemy.

"Mm-hmm," she said, "I've heard about the things you do." She ran her finger across the hood of the Jeep, leaving a thin curved line in the dust. "You seem to make appearances where some questionable things have happened. You visited Colin Rogers's auto body shop just after his building was vandalized, then you trot over to the stable just around the time several cars had their tires slashed." She inhaled and deliberately rubbed her thumb and forefinger together, letting the dirt drop back onto the hood of the Jeep. "Not to mention the more serious crimes that have occurred right here." She swiped her hands together and came closer to Susannah, narrowing her eyes as she leaned in. "I'm watching you, Doctor. It won't be long before you trip yourself up, running to and fro, trying to cover your tracks."

"Maybe you're the one who should be running to and fro," Susannah blurted, anger at the woman's arrogance bubbling up from inside, "looking for someone who is growing poison."

The second the words left her mouth, she regretted them.

Then the detective laughed, not the wheezy, rasping laugh Susannah had expected but a full-out guffaw that shook her shoulders and loosened a few more strands of kinky hair from her bun. "Are you finally confessing?" she asked, fingering her handcuffs.

"Of course not," Susannah forced through gritted teeth. "I'm telling you you're missing something important. Tina is still in the hospital. First, she was diagnosed with a heart problem and now there is concern about her kidneys. Why haven't you insisted she be tested for poisons?"

The detective's smile faded. "That's a very interesting question coming from a suspected poisoner. Do you need to get something off your chest, Doctor? Did you poison your assistant because she found out something that could incriminate you? Did you get to her before she could get to me?"

Susannah's heart froze midbeat at the accusation and then pounded so hard against her sternum that she became nauseated. How could she have been so stupid? She had been so wrapped up in discovering where the digitalis in Anita's blood had come from, she had let herself play right into the detective's hands. Detective Withers had to know by now that foxglove was available at any garden center. Did she suspect that Susannah was brewing up batches of poison and spoon-feeding them to her friends? A chill wracked her body. Sweat bloomed across her back and slimed the palms of her hands.

Just then, a black SUV charged down Piney Grove Road and careened into the lot, stopping hard next to Susannah's Jeep. The detective moved back, scowling at Bitsy as her passenger window descended.

"Morning, Detective." Bitsy smiled, nodding at Susannah. "I didn't know you did breakfast interviews. Dr. Shine and I were on our way to Waffle House, but we can just as easily go to the donut shop if you'd like to join us." She pressed a switch, and the door locks sprang open. Susannah took the opportunity to exit the Jeep and enter Bitsy's Explorer.

Without waiting for an answer, Bitsy gunned her engine and left the lot, waving at the detective in the rearview mirror.

CHAPTER THIRTY-SIX

Susannah pulled her Atlanta Braves cap down low and scanned the dairy case. She had made it through another day in the office without Tina. It had been almost three weeks since Anita's death, and her patient base was dwindling. Staring into the dairy case, she wondered if she was coming undone. Her need to make a peach cobbler resulted from a craving, which she was sure Bitsy had subliminally planted in her brain. Her friend's chatter about peaches was ceaseless.

Everything had looked perfect for a bedtime snack, then the smoke alarm was screaming, and a luscious-looking gluten-free peach cobbler was smoldering. She hung her head. Her inattention to details had intensified as she worried about Tina and pondered Anita's death. Not to be deterred, she had begun a fresh batch, only to discover a deficit in the shortening department. A simple stick of butter, and the cobbler would be melting in her mouth soon enough. Now, she grabbed the nearest brand, determined to exit the market before someone saw her in her baking clothes, disheveled and sticky with peach juice. Squeezing between a shopper and her buggy, she smiled at the ease of her escape. But at the corner of the aisle, flanked by stacks of egg cartons, she found herself blocked by a figure in the uniform of the Peach Grove Police Department.

Great, she thought, reluctant to look the officer in the eye. *What now?* Resolved to avoid confrontation and get home to her cobbler, she tipped her head down, using the brim of her cap to shield herself from any eye contact and sidestepped the dark figure. The officer would not cooperate and blocked her move.

She looked up.

It was Randy Laughton.

"Oh," she said, stepping back and bumping the cold case with the back of her knee. The other shopper moved her cart down the aisle.

"Susannah. I—"

"Excuse me." She frowned and tried again to step past him, but he moved, his heavy work shoes scuffing the tile floor. She sneered. "Either move or arrest me."

"Now hold on. You don't have to be so ugly. I only wanted to have a word."

"Here?"

"We could step outside."

Her eyelids fluttered at the thought of how much gossip would be generated if anyone saw her being escorted outside by Randy. Where would they talk? In his patrol car? She held her ground.

He said, "I wanted to ask about Tina."

Susannah was startled. She assumed that he would get updates from the detective. "There's no change. I expected the detective to keep you updated."

His face got that pink tinge that she knew meant he was

rattled. "I haven't seen her."

Susannah snorted. "I guess she's out trumping up charges against someone else."

"Susannah, I know you have some experience with law enforcement, but that was a long time ago. You have to trust us to do our job. Detective Withers is a professional."

"I don't think it's professional to assume things that you can't prove while ignoring other key aspects of the case."

"How would you know about key aspects of the case? I don't have to remind you that interfering with an investigating is a crime."

Susannah clenched her teeth and stepped away from the refrigerator case. She had said too much, but she didn't care. This was her life. "I'm not interfering. I'm talking common sense. Detective Withers thinks I sold Anita some herbal mixture that interacted with a medication she was taking," she blurted, "only I never sold Anita anything, and there's no proof that I did. Besides, she wasn't taking any medication."

A look of wariness crossed Randy's face, then vanished, replaced by a hard stare. "How do you know what medications Anita took?"

Susannah chewed on the inside of her lip. *Tread carefully*, she thought. She arched an eyebrow in mock offense, hoping it made her look wrongly accused. "I spoke to Dolores and Pilar at Anita's memorial luncheon. They told me she wasn't taking any medication. They also told me that Detective Withers didn't believe them, which is par for the course with that woman. She's a sloppy investigator."

It was Randy's turn to shake his head. "You know that's not true."

Susannah stiffened, pushing back her cap. Her fingers dug

into the cardboard packaging she held, and she resisted the urge to wave her hands in Randy's face. She had to remain calm. She didn't want to get carried away and be charged with battery against a police officer using a pound of butter. *Would that be considered butter battery?* The silly thought calmed her, and she faced him.

"No, it is true. Her theory of the crime is that I met Anita at my office, in secret, to sell her herbs that caused her death. Only you both know that I wouldn't have been at the office that day, except that the alarm company called me. I know you checked on this."

He didn't interrupt, and she took that as agreement.

"If I wanted a secret rendezvous, why did I park my Jeep in front of the building, in full view of anyone driving by? Why even go to the office? She could have come to my house."

Randy opened his mouth to answer, then shut it.

"Oh, I forgot, I was selling her the deadly herbs." She watched his face for any reaction, but his expression gave nothing away. "Well, you know what I think? Detective Withers is uneducated about herbal medicines and can't admit it. I also think Anita *was* meeting someone in secret, but it wasn't me. I think it could have been a man, someone she was in a relationship with."

"How can you say that?" This time, the color changed in Randy's face, and she knew she had hit a nerve. Had the investigators come to the same conclusion? Or maybe he had made this suggestion to Detective Withers and been ignored.

"Let me walk you through it. I know Anita wasn't there to see me, so I've been asking myself: Why was she there? If she was there for a legitimate reason—for example, she wanted to make an appointment—she would have parked in the front of the building and tried to go in the front door. Right?"

He nodded.

"When she realized the office was closed, she would have left. Or, if she was really determined to contact us, she would have called the office phone and gotten forwarded to Tina. She didn't do either of those things. Instead, she went around back to the staff parking lot, which can't be seen from the road."

Randy rubbed his chin. "That's exactly what makes it suspicious."

"Of course it does. But the detective is suspicious of the wrong person. She should ask herself why Anita was there, not why I was there. It's like she thinks up a theory and tries to prove it, instead of following the evidence to uncover the crime. Just like with Colin."

"What do you mean?"

"Colin told me she suspected him because of what Tomás said. She's trying to make the circumstances fit him."

"Susannah, you need to stay out of this investigation. You shouldn't be talking to Colin."

She realized her fingers were sinking into the butter and tried to relax. "I am not involved with your investigation. I went with Bitsy to get her truck inspected, and Colin was locked down tight. His assistant was a nervous wreck because they're being harassed. We saw the damage to the building, and he told us that someone broke into his shop and trashed his computer. And the police don't care."

Randy shook his head. "Susannah, don't take what Colin says too seriously."

"Why not?"

He lowered his voice. "Colin Rogers has a major drinking

problem. He's called us many times before, but there's never been any evidence that anyone other than him caused the problems. He gets so liquored up, he passes out in that back room. You ask me, he wrecks the place himself, but he's too drunk to remember." A thin, red-haired woman appeared at the end of the aisle and then turned away, dragging her toddler with her. "Course, we can't prove that either, so he walks around with a chip on his shoulder."

Susannah glowered at him. Who wouldn't have a chip on their shoulder when they know they are the subject of gossip?

Randy lowered his voice. "You would do well to stay away from him. His credibility is already low. You don't want to be painted with that same brush."

Susannah appreciated that the police had to be objective, but Randy's dismissive tone made her question that objectivity. Colin might have a drinking problem, but she had seen the empty parking lot and the dent in the bay door. "You think this is all in his imagination? What about the vandalism to his property?"

Randy shook his head. "We're looking into it."

"Stevie told me he saw two men in a pickup vandalize the garage door, and I saw the dent. The paint didn't match Colin's car. And why would he do that to his own shop?"

"We don't know what to make of it. A squad car was at his shop within five minutes of his call. Colin didn't see the car, and Stevie couldn't give us any details."

You mean, Detective Withers scared him out of his wits, Susannah thought.

Randy looked her in the eye. "Susannah, we're well aware of Colin and Stevie. Colin's been very good to Stevie, but Stevie would not make a good witness for him. Everyone

CHAPTER THIRTY-SIX

knows that Stevie is not quite right." He tapped his temple and tried but failed to make a sympathetic face. "He would say anything to keep his job, and everyone knows it. As for Colin, he's a talented mechanic and except for his battle with the bottle, he's a decent sort."

Susannah relaxed. This was probably the closest to an apology she would get.

Randy continued, "Nice people commit crimes all the time. The prisons are filled with them."

Susannah stiffened. "What does that mean?"

"It means you should stay away from him until we catch the killer."

With that, he leaned past her, picked up a dozen eggs, and, after offering a somber nod, turned and left.

Susannah stared at the butter in her hand, the hankering for cobbler gone.

CHAPTER THIRTY-SEVEN

Pilar Alvarez flicked her wrist. A silver demitasse spoon clinked on the porcelain cup, sending the bitter scent of coffee wafting to Susannah. The afternoon light streamed through the blinds and fell on Pilar, illuminating a wide swath of gray hair. Susannah stood in the house that Pilar had shared with Anita and observed her as she stopped stirring long enough to place a plate of cookies on the kitchen table. She fixed her dark brown eyes on Susannah, who sipped from her own porcelain cup, suppressing the urge to stick out her pinky. The coffee's pungent smell and dense flavor curled her toes.

Pilar inhaled evenly, pulling her eyebrows together, and said, "What do you think?"

"Delicious."

"Ah, *Doctora*, you sidestep the question."

Susannah inhaled. She could detect the cinnamon, but an unknown essence enriched the aroma and deepened the taste, giving it a barely noticeable twist of freshness. This coffee tasted superior to anything Anita had ever made. "Yes," she replied, feeling like she had betrayed Anita's memory. "It *is* the best cup of coffee I've ever had."

CHAPTER THIRTY-SEVEN

Pilar smiled, her smooth face revealing a few creases. "Anita and I tried to outdo each other in the kitchen. It was all in the name of *sabor*." She used the Spanish word for flavor. Susannah had heard Anita use this to express her joy in creating a new dish, and Susannah considered whether competing with this intense woman could ever be considered anything less than intimidating.

Susannah thought back on the phone call from Dolores confirming her visit this afternoon. She had not expected to see Pilar, but she welcomed the opportunity to learn more about Anita's private life. She was dying to ask if Anita had any enemies but held her tongue. When Pilar had welcomed her into the kitchen and tempted her with her own version of *café*, Susannah had readily agreed. She raised her cup to Pilar. "I can see that this is the kitchen of someone who loved to cook," she said, motioning around the room with the cup. She observed that Anita's colorful personality burst from every corner. There seemed to be little room for anyone else in it. Had this been Anita's way of overcoming Pilar's powerful personality and claiming the space for her own?

Pilar sipped, watching Susannah over her delicate cup, eyes twinkling with pleasure. "Ah, *mi Anita* put her heart into this room."

The kitchen had an expensive European feel to it. The wall that held stainless steel appliances boasted hand-painted tiles whose deep vivid yellows and burgundies contrasted with the white floor and countertops. The espresso maker shamed the one Susannah's family had bought her when she graduated from chiropractic school; she recognized it as an imported Italian model with solid copper fittings. Professional-grade saucepans hung from a gleaming metal rack. The floors, too, were tiled, and the cabinets were handmade.

"She was a perfectionist, and this was the room she was proudest of." Pilar gestured with a gnarled finger that encompassed the entire house with a small sweep. "In fact, she lived here alone the first few months before she let us move in."

"Oh, I didn't know that."

"Yes, she opened the Cantina Caliente first and spent many months commuting back to Atlanta where we were living. When she was sure that the restaurant could support them both, she built this house so that Dolores could come and live in the country." She smiled, and for the first time, her features softened. "She spent many sleepless nights worrying about the details."

Susannah recalled her conversations with Anita. "She made it look easy. I thought she enjoyed running the restaurant." The sounds of Anita shouting at Tomás resounded in her mind. Chalk up another white lie. "Did she ever mention any problems?"

"Problems?" Pilar waved her hand. "There are always problems in the food business. Servers quitting, suppliers running out of items, inspectors asking for bribes, deliveries gone wrong." She leaned in. "Which piece of gossip have you heard?"

Susannah sat back, flustered. She had underestimated this woman, who apparently had her own sources of information. She tapped her cup, her nail eliciting a pleasant ring from the porcelain. "All right. Yes, it's true, it is gossip. I heard that there was a problem with the inventory of the bar."

Pilar emitted a dismissive hiss. "Even I know this answer. Anita, *mi hija*, was a stickler. Wanted everything to balance to the penny. She didn't like that Tomás sometimes gave one or two of the laborers a little bonus drink."

"Laborers?" Susannah echoed.

"Oh, not the staff. Not the servers, they are only children, most of them." She waved again, this time with a sideways flick of the wrist. "You are a business owner. You understand that sometimes you need help after hours. Moving equipment, fixing the plumbing, or patching a leak in the roof where the rain comes in. Things tradespeople help you with. Sometimes you are there late at night after customers have left, or you must come in early in the morning before the day starts. So what if Tomás shared a shot of mezcal with one of these workers or slipped them a beer to drink at home?" She rapped her fist angrily on the table, and Susannah blinked. "That is a way to show your thanks and appreciation. That is not stealing."

"I understand."

"Anita was wrong about this, but it was an unimportant thing." She sipped at her coffee, her mood now somber. After a moment, she put down her cup and moved to a wooden shelf, which held two picture frames. She picked one up and showed it to Susannah. Anita smiled out at them, her white chef coat pristine with its double row of buttons and long capped sleeves. She was surrounded by a group of grinning faces dressed in identical coats, every head topped with a white cap.

"Who would want to hurt my daughter? Opening her own restaurant was a dream come true. She worked hard, barely had any time for herself." Her lips curled into a tight smile. "At first, she drove home every night. She would come in late, stinking of grease, and exhausted. Sometimes, I would find her curled up in Dolores's bed, fast asleep."

Susannah nodded. She remembered getting to know Anita in the early days of the restaurant but had no idea she was spending so much time commuting back to Atlanta.

"Other times, she crept into the house in the middle of the night and didn't wake for breakfast. I got Dolores off to school."

"That must have been hard for you."

Pilar's expression darkened. "That girl is my blood. She is my heart."

"Of course, I meant—"

Pilar raised an eyebrow, and Susannah went silent. She buried her face in the tiny cup and gulped the last of the espresso, listening for the sounds of Dolores returning home. All she heard was the tick of a clock on the kitchen wall. She looked at the picture again, imaging Anita in happier times, learning her craft, making friends with whom she would share her new life. There were five faces in the picture: three men and two women. Susannah's gaze stopped on one man. He looked familiar. Had she met him at the restaurant? She couldn't be sure.

"Managing the restaurant was hard on Anita," Pilar continued. "Early mornings and long nights took their toll. Sometimes I found her staring at this photo, lost in thought."

Susannah sipped her coffee and pored over the photo. Was there a clue there in the fresh, youthful faces, so eager to take on the world? Could one of these people be a key to the puzzle? "Did Anita keep in touch with her classmates?"

"No," Pilar replied, returning the picture to its place. Susannah tried to store the faces in her memory. Perhaps she should get in touch with the culinary school. Before she could ask any further questions, she heard the squeak of the front door opening.

Pilar gazed pensively out the window into Anita's yard; she inhaled and drew her shoulders back, as if she had come to a decision. She took Susannah's arm and whispered, "Anita had big dreams to cook in a five-star kitchen, but once she had Dolores, she gave up those dreams." Her words tumbled out in a long, deep exhale, spoken in a staccato volley as her gaze fell on the kitchen door. "This place cast a spell over her. I believe it was more than just the restaurant. I believe there must be a man here in this town." Her black eyes flashed, boring into Susannah's soul. "Find that man, and you will find who did this to Anita."

She released her arm, and the kitchen door opened. Dolores entered, a tentative smile on her face. Her eyes were dull and red, but they brightened as she inhaled the scents of espresso and cinnamon. She gave Pilar a peck on the cheek. "*Abuela*, are you tempting Dr. Shine with your *café con leche*? Did you make her guess the secret ingredient?" Her gaze darted between her grandmother and Susannah and then landed on the plate on the table. A grin transformed her face, twin dimples accentuating the mischievous expression.

"*No, mija*," Pilar answered, pulling the girl in for a hug, "and don't you tell her."

Dolores reached out while still ensconced in her grandmother's embrace and grabbed a cookie off the plate. Susannah was fascinated by how her dimples twinkled as she chewed. Then she stepped back and placed a hand on Susannah's arm, her face once again tinged by grief.

"I want to show you something and ask you what you think I should do."

CHAPTER THIRTY-EIGHT

Dolores retrieved her black book bag and unzipped the top as she walked. She pulled out an envelope, which had been slit open at the top, and handed it to Susannah

"This came yesterday." She bowed her head as if caught with her hand in the cookie jar. "Sorry, *Abuela,* you weren't home when I found it, and I didn't want to turn it over to the police yet."

Pilar frowned, moving so close Susannah could smell the coffee on her breath. "What is it?" she asked, reading the return address of a local insurance plan.

Susannah glanced up at Dolores.

"Go ahead." Dolores gestured at the envelope. "Open it."

Inside the envelope was a form letter with Anita's name and address at the top. Susannah scanned the letter and recognized it as an explanation of insurance benefits form. It listed a medical group, which Susannah didn't recognize, and gave the date of the visit as two days before Anita died. Susannah handed the paper to Pilar, who stared at it for a few moments.

"What does this mean?" Pilar asked.

CHAPTER THIRTY-EIGHT

"It means that *Mamá* did go to the doctor right before she died." Dolores pointed at the appointment date. "But it wasn't for her heart."

Susannah flipped the page over and scrutinized it. "How do you know it wasn't for her heart? This doesn't give a diagnosis."

"No, but her online account does."

Pilar pursed her lips. "What is an online account?"

"*Mamá* registered for an account with her insurance company through their website. They have all their documents online now, *Abuela*. You can see everything: what doctor you went to, how much your insurance company paid, and other things too." She paused and flashed a shy smile at Susannah. "Like what prescriptions you're taking."

"How did you get into her account?" Susannah asked, thinking of all the privacy laws that prevent unauthorized persons from gaining access to medical information.

Dolores addressed her grandmother. "Remember when I went through *Mamá's* desk looking for her checkbook? Well, I found all her important papers, including her insurance card, and a list of usernames and passwords. I didn't think of looking up her insurance company website until this letter came." She nodded at the paper Susannah held in her hand, which had a logo for the website in large green letters.

"What did you find online?"

"There are two doctor's visits and a prescription. I Googled the prescription, and it's a migraine medication." Dolores placed her book bag on the table and reached in, pulling out a slim notebook computer. "There are some other things I thought you could help me figure out before I tell the detective what I found."

A loud *bam* filled the room. Pilar, her palm on the table, glared at Dolores. "No!" Pilar shouted, her eyes hard. Clearly, loud outbursts ran in the family. "Don't give the police any personal information about *mi Anita*. They have no respect, they want to dig through her private life like she did something wrong, and I won't have it."

"I understand." Dolores touched her grandmother's sleeve and then glanced at Susannah. "That lady detective was so rude to us, to *Abuela*. She treated us like we were lying to her, like we wanted to keep things from her, but we both knew that *Mamá* didn't have a heart condition. We told her she never had that kind of problem, and she wasn't taking any medication for her heart. We knew she had complained about headaches."

"That detective said, 'Maybe she hid the medicine,'" Pilar continued, her face flushed. "She asked me, 'How would we know if she kept a bottle of pills hidden in her room?'" She removed her hand from the table and lowered herself into one of the wooden chairs. "I told her Anita had all the privacy she needed, but we are a family. She told me about the headaches. I knew she made an appointment to see the doctor, but she was busy right before…" Her words trailed off. She paused, then went on. "We are a family. We support each other. Why would she hide such a condition from her family? That is not how families work."

Susannah wondered if Detective Withers knew this about families.

Dolores placed her computer on the table. "She's right. Why would *Mamá* hide something like that? Besides, after the detective left, I looked in her room and bathroom for any pills." She blushed, and Susannah knew she had done more

CHAPTER THIRTY-EIGHT

than merely look. "There were none."

Susannah said, "Why don't we figure out what this all means and then we can decide about showing the police?"

Pilar nodded, and Dolores placed her computer on the table. A few minutes later, she had Anita's insurance account open, and Susannah read over her shoulder.

"I understand this." Dolores pointed to the first line, which listed a doctor's name. "That's the doctor we used to see in Atlanta."

Susannah read the doctor's name and address. The office was in Atlanta, approximately thirty miles from Peach Grove. If Anita's health was as good as her family believed, it made sense that she had returned to a doctor who she knew and trusted. If she didn't have a condition that needed regular monitoring, there was no need for someone local, although most people used a primary care doctor who was near their home. Apparently, the drive had been worth it for her. Some of Susannah's patients drove long distances to see her. This might also explain why the detective didn't have accurate information about Anita's prescriptions. The small-town grapevine didn't extend into Atlanta.

She resumed reading. A description of the service and the date Anita had been in the office came next. Running her hand through her hair, she continued reading. The web page displayed an electronic explanation of benefits similar to the document that Dolores had found in the mail, but with more detail. Not only did the screen list her insurance benefit and copayment for the doctor visit, but it listed other pending charges. This page gave an account of the medical treatment Anita had sought in the days before she died.

Dolores pointed. "Here's what I don't understand. What

does this mean? Laboratory? Why would *Mamá* need a laboratory?"

"It means the doctor's office sent something to a lab for analysis," Susannah answered, reading the name of the lab. "Most likely a blood test. Click on the line and see if there are more details."

Dolores tapped, and a drop-down screen opened, showing the date that the doctor had ordered a complete blood count.

"That's a typical screening blood test that any doctor might do as part of a checkup."

Dolores nodded, and Pilar exhaled, crossing to the sink with her cup and saucer.

"So, she went to her primary care doctor, and they drew blood and sent it to a lab. Nothing unusual there," Susannah commented, talking more to herself than to Dolores. "This is the same doctor, same date as in the letter. This is the lab where her blood was analyzed. The lab would send the results directly to the doctor. I don't think they would post the results here." She scanned the page, taking in all she could. Randy might think she was a half-assed investigator, but she wasn't about to act like one. "Where did you see the prescription?"

Dolores scrolled up and followed a link called YOUR PRESCRIPTIONS to another page, which displayed Imitrex as the one entry on her drug list.

"See?" Dolores said. "The only thing on the list is the migraine medication, but I didn't find it in the house."

"Click here." Susannah pointed to the words YOUR PHARMACY, and Dolores tapped the screen. A window opened showing the name and address of the pharmacy that had filled the prescription.

"If you didn't find the bottle, she might not have had time

CHAPTER THIRTY-EIGHT

to pick it up. You would have to talk to the pharmacy to be sure."

Dolores looked doubtful. "Would they tell me?"

"Not without some kind of proof that your mom has passed and you are her next of kin. The privacy laws are strict. I could research it for you. Or..." She glanced over to Pilar. "You could tell the police."

Pilar's eyes became stony, and Dolores stroked her grandmother's arm. "*Calma*," she said firmly. "We have to tell them sometime, *Abuelita*. This proves that the detective is wrong. *Mamá* didn't die because she overdosed on a medication, and they have to know it."

Susannah left the house feeling as if she had been granted a reprieve. Once Detective Withers had all Anita's medical information, she surely would have to change her beliefs about the manner of death. There was no way any of the herbs Susannah sold could have put the digitalis in her system. If she had been taking a digitalis-containing drug, the adrenal tonic Susannah sold her might have affected her potassium levels, making the drug more potent. Even this rare outcome would have taken a while to happen. But Anita had never bought the tonic.

Susannah knew now that Anita had never taken a heart medication.

She was murdered.

The question became how to convince the detective. Even Iris had known immediately that poisoning was a realistic possibility. Susannah hoped that Varina Withers lived in the realm of realistic possibilities.

CHAPTER THIRTY-NINE

Susannah arrived at the Peach Grove Independence Day Festival in the chill of the early morning. Several large white cumulus clouds speckled the deep blue of the eastern horizon. She unloaded her Jeep and was pleased to see Larraine maneuver her Grand Marquis over the pitted strip of grass used as parking for vendors' vehicles. Susannah hefted two folded camp chairs and threw the straps over her shoulder, then grabbed the pop-up tent and wheeled it toward the fairground. Larraine followed, and despite her energetic stride, Susannah could see the exhaustion in her eyes.

"Is Tina any better?"

"She is." Larraine frowned and stopped walking.

"But that's great news!"

"Well," she began, looking up to meet Susannah's curious gaze, "it's good for Tina, but not so much for you."

Susannah swallowed. "Why?"

"The detective finally checked Tina for digitalis, and the levels were high." A breeze rustled her well-sprayed coif, but she ignored it and placed a hand on Susannah's arm. Her light blue eyes brimmed with tears, and her words came fast and choppy. "The doctors changed her treatment and, praise the

CHAPTER THIRTY-NINE

Lord, it worked. She's stronger, and her kidney function is back to normal. She still has the arrhythmia and the doctors fear she may have to live with it, but it's treatable."

"That's all wonderful news."

Larraine's hand shook. She bobbed her head. "For Tina, yes. But the detective insisted you confessed to poisoning her."

"That's absurd."

Larraine moved to the side to allow a vendor pushing a cart to pass. She sighed and wiped her cheek with the back of her hand. "Keith and Iris have been bugging the doctors about this for days. They told us it was already done and nothing had showed up, and now they are backpedaling about false negatives because of her pregnancy."

Susannah tried to make sense of it all. "False negative?"

"That's what they said." Larraine pulled a Kleenex from her bag and blotted at her nose. "I'm just worried about you, is all."

Susannah hugged Larraine, squeezing her firmly as if she were her own mother. "I'll be fine." She took Larraine's hand and led her to their designated space. In a few minutes, they were sitting under the shade of a pop-up tent with the name of Peach Grove Chiropractic lettered on its side.

Susannah surveyed the fairground. There was no sign of the detective, and she took comfort in knowing that her blunder could not provide the hard evidence needed for an arrest. She bit her lip, pulled herself up in her chair, and vowed to use her time at the festival to monitor both suspects and the police. She pledged that if Dolores and Pilar did not contact the detective with Anita's insurance information today, she would do it herself. However, there was no guarantee that she would be believed.

Her stomach flip-flopped, but it was useless to worry. If the detective wanted to arrest her, she knew where to find her. She calmed herself by observing the rows of tents and tables laden with wares. It was a craft festival at heart, with local businesses' and churches' booths scattered amidst crafters who sold all manner of homemade goods. She noted trays of jellies and jams, embroidered clothing, and beeswax candles. PGBA members claimed prime real estate. Fiona would offer pony rides, Tomás hawked *té tamarindo* and fried churros, and Colin and Stevie handed out coupons for $10 off an oil change. And of course, Bitsy did double duty today; she had already arranged the Peachy Things signature peach-colored tent, hung heavy with fringe-covered shawls, and Susannah spied her across the fairground, organizing the pie-eating contest.

Then there was Marcie. Standing next to the children's inflatable toys that dangled from the sides of a brightly colored tent, a red-faced Marcie set up tables under a long Wing Shack banner. Susannah knew Marcie never missed a year, and the whole family, plus Zach, were there at her command. An aisle over, she saw the red tent with the logo of Colin Rogers's OK Automotive, but no sign of him. Susannah was certain that he would take the opportunity to get some new business. She strode down the aisle and noticed Tomás working with Nolan to put up a tent.

Adjacent to the municipal building, Bitsy grappled with an upended table. Her punishment for volunteering was to stage the peach pie-eating contest in a cracked and broken asphalt parking lot. Susannah made her way over the cool grass, dew gathering on her boots. Bitsy rushed to her side and seized

CHAPTER THIRTY-NINE

her arm. "Thank goodness you're here," she said, panting.

Susannah had never seen Bitsy so perturbed. Her face was scrunched into a painful expression, and she tugged on her ear as if she were in pain. She grimaced maniacally, and Susannah took a step back.

"Gettin' all this together is a lot tougher than I thought it would be," she moaned. "Roman was supposed to be back from his trip, but I haven't heard from him. I set up my booth for Peachy Things right quick and left Andrea in charge. I been here ever since, workin' like a dog. I've been lugging tables back and forth." She shot a glance down the main aisle, where Marcie and Billy were unfolding portable chairs, and then lowered her voice. "The mayor got all bossy about proper table placement, but I don't want Marcie to know that. I'm on top of it."

Susannah nodded. "Can I help?

"I thought you'd never ask. I need to put the finishing touches on these tables, then organize the sign-up sheets and get the pies from the refrigerator—"

"What can I do?"

"Move my truck to the parking lot." She motioned to her Explorer, which sat alone behind the tables, all four doors open, a cardboard box filled with supplies on its hood.

Susannah laughed as Bitsy rifled through her purse and presented her with her keychain. The peachy bob dangled as Susannah revved the engine and carefully wound the oversized vehicle out of the cordoned-off lot, across the back lawn and down a paved pathway that abutted the cemetery. The fairground was no more than a grassy field, part of which had been designated for inflatable bouncy houses and slides for the little ones. She drove along the grass and down a row of vehicles, and nosed the truck under a tall oak, pleased that she had caught some shade for Bitsy.

As she stepped down from the running board, she spied a man inspecting a small trailer that was hitched to a pickup. His Alabama ball cap was pulled down low, covering his face. Perhaps he had discovered a flat tire or locked himself out of his car. Susannah thought about offering him a hand, but at that moment her phone buzzed. Bitsy's face showed on her screen.

"I need you to bring me some fortification. Some of that hot cocoa from the PGBA booth would go down good right now. And a biscuit, maybe you could find me a chicken biscuit," she added, her voice fading out as she shouted instructions to someone, "but not from *you know where*." Her last few words faded into a whisper, and the connection was broken.

Susannah studied the parking area. The man in the ball cap was gone. Making her way to the vendors' booths, she examined the wares of the Peach Grove Gardening Club, traditionally the first booth. Valerie Underwood, the master gardener, waved her over, pointing at this year's crop of Better Boy tomato plants. Susannah waved back and promised to return, but she knew that she would not. Her bad luck with plants was legendary, having earned her the nickname *Doctor Black Thumb*, and she dutifully kept away from all greenery. Any homegrown veggies she ate were given to her by those with greener digits.

The line for cocoa was long; no surprise, as the PGBA made sure that they manned the only stall that sold hot beverages. Patience was not one of Susannah's better-known virtues, and she twisted to find her tent. Guilt pricked at her conscience. She had abandoned Larraine and needed to get back. She

CHAPTER THIRTY-NINE

grabbed a couple of packets of sugar and a handful of napkins and threw them in her shoulder bag. The cocoa and biscuit were hot in her hands when she felt a tap.

"Doctor Shine!"

She turned to see Dolores and Pilar. Dolores waved, a small flick of her wrist, an economy of movement Susannah had seen in her mother.

Susannah returned the greeting, a flutter in her belly urging her to ask if they had turned Anita's medical file over to the detective. It was more important than ever that Pilar relent and give the police department Anita's information. "What are you doing here so early? The parade is not for an hour."

"I was helping Tomás and Nolan set up the drink stand." Dolores stepped toward her grandmother and squeezed her hand. "Now I want to show *Abuela* some of the scarves that the Peachy Things shop sells. Do you know where her booth is?"

Susannah shifted the steaming Styrofoam cups. "Straight ahead. If you wait a minute, I'll walk you there."

She hurried over to Bitsy, who plucked the cocoa and biscuit from her hands as if she had been trained at the famous School of the Seven Bells for pickpockets. "Is this the biggest they got? I need my strength if I'm gonna be in the sun all day," Bitsy said.

"That's all they had. When I come back, I'll buy you lunch."

"Can I have a funnel cake? I really love funnel cakes."

"Anything you want," Susannah replied, not bothering to mention that Peachy Things' first customers of the morning were waiting for her to escort them to the booth. She hurried down the main aisle, where most vendors were set up and ready for business. She slowed as she found Dolores stopped at a booth that hawked handcrafted yard art. The welded metal had been sculptured into various whimsical animals. Susannah had noticed the vivid colors from fifty yards away. Up close, they were fun and comical.

"Look at this rooster," Dolores chuckled, pointing out a specimen to Susannah that stood four feet tall with a yellow body and bright red cockscomb. Its tail feathers were painted in alternating green and blue, and its eyes were black under small metallic lids. It was surrounded by a brood of smaller statues of exactly the same shape but in a dizzying array of color combinations. "My mother would have loved this."

Susannah agreed, remembering her glimpse into Anita's personality during her *tête-à-tête* with Pilar.

Dolores turned to her grandmother, her hand poised to touch a woman who was no longer there. *"Abuelita?"*

Scanning the aisles, Susannah spotted Pilar a few yards away, gazing up at a black-and-white photograph that Marcie had hung across one of the Wing Shack's three tents. The image, enlarged to the size of a poster, was daunting. A banner above it claimed 20 YEARS IN BUSINESS. Susannah could not make out details, but it appeared to be a typical grand opening ribbon cutting ceremony. She'd had one when she had opened her chiropractic office.

Pilar stood alone, gazing at the photo. Susannah noticed Marcie Jones standing outside the tent talking with Hayle, who bobbed her head and pointed back toward the parking lot.

"What is it, *Abuela?*" Dolores asked.

Pilar turned and studied Dolores, and her posture changed; her shoulders sagged slightly and she shook her head, a small movement. *"Nada, mi amor."* Color suffused her cheeks. "I was hungry, so I went over to see if they had anything ready, and the size of that photo impressed me. That is all."

Dolores looked doubtful, but she put her arm around the old woman's shoulder and gave her a protective squeeze. She glanced back at the Wing Shack. "I think that they're selling chicken biscuits now. I can get you one."

Pilar again shook her head ever so slightly, her face a tightly drawn mask. Susannah noticed how stiff she held herself, like her posture when she'd banged her fist on the table, swearing she would not give Anita's personal information to the police. "No. *No es necesario.*"

"It's no trouble."

"I said no!" she snapped, then relented, her face softening in a gesture that Susannah recognized as fear. "I'm sorry, *mijita*. I can't eat fried food."

"Are you sure?"

"Chicken biscuits—*me hace dano.*"

Susannah knew enough Spanish to understand that the woman had said that chicken biscuits didn't agree with her, but the way her face had darkened made Susannah suspect she was hiding something. Dolores didn't notice.

"Let's go then." Dolores smiled. "No more getting sidetracked. I promise."

Susannah continued down the row, passing Colin and Stevie, who were now sitting behind a table piled high with discount coupons. Unlike the Wing Shack, whose aspirations for the Independence Day Festival overflowed three spaces, Colin had one tent, which was empty, behind the small plastic folding table. He sat, his head tilted toward Stevie, deep in conversation. Though the morning was still cool, his face shone with sweat. His red tent, emblazoned with the OK

Automotive logo, backed up to one of the few shade trees that ringed the fairground, and Susannah hoped his condition resulted from the exertion of setting up the tent and tables and not because he was drinking so early in the day.

She hurried past, not wanting to get caught up in a conversation with either man. Colin had not been quite the same to her since the day she and Bitsy took her Explorer for the oil change, and she wondered if her prying had angered him.

As they neared Bitsy's booth, Susannah stopped and faced Pilar. She knew it was self-serving to make demands on someone who had recently lost a loved one, but at this point, she had no choice. "I want to ask you to turn over Anita's insurance records to the detective today. It's vitally important that she knows Anita did not take heart medication."

Pilar's eyes flashed. "No," she said, and let fly a few words in Spanish. She walked into the Peachy Things booth and didn't look back.

"What was that?" Susannah asked Dolores.

"Uh, it doesn't matter, Dr. Shine. I'll talk to her. She knows it's the right thing to do. Anyway, I don't need her permission to talk to the detective."

Susannah said nothing. She hoped the girl intended to keep her word. She nodded at Andrea, who raised her eyebrows as if to ask *What's going on?*, but she made no comment and welcomed Pilar. Susannah watched as Pilar chose an intricately woven shawl in dark blues and greens. Exotic and alluring on its own, on Pilar it took on her aura of strength and mysticism. Susannah felt the woman's energy amplified in a way she did not know was possible, and she pondered this revelation.

A cry in the distance caught her attention. It came again.

CHAPTER THIRTY-NINE

Someone was screaming for help. Susannah turned from the Georgia Peach aprons and ran.

CHAPTER FORTY

Susannah sped down the aisle without thinking. Since the day Anita died, she had been on edge, and Larraine's comments earlier had unnerved her more than she wanted to admit. Now her heart raced, and her adrenaline levels propelled her toward a crowd that had formed around the tomato plants that ringed the Gardening Club's booth. Drawing closer to the crowd, she recognized Marcie's voice.

"Don't stand there staring!" Marcie yelled. Her slender hands trembled. "Call an ambulance!"

As Susannah pushed her way through the crowd, she held her breath, dreading what she might see. Marcie and Hayle had been together earlier and the thought that something had happened to the girl sent a chill down her spine. Then she spied Billy sitting on the ground, his hand to his head.

"Let me through." She pushed her way past a heavyset man in overalls who was scratching his shaved head with dirty fingernails. Kneeling down next to Billy, she fished a few napkins out of her bag, glad she had forgotten to give them to Bitsy. Blood smeared Billy's fingers and dripped from a wound on his left arm.

CHAPTER FORTY

"He stabbed me."

"Who stabbed you?" Susannah asked, placing the napkins on his arm and pressing firmly. "Did someone call 911?" She shot a glance at Marcie, who looked like she would faint.

"Y-yes," Marcie said. "Is he all right?"

Her voice sounded like that of a frightened child, and for the first time since she had known the woman, Susannah felt sorry for her.

"I think so," she lied, not at all sure what his condition was. Her experience as a first responder was limited, but she did know that there were a lot of nerves in the arm that could be easily damaged by a knife. The napkins were already soaked through, but the bleeding was slowing. Marcie moaned as a siren rose in the distance. Peach Grove Fire and Emergency was less than a mile away.

"Ow," Billy said. "That hurts."

"Get me more napkins," she ordered Marcie, hoping she would step away and give her a minute alone to question Billy. Marcie gave a squeak and turned, racing back toward her booth. A man stepped out of the crowd and handed Susannah his handkerchief; it felt moist, and she hoped it hadn't been used. She put it on top of the napkins, vowing to scrub her hands with disinfectant soap as soon as possible. "What happened?" she asked Billy.

"I can hold it." He blinked at her, dazed. "I'm not sure. Hayle told me she saw someone hanging around the truck, and I went to check. He must have been hiding behind the trailer. He rushed me, and we tussled. I reckon I haven't been tackled like that since high school." He forced a smile, but the usual twinkle in his blue eyes was gone, replaced by a stark gray look. "Then I was on the grass."

He twisted his arm, taking in the blood, his face pale, his expression grim. "I didn't even realize I was hurt until I tried to get up and saw all the blood. I called Marcie to come help me, and she went to screaming."

The crowd parted as the ambulance approached, the driver negotiating her way across the grass. At the same time, Susannah saw Randy pushing his way through the crowd. She had to make it quick. "You didn't see who it was?"

"No, it happened so fast. It was a big blur."

An EMT in a blue uniform climbed out of the passenger side of the truck. Susannah stepped back as the woman placed her orange gear bag on the ground and pulled a pair of gloves from the waist of her pants.

"What happened?" she asked, glancing from Billy to Susannah, as she removed the bloodied handkerchief and probed the wound. Randy arrived at her side, giving Susannah a menacing side-eye before peering down at Billy. Susannah backed away without a word and slipped into the crowd. She watched the attendant pull a bandage out of her bag, ripping open the package.

"I was jumped," Billy finally answered, fixing his gaze on Randy, unaware that Susannah had deserted him, "but I didn't see by who. He must have had a knife."

At that moment, Marcie reappeared, her lipstick standing out on her pale face. She clutched a roll of paper towels to her chest like a child holding a security blanket.

Susannah made her way to the edge of the crowd, observing the scene. *Could Anita's killer be here? Was there some reason the killer wanted to hurt Billy?* Susannah felt overwhelmed with questions. *Who was this person, and what did he or she want?* Anita and Tina had been poisoned, Susannah was almost killed, the stable was vandalized, now Billy had been stabbed, and no one had seen anything. How was it possible for one person to move so stealthily in such a small town? And what was the connection?

Susannah found herself in the parking lot, a few spaces away from Bitsy's vehicle. She examined the white pickup truck, the same truck around which she had seen the man with the ball cap loitering. She now saw the door sported a small decal with the Wing Shack logo; she had not noticed it earlier. It towed an enclosed trailer with the Wing Shack name emblazoned on the side. In a rush to get back to Bitsy, she had not noticed the trailer when she parked her Explorer only an hour ago. She moved closer to examine it.

The trailer resembled an enclosed box, smaller than a car length, the kind that college students rent to move their belongings. It appeared to be in fine condition. Susannah couldn't see any damage; there were no scratches or any sign that the man had been trying to force his way into it or steal it. The ground had not been disturbed.

She walked back to her booth, considering the possibility that this was unrelated to Anita's death. She shook her head. The man with the ball cap had been lurking around before she parked Bitsy's truck. What had he been doing? If he wanted to steal a trailer, this seemed like an odd time to do it. The parking lot was empty except for the vendors' vehicles, and in an hour, families would arrive, and both the pathways of the Festival and the parking lot would be inundated with people and noise. One person standing around a parked truck would not generate a second thought. Besides that, the vendors would be involved at their booths and not inclined to leave. If someone wanted to steal anything from the parking lot, that would be the time.

Why hang around until the owner showed up? Unless the motive was not theft. Was the motive personal? Could Anita's killer have a grudge against Billy? Or harbor ill will toward both Billy and Marcie? Billy, Marcie, and Anita were all restaurant owners. Could that be the connection? As far as Susannah's investigation had gone, a motive for Anita's murder still eluded her. Could Anita have been murdered because she was a restaurateur?

She stopped. Anita, Fiona, Marcie, and Billy were all members of the Peach Grove Business Association. Was there a connection there? Susannah was convinced this was not a random attack.

CHAPTER FORTY-ONE

Susannah strolled back to her booth, on the lookout for anyone wearing an Alabama ball cap. The more she pondered it, the more she felt certain that this attack on Billy was related to all the others. Anita's death, the vandalism at the Long Branch Stable, and the attempt on Tina's life had to be connected. She just had to work out how.

It was 9:45 a.m., fifteen minutes short of the parade start time, but the aisles were filling with people. At the Wing Shack booth, there was a line for breakfast orders, and the smell of hot buttered biscuits filled the air. Hayle, her small frame swallowed up in one of the Wing Shack's plus-sized aprons, handed a cup of cocoa and a biscuit wrapped in waxed paper to a matronly woman who lumbered away, eating as she walked. Susannah queued up for coffee.

Hayle leaned over the plastic folding table, tears welling in her eyes. "Dr. Shine, thank you so much for helping my dad."

"I was glad to, but I didn't do much."

"Mom told me she was grateful to you, and I am too."

Susannah fumbled her wallet out of her bag. Billy hadn't been badly hurt, and her ulterior motive of snooping around the festival grounds had led her into her role as a Good

Samaritan. "Did the EMTs take your dad to the hospital?"

"Yes," she said, a worried frown furrowing her cheeks. "My mom called and told me he would need a few stitches, but he'll be okay."

"That's good news." Susannah made a gesture with her hand indicating the cooking operation. "How are you doing?"

"I'm okay," she said, tilting her head to Zach, who stood behind her fiddling with a knob on a portable fryer. "Zach and I can handle the breakfast crowd, no problem."

At that moment, a gust of wind shook the canvas tent, sailing cups and paper plates into the air and lifting the large anniversary photo. Hayle and Zach made chase as the photo bumped against the tent and then settled. Susannah's gaze took in the picture, this time stopping to examine the black-and-white photo. It had been blown up from a less-than-perfect original, revealing an image that was grainy and pixelated rather than lifelike. Perhaps that was why they had chosen to go with black and white. *Or maybe Marcie didn't want to spring for the extra money for color*, Susannah thought snarkily. In the center of the photo, Marcie stood behind a grand opening ribbon, holding the requisite giant pair of scissors and wearing a loose-fitting, billowy dress. On her left, a younger, slimmer Billy posed in a starched white apron, wearing a chef's hat, flashing a cat-that-ate-the-canary grin.

Susannah blinked, suddenly feeling disoriented. The face gazing at her from under the chef's hat was one that she had burned into her brain the day she had coffee with Pilar. Billy Jones was one of Anita Alvarez's culinary school classmates! She felt lightheaded and took a deep breath. No wonder Anita kept her private life to herself. Susannah had blamed herself for being aloof. And she had wondered, more than once since

CHAPTER FORTY-ONE

Anita's death, how it came to pass that she could consider the woman a friend but have never met her family or gone to her home. Here was her answer. Anita had a secret.

"Dr. Shine, are you okay?"

Hayle had come around the table and stood by her side. Susannah observed the girl while trying to hide the shock and suspicion that she felt on seeing the slimmer Billy, his cheekbones chiseled under the white hat, the charming dimples now front and center in a jowl-less, angular face. She removed her gaze from the picture. "Sure, I'm fine."

"You look kind of pale," she said, glancing up at the picture and then back at Susannah.

"I haven't eaten—that's why I came over. But I guess when I glanced up I got lightheaded," she lied and pushed away the guilt that came from a Catholic upbringing. It had become too easy to lie.

"Well, come on." Hayle smiled, her dimples sparkling out from both cheeks, matching Billy's grin in the picture.

Dimples. An attribute she had also noted in Dolores Alvarez. Susannah gasped, watching the picture of Billy sway in the warm breeze as an idea spread across her mind, tucking its fingers into the tiny, lazy spaces at the edges of her brain. Pilar must have recognized it too. This was what had distracted her earlier. The broad smile, the deep dimples: Dolores was also Billy's daughter!

That was Anita's obsession with Peach Grove. It wasn't the restaurant. It wasn't life away from the big city or from an overbearing mother. She had settled here to be near the father of her child. Susannah glanced at the picture again, making note of Marcie's swollen belly under the loose dress.

"I'll get you a chicken biscuit," Hayle said.

Susannah nodded and followed Hayle into the shade of the tent, taking a seat at one of the folding tables. This was the reason Pilar wanted to keep Dolores away from the booth earlier. When she had snapped at Dolores, Susannah thought that Pilar was being unreasonable, but that was not the case. She wanted to protect Dolores, and the enormity of the situation dawned on Susannah. Dolores and Hayle were *both* Billy's daughters. The friendly man whose genial, almost buffoonish behavior had charmed and intrigued Susannah was the father of an out-of-wedlock child who went to the same high school as his legitimate daughter.

She gulped. Perhaps she was wrong. After all, a lot of people had dimples, and going to the same cooking school as Anita Alvarez could just be a coincidence. She remembered the freezer-sharing situation that had seemed so odd. Maybe it was the kind of favor that cooking colleagues did for each other. Or maybe it indicated a more intimate relationship.

She thought about Marcie. Many times after a Business Association meeting, Susannah and Bitsy had held gripe sessions about the curt and rude way that Marcie addressed various members. Many times, she had thought of Marcie as mean-spirited and vindictive, and she often wondered why a nice guy like Billy put up with her. She never gave Marcie credit for raising Hayle, who appeared to be a good-hearted and kind girl, or for having married the most affable and good-natured man in the town. Susannah assumed that whatever had attracted Billy to Marcie was long gone, buried deep under her hard-boiled exterior.

But perhaps she had read the whole relationship wrong. She had seen firsthand Marcie's concern and worry over Billy. Did Marcie have a softness under that tough outer crust? Was

CHAPTER FORTY-ONE

her grumpy exterior warranted? The picture of the grand opening showed Marcie as clearly pregnant. Had they been married at the time? She tried to do the math, but without knowing the date of the picture, she could not. Did she dare ask Hayle? The last thing she wanted to do was to tip off this innocent teen to a possible family scandal. She bit her lip, stepping to the side as a young boy pushed past her, a crumpled dollar bill in his fist.

"I'll be right with you," Hayle said to the boy, nodding at his parents, who were standing to the side, supervising his purchase. She exited the tent again, bringing the smell of fried chicken and hot sauce with her, and touched Susannah's shoulder as she handed her the paper-wrapped biscuit.

Susannah absentmindedly took a bite, too late realizing that she was chomping on a wheat-laden biscuit. She refrained from spitting and gave Hayle a weak smile, knowing she would deal with a migraine if she swallowed any of the dough. Hayle returned the smile and rejoined Zach tending to the line. Susannah grabbed a napkin and discreetly emptied her mouth.

From what she remembered, Dolores and Hayle were about the same age. Could Billy have been cheating on Marcie with Anita? Was this the reason for Marcie's permanent bad mood? Or was there another, blander explanation for it?

"That photo is amazing," Susannah began, not knowing how to open the conversation.

"I know, right? My dad was so handsome." She peered up at the photo, grinning. "It was his dream to open a restaurant"

"He looks like a proper chef, dressed like that."

"Oh, he is. He graduated at the top of his class in cooking school. Mom always kids that she stole him away from a life as a French chef." She giggled.

"Is that what he studied?" Susannah asked, trying to keep her talking.

"I think so." She wiped her palms on her legs, staining the trademark Wing Shack red apron with smudges of white. "I mean, you learn different techniques at culinary school, and he studied French cuisine for a while. You know, like in the big five-star restaurants? He always says he couldn't ignore his small-town, country-cooking roots. So he came home and married my mom, and the Wing Shack was born right before I was." She rolled her eyes at the last statement, clearly a family joke. Susannah watched the grin spread across her face; she enjoyed telling the story. "I was born three months later."

Susannah tucked that info away for later comparison to Dolores's birth date.

"Feeling better, Dr. Shine? You still don't look right."

"I'm okay." She stared into the distance, looking for Pilar. "The dizziness is gone." She thanked Hayle and pulled a few dollars out of her back pocket as her cell phone rang.

Larraine's voice came through, barely above a whisper. "Dr. Shine, you can't miss this," she said. "Randy is making an arrest, and you'll never guess who."

CHAPTER FORTY-TWO

Susannah raced away from Hayle, pausing only to throw the chicken biscuit in the nearest trash can. The aisles were becoming crowded, and she had to zigzag between a scrawny teenage girl pushing a stroller and a tall man in blue work pants.

A few feet past the metal lawn animals, she found Larraine standing at the rear of a crowd, her back straight, her hand to her mouth. Susannah sidled over and took her hand. They stood together, craning to see over the crowd. Under the red canvas of the OK Automotive logo, she saw Randy leaning in, speaking to Stevie, whose tear-streaked face was twisted in anguish, snot dripping from his nose. Randy did his best to calm him.

"He's arresting Stevie?" Susannah asked, unable to keep the contempt from her voice. What could have prompted this?

"Not Stevie," Larraine answered, pointing with her chin. Susannah looked to the area past the tent, where two figures struggled under the large shade tree. The uniformed figure was unmistakable—partially hidden behind the tree's enormous trunk, Keith's large frame towered over Colin Rogers, who glared out at the crowd with an expression of unmitigated hatred, an Alabama ball cap on the ground at his feet.

Susannah gasped, recognizing the cap she had seen on the man lurking around the parking lot earlier this morning. She recalled the brim of his ball cap had been pulled down low, but now that she made the connection, she was sure it had been Colin.

"Colin attacked Billy?" Susannah asked incredulously, as Keith appeared from behind the tree and jerked up on the restraints on Colin's wrists.

"I don't know why he's gettin' arrested," Larraine answered.

A loud moan filled the air as Stevie jumped up from his chair and in two uneven steps crossed the distance and flung himself at Keith. Alarmed, Randy leaped over the table, his arm outstretched to grab Stevie, but he fell short and stumbled. Stevie flopped forward and latched on to Keith's arm, howling. Keith's Herculean frame absorbed the collision without flinching, and a slight rise of the shoulder dislodged Stevie, who landed on his knees in a heap, like an overgrown child.

Colin's angry demeanor vanished in an instant, and he turned toward Stevie, his face soft and his voice firm. "Stevie, you calm yourself now."

Stevie looked up at him, his face contorted. "But, Colin," he said, with a hiccup.

"No, sir. You get ahold of yourself." Then to Randy, who had one hand on his Taser and the other on his cuffs, he said, "He didn't mean nothin' by it. You know that. You cain't arrest him, he's got the mind of a young'un."

"Colin, I ain't a young'un."

"You hush," Colin scolded, "and stay where you are."

CHAPTER FORTY-TWO

Randy pulled Stevie to his feet. "I have a right mind to bring you in—"

Stevie's face fell, and he began to bawl.

"Now why'd you go and do that?" Colin said, his face pained.

"He didn't interfere with me," Keith said to Randy. "Leave him be. I'm fine." He pushed Colin forward. "Tell him to stay where he is and not to make a fuss."

"It's gonna be auright," Colin said. His voice had a soothing quality to it, but there was fear in his face. "This is a mix-up. I'll be back at the shop directly. You go over there and wait for me."

"Don't leave me, Colin. I'm scared by myself, you know that."

At that, Larraine could restrain herself no longer. She pushed through the crowd and jammed herself against the leg of the OK Automotive tent. "Steven Duncan, you come over here," she called, and Stevie raised his head, rubbing his eyes. "It's Miss Larraine from church. You come on over here."

"Go on," Colin encouraged, "you know Miss Larraine."

"Yessir, but I don't want to go to church. Today's Saturday," he whined, hanging his head like a child. Several in the crowd chuckled.

"No one's goin' to church, Stevie," Larraine said, "but you have to let Colin go with the officers. I'll call your mama, and she can come and collect you, if you want."

"No, ma'am, I don't live with my mama anymore." He stood up and ambled over to Larraine. "I rent my own room now."

"Well, that's fine," she said, taking his large, calloused hand in hers. "We'll figure it out, but first I'll get you a biscuit. How about that?"

Stevie nodded slowly, and Larraine walked him away from Colin.

Susannah felt a nudge, and she turned to see Bitsy, who asked, "What all is goin' on here?"

"I'm not sure, but I think Colin is being arrested for attacking Billy."

"Well, I'll be." They watched as Keith walked away with Colin, and then Bitsy said, "I need your help."

"What for? I have to get back to my booth." Susannah had put up a booth so that she could advertise her practice and had spent less than five minutes there all morning.

"You have to go get me a few more pies. Marcie put them in the refrigerator at the Wing Shack. It will only take you a minute. I've had four more sign-ups than I planned for. I can't leave right now, and Marcie hasn't got back from the hospital yet."

Susannah hesitated. Now that she knew Billy's secret, she dreaded bumping into Marcie or Billy. As long as they were still at the hospital, she could get into the Wing Shack without seeing either of them. She glanced down the aisle where her pop-up tent sat unmanned and shrugged. It could wait a little longer. "Gimme the key."

CHAPTER FORTY-THREE

In the short drive from the fairground to the shopping center, Susannah tried to fit the puzzle pieces together. Pilar told her that Anita lived in Peach Grove alone for months, biding her time to ensure that the restaurant turned a profit before she built a house and moved Dolores from Atlanta. But maybe there had been more to it than that. Pilar also told her she had watched over Dolores in the morning and after school. Had Anita been searching for Billy during that time, or had she known exactly in which small town she would find him?

Susannah pulled up to the back entrance of the Wing Shack, suddenly feeling a chill. When she first got involved with this, she believed that Anita was an innocent victim of a violent act. But now she knew there was a volatile, even manipulative side to Anita. What had Fiona said? Anita would declare that someone was her enemy until she had gotten what she wanted. Had she stalked Billy, hoping he would give her what she wanted? A wedding ring, perhaps?

Susannah turned off the car and dug around the rear pocket of her cargo shorts for Bitsy's keys. "Where are they?" she mumbled, exiting the vehicle and absentmindedly setting the alarm. She relocated her phone to a side pocket and found the key, all the while wondering: If Anita wanted a relationship with Billy, she obviously had not gotten one. So why did she stay on in Peach Grove? To share a freezer?

The answer came to her with a jolt. Anita and Billy were having an affair. Pilar's words echoed in her head. *Find that man, and you will find who did this to Anita.* Billy knew that Susannah's office would be closed the day Anita died because he was a patient. Billy was also a trained chef. He would know how to make some kind of edible concoction out of a poisonous leaf.

Susannah spun back to her car, her hand shaking as she gripped the key fob. She had to get out of here, now, and get to the police. Before she could unlock the car, a thick hand had hold of her wrist. A square bandage covered its forearm. She winced, trying to pull away, but she could not.

"Fancy meeting you here," Billy said, grinning. "I heard your car and came to see who was out here."

"Oh, I thought you were at the hospital," she said, too quickly. She held up the key Bitsy had given her. "I came for more pies. Is Marcie with you?"

"Marcie had to get back to the fair. She sent me home to rest, but I needed to pick something up first." He swept his arm in the grand, inviting gesture she had seen many times before and tugged her arm. "Come on in."

"I, uh, I forgot something at home," she replied, twisting free of his grip. "I'll stop on the way back."

"Nonsense." The sunlight changed as a cloud passed overhead, and for a moment Billy's eyes appeared flat and cold. Then the light returned and he smiled, gently pulling her away from the car and into the restaurant. *Maybe I'm*

CHAPTER FORTY-THREE

overreacting, Susannah thought, but her mind soon changed as he shut the door and immediately wrapped his arm around her shoulder and ushered her into the kitchen. He squeezed her closer, pushing her ahead of him and sliding open the door to one of the refrigerated cases without releasing his grasp.

"Bitsy's peach pies." He pointed at the cardboard boxes, which Marcie had bound with red-and-white baker's twine and stacked three high. He delved deeper into the case, and his expression hardened as he felt around until he finally located what he wanted. He closed the door and set a clear plastic bottle on the counter beside two plastic tumblers filled with tea. "First, a drink. I know you are as warm as I am from being outside all morning." He poured a glass and pushed it toward her. "You drink your tea unsweetened, right?"

She nodded slowly, uncertain what to do next. She did not want to drink. She left it untouched.

"Drink up," he said, watching her.

Susannah scrutinized him. Though he was one of the first people she had met when she moved to Peach Grove, she had not noticed how he much had changed over the years. The old photograph emphasized how his face had swelled as he gained weight. Bloodshot eyes gazed out from a puffy, splotched face, and she wondered if it were the result of the assault or if she was seeing him a new light. The change in his attitude alarmed her; she felt certain that he was capable of cheating on Marcie. She scrutinized the liquid he wanted her to swallow.

Was he also capable of murder?

"Aren't you going to drink?" he asked, poised with the bottle in his hand.

"No, I'm fine."

For over a decade she had thought of him as a warm-hearted man who went out of his way to be friendly and gracious. He glared at her, and a cold chill jolted her to her senses. She leapt for the door, but he quickly reined her in and pressed the cup to her lips. She shook her head, but he twisted his fingers in her hair and yanked her head back. When she opened her mouth to protest, he poured the liquid in.

It was cold and she swallowed, coughing. "What are you doing?" she sputtered, the tea coming up and burning her throat.

He yanked her hair again. "I'm being hospitable, and you are acting rude and uncultured."

She was shocked at his voice—his accent had thickened and the timbre had deepened. But it was the malice in his eyes that chilled her. He put the cup to her lips again, and this time she opened her lips but let the liquid flow out of her mouth, wetting her blouse. The taste was bitter, but it had a familiar tang. He poured faster. She swallowed and coughed. *What in the hell is happening?* It was like being waterboarded by Lipton.

He eased off and stood back, leaning against the counter with a crooked twist to his mouth. "Would you like to sit down?"

She felt her knees quiver, and a wave of nausea flooded her gut. Instead of cooling her down, the foul-tasting tea had heated her up, a sheen of sweat obvious on the palms of her hands.

Billy seemed genuinely pleased to see her sweat. "You're sweating like a whore in church," he grinned, swiping the back of his arm across his brow.

CHAPTER FORTY-THREE

Susannah's hand began to shake, and a pain smashed into her abdomen. Her knees gave way and she sat down hard on the cool tile floor.

"I asked you if you wanted to sit," he said, as he watched her crumble.

"What did you give me?"

"It's my own personal stash of *té tamarindo*." He lifted his untouched cup and poured the liquid back into the container and resealed it. "I never touch the stuff, myself, but Anita really enjoyed it the last time we met."

CHAPTER FORTY-FOUR

"Up we go," Billy said, using a tone of voice that one would use to soothe a sick child.

Susannah's breath came with difficulty, and she knew without a doubt that she had been poisoned with digitalis.

Billy tugged on her arms, attempting to pull her to a standing position. "Come on now," he said impatiently. "You're much stronger than she was, and that was a small dose."

Another wave of nausea tore through her; she heaved, but nothing came up. She stuck her finger down her throat, hoping to disgorge some of the liquid and slow the poison. All the speculation she and Bitsy had done about opportunity and method, and it turned out that the vector of the poison was a simple one. Billy had poisoned Anita's tea. Betrayed her with her own creation. A sharp pain tore through her ribs. It took a moment to comprehend that Billy had kicked her.

"Don't hurl," he ordered, as if she could control the serpent that slithered upward from her gut. He yanked her again, and she resisted, hoping to rest for another moment and gather

CHAPTER FORTY-FOUR

her strength. She needed to ignore the sensations of pain and the prickly fingers of vertigo that played at the edges of her mind. She had to form a plan. She had to fight back.

Inhaling with difficulty, she recalled that the effects of digitalis were primarily cardiovascular. Her heart could be skipping to any one of a number of irregular beats, which would cause shortness of breath. The strength in her muscles should not be affected. She steeled herself; she needed to coordinate her body and mind. Her eyes darted around the room. Her best chance was to get to the back door and outside.

She willed her legs to move, but they trembled so furiously she could not take a step. The page in the *Compendium of Plants* came back to her clearly. Along with nausea, vomiting, and cardiac arrhythmias, digitalis toxicity caused tremors, but it didn't cause weakness or loss of muscle tone. She should be able to muster the strength to stand and run. Unless of course, she had ingested enough poison to kill her. She pushed that thought away. She had to concentrate on getting away from Billy.

He kicked her again. "Don't try anything." The expression on his face told her that he expected cooperation. She got to her feet, the shaking in her legs subsided, and she felt steady.

"The flowers on her desk were from you."

His grin became a grimace. "Anita loved flowers. I was more than pleased to give them to her. It was one of our little rituals, and she ate it up." He laughed. "Ate it up, get it?"

His face was red with exertion, and he twisted her arm fiercely and spun her around, pushing her belly into the counter, frisking her roughly. He yanked her phone from her shorts so violently he ripped the pocket.

"You won't be needing this." He threw her phone on the countertop, where it skidded to a stop next to the coffee maker, and snatched the baker's twine from the shelf.

She bit back a groan as he pulled her wrists behind her back. Remembering the games she used to play with her brothers, she quickly placed her palms together as he bound her wrists.

"I saw you hiding behind the dumpster the day of her memorial." She could feel his hot breath on her neck. "You might be smart, Doc, but you are clumsy."

Susannah's thoughts flashed back to the alley. Squatting behind the dumpster, she remembered how the smell of the garbage had assaulted her nostrils. He had been one step behind her all along. Her heart sank. "The blue sedan." She twisted, determined to see his face.

He shoved her forward, her face now inches from the counter. "Bingo. Once I saw you out there cowering in the trash, I knew you had been prowling around the restaurant and probably had stuck your nose in the kitchen *and* Anita's office. Ignoring the crime scene tape like you're above the law. Just like Anita, always justifying her actions, no matter who she hurt."

"A man doesn't look behind the dumpster unless he has hidden there himself," Susannah said, paraphrasing an old French saying. She was babbling now, trying to keep him occupied, hoping there was some way she could retrieve her phone without him noticing.

"I made sure I dumped the vase she kept on her desk." His breath was on her neck, and she reflexively shrank away. He pushed her down harder, and she found herself staring at her phone. She could not discern if the pain in her gut came from the digitalis or from the desperation of knowing her phone

CHAPTER FORTY-FOUR

was in arm's reach, but she could not get to it. She struggled against him but couldn't move. "She thought she was so smart. She used to gloat about how much more money her Cantina Caliente made than the Wing Shack. She thought it meant she was some kind of business genius. But she never figured out why I gave her flowers every week," he said. "No one else did, either. I knew that detective would never suspect me on her own. She's a two-dimensional thinker. You, on the other hand, understand that medicines can grow in your backyard. But one man's medicine is another man's poison."

The pain in her gut was hard to ignore, but she had to keep him talking. The more he talked about Anita, the more agitated his voice became. Could she distract his attention and get him off balance? He outweighed her by over a hundred pounds, but there were ways to use an opponent's weight against them. She moved her foot back, trying to find his. If she could trip him, she might have a chance.

"It wasn't just the flowers." She took a breath, wincing in pain. "I know the herbs I sell are safe. If she was poisoned, it didn't come from my office. I had my suspicions about Anita ingesting digitalis from foxglove. When I saw flowers in the dumpster, I knew I was correct. But they fell apart before I could get them out. Even then, I couldn't figure out how someone could slip her poison without her noticing."

"Enter *té tamarindo*, that disgusting substitute for sweet tea," he sneered. "She'd swill that crud any time of day. She wasn't picky about what she put in her body." He worked the twine around her wrists, and she took the opportunity to strike with her foot, a spark of hope igniting and then going out, as she connected with a stiff leather boot which didn't budge. He responded by bashing the back of her knee with his, forcing her foot back into line.

Instead of tripping him, she had caused him to get even closer to her, his leg now on hers. He shoved his heavy boot between her feet, and she lost her footing and flopped forward, her cheek now flush with the countertop. Her breath fogged the metallic surface. Her phone was only inches away.

He continued, "Not like those crunchy assholes who want me out of business so they can eat only organic, free-range puffs of kale."

Susannah grunted as he pulled her up and spun her to face him. She let the momentum carry her to the side, her body blocking his view of her phone. Salvation in the form of a mobile phone lay on the stainless steel behind her, and she had to keep his attention off it. She forced herself to glare at him, not daring to move her hands, which had landed palm up on the counter. There was rage in his eyes, and she hoped that it worked in her favor.

"Present company not excluded." Spittle gathered at the edges of his mouth, a few drops landing on her face. "Don't think for a second that just because you helped my back, I respect your ridiculous, self-absorbed ways. You're what's wrong with this country. People like you are the reason why I have to work six days a week to make a living. Used to be, a man knew what to expect when he got up in the morning."

"Not everyone eats wings," she offered.

Billy's face flushed. "And not everyone convinces people to buy high-priced supplements to take instead of eating real food." He leaned in. His face was now contorted from anger, inches from hers. "But you do."

She leaned away from him, using the opportunity to move her hands closer to her phone. She had to keep him talking.

CHAPTER FORTY-FOUR

He and Anita had engaged in a romantic relationship, but everything he said spoke of professional jealousy. He was angry because the Cantina served a much larger clientele than the Wing Shack, and Anita made more money. His anger even spilled over into resentfulness that Susannah counseled her patients on nutrition and sold supplements to them—as if she were stealing his business. If it weren't so frightening, it would be preposterous.

Susannah said, "Trust me, more people in this town come here for wings than buy vitamins from me."

"I don't trust you. You tell your patients to stop eating wheat. Bread is the staff of life." He swung his arm wide, palm open, indicating the dining room, and looked away. Susannah felt for the phone and grabbed it, her wrists bent awkwardly on the counter. He knit his brow and stabbed his finger in her direction. "Bread is the working man's food. Only overeducated morons like you don't understand that."

He raged past her, ripped open the door to the oven and pulled out a biscuit. With his back momentarily to her, she quickly dumped the phone into the cargo pocket of her shorts. He winged a biscuit at her, and it hit the side of her face and crumbled. He threw another so wildly that it sailed over her head. He removed one more, slamming the oven door so hard it bounced open again. He heaved his body against it, and it closed with a sucking sound. He reached out and jerked her away from the counter, smashing the biscuit into her face.

"How did you like that? I should force-feed you those crumbs, kinda like a last meal. But we're outta here." He squeezed both her wrists in one huge hand, the bulk of his pendulous gut leaning on her, his scent making her dizzy. Could the vertigo be returning when she needed it least?

She knew that digoxins could cause hallucinations along with nausea, but she wasn't prepared for the clumsiness and sluggish thoughts. She was grateful she'd had the coordination to stow her phone. Only a minute or two could have passed since she had snatched the device and slipped it into her pocket, but suddenly her feet felt disconnected and she stumbled, earning another yank from Billy, which sent a searing pain into her shoulder. At least the pain dulled the nausea.

"You were jealous of Anita," she blurted, her tongue thick. Her words slurred, and she felt his body stiffen.

He spun her around, sneering. His fingers dug into her so tight his knuckles blanched, tiny brown freckles standing out like specks of cinnamon on his hand. "You have no idea, nobody does," he exclaimed, his voice softer, choking back a sob. His eyes darted around the kitchen, and Susannah recognized a glimmer of satisfaction and pride that immediately disappeared, replaced by fury. "She was bleeding me dry. She was ripping handfuls of profit out of my business." He slid his tongue over his lower lip, pausing, and Susannah seized the opportunity and ripped her arms from his grip.

She threw herself at the back door, twisting to reach the handle, but she was unable. The effort taxed her heart, which started fluttering wildly in her breast. It was all for nothing. Her legs shook and wobbled, and the last thing she saw was Billy peering at her. Then all was black.

CHAPTER FORTY-FIVE

Susannah's thoughts were hazy as a rattle woke her. She lay on her side in the darkness of a moving vehicle—the trunk of a car. Her heart tapped, adding a glitch to its beat that made her chest feel hollow and weak. She recalled Larraine's admonition, *"It wouldn't hurt you to pray."* Prayer and faith came so easily to Larraine; Susannah had always made her own miracles.

She had faith that Bitsy would soon miss her. How long had she been in the Wing Shack? The confrontation with Billy seemed to have taken an eternity, but it could have been ten minutes. Sweat slicked her body, and she sent out a silent prayer that someone would notice she had not returned.

"Well, Miss Larraine," she said, crinkling her nose at the rank air in the stuffy trunk, "some divine intervention would be welcome about now."

A faint sound of music filtered in and she focused on it, pushing away the panic. Billy was playing the radio as he drove. She forced herself to take a long, slow breath, fighting the poison that made her heart ram against her rib cage. Tears welled. He was taking her somewhere to die.

Her arms behind her back, she squirmed, assessing the

space she had around her. Her maker had graced her with long arms, and as a child she could readily step through her interlaced fingers, a characteristic that came in handy during cops-and-robbers games with her brothers. In this cramped space, she had to contort herself to attempt this trick. Her shoulders ached, and she banged her head as she stepped through her bound hands and forced her arms forward. The volume of the music increased.

As her eyes adjusted to the dark, she sawed the thin baker's twine between her teeth and soon her hands were free. She placed her palms against the lid of the trunk, formulating a plan. Taking stock of herself in the cramped space, she wiggled her fingers to shake off the tingling sensation, but they were thick with numbness. Unable to stretch her legs, she wiggled her toes and flexed her feet, determined to get the blood flowing Something sharp jabbed her right leg, and she shifted her weight, pawing at it, but it didn't move. It was solid and rectangular.

Idiot! Her spirit soared with hope. It was her phone, tucked into her right cargo pants pocket. In all his rage, Billy had missed it.

The car turned, and the road took on a rougher aspect. She pitched to and fro as the car bounded out of a pothole. They were on a dirt road, she was sure of it. Panic enveloped her. Was he going to dump her somewhere and leave her for dead? She pawed her pocket with her numb hand. She had to get to the phone.

The car slowed, and she grunted, forcing her hand under the flap of the pocket where the snap was now engaged. In any other place this would be an easy procedure, but the numbness in her fingers made it agonizingly slow. The

CHAPTER FORTY-FIVE

vehicle came to a shuddering halt. She heard Billy's footsteps nearing. Even if she removed it, how could she hide it from him?

With uncoordinated fingers, she flipped the snap and grasped the phone, forcing her hand beneath her blouse, shoving the phone deep into her bra. This was her lifeline now. She wouldn't give it up without a fight. Rolling flat on her back, her knees pulled in, she was ready to spring as soon as the latch released.

Rap, rap, rap. Billy banged on the trunk. "You hear this?" he demanded.

Susannah recoiled but didn't answer.

"I know you can hear me." He rapped again, this time harder. "That's the sound of my Glock. You give me trouble, and it'll take a nice bite outta you."

The lid popped open, and Billy's fleshy hand maneuvered the barrel of the semiautomatic Glock 19 toward her nose. "Get up."

Susannah moved, but her sluggish muscles were too slow for him, and he wrenched her upright. She squinted, the subdued lighting blinding after her after her time in the dark. She had to find something that could help her escape. Billy had brought her to a wooded area. She glimpsed trees and pine straw and dead leaves. The view was similar pines and paper birch that surrounded her home and office, thin-trunked trees, too slight to hide behind. She couldn't be far from Peach Grove.

"Don't even think about it," he growled, moving the barrel of the gun even closer, groping her face with his other hand and forcing something hard into her mouth. It was the plastic bottle of *té tamarindo*. She writhed away. Wetness dribbled over her lips. Sputtering, she slapped the bottle away in an uncoordinated, spastic motion.

"Stay still, or I'll shoot," Billy snarled.

But Susannah had no intention of staying still. If she was going to die, she would go down fighting. She twisted to get her legs free and kicked Billy in the gut.

Unperturbed, he rammed the gun into the soft spot under her collarbone, and she backed further into the trunk. "No!" she cried. He had pushed her in the wrong direction. She had to keep balled up with her muscles taut if she were to lash out with all her might.

But her might was failing.

She glared at him, noticing the droplets of sweat dotting his brow.

Good, she thought, *I'm making him sweat. I can wear him down.*

He fought more liquid into her mouth. The sweetness flowed over her tongue, but she refused to swallow, instead spitting it into his face. He shook his head like a dog coming in from the rain. She saw her chance and kicked again, feebly. It was as hard as she could manage, and by some miracle, her foot found purchase in his groin and he gasped, dropping the bottle.

"Nooo," he howled, lunging for her as she tipped herself out of the vehicle.

Panting, she reached the bottle but it slipped out of her grasp, the tips of her fingers grazing the bottom. Tea leaked slowly from the opening. With a thrust of the shoulder, she propelled the bottle under the car where Billy couldn't reach it.

He fell on her, shoving her legs into the rock-hard soil

CHAPTER FORTY-FIVE

with such force it brought tears to her eyes. He shook her furiously, and her head hit the underside of the car. Her ears reverberated with a high-pitched sound, her vision blurred, but she felt satisfaction as the last bit of iced tea spilled onto the dry earth.

CHAPTER FORTY-SIX

Susannah did not know how long it had been since she'd been poisoned, but the stabbing pain in her abdomen reminded her she was still alive. Digitalis could kill quickly, or its effects could linger if the dosage was not high enough to kill. She credited her mother's daily rosary that she was still alive. But for how long?

She had barely felt anything as Billy dragged her from under the car, his grip on her ankle only now transforming into a gnawing pain. The drug had given her a kind of distance, and she watched through a halo of yellowish light as he hauled her up, huffing with effort. Sweat beaded across the large pores of his forehead, and when he shoved her through the door of an old shed, her five-foot-ten frame collapsed upon itself like an oversized rag doll. A clap of metal on wood sealed the shed, and a lock snapped into place. "I'll be back," he growled. Minutes later, the hum of his car faded into the distance.

She had to get help before he made good on his threat to return. Removing her phone from its hiding place, she swiped at it with twitchy fingers but got no signal.

A rustling noise came from outside the structure, and adrenaline coursed through her body, covering her with

CHAPTER FORTY-SIX

sweat. Moving was an effort, and a new wave of pain roiled through her belly, this time making her fear that she would soil herself.

"Hell no," she said aloud, sounding braver than she felt. "Being poisoned and kidnapped is one thing. Being fodder for rats and snakes is another."

The structure in which she found herself was not a prefabricated shed like the Dutch dollhouse in Bitsy's yard but rather a shack constructed from panels of plywood screwed into a wooden frame. The air inside was thick with a moldy stink permeated her clothes and seemed to nest in her hair. She swiped the home screen on her phone to bring up a light. There had to be a weakness in the moldering wood.

Holding her breath, she considered the possibility of picking up some weird disease from an airborne fungus. During chiropractic school, she had studied pathology and microbiology, and the names of rare diseases tumbled through her brain. Microbes that hid in musty, disused places.

Coccidiomycosis.

Hantavirus.

The plague!

The rustling noise returned. She shivered and put thoughts of the plague aside. A thread of light streamed through a small chink in the wood, and she pressed her eye to it, searching for what could be making the rustling sound. Nothing moved in her line of sight, and the dirt path Billy had driven down showed no sign of their struggle. This spot was secluded, a perfect place to let poison do its work. She sagged and turned back to the darkness. Misery leeched into her body and soul. She would die alone, be erased from this earth permanently. Forgotten, even by Henry the Eighth. A tear dripped down her cheek.

But instead of depressing her, it made her angry.

"Stop feeling sorry for yourself," she said out loud and turned back to the darkness trying to work out how Billy had outsmarted her—and the police.

The arrangement he had with Anita, sharing the freezer space and visiting the Cantina on a regular basis, should have set off alarm bells in her mind. Not only was it odd, but it was the perfect excuse to get closer to Anita and administer the poison. Could he have put the poison in other drinks too? Had he shown up in the morning and slipped it in her coffee, something else she drank with gusto?

Susannah recalled Anita's hand trembling as she drank her *café con leche* at the last PGBA meeting. Could Billy have poisoned her that morning? Was he in the kitchen with her, meeting her at the service entrance, bringing her fresh flowers with a side of poisoned iced tea?

No wonder Marcie was ornery all the time; she must have suspected that Billy had more than a business relationship with Anita. Hadn't Zach pointed out that they frequently argued about it?

On knees burning from the scuffle on the hard earth, she crawled forward, scanning the walls with the light from her phone, searching for an opening. The corners were filled with spider webs, and she grimaced at the thought of crawling into a brown recluse, or worse, a black widow. A bite from either could interfere with her escape plans permanently. She bumped a dust-laden object, and it fell to the floor. Examining it in the light, she realized it was a three-legged collapsible camping stool, designed to be carried on a backpack. Picking it up, she held it out and flourished it like a sword. *En garde*,

CHAPTER FORTY-SIX

she thought, remembering the sword fights in the old Three Musketeers movies her Nana loved.

"This might work," she told the darkness. Feeling braver, she stabbed it into the corner to clear the webs.

Remembering Bitsy's complaints about how often she had to repair the wood of her raised beds due to dry rot, which was accelerated by the Georgia heat, she continued jabbing her way around the perimeter, poking with the plastic legs of the stool at the wood panels and prodding into the dirt floor, feeling for any softness. There had to be a way out. Musty air made her nose twitch, and she rubbed at it, her fingers tingling.

Sweat collected on her brow. It wasn't only the humidity that was affecting her—the digitalis made her stomach sway and her head spin. But she kept at it until, in the corner of the shed, a crack revealed a spider's web in which a bug wriggled and twitched, trying to get free. Like her, it was stuck in Billy's web, but unlike her, it could wriggle its way out of here. She peered at the web and in the light of her phone, she noticed other strands of the web. Two familiar insects were snared within.

"Eureka!" Susannah yelled, brandishing her faux sword. "Termites and fire ants!"

Termites ate at the wood and turned it to sawdust. Fire ants loosened up the Georgia clay by creating an extensive network of tunnels and removing a sizable amount of hard-packed dirt. There had to be a weakness here that she could exploit.

She banged at the boards where they touched the ground. A corner of the wood gave way under her hand, and she collapsed in a hiccup of happiness.

CHAPTER FORTY-SEVEN

She had no strength left in her body. Freedom was only inches away, but hammering away at the rotted wood with the camp stool had exhausted her energy, and the opening she had made was barely the size of a tennis ball. Her mind raced.

An old rotting piece of wood could not beat her.

She felt a tickle. Termites were climbing on her arm, mocking her gargantuan size and inability to fit through cracks. Placing her feet against the rotting wood, she rested a moment.

"I don't have an Ant-Man suit, but I can use my superior size to defeat you," she taunted the bugs. Her voice sounded slurred, and she knew she had to rally her strength and get some medical help before the digitalis ended her. Leaning back, she kicked the wall with all her might. Her foot flew through the wood to the outside world.

Woo hoo, she thought, too drained to cheer. She slumped, her breath coming in short, heavy rasps. She counted to thirty and kicked again. Over and over, she kicked and rested, widening the opening bit by bit, until she came to the end of the rotted wood. It would give no more. She had managed

CHAPTER FORTY-SEVEN

to clear a small hole, possibly enough space for her head. Outside was an ant mound. She would have to brave their stings to tunnel under the plywood, like a cat squeezing under a fence.

Grabbing the camp stool, she began sawing back and forth in the earth, ants pouring onto the plastic legs and up her arm. She shook them away, their stings making her twitch and flail. She continued until the dip under the wall took shape as an actual hole in the earth. It was small and irregular, but it tunneled under the shed wall, and that was all that mattered.

Squeezing her eyes shut, she crawled, determined to ignore the ant bites until she was completely free. They were on her face, in her hair. She jammed her shoulders through, splinters of wood scraping her neck and back. Digging in with her elbows, she twisted her hips and pulled herself free. Flat on the ground, she brushed her face maniacally, rubbing and slapping at the insects.

Inching forward, she pulled her shirt over her head, shaking it to dislodge the stinging pests. Frantically, she wiped her face, arms, and legs. At last, the stinging ceased and she flopped to the earth, sweating. Except for the sound of the breeze rustling the trees, all was quiet. She grabbed her phone, stabbing at the screen with still-numb fingers.

"Nooo," she moaned. There was no signal.

There were no towers out here—that's why Billy had chosen this place. A sob escaped her. It must be an old hunting camp. Deep in the woods. No one would hear her, and no one would find her. Tears filled her eyes.

She was spent. He would win.

She closed her eyes and exhaled. A burning pain seared her ankle, and she propelled herself forward, slapping at a persistent pismire.

"No."

She had gotten this far. He would not win.

She had to get away.

Susannah forced herself to stand. The effort made her dizzy, and she coughed weakly. Staggering to a thirty-foot pine, she leaned heavily, glanced into the woods, and chose a direction away from the road. She ambled on, dizziness and shortness of breath plaguing every step. After a few minutes, she could no longer see the shed. Increasing her pace, she moved as fast as she was able. Not knowing where she was or how deep in the woods this property lay unnerved her. If she had chosen the wrong direction, she would certainly perish alone.

"Okay, Larraine," she mumbled, "your prayers are up. Help me find my way out of here."

She carried on putting one foot in front of the other and touching each thin pine for support. Stumbling over a root, she lost her balance and slipped onto her knees. Bowing her head, she fought the urge to give up. She would take a brief rest. Only a few seconds to gather her strength.

The slam of a car door echoed through the trees. His words came back to her: *"You're much stronger than she was, and that was a small dose."*

Anita had survived worse and managed to keep moving, and so would she. Her knees ached as she pulled herself up and continued on, layers of pine needles slowing her as if she were in a bad dream. At last the light changed and she perceived a thinning of the trees. She was near the end of the wood!

Breath ragged, she faltered, listening for any sound that Billy was on her trail. The air here felt lighter, not heavy

CHAPTER FORTY-SEVEN

with musty pine, and was easier to breathe. She heard no human sounds and moved forward. A few labored steps and she stopped, blinking against the sun. A lone horse stood in a field a few yards off, chewing on a mouthful of grass. It eyed her and twitched its tail. Hope sprang to her heart. Civilization was near. She was safe.

The horse came closer, curious. He must have been familiar with human females covered in ant bites and sweat. Susannah wheezed in relief and reeled into the clearing, clung to a wooden fence post, and checked her phone.

No service.

She sagged, the muscles in her knees and thighs finally giving way. Holding the post, she sat heavily on the hard-packed earth. The field was deserted except for the animal, who had gone back to grazing. The sound of his lusty chewing filled the air. The area seemed familiar, and she shook her head, trying to make sense of what she saw.

"I know where I am," she mumbled, raising her fist and pumping the air feebly. Susannah had ridden Ginger across this very field with Fiona. During that ride, she had seen a house yard with a row of crepe myrtle trees, and she searched for the vibrant color, trying to remember where that house had been. It was close to here. She was sure of it, but where?

The horse stared, not taking its eyes off her. She observed the animal as it chewed. Was this field part of the Long Branch Stable, or was her mind playing tricks?

"I've got to get outta here!" she told him. Large and intimidating, the horse looked like Shadow, Fiona's mount. She recalled how spirited he was. He had ridden fast and kicked water up at them as he drank. Did she dare try to ride him?

"Nice horse," she called as she crept under the fence, swallowing hard. Her whole body trembled, and she wasn't sure if it was from the drug Billy had forced on her or from good old-fashioned fear. She stood and patted the animal gently. He shook his head, and she stepped back, suppressing an urge to flee. But she had to hang on. She couldn't go much farther on foot. Even if this wasn't Fiona's property, she needed to use this animal to get away.

Her first obstacle was mounting a horse with no saddle or bridle. She forced herself to think. Fiona had told her that Shadow was obedient, and indeed the horse followed her lead as she maneuvered him toward the fence. Tentatively, she twisted her fingers in his mane, expecting him to balk, but he didn't. She placed one foot on the fence and swung the other foot up, the field suddenly spinning, the horse tilting out from under her. She found herself on the grass, the sky whirling. Shadow stared down at her.

Vertigo.

Squeezing her eyes shut, she pawed her way back to the fence and used it to pull herself up, waiting for the spinning to stop. She breathed deeply, opened her eyes, and again approached Shadow, guiding him back to the fence. She repeated the process of mounting the animal; this time, she shut her eyes and gripped his neck with both hands. A wave of nausea shot through her, but she stayed on the horse's back. A tiny triumph.

Without peeking, she had managed to straddle the animal and remain on his back. Focusing intently, she ignored a clicking sound that niggled at her brain. She couldn't worry about a katydid landing in her hair; she had real problems here.

CHAPTER FORTY-SEVEN

Twining her fingers into the horse's mane, she centered herself, pleased that the animal had not fled across the field with her hanging off. She slitted her eyes, getting her bearings without the world spinning. Shadow stepped as the clicking intensified. A sharp kick should send him away from the noise and across the field.

"Stop right there."

CHAPTER FORTY-EIGHT

Startled, Susannah twisted toward the voice, sitting up sharply as she saw the voice's owner. Immediately, the field began to whirl. She plastered herself against the horse's neck, eyes clamped shut, the image of Billy, red-faced and wild-eyed burned in her brain.

He had found her.

"Don't move," he growled.

She squinted as he raised the Glock and aimed it at her head. One foot on the fence, he extended his other hand toward Shadow, a small apple in his palm.

Susannah dug in her knees, unwilling to lose her seat. As if reacting to her tension, the gelding shifted away from the fence, tossing his head. Billy pursed his lips, emitting a series of soft clicks, which calmed the animal.

She felt her cheeks get hot. It hadn't been katydids sounding in the field. Billy had been calling Shadow. Overwhelmed by the disorientation of her vertigo, she had completely misinterpreted the sounds. At that moment, she knew she had made the right call years ago to leave the police force. Her brothers' opinion of her didn't matter. Neither did Randy's. She hadn't been a bumbling officer. She had a condition that made her unable to function in certain situations and that could put others in danger. With the calmness of acceptance came the anger of being conned by this impostor. Her rage churned, and she held tight to Shadow, knowing that whatever it took, she would not leave this field with Billy.

He continuing the clicking, and Shadow slowed, turning to accept the apple, his muzzle getting so close that Billy placed his own head against Shadow's neck, giving him a gentle hug that Marcie would have been jealous of. The apple disappeared in three crushing bites, and Shadow placed his nose under Billy's chin in a familiar gesture. Billy patted Shadow and then held out his hand. The gun didn't waver. "Your phone."

Susannah froze, playing for time. If he wanted her phone, maybe there was a signal out here. "You took it away from me. Remember?"

"I met your ditzy friend Bitsy back at the fairground. When she told me she had been texting you, I went back to the store to look for it. Imagine my surprise when I couldn't find it."

Susannah blinked. Would he really shoot her here and take the chance of spooking the horse and having him run off with her?

As if he read her mind, he placed the pistol against Shadow's muzzle. "Now! Or I'll put a bullet through his brain."

She extracted the device from her pocket, contemplating her options. She couldn't allow him to harm the horse. Straightening her spine, defying the vertigo, she raised her hand. "You want it? Go get it."

Before she could release it, the strains of "Girl on Fire" blared from its speaker. Shadow snorted and shook his head, slapping Billy's gun askew. He patted at the horse, trying to calm him, but the volume of the music intensified, and the animal became more and more agitated. He took another wild step, and Susannah eyed the gun wavering in Billy's hand. She stowed her phone and dug her fingers deeper into Shadow's mane as he shook his head, smacking Billy in the face.

"Good boy, Shadow!" Susannah cried.

It was now or never!

She yanked the pistol from his hand as the music resumed, now even louder. Shadow reared, and she held on for dear life as he clipped Billy in the face with his hoof. There was a sickening crunch, and blood spurted from his nose. He crumpled to the ground.

She wanted to cheer; instead, she kicked Shadow hard and fast with both feet. The horse took off. She thought about kicking him again, but that was not necessary. Once he was off, even the cessation of the music could not slow him.

Susannah hung on, bouncing out of sync with the horse's gait as she desperately clung to the gun and Shadow's mane, fearful that Billy would find a way to give chase. She spoke soothing words to Shadow, but he did not slow his pace. Over her shoulder she saw Billy, standing now. Would he pursue her? At this pace, he couldn't catch the horse.

Suddenly the music blared again.

"Whoa, Shadow! Slow down, boy." She tried to make kissy sounds to calm Shadow, but she didn't have Billy's talent as an equine traffic cop. He ran on with her laid flat along his spine, the warm air dusting her face. They crossed the dry grass, clods of orange soil flying behind them, the gun hot in her hand.

As they came over a knoll, Shadow slowed.

CHAPTER FORTY-EIGHT

Three large horses galloped into view. Susannah dug into Shadow's mane, her fingers stiff with fear, glad she held the gun.

Did Billy have accomplices?

She squinted at them as they closed in and understood immediately. A smile tugged at her lips. Bitsy sat atop a horse even larger than Shadow, one hand on the reins and the other waving her phone wildly.

"I found my friend," she crowed, riding up and thrusting her phone, which displayed a map, under Susannah's nose. She recognized the activated Find a Friend application on Bitsy's phone.

Beside Bitsy, Fiona rode a black steed, and Roman rode just behind her.

Susannah blurted, "It was Billy, he's still in the field!"

Roman placed two fingers in his mouth and whistled, and two more riders came into view. Detective Withers sat a chestnut mount, holding the reins in gloved hands. Next to her, Ginger swept into view, carrying Randy Laughton.

"He's that way." Susannah waved the gun in the direction from which she had come as Shadow fidgeted. She tried to calm him, but he skittered to the side as Roman's horse broke into a run. Ginger followed Roman's mount, nodding at Susannah and whinnying in approval before he trotted off with Randy in tow.

Fiona edged Bitsy out of the way and calmed Shadow, stroking him as she maneuvered a rope halter over his head. She cooed, "There's a darlin'," patting his cheek as she fastened the halter.

Detective Withers moved her mare next to Shadow and removed the gun from Susannah's trembling hand.

"Get her to the ambulance," she said to Fiona, pocketing the pistol before she disappeared over the hillock.

"Come on," Fiona said, holding Shadow's rope and her reins in one hand. She directed them both back toward the barn.

Susannah sighed, throwing her arms around Shadow's neck and finally allowing the tears to flow.

CHAPTER FORTY-NINE

"So you're telling me that Mr. Billy tried to poison you by giving Tina a supersized unsweetened tea." Bitsy blinked at Susannah while licking chocolate frosting off her fork.

"Yup." Susannah nodded solemnly, yawning. "That's what I'm saying."

She gazed around Bitsy's kitchen and inhaled, pulling in every scent the room offered. Her favorite people gazed back; the family-sized table brimmed with smiles and laughter. The ER doctors had kept Susannah overnight, testing her blood every few hours to determine how much digitalis she had ingested and treating her accordingly. She was thrilled to be here. Even the elusive Roman Broady was present, holding hands with Bitsy as she manned her dessert fork with the other hand.

Tina, who had experienced worse at the hand of Billy and come out smiling, leaned into Keith, fitting perfectly into his side. Roman finally released Bitsy's hand and sat back in his chair, folding his arms across his chest. A lopsided smile brightened his face as he watched Bitsy make easy work of a second piece of chocolate cake. Larraine yawned, her glasses perched on the end of her nose, and peered at her watch. Susannah knew she had been up for early service and still had coordinated this supper with Andrea. Bitsy, despite her fervent desire to stay away from germs, had remained by Susannah's side through the ambulance ride to the hospital and her treatment in the Emergency Department.

"It would have worked, too," Tina said, looking wide-eyed at Susannah. "But Billy didn't know that I was pregnant and had given up sweet tea."

The last twenty-four hours had been difficult on all of them, particularly Tina, who had barely opened her eyes when Detective Withers began a nonstop line of questioning designed to implicate Susannah in Anita's death but instead implicated Billy Jones in Tina's illness. Once the detective had latched on to Billy as a suspect, Bitsy did not have to convince her to lead the search for Susannah using her Find a Friend app.

"Stop right there. This here is the part where I don't follow," said Bitsy.

"Auntie Bitsy," Andrea said, picking up her cake plate and taking the fork out of her hand. "Listen up."

"I swear," Roman laughed, his freckles standing out across his cheeks, "this girl is a food-lovin' fool."

"I'm a fool for you," Bitsy said, her freckles matching his as a smile lifted her cheeks. "I guess I was more interested in the dessert than the details." She touched Roman's arm, turned back to Susannah, and batted her eyes innocently. "Go on."

"Like I said before, Billy knew I drink my tea unsweetened," Susannah said, "so when Tina told him she was ordering for the office, he naturally thought the unsweetened tea was for me and put a load of his foxglove brew in it."

CHAPTER FORTY-NINE

Larraine shook her head. "Lord forgive him."

Keith pulled Tina closer, but she sat up energetically, taking up the story. "But they were both for me," she said, continuing the narrative in one breath. "On account of the doctor made me give up sweet tea, but I had a really bad hankering for one and—"

"And you snuck-drank the sweet tea in the car by yourself," Bitsy finished for her, picking up Roman's fork and taking a sliver of Larraine's peach cobbler. "I gotcha."

Tina nodded.

"But what were you doing with the unsweet tea? It don't make no sense to sneak-drink an unsweet tea on top of the sweet one."

"It was my decoy tea."

Bitsy's mouth fell open, her fork dangling in her hand. "I never heard of decoy snacks. Tell me more."

Tina looked up at Larraine, her brown eyes watery under dense, dark lashes. She grasped Keith's hand and squeezed. He squeezed back and dipped his head, indicating she should go on. There was a cheerful gleam in his eyes.

"I thought if I walked in with no drink, Ms. Larraine would notice I didn't have one and ask me about it." Her words came in one long, unbroken stream. "And I'm a terrible liar, and she knows how hard I've been trying to be good. She's helped me so much; I didn't want her to be disappointed in me."

Larraine looked over her glasses at Tina. "Oh, sugar, you wouldn't ever disappoint me."

"So I got the unsweet tea to pretend I was being good."

"I follow, I follow," Bitsy nodded. "But why did you actually *drink* it?"

"Because I reckoned if I didn't drink it at all, and it sat on the desk all afternoon, Ms. Larraine would notice that, and if I spilled it all out on the ground, she would notice that too."

"Oh darlin'." Larraine shook her finger at Tina. "What a tangled web we weave."

"So I sipped a little, and I spilled a little. And then I fell a little!"

Laughter erupted from around the table.

"Well, thank goodness the doctors finally listened to Keith and did the right tests," Roman said.

"Oh, they didn't listen to *me*," Keith grumbled. "They claimed they did the tests, but it wasn't until Iris convinced the detective that they really took notice. She let her know that Anita's labs were irregular, and the detective went on a rant about how Dr. Shine had poisoned them both." There were murmurs of disbelief around the table.

Andrea leaned against the sink, which was filling with soapy water, a mound of bubbles growing behind her. "So that means Billy became suspicious of you way before you realized he was the one who poisoned Anita?" She looked at Susannah, folding her arms across her chest, one hand covered by an elbow-length pink rubber glove.

"Yup," Susannah said. "I only suspected him after I saw the enlarged photo at the Independence Day Festival. But he had been keeping tabs on me because he thought I was the perfect fall guy." Her face darkened as she looked from Larraine to Tina. "When I told him that I had met Hayle at the high school on Career Day and that she was going to give me riding lessons, he snapped."

Bitsy pointed at Susannah with her fork, crumbs of cobbler flying across the table. "He didn't want you going to the stable because it was too close to his house?"

CHAPTER FORTY-NINE

When Detective Withers finally made it to Billy's house, she had discovered, hidden behind a row of crepe myrtle trees, a healthy foxglove garden in the far corner of his yard—the same yard Susannah had seen on her horseback ride with Fiona, and the same house she had considered fleeing to when she escaped from his camping shed in the trees. She shivered. Thank goodness she hadn't been able to locate it in her terror.

"I think that was part of it," Susannah answered slowly, biting her lip, deep in thought. "He also didn't want me seeing Hayle's car because I had seen it the day of Anita's memorial lunch. Colin also mentioned seeing Anita get into a blue sedan, so I was on the lookout for it."

Bitsy stood. "Well, I am done running pie-eating contests," she said, shaking her head. "If I hadn't let Marcie keep those pies at the Wing Shack, none of this would have happened. I never would have asked you to go get those pies—"

"I wouldn't have gone either," Susannah interrupted her. "But he wasn't supposed to be there." She shivered again and scratched at the back of her hand, where the ant bites had swelled. "I thought he was still at the hospital. Even though I hadn't worked it all out, I had him figured for a cheater, and it made me rethink everything I thought I knew about him and Marcie. I wouldn't have gone if I knew he was there."

"That must have been horrible, locked in that shed, bugs and varmints climbing all around," Larraine said, hugging herself and then rubbing imaginary bugs off her arms.

"It wasn't a picnic." Susannah looked at her fingers and wrists, which were bruised and abraded. Tiny red welts from the ant bites decorated her arms, shoulders, and face. "Thank goodness for dry rot and termites."

"And your equestrian skills!" Bitsy said, holding up her

phone, which displayed a picture of Susannah sprawled lopsided on Shadow's back. Susannah blushed, grabbing at the phone, but Bitsy held it out of reach, grinning.

There was a knock on the door. Susannah, who sat at the end of the table, stood. "I'll get it, don't bother yourself," she directed to Bitsy, who had already handed the phone off to Andrea and was beaming at Roman. Susannah was pleased that he and Bitsy had put their differences aside. For now, at least, all talk of moving had ceased.

As she opened the door, laughter erupted from the kitchen, and Susannah glanced back to see hands reaching across the table, vying to see who would get Bitsy's phone next. Turning back to the door, she was startled to see Detective Withers standing there with her thumbs hooked over her belt.

CHAPTER FIFTY

"Dr. Shine, I thought you might be here. May I come in?"

Susannah backed away, letting the door swing open. A commotion rose from the kitchen as chairs scraped and mumbled apologies filled the air. Suddenly Bitsy appeared at her side.

"You have some nerve coming to my home," Bitsy spat, one arm raised to block the detective's entry.

"I understand that I haven't made the best impression, but I'm here to apologize for any misunderstanding."

Bitsy's eyes widened. "Misunderstanding, I—"

"Come on in." Susannah nudged Bitsy to the side and allowed the detective to enter. The group at the table gathered around the kitchen door, peering at them, Tina grasping Keith's hand and scowling so deep that Susannah thought she would permanently crease her face.

The detective shoved her hands into her pockets, glanced at the crowd in the doorway, and nodded. "I only now came from the interview with Billy Jones. He confessed to everything, including damaging Colin's garage and slashing the tires at the Long Branch Stable."

"Why on earth did he do that to Colin?" Larraine asked.

The detective pulled her hands from her pockets and tapped a finger into the opposite palm as she spoke. "To cover up. You see, Billy used Hayle's car when he met with Anita because he didn't want to be recognized in his truck. He knew Colin frequented the bar at the Cantina and worried that he had seen him with Anita one night. She had arranged a rendezvous, and apparently, she had lost track of time and Colin was still drinking at the bar when Billy pulled up. That was the same night Tomás thought he witnessed Colin knock Anita down. She told Billy that she slipped trying to get Colin away from the door so he wouldn't see him. According to Billy, Colin had done some work on Hayle's car, and he was convinced the mechanic would remember who owned the car. He wanted to ruin Colin's credibility. Ironically, Colin didn't realize that it was Hayle's car, but he did remember the model and color."

"With the amount of drinking he does on the job, I'm not surprised about that," Keith interjected.

The detective nodded and continued. "After that, Billy had it out for Colin." The detective looked at Keith, then back to Susannah. "A lot of people knew about Colin's drinking, and Billy was one of them. It wasn't hard for him to start spreading rumors about Colin. He thought if he rattled Colin, it would push him over the edge and make him act crazy, and it did."

"So he cracked and stabbed Billy at the festival, then got himself arrested," Bitsy commented.

"Correct," the detective replied.

"What about the stable?" Larraine asked. "His little girl worked there. Why did he want to damage those cars and frighten everyone?"

CHAPTER FIFTY

"To keep Dr. Shine from seeing Hayle's car. When she told him that she was going to take riding lessons, he became afraid that she was on to him." She faced Susannah. "He's been stalking you since Anita's death. He wanted to find out if you remembered anything from that day. He became obsessed with the thought that you would remember seeing him at your office. He swore a blue streak, blaming you for messing up his plan."

Susannah stepped back, perplexed, and the detective stepped further into the entrance. "How could I have messed up his plan? He had been poisoning her for a while, right?"

"Correct. But when you showed up to your office, Anita was already quite ill from the dosage he had given her earlier that morning, and he was trying to convince her to go home and lie down. He hoped if she died in her own bed it would look like natural causes, and there would be no investigation."

"So I interrupted that conversation," Susannah said, more to herself than to her friends who were oozing further out the kitchen doorway with each word. "But what set the alarm off?"

"Ah, Billy didn't have a direct answer for that, but he did mention that he doesn't like cats," she shrugged. "I think he threw a rock at your tabby and probably hit the back window. When you showed up, he heard you walking along the side of the building, and he grabbed a flashlight he keeps in the truck and hit you with it."

"My goodness," Larraine exclaimed, grabbing the nearest hand, which happened to belong to Keith. He swallowed her up with a reassuring hug, which she had to extricate herself from to keep up with the story.

"When Anita saw what Billy had done," the detective

continued, "she got so upset, she collapsed. He thought about trying to revive her to get her home, but she didn't respond." She shook her head, a few frizzy blond hairs falling over her eyes. "He's a sick man. He left her there to die." She paused, and the house went silent as everyone digested this tidbit. She picked up the report in a subdued voice. "He loves his daughter but seems to despise every other woman he knows. Especially his wife."

"If he despises his wife," Bitsy said, moving to Roman's side, "and I'm not saying I blame him there, why did he kill Anita?"

"It was all about money, Ms. Long." Detective Withers shifted her gaze to Bitsy, who seemed to have forgotten she didn't want the woman in her house. "I've seen it dozens of times."

"Not *all* about money," Susannah spoke up, and every eye shifted to her. "She killed his dreams of opening a classy restaurant. They went to culinary school together, where he studied French cuisine and dreamed of running a five-star restaurant."

The detective shifted her weight and lifted her hand as if she was going to interrupt, but Susannah continued. "I managed to track down an alumni website from their cooking school and spoke to two classmates this morning. Neither of them knew that Anita had gotten pregnant. She dropped out of school suddenly at the end of the term, very close to graduation. They were both saddened to hear that she had passed but thrilled to learn that she had achieved her dream of running an authentic Mexican restaurant. They were both stunned to find out that Billy ran a takeout joint. When they graduated, he told them he was going home to arrange the financing to open a bistro in Atlanta, and they both thought he was being modest. One of them said she wouldn't have been surprised if he earned a Michelin star within two years."

"Then why did he stay here? Why didn't he leave?" Andrea asked, while removing the pink rubber glove and folding it over her arm.

"I seem to remember his mama and daddy talking about giving him a trip to Europe as a graduation present," Larraine offered, "but now that I think on it, they had some kind of emergency come up and couldn't afford it."

"True," the detective cut in. "We've done some digging and learned that the Jones family owned land but had little money. When Billy's father had a stroke, the family's savings were eventually depleted. They kept the land, which included that shed where he kept you." She nodded at Susannah. "Billy called it an old hunting camp, but it was more of a storage shed."

Roman laughed, and all eyes turned toward him. "I'm sorry, but I've been at a few of those backwoods 'hunting camps.' They only get used after the hunting is all done. They're usually just big enough to store some chairs and keep a few bottles of moonshine to nip on. Keeps the seedy behavior away from the wife and kids."

Bitsy quirked one eyebrow. "Kinda like a man cave."

Detective Withers continued, "Billy's family had already sold some land off to a cousin who built the stable. In the end, his family had some land to hunt on, but not enough to finance the kind of operation he believed he deserved."

"So he married Marcie for her money?" Andrea asked.

"Marcie's family is wealthy. Billy knew that Marcie had inherited a substantial amount of money from her grandmother, which she would gain control of when she married.

I think he found the money more attractive than he found Marcie, but he must have put on one heck of a show." She shook her head, and Susannah was surprised that what she had thought of as a serpentine movement on closer inspection appeared a tad graceful. Just a tad. The detective addressed Andrea now. "However, after they married, Marcie balked at laying out the amount of money he wanted, and once she found herself pregnant, she refused to leave Peach Grove."

"I reckon Billy resented Marcie for keeping him here," Larraine said. There were murmurs of agreement around the doorway.

"Pilar told me that Anita used to spend a lot of time here when she was establishing her restaurant," Susannah said. "She thought there must have been a man in her life, but Anita never spoke of one. I suppose a mother knows."

"Maybe she never got over Billy." Andrea sighed. "How romantic."

"Never got over being run-out on, is what I think," Bitsy said, smacking Andrea in the back of the head. "You read too many of them romance novels. Abandoned, pregnant, and without a job is not romantic."

"Whatever their initial relationship was, I believe Anita began to blackmail him," Susannah said, thinking aloud. "Not that I excuse him, but when he had me in the Wing Shack, at one point he sounded inconsolable. Anita must have backed him into a corner financially."

"Correct," the detective said. "Marcie started an audit of the Wing Shack's accounts, and Billy decided it was time to take some huge risks. He claims at first he just wanted to make Anita ill. Get her off his back, as he put it."

"How did he decide to poison her?" It was Keith's turn to

ask a question, and he pulled Tina in so close that she had to wedge her chin over his forearm to hear the answer.

"He wanted to prove that he was a better chef than she was. He kept gloating that she never suspected anything was wrong with her tea. Apparently, he loved to garden and has quite a green thumb. No one gave a second thought to his selections for his flower garden."

"Who would ever suspect something like that?" Larraine said, shaking her head.

"I did suspect poison, but it turns out I suspected the wrong person." She turned to Susannah and offered her hand. "I want to offer my apology, and I hope we can get past this."

Susannah studied her angular gray eyes before taking her hand and shaking it. *Now maybe things can get back to normal.* "You owe me one," she said, smiling. "Now come on in and have some dessert."

"Yeah," Bitsy smiled. "Try some of Miss Larraine's cobbler. She puts the peach in Peach Grove."

Roman chuckled and gave Bitsy a tap. She jumped, bumping into Tina and Keith, which started everyone laughing. Susannah stood back and watched the group escort Detective Withers to the kitchen. It was good to have family.

***

If you enjoyed this story, **Learn how Dr. Susannah met BFF Bitsy Long In the prequel novella:**
Susannah Shines Through
An armed robbery, an invisible gun, and two new friends fight to solve a mystery!
In this exclusive prequel to the ChiroCozy Mystery Series,

recent graduate, Dr. Susannah Shine, moves to Peach Grove, Georgia. With her best friend, Henry the betta fish, in tow, she soon discovers that Peach Grove is a small town with BIG secrets.

Susannah meets gal pal Bitsy Long, and together they stumble upon a mysterious robbery. Working together, Susannah and Bitsy must make snap decisions to uncover the truth.

Will they find a felon, or fall prey to the robber's deadly twist?

Join my Cozy Reader's Club Newsletter and Get a **FREE** ebook version of **Susannah Shines Through** via BookFunnel: at https://dl.bookfunnel.com/oywdl45g4c

Find Cathy Tully on her website or your favorite social media.
Website: https://ectully.com
Twitter: @ChiroCozy
Facebook: CathyTullyCozyAuthor
BookBub: Cathy-Tully
Goodreads: Cathy_Tully

Gluten-Free Recipes

Huevos Rancheros Susannah

- 1 Tablespoon avocado oil or coconut oil
- 4 large eggs
- 4 corn tortillas
- ¼ onion, chopped
- 1 cup black beans, drained and rinsed
- 1 teaspoon cumin
- 1 teaspoon chili powder
- 1 avocado, sliced
- Salsa (homemade or store bought)
- Sea salt
- Hot sauce (optional)
- Sour cream (optional)

In a large skillet, sauté the onion in the oil of your choice. Cook until soft, about 5 minutes. Add cumin, chili powder, and sea salt.

Add the black beans and mix well. Create 4 wells in the mixture with a spoon and crack eggs into the wells. Cook eggs until whites are firm and yolks are runny.

Plate on tostadas and cover with salsa. Add hot sauce and sour cream.

Gluten-Free Flaxseed Crackers

- 1 cup flaxseeds
- 3 Tablespoons chia seeds
- 1 cup water
- 3 Tablespoons sunflower seeds
- 3 Tablespoons pumpkin seeds
- 1 teaspoon sea salt
- 1 tablespoon garlic powder (optional)

Preheat oven to 200 degrees. Line a 9x13 baking sheet with parchment paper.

In a large bowl, soak flax and chia seeds in water for 15–20 minutes. After soaking, the mixture should be slightly gelatinous. Add pumpkin and sunflower seeds and mix well. Add salt and garlic powder or other seasonings to taste.

Turn the mixture onto the parchment paper and use the back of a spoon or spatula to flatten it down and smooth it out evenly across the baking sheet. This will take several minutes.

Place the tray on the bottom rack of the oven for 90 minutes. Remove the tray and turn the mixture. If it has sufficiently "dried," it will peel off the parchment paper easily and you should be able to flip it over in one piece.

If you want your crackers to come out in even pieces, score

the cracker dough now with a sharp knife.

Place the tray back in the oven for another 90 minutes. Turn the heat off and let it cool inside the oven. Once cooled, remove from the oven and break into pieces.

Gluten-Free Blueberry Muffins

2 cups almond flour
   3 eggs
   ⅓ cup raw honey
   ½ teaspoon baking soda
   Pinch of sea salt
   1 teaspoon vanilla extract
   5 Tablespoons coconut oil or ghee, melted
   1 cup fresh blueberries

Preheat oven to 350 degrees.

In a bowl, combine almond flour, baking soda, and sea salt. In a separate bowl, combine eggs, honey, vanilla, and coconut oil/ghee. Combine both mixtures together. Once well incorporated, add blueberries and mix. Fill a muffin pan with liners. Fill each liner with batter. Bake in oven for 15–20 minutes.

*Healthy Baking Tips

1. Gluten-free baking flour is available and can be used in place of the almond flour.
2. Gluten-free baked goods may rise a little less than what you might expect, so don't omit the whole eggs as they

will help make your muffins fluffier.
3. Raw honey is thicker than regular honey. Put a dab of coconut oil or ghee in the measuring cup, and the honey will release much easier.
4. Coconut oil and ghee are solid at room temperature. You can bring your eggs to room temperature to prevent the melted coconut oil from clumping when added to refrigerated eggs, but in the end it will melt again as soon as it's put in the oven.

Gluten-Free Peach Cobbler

Batter
  4 tablespoons butter, cold
  1 cup gluten-free baking flour mix
  1/2 cup granulated sugar
  3/4 cup milk, at room temperature
  1 large egg, at room temperature

Fruit
  2 1/2 cups fresh or frozen Georgia peaches (about 3 or 4 peaches)
  1/2 cup granulated sugar
  pinch of salt
  1/2 teaspoon cinnamon

Instructions

1. Preheat the oven to 375°F.
2. To prepare the pan: Melt 4 tablespoons butter in the bottom of an 8" square or 9" round pan; set the pan aside while you make the batter.
3. **To make the batter:** Mix the baking mix and sugar.
4. Blend in the milk and egg; pour the batter over the melted butter in the pan.
5. **To prepare the fruit:** Peel, pit and slice fresh peaches.

If using frozen, thaw them.
6. Mix the sugar, salt, and cinnamon into the peaches.
7. **To assemble and bake:** Spoon the peach mixture over the top of the batter.
8. Bake until the top is lightly browned and the fruit is bubbling, about 40 to 45 minutes.
9. Remove the cobbler from the oven, and allow it to cool for 5 to 10 minutes before serving.

Misalignment & Murder...Sneak Peek

All Hail the Nephew's Here

"Here comes trouble," Dr. Susannah Shine commented to Henry the Eighth, her betta fish, who was swimming circles around the green Marimo moss ball in his tank. Her seven-year-old nephew leapt out of her sister's car and careened toward the front door of Peach Grove Chiropractic. Susannah left her desk to intercept him before he could commence banging.

Caden Rossi ran in, breathless. "Halloween is almost here!" he cried. "Can you take me to the Halloween camp-out this weekend? Jamal and his auntie are going to be there. Can you, can you?" Caden scooped up Rusty, the marmalade cat who called the office his home, and gave him a squeeze.

"Mrow," Rusty said.

Caden ignored him, stroking him with one dirty hand and holding him tight with the other. "I get to sleep in a tent, and cook over a campfire, and go on a haunted trail."

"What's this now?" Susannah turned to her sister, who appeared in the doorway, Caden's backpack and juice box in hand. "Camping? In the woods?"

Angela Rossi ignored the question. "Caden, let go of the cat."

Rusty's golden eyes remained placid as he wiggled until he was dangling by his front paws. He squirmed out of Caden's grasp and sprinted past Angie, who jumped back, grabbing the wall for support. The cat was across the parking lot before she regained her balance. "Only you, Suzie. A bone cracker and a cat rescuer."

Newly relocated from Brooklyn, Angie pronounced the word cracker as *cracka*. Susannah smiled. "We adjust spines, Ange. We don't crack bones."

"Uh-huh." Angie peered down the hall toward the adjusting rooms. "Are ya sure Caden won't bother anyone? I could put off my errands—"

"It's fine." Susannah took Caden's book bag and walked him to the break area, where he placed the book bag on the table. "We have plenty of space away from the patient treatment rooms. Now about this camp-out."

Angie rolled her eyes. "Caden, go wash your hands."

Susannah watched her nephew walk down the hall to the washroom. Asking her newly divorced sister to move in with her had been a spur-of-the-moment decision, and she was shocked and pleased when Angie took her up on it. She and Angie had never been particularly close, and Peach Grove, Georgia, was a far cry from the family home in Brooklyn, New York. After two months, Angie's post-divorce funk was starting to lift, and Caden seemed to be thriving. He had confided in her that he didn't want to go to the Fall Festival, but Angie made no mention of that. Being an aunt was sometimes more than Susannah had bargained for. "You know I hate being in the woods."

"Yeah, about that. Ya know I wouldn't ask if I didn't have to." Angie shook out her black hair and gazed up at her younger sister. Her Brooklyn accent caused her to pronounce ask as *axe*. Susannah shuddered. She had lived in small-town Georgia for a long time—so long that a soft country accent sounded more familiar than Angie's New York City Yankee twang. "The hospital scheduled a CPR and Advanced Life Support training for Saturday morning, and I hafta attend."

Susannah chewed her lip. She'd been thrilled when Angie found a position at Henry County Hospital. She was a little less thrilled now. As for the camp-out, after an unpleasant incident over the summer, her appreciation for the outdoor life had waned. Fearing an Italian-American intervention featuring her mother's Rosary Society, she had kept the details of the unpleasantness from her family in New York, and she wasn't going to mention them to Angie now.

Angie squinted at her, a trait Susannah knew meant she was ready to argue. "Bitsy is taking Jamal. Maybe you can share a tent. Keith will be there too. You have nothing to worry about."

"I'm not worried. I—" Susannah stopped. Caden appeared in the hallway, and Angie rushed to him; she planted a loud kiss on the top of his head and led him back down the hall to the break area. Susannah noted a fleeting expression of doubt sweep across Angie's features and then disappear. It was her turn to reassure her sister. "He's going to be fine."

Angie nodded at Susannah and pulled a lipstick from her purse. She looked around. Susannah knew Angie was searching for a mirror. Foundation, eyeliner, and blush were what Angie called her first line of defense. Mascara, eye shadow, and a custom lipstick color, which Angie called Marvelous Magenta, finished the tableau. Susannah would have looked like a clown with that much makeup on, but set off by Angie's olive skin and black hair, it looked amazing. "Don't forget, the Fall Festival is tonight at school." She dropped the lipstick into her bag and pointed down the hall to the break area. "I already stocked the fridge so yas can have a hot meal before ya go. I know me leaving early for my shift is throwing a monkey wrench into your schedule, but once I'm done with training, I won't need you to watch him as much." Like most in her family, Angie was a lover of Italian food. But Angie was also a tireless cook, using all the family recipes and updating and inventing her own gourmet takes on them. She laughed at Susannah's simple way of eating and food sensitivities. "Go to work."

Twenty minutes later, Susannah entered treatment room two where Gus Arnold, the assistant principal at Peach Grove Elementary School, sat. His blond hair and deep-set gray-blue eyes gave him a Ryan Gosling look, only blonder.

"Dr. Shine." He smiled at her. "That last adjustment fixed my knee pain. I've felt better in the last month than I have in the last year. And I've gotten off all my pain medications."

"I'm glad to hear it." Susannah held up her hand for a high five.

"Me too." He laughed as he high-fived her. "But yesterday, I was walking around my yard and stepped in a hole, and I think I misaligned my knee. The pain is back. I need another adjustment."

"I can arrange that." Susannah faced Gus and positioned his leg for the adjustment, wrapping her hands around his knee while he lay on his back. A low, deep click signaled a successful adjustment.

Gus sat up, tentatively putting his weight on his leg. "I can't believe the difference. I wish I had done this years ago."

"That's what they all say."

Gus took a few steps, placing more and more weight on the joint. "Thank goodness, the pain is gone. You have no idea how much this helps me. Tonight's the Fall Festival at school. I've been on my feet constantly the last few days."

Susannah took a moment to ask Gus about what to expect at a Fall Festival, and he filled her in. His gracious manner and infectious smile put her at ease.

"I'll see you there." He did a herky-jerky step and laughed as he left the room.

Peach Grove was in autumn mode, and this year she would have the added enjoyment of accompanying Caden to the festival. As she watched Gus leave the treatment room, another thought came to her: in addition to the Fall Festival tonight and the camp-out this weekend, tomorrow morning another local institution was meeting. The Peach Grove Business Association would elect a new president, and her best friend, Bitsy Long, was running. Whatever the outcome, this was going to be an interesting week.

A Zombie in the Sand

Susannah entered her office and was startled to see Caden with his cheek pressed against the glass of Henry the Eighth's fish tank. Henry swam his usual route as Caden watched, wide-eyed, his small body slumped sideways in a chair, one finger tracking the fish as he swished by. The glass on the tank fogged from Caden's breath.

Susannah said, "You never told me why you don't want to go to the Fall Festival."

Caden blew on the tank and ran his finger through the condensation. "Some of the kids are mean to me. Dylan S. laughs at me. He says I talk funny."

Susannah felt her stomach sink. His New York accent was not as pronounced as Angie's, but it was clear he wasn't from around here. She put her hand on his shoulder. "Don't pay attention to Dylan S., he sounds like a real doofus."

Caden sat up and smiled. "Yeah, he's a doo-puss."

"Not doo-puss, doofus. It means he's dumb."

"Oh. I think he's a doo-puss too."

Susannah shook her head, not sure if she had just made the matter worse. "Come on, let's go have some fun." She grabbed his backpack and loaded him into her Jeep.

Her last patient had been running late, and they were behind. Luckily, Peach Grove Elementary was only minutes from the office. When they arrived, a Peach Grove Police Department patrol car blocked the entrance to the parking lot. Officer Owen Chaffin, who Susannah had met over the weekend at Tina and Keith Cawthorn's Halloween party, waved her toward the other cars parked behind the school.

Caden pressed his nose to the window. "Are we really allowed to park on the lawn?"

Susannah chuckled. The overflow parking was in the grassy field past the playground. In Brooklyn, where Caden came from, the only wide-open green spaces were parks surrounded by cement walkways and chain link fences. In fact, some of the parks in Brooklyn *were* just cement walkways and chain link fences. "Only tonight, kid. Too many cars to fit in the lot."

The Jeep bumped over the rutted grass, and she squeezed into the last spot next to some cedar trees. She led Caden across the playground, toward the gymnasium, passing Bitsy's SUV on the way. The air smelled of hay and freshly popped popcorn. Bales were stacked two and three high, with gap-toothed jack-o'-lanterns and scarecrows lounging on top. Strains of "Turkey in the Straw" filled the air, and children and adults lined up to play games along a midway. At the far end of the building were a dunking booth and a bouncy house.

She looked around for Bitsy, who would be accompanying Jamal, but didn't see her. Caden found his classmates and queued up to try his hand at knocking down a pyramid of empty soda cans with a tennis ball. As he took his turn, a loud whoop caught Susannah's attention, and she proceeded down the midway. When she saw the source of the whoop, she laughed out loud and called Caden over.

Bitsy stood in the dunking tank, water cascading off her body. She was dressed as a scarecrow, her straw hat drooping. Jamal stood in front of the booth, and Caden ran to his side.

"That's Jamal's auntie," he giggled. "She looks funny. She's got straw in her hair."

Susannah watched as Bitsy's colorful costume and lively banter kept the adults around the dunk tank. A few moms cheered delightedly when she splashed down. Each time a bull's-eye pitched Bitsy off her perch, Caden and Jamal capered to and fro in front of the tank, like oversized puppies, soaking up almost as much moisture as she did. After an hour, Bitsy had raised $300 for the PTA and was as wrinkly as a box of raisins. She exited the booth with a lopsided smile and a wilted straw hat. She was immediately set upon by the boys, who, if they'd had a dry spot on them, immediately lost it. Susannah kept her distance as Bitsy rained on the pavement.

"That dunking tank is hungry work." Bitsy hugged Jamal and winked at Caden. "What do you say we go get ourselves some kettle corn?"

The boys nodded enthusiastically.

"Can I, Aunt Suzie?" asked Caden.

"Sure, you stick with Ms. Bitsy while I get you some dry clothes out of the car."

Susannah hurried away, crossing the playground quickly. The streetlight from the parking lot shone an orange haze across the swing set and sandbox. Digging in her purse for her keys as she went, she stopped. Had she heard a noise? She looked around, but all she saw was a teacher cleaning up her game station in the parking lot. Glancing at the row of cedar trees, she reached her Jeep and jumped in. As she pulled the door shut, "Girl on Fire," the ringtone she had assigned to

Bitsy, sounded from her purse.

"Kettle corn's almost all gone," Bitsy crowed. "What's taking you so long?"

Susannah wedged the phone between her shoulder and ear as she twisted to reach the back seat. "I'm coming. Save me some," she replied, grabbing the gym bag jammed with emergency supplies.

"You snooze, you lose," Bitsy replied. The call ended and Susannah tossed the phone into her bag, shaking her head with a smile. As she pulled out a pair of blue jeans and a T-shirt from the gym bag, she had the feeling that she was being watched and again gazed down the row of cedar trees. Not a soul graced either the paved lot or the grassy overflow parking.

Suddenly a scream split the quiet. Her heart began hammering so strongly, she could hear her pulse in her ears. She shouldered her bag and grabbed her keys. The slam of the door fell flat in the still night air. Hustling across the parking lot, she passed the sandbox and swings. A loud groan sent the hair on her arms standing straight up. She turned and saw someone dressed as a zombie coming from the trees. Trembling, she forced a smile. *Probably some middle schooler trying to scare me.*

"Dr. Shine."

The zombie had called her name. She stopped, watching the costumed teen shamble toward her, one leg dragging behind in a classic zombie cadence. Suddenly the zombie tripped and fell face down into the sandbox. Susannah clutched her keys, her hand shaking. Again the zombie called her name and she drew closer, horrified to see a dark substance seep into the sand beneath its hips.

That's blood!

She rushed over. "Ack!" she blurted. This was not a teen. It was a man, face down, sprawled with one arm pinned underneath his body. She turned him over and gasped.

"Gus!"

Blood seeped from a hole in his chest.

**

Misalignment & Murder: ChiroCozy Book 2 is available on Amazon in paperback, in the Kindle Store and Kindle Unlimited.

The **ChiroCozy Mystery Series** has been a finalist for the Silver Falchion Award for Best Cozy in 2021 and 2022.

About the Author

Cathy Tully is the pen name of USA Today Bestselling author E.C. Tully, a chiropractor and writer.

She is a graduate of Georgetown University, in Washington DC, where she studied foreign languages and linguistics. She lived abroad in Quito, Ecuador and worked for an international trademark and patent law firm in New York City, before changing careers and graduating from Chiropractic School.

Her award nominated novels, **Dr. Shine Cracks the Case**, and **Fixation & Fraud** feature a chiropractor practicing in small town Georgia. She is a member of the *Atlanta Writers Club* and *Sisters in Crime Atlanta.*

She has written seven books in the ChiroCozy Mystery Series. She lives with her husband and gets bossed around by their three rescue cats.

Also by Cathy Tully

USA Today Bestselling author **Cathy Tully** brings you quirky characters, hilarious situations and plenty of twists and turns to keep you hooked and reading into the night.

When former NYPD officer, Susannah Shine, changes careers and becomes a Chiropractor, her path leads her to the small Georgia town of Peach Grove. After meeting her BFF, entrepreneur and shoe hound, Bitsy Long, the women tackle a treacherous murderer by forming the **Ladies Crime Solving Club**.

Fixation & Fraud: ChiroCozy Book 3

It's Thanksgiving and foul play has been served along with dessert. Though Dr. Susannah Shine expected a relaxing holiday, the mysteries keep piling up. A stranger is found dead, a stray dog appears in the dark, and a precocious pig calls at her door.

With BFF Bitsy's Gramps as a primary suspect, *The Ladies Crime Solving Club* jumps in to help Susannah figure out who killed the real estate agent.

Thanks to the **Long Family Dessert Contest**, tasty tidbits pile up along with confounding clues - all leading back to Gramps' Pecan orchard. Misadventure manifests in the blueberry patch as Susannah, Bitsy, and Little Junior parlay a porker's visit to the vet into the undercover adventure of the century. Or at least of the last week.

Fixation & Fraud is a light-hearted cozy mystery featuring quirky small-town characters, a rescue dog with special abilities, and a pot-bellied pig!

Fixation & Fraud is a 2022 Silver Falchion Award Finalist for Best Cozy.

Fixation & Fraud is available on Amazon in paperback, in the Kindle Store and Kindle Unlimited.

The Purloined Poinsettia: A ChiroCozy Christmas Novella

When former NYPD cop, Dr. Susannah Shine, and office manager Larraine Moore search for a canceled flower order for Larraine's church, they dig up a deadly discovery: A bloody body surrounded by the poached poinsettias.

Together again, *the Ladies Crime Solving Club* unwraps clues that lead them from shrouded secrets to hidden heartaches, with a dash of deliciousness thrown in.

From Silver Falchion Award Finalist Cathy Tully, **The Purloined Poinsettia** is the 4th in the Dr. Susannah Shine ChiroCozy Mystery series. A Christmas Novella, it can be read anytime as a stand-alone.

The Purloined Poinsettia is available on Amazon in paperback, in the Kindle Store and Kindle Unlimited.

Coming in late 2022: Disco, Disguises and Deception
Dr. Susannah Shine is getting ready to take a much-needed vacation to Florida to see her ex-NYPD partner, Anthony "Tone" Mancuso, when she receives a cryptic text message from him.

Alarmed at what it might mean, Dr. Susannah, heads to Florida with BFF Bitsy Long and Bitsy's pot-bellied pig, Priscilla. Once they arrive, it becomes clear that Tone is nowhere to be found, and his wife, Irma, is growing concerned.

When Priscilla discovers a clue in a potted palm, Susannah encourages Irma to investigate, and our chiropractor turned sleuth follows the trail of an enigmatic message, a burglar in Birkenstocks, and a disco dance contest for an exhilarating adventure in the Sunshine state.

Check Amazon for more details: https://www.amazon.com/dp/B08L4VRRG9

Made in the USA
Monee, IL
16 November 2024

70268954R00215